Imperfecta

by

Robin Martinez Rice

Sandra –
Enjoy!
R Martinez Rice

Thank you, Dad, for telling me I could be whatever I dreamed of and for playing all those funny word games with us whenever we were out on Sunday drives that lasted until Tuesday.

A special thanks to my grandmother, my aunts and my uncle, for letting me make up a story about their lives.

CONTENTS

Thunder Gods

One

"La Bruja," Perfecta shouted, as soon as she was clear of the classroom door. Sister Maria was such an evil witch.

Now I'll burn in hell for sure. Perfecta glanced over her shoulder at the white building that served as school to her small town. Her head felt like it might burst if she didn't put some space between herself and her teacher.

No, La Puta—a bitch, that's what the nun was.

Perfecta ran from the school house and down the packed dirt road. She raced past the row of houses, the market, the construction of the new courthouse.

At the edge of town she turned right, down the road that led to the massive Martinez property which surrounded the south end of town. She heard the boards of the old wooden bridge groan as she pounded over the irrigation ditch. The lifeline of Tierra Amarilla, this ditch provided water to the crops, the cows, the sheep and the people of T.A.

She slowed as a sharp pain welled up in her chest. Bending down she clasped her arms tight around her body, pulling the warm desert air into her lungs.

"*¡Nunca volveré a esa escuela!* I'm never going back to that school." She screamed the words to the empty desert, using her recovered breath to share her rage. The desert had no echo; it sucked up her words and kept them, leaving her with a feeling of emptiness.

Another note from the nun. Papa had warned her that she would pay a high price if it happened again.

Her father, Primitivo Trujillo, was a strong man. He was also the sheriff of Tierra Amarilla. He rode around on his tall gray gelding making people obey laws of the town. *No fights, keep your animals under control, pay your taxes*. Silly things that made him important. He made stupid rules at home; he needed to be important there, too.

People said her father was handsome. They admired his broad shoulders and his brilliant gray hair which drew their attention to his light eyes. Perfecta thought his ears were too big, and he had a funny hook on the end of his nose.

Arms crossed in front of her chest, she considered her situation. She would no longer obey him. She had outgrown his power and wasn't afraid of his sharp words or his sharp blows anymore. She could run away. She *would* run away.

She wasn't afraid of God either, even though she thought bad things about a nun. Her mother's constant warnings swirled around like tiny angels chanting into her ears. "You must pray for forgiveness, pray to God so that you can go to heaven. Be a nice girl." This was the only advice Avelina ever gave. Perfecta discovered it didn't seem to matter what she did; God never noticed her at all, in spite of what her mother said.

People noticed her, but not in the way she wanted. *Los ojos tristes.* Everyone said she had sad eyes. Maybe it was the way they drooped down on the outer corners, her lids folding half way closed when her face was at rest. Perhaps it was the crease that lived on her forehead, even when she thought of nothing at all. It could have been because her pupils were large, never shrinking all the way to pinpoints in her cloudy green eyes, even on a sunny day.

Perfecta's eyes glared, the wrinkle on her forehead a mountain rather than its usual crease. It just wasn't fair. She was always in trouble.

The pain in her chest eased. The soft desert wind blew a fine dust. She watched a tiny whirlwind spiral up the road. It raced along, changing direction as if it were a ballerina twirling across the dance floor, bending to pick up bits and pieces of the earth, then dropping them again for no reason.

She closed her eyes and stood still. There was something satisfying about the sharp sting of the sand, tiny needles poking her bare legs. It wasn't really painful—just a hint, like scratching a mosquito bite hard enough to draw blood. She needed the pain, punishment for this latest disaster.

The words of Sister Maria Esther pounded inside her head.

"Perfecta, this work is ridiculous for a girl nearly ready to go to high school. My first graders can do better than this. *Tienes que trabajar más duro.* How much time did you spend on this? *¿Diez minutos?* What do you do with your time? Moon after the boys? You are too young for that. What boy will want a girl who can't even write a simple essay? *No sé que sera de tí.*"

Sister Maria Esther didn't seem to care that the whole class had stopped working and were listening to the angry words she spoke as she paced back and forth in front of Perfecta's desk. Sister didn't seem to expect her to answer the tirade, never pausing as she switched from English to Spanish and back again. If the students did such a thing they were punished.

"We have talked about this before. You must work every night, and you need to listen in class, not daydream."

"*Trabajé demasiado duro en éste papel.* I worked so hard. The ideas just wouldn't come last night." Perfecta lifted her chin and raised her eyes to stare straight at Sister Maria Esther's. "*Es un idioma dificil.*" English was a difficult language. But she could switch back and forth too, although it made her head hurt to do this.

It wasn't fair Sister made her write in English. Perfecta had spoken Spanish all her life, just as everyone else in town. Last year Father Tom, a new priest, came to Santo Niño Church. He didn't speak the language. Sister Maria Esther arrived soon after that to teach the school children to speak, read and write. English felt like being without water for a week, the words brittle, striking her teeth and sticking to the roof her mouth. Perfecta preferred the soft rolling Spanish, more like the song of the oriole than the croak of the frog.

She shifted her eyes away from the furious stare that had taken over Sister Maria's face and looked at the tightly pulled wimple which bordered the nun's red skin. There were no stray hairs to give a clue of the woman who lived underneath. How old was Sister Maria anyway?

Perfecta looked away quickly, realizing she'd done it again—forgotten to pay attention, trying to guess at the color of hair, the age, the past of this angry woman instead of listening to what the nun had to say. She tried to focus on Sister Maria's words.

"You'll have to do better. I'm sending a note home to your father. You will not move on to the ninth grade unless you do as I say and improve this work. Pay attention to me. I expect your eyes to be on me when I am talking to you."

It was then Perfie had fled the glare of the nun and raced as far as she could from the stifling classroom.

The stinging sand stopped. The wind had passed, the spiral swirling down to nothing as it left the road and headed into the brush. Perfecta remained as she was—standing still—her breath soft, eyes closed, staring at the inside of her eyelids.

They weren't black at all. Tiny splashes of yellow, red, even blue, like stars and planets, floated and rotated past one another. The colors distracted her from her thoughts about the note she had crumpled and thrown into the brush as she fled the school room.

Infinity. There it was, inside her closed eyes like the endless space surrounding the world. Joe, her brother, had taught her about the night sky —not heaven like the nuns taught, but a vast expanse which never ended.

She questioned the nuns, "But what is on the other side of that?" They simply referred to heaven and belief and too much curiosity not being proper for a young lady. They punished her for asking questions, just as they punished her for not knowing the answers.

Joe, on the other hand, loved to explain things to her. He waited for new books to be delivered to the mercantile each week when the truck came the sixty miles from Española. He devoured information about the heavens and tried to pass all this knowledge on to her—knowledge about Copernicus, nebulas, the spiraling universe and stars that were different, even though they all looked the same from here.

She thought he liked the stars because they were romantic, an excuse to get girls to go out at night, but he brushed away her teasing, telling her to grow up. Just because he was twenty-four years old he thought he knew everything, but he didn't know she spied on him. She could climb out the window of her attic bedroom as quickly as he could go out the front door. The old ash tree had branches sturdy enough for her to jump on and swing down to the ground. He was handsome and played the guitar; his voice crooning love ballads was enough to convince any girl to look at the stars with him.

Even though she loved listening to Joe, Perfecta did believe what the nuns said about heaven. Her mother told her the same stories. It must be up there in those fluffy white clouds, where angels played harps and Saint

Peter waited at his gate, checking to see who would shake hands with Jesus.

But on the other side of that, out the back gate of heaven, there was Joe's infinity. Maybe if you behaved in heaven you got to go out that back gate and explore.

Perfecta pressed the heel of her shoe with the toe of her other foot, and slipped smoothly out of her worn leather loafers. The road turned to fine dust through the wash, and she liked the soft feel between her toes. Her father had warned her about walking out here with bare feet; rattlesnakes and the sharp cholla thorns were everywhere. What did he know? He never removed his boots, thumping around the house and tracking dirt all over the floors she had just swept. He was too hard to appreciate the softness of the sand.

She kept her eyes down, sliding her feet through the dust as she examined the snake-like tracks she left on the road. Would someone think a strange creature had made its way across the land?

I am a strange creature.

She stopped and leaned forward, pressing both hands into the sand.

This is my hand, a hand like no other.

I am like no other, she repeated to herself, suddenly realizing what this meant.

She heard that no two fingerprints were alike. She studied the tip of her finger, following the swirls and twists until her eyes ached.

"You have a curious mind, *Hermana*." Joe was the only one who understood she wasn't *estúpida*. She tried so hard at school, but no one believed her. Everyone thought she was lazy. They didn't understand that no matter how hard she worked she couldn't find the information when she needed it. She remembered things, just not when someone else demanded she remember. Daydreamer, her mother called her. But it wasn't like dreaming; it was just that her mind went where it wanted to go, and nothing she did seemed to change that.

She could learn from her brother. He was a better teacher than the nuns. He told stories, weaving lessons and information into amazing tales which held her mind captive. She never drifted off when he was talking to her. If she quit school Joe could teach her—that's what she'd tell Mama and Papa.

She wasn't going back, no matter what they did to her.

At the top of the slope the road turned to rough yellow soil. There were rocks here, churned up by the wagons and horses as the men headed out to toss feed to the cattle.

Slipping her shoes back on, Perfecta turned her gaze to the dark bluffs outlined against the bright clouds. I'd love to paint this scene, she thought. She imagined herself dipping the brush into the blue paint and slashing it over the top of everything. Not too many clouds today, but the horizon held a dark hint of a spring storm. Thunderheads were starting to move in. A tinge of black paint would go in the corner of her picture.

She craved the crash of thunder and bright flashes of lightning that could arrive unexpectedly, playing their violent song for just a few minutes as they traveled north. She would stand with arms stretched, palms facing the heavens, worshipping this god of thunder as the rain surrounded her for those few minutes.

The air would become cool and fresh and the smell of the sage strong, as if the many scattered bushes also stood with arms spread to welcome the rain, and they too had a renewed spirit.

I understand that god, the thunder god, she thought. He shows his face to me. His presence is gruff, but he sees how I need his cooling rain. Why can't I see Mama's God?

As she prayed for a storm, she heard her father's warning stuck across the back of her mind like a song that gets caught in your head, the same lines playing over and over. "You're going to be struck by a bolt of lightning! One day you won't be here. Just a black grease stain on the road, that's all I'll find. My daughter, I will say, this is her, all that is left. Do you think I will plant flowers for you? A cross? We won't even have a funeral. Why waste money on a casket for a grease stain?"

"Plfft, caw, caw." Perfecta jumped at the sound of a raven scolding as he landed next to her. Had the spirits sensed her thoughts about her father and sent the raven to chase them away? The huge black bird hopped in the dust beside her, head cocked to one side, black eye shining as he inspected her. The expression on his face scared her. This bird frowned, just like her father.

Her shoulders tightened. Ravens could mean bad luck. She relaxed a little. They could also mean good luck. What did this one mean for her?

"Ssshhhh," she hissed and hopped toward him. He rose with a flap of wings, tossing a final scolding "cwaaaee" at her as he flew off.

But even though the bird flew away, Perfecta couldn't shake the thoughts of her father. Had there ever been a time when he didn't criticize everything about her?

When she was younger she asked her mother. "Why did you name me Perfecta? He thinks that to have the name is to be perfect. I can't be perfect; no one can."

Avelina had avoided Perfecta's stare as she continued to brush her daughter's thick hair. "*M'ija*, he loves you. He wants a good life for you."

"Does he have to be so mean?"

"Not mean, concerned. Be thankful, many people have no father at all."

Why was it that people always told her to be thankful when she complained about something? She couldn't think of any reason a person would choose to suffer, choose the bad things. So why did it make sense to be thankful for them?

Life would be different now that she was nearly fourteen years old. She was just going to *live* from now on. If she wasn't supposed to do something, why then, she wouldn't. Her gut would tell her not to do it—not her father, or her mother or some stupid rules someone made up.

Perfecta lifted her chin and balled her hands into fists, a surge of energy moving from the yellow earth into the soles of her feet and up to her heart.

I won't be Perfecta any more. From now on I'll be Perfie. She glanced around as if she were on a stage, the tall cholla, spiny arms reaching up to the sky, her audience. She pulled her shoulders back and lifted her chin.

"Perfie. Perfie Trujillo I am called." Wrapping one arm in front of her and tucking the other behind her waist, she bowed to the cholla audience, pleased with her new name.

Finished with her performance, she headed up the road. Dust had stuck to her legs during her dance with the whirlwind. Not only that, but the nuns kept the classroom windows shut, as if fearful the light breeze or sound of birds singing might interfere with the boring lessons. On a hot day like today it seemed they felt the brains of children should be cooked to perfection in order to earn a diploma.

She knew how to cool off.

She glanced over her shoulder to make sure there was no one in sight, then veered off the road.

The path was faint. Deer walked here, not the cattle who made their way to the water each night, creating a wide dusty trail farther along the road. Perfie stood taller than the sage, her head like a flag alerting her presence. She didn't want anyone to see her, so she crouched and walked hunched over like an old woman with a bad back.

The hidden trail that wound through the prickly bushes was not wide enough to keep her dress from catching, so she grabbed the sides of the skirt and pulled them together in front of her, holding the fabric close to her body. It wouldn't do to come home full of burrs and stickers—or worse yet, with a torn dress.

Perfie felt the moisture in the air—the ditch was just ahead. This water flowed from high in the Los Brazos range which surrounded the valley, maintaining its melted snow temperature for the first few weeks of the season, then warming slightly as summer months passed. But it stayed cool, even during the hottest part of summer.

She inhaled, tilting her head back and filling her lungs. Such a wonderful smell, this odor of dampness, the hint of sage, cattle, pine. It refreshed her, not like drinking the cool water, but every bit as thirst quenching.

She ducked under the claw-like branch draped over the trail, then stood in the shadow of the spiky piñon tree. Her eyes flicked around, checking for danger as if she were one of the deer who poked a nose out of this trail at dusk.

The broad expanse of brush stretched up the hill, and the piñons didn't offer much shade. The few head of cattle kept here in the summer spent their days down by the cottonwoods, meandering up the hill in the early evening to sip the water. A thick layer of short green grass covered the bank, which sloped slightly to the abrupt two foot drop into the ditch. She looked at the clear water. She could see the rocks which settled into the clay on the bottom. You weren't supposed to swim here; the water was headed to town to quench the thirst and supply the households of the people of Tierra Amarilla.

Just the place for her.

She pulled her arms from the sleeves of her yellow cotton dress and shrugged it off. As it slid down her thighs, she stepped out of dress and shoes in one quick movement, slid a finger under the waist of her panties and removed them. She reached up and pulled the tie from her hair.

"Water, water, water, here I come." With a shake of her head, her braid came loose and she slipped off the dirt wall of the ditch as smoothly as one of the speckled snakes who sometimes shared this spot.

She lay flat in the two feet of water, head tilted back. She used her fingers to scrub her scalp, hair floating in the current. With a sudden splash she flipped over to her stomach, plunged her face into the water and swirled around onto her back, head down stream.

Where is that rock? She groped around on the bed of the ditch until she felt a large stone and held herself in place. The water wasn't deep, but the flow was strong.

She gazed upward into turquoise so bright it seemed unreal. If I could only be as pure as that sky, I wouldn't have these problems. I could be so happy.

As she kept her eyes on a slow-moving cloud her thoughts went back to her troubles. If I stay very still I don't have to think about those things. I can forget about Sister Maria Esther's words. I don't have to think about Papa's lecture or Mama's face when she finds out I'm in trouble again.

She felt as though she were lying in a bed of something magic. The water didn't just flow around her, didn't just wash away the sweat and dust, it flowed through her. She felt as if each cell was refilled with a cool spirit, her body growing bigger and stronger. Her despair and frustration were replaced with a sense of purpose. She was right; those other people were wrong.

Slowly her mind cleared, her stomach relaxed and the pounding behind her right eye stopped. She was alive again, drinking in the strength of the ancient New Mexico spirits.

Peace at last.

Safe in this world of her own, she didn't feel the penetrating stare of the bright blue eyes or sense the presence of the young man who peered out through the brush on the hillside. His gaze flowed over her body, just as the water did.

Two

Isaac Martinez lay awake listening to Benjamin's steady breathing. The two brothers slept in the loft of the big house, separate from the rest of the Martinez clan. Enoch, Eli and Levi slept in a large room below, while Naomi, the only girl, had her own small room on the second floor. The bit of privacy this cramped space afforded them was worth the low sloped ceiling and hot summer nights.

Isaac wasn't usually bothered by Bennie's gentle snores, the occasional mumbles or the odor of his brother's stale cologne. But tonight he couldn't get the image of the girl at the ditch out of his mind.

He'd come home from the University in Santa Fe, finished with his two years of study at last. He was twenty-one years old—a man ready to start his life of labor.

Three days had passed before he had a chance to hike out to the family property. After greeting the few cattle who stayed behind when the vaqueros drove the herds to the summer pastures, he wandered around the ranch, absorbing all that he'd ached for while he was gone. He didn't like to work the cattle, but he liked to be out here. This was really home: the yellow earth, the sage, the gentle slope of hills leading up to the steep bluffs. For nearly an hour he sat and gazed across the land of the high mesa which marked the south end of the Chama Valley. He refilled his soul with the strange spiritual energy which only existed here, in this place of his birth.

He'd headed for the ditch, following the path along the winding edge high enough on the slope to give a view of the twisting Las Nutrias creek. He hummed softly as he walked, his mind on the coming year. In September he would teach at La Academía, the school his father had started here in T.A.

A quick movement of something bright across the ditch stopped him.

It was a girl.

He was about to call out to her, when she slipped out of her dress and into the ditch in one quick motion, giving him a flash of her naked body before she disappeared behind the brush.

"Sweet mother of God," he whispered. Before he thought about what he was doing, he bent his knees and pulled his head down. He crept forward, slipped behind a large cholla bush and looked down on the flowing water.

He watched as the girl floated for a moment on her stomach, her face down. His eyes went to her smooth buttocks, bobbing above the ripples of water like the skin of a summer melon. Saliva gathered in the bottom of his mouth, which dropped open. Suddenly ashamed, he closed his mouth and swallowed.

When she flipped over with a splash, revealing her body to him, he clutched the branch and sharp thorns stabbed his hand. He bit his lip and held his breath, ignoring the pain in his punctured palm.

This can't be real, he thought. My mind is desperate, giving me strange visions. He blinked and shifted for a better look.

Her eyes were opened to the sky. Her hair floated and swirled in the water. It seemed strange she would lie with her head down stream. No matter; it gave him a perfect view of her pale, round breasts and the small dark patch between her legs. The clear water flowed over her body, and she shimmered as if she were a mysterious apparition.

His legs quivered, cramped from this bent position, but he didn't dare move. If she saw him now he would be known as the town pervert. No one would believe he'd stumbled upon her by accident.

All too soon the girl pulled herself out of the water and perched on the ditch's edge. The sun glistened off the drops that covered her skin, like tiny jewels.

He didn't move as she dressed and ducked back up the deer trail, not as quietly as she had arrived, for she sang a little song. He couldn't make out the words, but he caught the laughing tune on the breeze that picked up her magical voice and carried it across the distance, teasing him with the sound. Slowly he stood, keeping his face behind a tall bush and trying to catch one more glimpse of this amazing girl.

Who was she?

He had lived in Tierra Amarilla his whole life. It was a small place, yet he didn't recognize her. Someone new in town? Bennie hadn't mentioned anything. And Bennie had a nose for women; he could sniff out a pretty girl from miles away. Isaac had planned to ask his brother about the girl, but Madre invited Tío Miqueas and all his kids to supper. There hadn't been a chance to get Bennie alone.

Isaac pushed the pillow into a tight bunch under his neck. The memory of the girl kept him in an excited state. He pictured himself sitting next to her, both of them feeling the sun as it warmed their skin, cool from the water. He leaned to touch her rosy cheek, kiss her perfect lips, let his hands feel her pale skin. He felt his body take charge, responding to the stimulating thoughts. He shifted carefully, so as not to disturb Bennie, and let the fantasy take over.

"Wake up."

Isaac felt a sharp poke in his ribs.

"Okay, okay, I will." He forced one eye open to barely a slit, just enough to look at his brother.

Bennie stooped in the tiny space, pulling on a long-sleeved shirt and denim overalls. "We have a lot to do today. We told Padre we'd help with the painting, remember? If you want to eat before we go, get up. That man waits for no one."

Isaac closed his eyes. He wasn't ready to wake up. A smile came over his thin lips.

The girl.

Maybe today he could find out who she was.

He whipped the blanket to one side and swung his legs over the edge of the bed.

Bennie stood in front of the tiny mirror on the wall, a glob of pomade on one hand and his comb in the other. Isaac watched as his brother primped his perfect hair. Bennie's hair was darker than his, nearly black and shiny from the grease he applied. Isaac's hair was a dull brown.

They both had the Martinez light eyes, a definite magnet for women in this brown-eyed town. Bennie had perfect features: square jaw, smooth skin, slender nose. Isaac shared these features, but somehow on his face they didn't come together. Bennie was described as "handsome," while Isaac only merited "interesting."

Bennie kicked Isaac's boots toward him. "Come on, Ike, move it. I don't want to start the day making Father mad. I can't take that look of how-much-I-disappoint-him this early in the morning."

Isaac slipped into the pants he'd slung over the chair the night before and pulled on a soft cotton shirt, the blue of the plaid the same as the blue of his eyes. Although the weather was hot, he chose long sleeves. He didn't want his arms covered with paint. He stood on one leg as he pulled on his boot.

"Hey, Bennie. Have any new families moved into town?"

Bennie's hand paused. He squinted his eyes and tipped his chin. "Not that I can think of." He added more goop to the cowlick which stuck up on the side of his head.

Isaac leaned on the bed post as he pulled on his other boot.

"I saw this girl yesterday. I didn't recognize her."

"Ahhh . . . a girl. Of course. What was she like?"

"She was beautiful. Light eyes, shiny hair. Brown. She wore it in a long braid down her back." If anyone understood girls it was Bennie. "When she shook the braid loose you could see hints of gold and red shining in the sun."

"Whoa there, Brother. When she shook the braid loose? What were you doing with this girl?"

"Nothing. I was just watch—" Isaac felt his face grow warm, embarrassed to let Bennie know he had been spying on the girl. "I just saw her."

Isaac was saved from answering any more questions by the sound of their mother's stern voice. She called up the stairway to the loft as if her words could reach out and cuff the side of each head.

"Isaac. Benjamin. Your father is waiting."

The two young men dashed down the wooden stairs. Carlotta stood in the hallway with arms folded across her chest like an Army commander waiting for the troops to line up. Through the open door Isaac could see his father loading the wagon with buckets and paint brushes. A tall wooden ladder leaned against the back of the wagon.

Bennie headed out the front door, but Isaac stepped sideways around his mother and slipped into the kitchen. He snatched up a slice of toast from the stack on a green plate. He turned to the iron skillet on the stove and slipped an egg onto the toast with his finger. He ate his breakfast in three large bites as he headed out to join his father and brother. His mother would be happy he took the time to eat what she cooked, even if he slept too late to join her for breakfast.

The image of the naked girl continued to push all other thoughts from his mind.

It was just after two o'clock when Isaac washed off his brush and helped Bennie stack the extra paint into the wagon.

"I'm taking off, if that's okay." Isaac looked to his father. "I finished all the trim."

Lucas stepped back, examined the building and nodded. "Thanks for your help. Your mother wants you home for supper."

After promising he would make it back in time for the family meal, Isaac hurried to the edge of town. He was in luck. There was the girl making her way up the dirt road toward the ditch. He took the upper route, just over the small ridge which bordered the Martinez property. He clattered through the brush singing, arriving on the north side of the ditch just as she ducked under the hanging branch which guarded the south side.

"Hello." He called out loudly, hoping his feigned surprise would sound genuine.

The girl looked across the ditch. Her eyes widened and she stood very still. She hadn't heard him, in spite of his noisy approach.

She was every bit as beautiful as he remembered—even with her clothes on.

He sat on the edge of the ditch and pulled off one of his boots. "Are you coming here to cool off? I love to dip my feet. Cools off the whole body." He pulled off his other boot and his socks, then slipped his feet into the water.

She stood still for a moment, then sat and removed her shoes. A smile crept onto her face. First her mouth turned up at the edges, tiny commas on each side of the heart-shaped lips. Next the corners of her eyes crinkled as her eyebrows arched. Isaac felt a broad grin take over his face; there was nothing subtle about how happy he was.

She peered across the ditch for a moment. Her eyes bore holes into him; she studied him as if she had never seen a man before. Finally she spoke.

"It's hot today."

Her voice was as sweet as her face. The lilt at the end of that one sentence went straight to his gut, which clenched in anticipation.

"I'm Isaac Martinez."

"I know. I mean, I know you're a Martinez, I just didn't know which one."

How did she know who he was, yet he didn't recognize her? "There are a lot of us. I'm the youngest. I've been away at school." Isaac paused. "And you are?"

"Oh, Per—Perfie Trujillo" She dipped her chin, a slow flush moved up her neck and onto her cheeks.

Trujillo? As in Primitivo Trujillo, the rude lawman? Isaac racked his mind. There were some stepsons, Joe and Manuel, but a daughter?

"Is your brother Joe Chavez?"

"Sí, Ramaldo, my half brother. He likes to be called Joe." The girl looked across the ditch, staring into Isaac's face. "I have another brother. Mannie. Do you know him?"

"Yes, I've met him." Isaac remembered Joe's older brother. He had left T.A. some years back after a fist fight with Primitivo.

"Do you come here often?" Her question caught him by surprise. Weren't they talking about Joe and Mannie?

"No, this is the first time. I don't walk much." Isaac felt his voice waver slightly. What a stupid thing to say. As if this was the first time he came to his family's property. He continued, with the hope he wouldn't be caught in the lie. "Do *you* come here often?"

"I like it here."

Isaac felt a strange flush move down his neck and through him, until even his toes felt like they were vibrating in the cool water. He turned his eyes away for a moment. He couldn't look at her without imagining her naked body. He wanted to jump across the ditch and grab her, kiss those pink lips, hold her tight against him.

The thought was so strong, he felt as if he really had just kissed her. He licked his lips.

He suddenly recalled a little girl, a child. Joe had a much younger sister. Isaac realized this girl was probably about thirteen or fourteen years old. He paused for a moment, but realized that even knowing how young she was didn't change how he felt about her.

The sun dropped in the west and a sharp glare hit his eyes, turning Perfie into a dark outline. He raised his hand to his brow and peered toward her. He wanted to see her face. If only he were on the same side of the ditch. He slipped his boots back on.

There was an old board for crossing the ditch just past the curve of the hill. "Will you wait while I come around?" Not waiting for a reply, he jumped up and started down the ditch's edge.

It only took a few minutes to reach the board, but when Isaac came around the curved hillside to the spot where Perfie had been sitting, he saw only the flash of her yellow dress as she raced down the narrow path.

Late Friday afternoon Isaac headed out of town. He'd been to the property every day. He walked the south side of the ditch, hoping to catch a glimpse of Perfie.

He hadn't seen her all week.

I scared her. I shouldn't have moved so fast.

Today he walked slowly, not really expecting to see her. As he came close to the ditch he heard the sound of a horse pounding up the road. A white horse with a rider tucked tight against its back raced toward him.

It was Perfie. She slowed when she came to the trail, moving the horse easily through the sage. She raised her bare feet up onto the horse's shoulders, keeping them clear of the prickly plants.

Isaac knew she could see him. Her eyes met his as she wound her way toward the ditch.

She stopped the horse at a low spot just across the water from where he stood. The animal lowered its head to drink, balancing on the ledge with front legs spread wide. The gelding must have done this before; it seemed he knew just how far to bend to get his lips to the surface of the water.

The horse wasn't truly white. It was covered with brown splotches as if someone had splattered paint over the withers and rump. A black mane and tail, as well as two black legs, the left front and the right rear, gave the horse an unbalanced look, as if it might tip over at any minute.

She didn't smile. "Why were you on my side?"

Isaac was surprised by her accusation. This property belonged to his family.

"Your side?"

"I watched you. You aren't a very good tracker. You were looking for me."

"I like to walk here. This is my property, you know."

She wasn't fooled. "Yours? Your father's, you mean."

"My father's, mine, what difference? It'll be mine someday."

She scowled. "You must think I'm foolish. I know you have four brothers."

"Five brothers." He didn't like the way the conversation was going. "Nice horse." he said.

At last she smiled. "He is a nice horse, even if he isn't much to look at." She leaned forward and patted the spotted neck. "He's my best friend, aren't you Cimmaron?"

Isaac spoke up before he lost his place in the conversation to the horse. "Okay, you're right. I was looking for you. I wanted to talk to you again."

"Fine. But you stay over there and I'll stay over here."

"That makes it hard to talk, but if that's what you want, okay." He walked to the edge of the ditch and sat on the grassy bank.

The horse finished drinking and nibbled at the green sprouts poking out of the mud. Perfie swung her legs to one side of the gelding, sitting on him like a chair, one hand holding the rope of the halter, the other rubbing the long white neck.

Isaac noticed the horse didn't have a bridle or a bit, only the slim rope halter around the nose. "You ride like an Indian."

She scowled at him and slid off the horse. "I am *not* an Indian."

"Not Pocahontas? A beautiful maiden astride her trusty steed?"

She didn't seem to appreciate his poetic flirting. "I'm Spanish, through and through."

"Of course. Isn't everyone in this town?"

"Not the Martinez family."

Isaac was surprised. Not his family? Why did she think he wasn't Spanish?

"I am Spanish, descendent from Martín Serrano de Narvo Martínez. Do you want to see my pedigree?"

"You're not Catholic."

He shook his head. "Spain is a big country, filled with people of many beliefs."

"Have you been to Spain?"

"No, but I can read. I learned a lot at the University, believe it or not."

Isaac and Perfie talked on. She was curious about the world outside of T.A. The farthest she had traveled was Española. Imagine, he thought, fourteen—or however old she was—and never been to Santa Fe or Albuquerque.

"Someday I will show you the world. Would you like that?"

"What are you saying?"

"What I am saying is that I would like to be over there, on that bank, next to you."

She shook her head and jumped to her feet, whistling for the horse, who had nibbled his way up to a bend in the ditch. He lifted his head and trotted to her, snorting in anticipation. Isaac watched as she took something from her pocket and fed it to the horse, whose soft lips gently lifted it from her hand. She jumped onto Cimmaron's back and set off down the trail.

No goodbye. She had disappeared again.

For the next two weeks Isaac walked out to the ditch every day. Perfie was there, keeping to her side and making sure he kept to his. Sometimes she was on the young horse, other times on foot. Each day he tried to convince her to let him come to her side.

She would shake her head firmly. "It's not proper that way. It's better like this."

"Better for who? It's not better for me."

Today he would try something new. He waited by the bridge where the road split, to the right for the south side of the ditch and to the left for the north. He held an odd-shaped package wrapped in brown paper.

He called out as soon as he saw her walking up the road. "Hello."

She stopped where she was. "*Hola*. What are you doing here?"

He held up the package. "I have something for you."

"What is it?"

"A surprise." He could see she was torn. She wanted to know what he had for her, yet she had been firm in her demand that they stay apart. "Come on. I won't bite. I promise to go to my side when you have your gift."

She walked toward him, stopping just in front of him. He studied her green eyes as they peered first into his arms at the package, then met his stare.

"Why do you want to give me something?"

He held out the package and shrugged. "I saw it and I knew it was for you."

He watched her face as she took the package and carefully removed the brown paper without tearing it, uncovering the smooth felt of the hat he had bought for her in Chama. It was like those the vaqueros wore, but more delicate. The sueded leather was a warm brick color, and the band had a tooled design of flowers and leaves. Her eyes glowed as she ran her hand over the brim.

"It's like the soft skin of a calf."

"Put it on."

She placed the hat on her head, smoothing her hair back out of her eyes and tucking it inside. Placing her hands on the brim she wiggled the hat back and forth until it was snug on her head, a slight tilt to one side low over her eyes.

"How does it look?"

He took a step forward and reached to lift the brim out of her face.

She took three steps back, and he dropped his hand to his side.

"It looks beautiful. Do you like it?"

"Yes, I like it." She smiled. "But that doesn't mean you can come to my side of the ditch."

"Why are you so scared of me? All I want is one kiss."

"I'm sure that's all you want." Her voice dripped in sarcasm. "If I give you one kiss, then what next?"

"I promise. One kiss. Then I will be good. I will sit across from you every day for a year, for five years, if that's what it takes."

She tipped her chin, then reached up and adjusted the hat, uncovering her eyes. "Five years? What are you waiting for all that time? For a kiss? To sit next to me?"

"I wait for you to be *mi novia*, my sweetheart."

He watched as she stood in silence, one hand rubbing back and forth over the fabric of her shirt along the side of her abdomen. She pressed her palm to her stomach, then stepped forward and smiled from underneath the brim of the hat.

"Okay. One kiss."

Three

Perfie kept her head down as she watched her father stride through the back door and slip his jacket onto the hook. He pulled his hat off and perched it on top of the jacket. His white hair was mussed, curls sticking up like the branches of a tumbleweed. Her father was an old man, in his fifties at least. His heavy brow was creased, and his steely green eyes looked past people when he spoke. He stood tall, both in his height and his posture, always erect, chin held high.

He walked across the kitchen and stopped behind his wife.

Avelina worked in front of the small black stove, stirring a pot of lamb stew. The scent of the chili and meat filled the air.

He leaned over her shoulder and peered into the pot. "The ditch is down another three inches," he mumbled as he inhaled the rich aroma.

"That much?" Mama turned from the stove and picked up a basket of sopapillas. She looked small and frail next to Papa. Her shoulders pushed forward and her back bent, as if she were a peasant who had carried a heavy load for many years.

Perfie didn't know what her mother worried about. She rarely saw her father be mean to her mother; he saved his anger for her. If only once he would put his hand on her shoulder with the soft caress he now placed on her mother's arm. If he would only look at her, instead of through her.

She had watched those hands squeeze into fists of rage. He slapped her when she didn't keep her words to herself, and her arms often ached from the twisting he gave them while he lectured. When she was younger a flat paddle hung on the back porch, but it had been over a year since her father had used it to beat away her sins.

"Why aren't the girls helping you?" He looked around the room, his gaze settling on Perfie. She flinched and felt guilty, even though she was helping Mama.

Avelina didn't turn as she spoke. "They are helping. Perfecta, go get Isabelle and Joe. Dinner is ready."

The table was set with white plates, embroidered napkins and a smooth linen table cloth, its green the color of new grass. Perfie helped her mother place sliced tomatoes, fried patatas, roasted chilies and a bowl of field greens out in preparation for the meal. At least they were having stew with meat tonight, not the usual beans. That should make her father happy.

She loved her mother's savory beans. There was just enough red chili to burn your tongue, and the fried potatoes served with them would cool everything down. But Papa complained about not enough meat, so Avelina tried to serve the beans when she knew he wouldn't be home for dinner.

As Perfie left the kitchen in search of her cousin and her brother, she heard her father continue his conversation. "The majordomo is walking twice a day."

Her father was still talking about the water problems. This must mean Sister Maria Esther hadn't spoken with him yet.

Isabelle and Joe followed Perfie back into the room. They stopped short of the table—Primitivo must sit first.

"Smells good." Joe waited for his stepfather. When Primitivo pulled back his chair at the head of the table, Joe and Perfie moved into their chairs.

Isabelle turned to Avelina. "Do you need help, Tía?"

Of course Isabelle offered to help now, once Primitivo was here, Perfie thought. Her cousin had managed to avoid all the work before dinner.

Perfie snorted. Joe heard it and crinkled his nose at her. Her brother knew about the rivalry between the cousins.

Isabelle could never be described as beautiful. Her lank brown hair failed to curl, hanging to her shoulders with a lack of energy. It wasn't thick enough to shine, and no amount of brushing or lamb's grease could brighten the flat, dull look. Her eyes were of no particular distinction, a light brown set between a nose which was not large or small. Perfie's cousin was slim, not athletic or skinny. At five feet four, she was not tall or short.

Yet not a day went by without Perfie hearing someone tell Isabelle how wonderful she was.

Perfie couldn't understand this. Although she hated her own looks— hair too curly, eyes set too wide in her face, ears stuck out of her head like bats had landed there, legs too short and waist too low—she secretly thought she was much better looking than Isabelle.

So why didn't old Mrs. Burns or the beaky Kate Simms tell her she was looking fine today? Why didn't the boys look her way and smile? Why didn't Father Tom walk up and clasp her hand and thank her for coming to mass? No, that was all saved for Isabelle.

It must be the curse, Perfie thought—some evil ancient spirit floating in the room on the day I was born, waving an eagle feather over my head. No, that seemed like strength. More likely the feather was of the raven.

"Sit, sit, I have everything." Avelina instructed Isabelle, interrupting Perfie's envious thoughts.

The family ate the stew in near silence. Avelina fussed a little, making sure everyone's plate was served before scooping a tiny spoonful into her own bowl.

Perfie worried about her mother. Avelina seemed to be shrinking, barely eating a thing these days. Her mother's shiny brown hair was thinning and filling with gray. Perfie noticed that the tortoiseshell combs used to hold the loose swirl of hair in place slid out several times a day, Mama's hair too weak to hold them. The beautiful dresses her mother always wore, even when working, hung from her shoulders like the sacks the beans came in. The fabrics, shiny silks and smooth cottons, had lost their color. How long had it been since her mother made herself a new dress?

Avelina broke the silence. "School reports came home today."

Primitivo stopped eating, his gaze moving between Isabelle and Perfecta.

Joe used his sopapilla as a scoop; filling it with the vegetable and lamb mixture, he took a large bite and chewed vigorously. "I did great."

Perfie knew her brother was trying to lighten the mood. He had been out of school for six years.

Primitivo turned to Isabelle. "How did you do?"

Isabelle looked down at her plate. Perfie could see her cousin was puzzled. She had moved in with the family three months ago and was unfamiliar with the tradition of discussing grades over supper. Her own parents were uneducated. It wasn't likely they ever asked about her grades.

Perfie remembered the day Isabelle had come to stay. She was excited to have her cousin live with them. People said the two were like twin sisters, not cousins. Best friends since infancy, they learned to sew, to knit, to paint and to ride together. Isabelle wasn't as daring as Perfie, but she never failed to dive into the adventures. An excellent tree climber, she could run like the wind, and she wasn't afraid of snakes.

But Perfie hadn't imagined that Primitivo would spoil Isabelle so much and never dreamed her father would flatter and care for another girl while he nagged his own daughter about every little detail.

Isabelle was everything she was not. Isabelle was smart. She always behaved and never sassed the nuns. When she came to live with them she started in the eighth grade, same as Perfie, but was quickly moved to the high school class when it became apparent she was so intelligent. Papa seemed excited to have a girl in the house who would go to college, make something of herself.

Avelina spoke up. "She did beautifully. Top marks in all areas. She's a wonderful student."

Isabelle blushed and kept her eyes down. Beautiful and pious, too, Perfie thought with disgust. She loved her cousin, but right now a surge of spite welled up in her throat. Isabelle could be just too perfect sometimes. Too bad she wasn't named Perfecta.

Perfie sneaked a glance at her father's face. His eyes seemed to glow when he looked at Isabelle. His chin was held high as he waved his fork in front of him, complimenting her cousin on the meal. Isabelle never said a word, soaking up his praise with a smarmy smile, lowering her eyes and staring at her folded hands. What about all that Perfecta had done? She had gone to the market and carried back the heavy load of groceries along with everything else they needed. She had chopped all those vegetables, hauled the water from the ditch and set out the clean table cloth, arranging the dishes just so. Perfie chomped down on a chunk of meat, biting her cheek in the process.

Primitivo nodded his head. Then he turned to his daughter. "And you, Perfecta? Did you keep your promise? Am I to hear about all the improvement over the last report?"

Perfie was silent. Through some miracle the news not only of her failing, but of her missing school for a week hadn't made it to her father yet. But it was about to make its way to this dinner table. She thought about the huge fight the last time she brought home poor grades. The promise she made to herself that day out at the ditch surged into her.

She pushed her chair back, set the tips of her fingers on the edge of the table and leaned forward, chin jutting out. "Those Sisters hate me. I don't know what you expect me to do." Perfie looked straight into her father's face, her brow creased, puffs of air huffing from her nose as she waited.

His back straightened and he stared at her, his brow creasing to match hers.

Avelina pulled a folded paper from her pocket and handed it to Primitivo. He picked up his glasses from beside his plate and bent his head to read the report. When he was finished he slowly set it down.

"Failing math, failing English, failing domestics? These comments, Perfecta, do you even bother to pay attention at all? And absences? When were you not at school? You haven't been ill."

Her father's voice was quiet, a bad sign. The calm before the storm. Perfie imagined a coal miner calling out "Heads up!" before the dynamite exploded. It was now or never.

She raised her hands from where her fingers touched the edge of the table and slammed them down. Plates, glasses and silverware rattled. "I hate school. I hate it. I'm not going back. Never. I'm done with them. They hate me no matter what. When I do the work they fail me, so why should I do the work? You can't make me go back. I won't."

Every inch of her body told her to run. She would pay for this outburst. Her shoulders tightened anticipating the squeeze of her father's huge hands.

But she kept her gaze on his face.

Primitivo was silent and still for a moment. Then he picked up the report and looked at it again. He rubbed his forehead, and his frown deepened.

He set the report back down, picked up his fork and took a bite of stew. He continued eating without a word. Joe took advantage of this and went back to eating. Isabelle glanced around and picked up her fork, poking a single slice of potato and putting it in her mouth.

Avelina looked across the table at Perfecta and gave a slight shake of her head. Perfie sat without moving, hands beside her plate as if they had stuck to the table when she banged them down.

She didn't move while Primitivo finished eating, then stood, folded his napkin and turned from the table. He took his coat from the hook and walked out the back door. The screen door did not slam; he shut it slowly. The wooden steps creaked as he left the porch and went to stand in the yard.

Perfie looked out after him, watching as he lit his pipe and stared off toward the mountains.

"Oh Perfecta," Avelina sighed, but didn't say more.

Joe quickly finished his last bite, pushed his chair back and stood. "*Me voy*. I'm leaving," he said as he rushed out of the room.

Isabelle stood, her plate in one hand. She reached over for Primitivo's plate, walked around the table and added Joe's plate to the stack, then went to the sink.

Perfie and Avelina sat at the table in silence, the only sound the clink of the dishes Isabelle was washing. When her cousin was finished, she fled the kitchen, leaving them alone.

It worked, Perfie thought. I stood up to him and he didn't hit me or grab my arm. No lecture, either. She looked at her mother.

"I'm not going back." She tried to keep her voice steady, but there was a slight quiver.

"What will you do?" Her mother's voice was soft.

"I'll get a job."

"Perfecta, there aren't jobs for the men in this town. Who do you think will give a job to a fourteen-year-old girl, a girl who only knows how to run around the hills, iron wrinkles permanently into shirts, burn the beans and sass her parents?" Mama's tone was rising.

"I can embroider. I can work at the mercantile. There are a lot of things I can do. I know I can find a job."

"What about later? The future? What then?"

"I'll marry Isaac, that's what!" Perfie instantly wished she could take back the words. What was she thinking? Why was she telling her mother she was going to marry him?

Her mother's face turned white. "Isaac? Isaac Martinez?"

Perfie was silent.

"What do you mean you'll marry Isaac Martinez? He's a grown man, nearly as old as your brother. Perfecta, tell me what you have done?" Mama's pitch grew higher with each word.

Perfie chewed on her lip.

Avelina covered her eyes as she slumped forward. "Have you, have you—oh no."

"I'm still a virgin, if that is what you are trying to ask. I *am* a good girl, in spite of what you think."

Her mother lifted her head and studied Perfie. "There was once a beautiful Indian maiden called White Blossom."

Perfie sighed. Another story. Mama could never tell her something directly. Instead she would tell an intricate tale, expecting that some lesson would be apparent to Perfie.

"She was the daughter of a fierce chief."

"What was his name?" Perfie interrupted her mother, knowing she would be ignored.

"This chief had many duties and obligations. The responsibility of keeping the tribe safe from harm, making sure there was enough food, resolving arguments, knowing when to plant and when to hunt—these all fell to him."

Her mother never looked at her as she told these stories, assuming a sort of wise sage expression, her eyes gazing off at a wall or out the window as if she read the story out of thin air.

"There were so many dangers in those times—not only the wild animals such as mountain lions, bears and wolverines, but men who were coming to the secluded lands where the tribe lived. This chief, he wanted to keep his daughter safe, but he had so much to do. He needed to trust her to do the right thing. He tried to explain this to the maiden, to tell her what she needed to do to be safe. But the maiden didn't listen. She loved the land and would wander off to pick flowers or find reeds to weave into the baskets the tribe made."

Perfie turned her head away from her mother. She didn't want to roll her eyes at this ridiculous story. Mama didn't even bother to hide the lesson anymore.

"One day the maiden wandered far from home. She didn't notice the day was growing dark. She didn't think about all the warnings her father had given. A thunderstorm blew in and it started to rain. A thick fog came into the valley where the maiden had wandered. She couldn't see anything, and when she tried to find her way home, she slipped on some rocks and fell into a deep ravine.

"Night time came. The rain turned to snow. The maiden was soon covered, shivering, cold, freezing. As she lay there, her teeth chattering, she thought about her father's warnings. She realized he had told her how to avoid this situation. 'Oh, if I only listened to him, she cried out, as she lay there." Avelina paused, turned and looked at Perfie.

"Meanwhile, her father was looking for her. He rode his horse through the hills, calling her name. The rain and snow had covered her tracks, but he knew of the valley where she liked to go. He rode up and down for days, but he couldn't find his daughter. Finally the winter snow was too thick and he had to give up his search."

Perfie kept her smart remarks locked inside her head, her lips pressed tight together as she thought about her mother's story. At least White Blossom's father loved her. She doubted Primitivo would search for her if she failed to show up. She imagined herself on Cimmaron's back, riding high into the mountains, the snow coming down on them. She would find a cave and live with her horse. He was her only true friend anyway.

Her mother continued. "When spring came to the mountains the Chief resumed his search. He hoped he had trained his daughter well and that she had survived the cold season, keeping herself alive in some cave."

Could Mama read her mind?

"He rode up a narrow ridge until he saw a spot where there had been a rock slide. He made his way to the bottom of the slide. There was no sign of the maiden here, but there was something strange. A tall plant was growing, one he had never seen before in all his travels. It had a thick green stalk, white flowers growing up both sides."

White Blossoms. Of course, thought Perfie. She waited for the rest of the story.

But her mother stood and walked out of the kitchen. She moved as if her body was in pain. She went to sit in her rocking chair in the front room near the window facing the road.

Perfie saw her mother sit, the chair not rocking. The stillness of her body announced her displeasure.

That must be the end, Perfie thought. What now? Her father and mother both silent. No threats, no punishment, no harsh words. Just one vague story. She couldn't keep a tiny grin from pinching at the edge of her mouth.

It had worked. She had won.

Perfie lifted her hands from where they were still pressed against the table, picked up her fork and finished her lamb stew.

Four

"Come out here on Cimmaron tomorrow."

Perfie turned her head and looked at Isaac. Her eyebrows lifted into twin question marks. He had never asked her to do this before.

"Don't be so suspicious. Just do it."

She nodded. Isaac must want to go for a ride. She'd never seen him on a horse, but she knew the Martinez family had several. The small barn behind their tall house was visible from the church. She admired a shiny bay who liked to poke his nose over the fence and search her pockets for the treats she hid there. Why couldn't Isaac just come out and ask her to go for a ride?

She was beginning to know him, but big holes filled the picture she painted in her mind. When they met at the ditch each day they talked—and talked. He reminded her of Joe in that way, willing to teach her about the rest of the world. She realized she was even more sheltered than she thought. The trips to Española hadn't really taught her anything. She had been to Chimayo once but that was when she was six, and she didn't remember much—only Aunt Lucianda's funny dog and a big church. They had waited in the wagon while her mother went into the tall adobe building to pray and light a candle. These vague snapshots left her no real sense of the town.

Isaac told her about all the things she was missing. People in big cities had electricity in their houses, water that ran clean out of faucets and toilets that flushed. Cooking and cleaning took city women barely any time at all. This meant they had time to go to the movies or have their hair styled. Huge mansions lined the streets—houses with closets full of beautiful dresses and pantries filled with food.

"I will have all that one day," Isaac told her. "It will be for you."

Each night when she lay beside Isabelle and closed her eyes, she pictured what life would be like in one of those houses. Isaac would come home wearing his fine suit and hand his hat to the butler, just like in the books that she read. She would be wearing a green silk dress, her hair cut short in a shiny bob. She would be like the women in the magazines she and Isabelle poured through when Mrs. Hughes was done with them: McCall's, Good Housekeeping and Nash's. Dream books.

The next morning she reached under the bed and pulled out a pillowcase. She slipped the brick-colored hat out and put it on her head.

"Where did you get that?" Isabelle's voice startled her. She thought her cousin was down in the kitchen with Mama.

"It's mine. Don't worry, I didn't steal it."

Isabelle reached forward and snatched the hat from Perfie's head, swooping it onto her own as she hopped over to the mirror.

"It's beautiful."

Perfie nodded. She had never seen the hat on anyone else, although she had spent time gazing at her own reflection in the mirror.

Isabelle spun around and took the hat off. She rubbed the suede with her hand. "Where did you get it?" She wasn't going to let it go.

Perfie hesitated. She had been careful to keep her meetings with Isaac a secret, even from Isabelle. But she had spilled the beans with Mama, and she was dying for someone to talk to about the things she felt when she was with Isaac.

"Isaac Martinez." She watched Isabelle's face.

"A beau?" Her cousin's mouth pursed into a little "o", as if to accent the word.

Perfie nodded and reached for the hat. "He's really nice. We're going riding today." She slipped the hat back onto her head.

"Which one is he?"

"The youngest."

"The really handsome one?" Like every other girl in town, Isabelle must have been checking out the Martinez boys.

"I think he's really handsome, but I imagine you're thinking of Benjamin."

Isabelle sat on the edge of the bed and smoothed the quilt with her palm. "Have you kissed him?"

"Yes." Perfie sat next to her cousin. "Have you ever kissed a man?"

Isabelle shook her head.

"It feels funny. Wonderful. Warm. Some sort of weird magic flows through my whole body when he kisses me."

"You best be careful, Perfie. You know what can happen."

"I know. I am careful. We only kiss. And talk." She leaned forward and pressed her hands on her knees. "Even talking feels magic with him."

She stood quickly and faced her cousin. "I have to go. He'll be waiting. You can't tell anyone, not anyone. Papa would kill me if he found out."

"I won't tell." Isabelle stood and hugged her cousin. "I think you're lucky. Now go. You don't want him to leave without you."

Twenty minutes later Perfie and Cimmaron galloped up the road toward the ditch. She spotted Isaac on the shiny bay, just beyond the bridge.

She pulled to a stop beside him. "Where are we going?" The two horses snorted, nostrils flaring out as they sniffed at each other.

"It's a surprise."

"To the bluffs?"

Isaac shook his head. "You spoil it, my dear. I suppose you've been there already."

Perfie grinned. "I've been everywhere. This is my town, remember. I haven't been to any cities, but I know every inch of this land."

"Then we'll have to take my secret route. You probably haven't been there." He kicked the bay and raced up the road.

She had been the route he was taking her. But she hadn't discovered the spring set back against the canyon wall. It was cool here, even in the heat of mid-day. Isaac sliced apples and fed them to her, while the horses drank and nibbled at the plants growing near the spring.

"Have you seen a movie?" He sucked on the wedge and picked up a smooth rock from beside the spring.

"Yes. Once. In Española. It was hard to see because it was a sunny day. I guess it's better at night. It was about a man who invented a machine to travel in time."

"That's how I'll do it, Perfie. That's how I'll get our fortune."

"Show movies?" This apple was bitter. She felt her mouth pucker as she bit into the wedge.

"Be *in* movies. Be a star." He tossed the rock into the spring with a splash. "They make as much money for one movie as I could make in five years working at La Academía."

"How do you do it?" She tried to imagine a movie being made. She thought there was a stage and a special camera, but sometimes the movie seemed to be outside. Maybe there was a camera mounted on a wagon. Would Isaac have to buy a movie camera?

He turned to her and took her hand in his. "I have to go to California. Hollywood. That's where they make movies."

"What do you mean?"

"I have to leave T.A., Perfie. Go live in California."

This was the surprise? He was leaving? She jumped to her feet and stumbled to her horse. Grabbing a handful of Cimmaron's long mane, she pulled herself onto his back and pressed his sides with her thighs. "Gee!"

"Wait!"

She heard Isaac scramble to his feet. She leaned forward as Cimmaron raced through the trees. She heard hooves pounding behind her, but she didn't look back.

At the bottom of the hill a rock wall surrounded a pasture. They had ridden around it on their way to the spring, but she wanted to get out of here fast, so she reined Cimmaron straight toward it. She had jumped bigger. The hoof beats still sounded behind her. Maybe Isaac wasn't as good at jumping as she was.

The spotted horse gathered his strength into his hindquarters and stretched over the wall. Perfie saw the elk just as the horse twisted mid-air, flinching away from the big animal that stood on the other side of the wall. She gripped Cimmaron's mane, but her weight pulled her up over his shoulder and she felt herself fly directly toward the elk. The last thing she saw was the brown hide as she covered her head with her arms and hit the earth.

A hazy fog surrounded her. She felt something warm on her eyebrow. Blood? But when she opened her eyes it was a big brown nose. Isaac's horse sniffed at her.

"Ohhh." Everything hurt. Her shoulder, her back, her arm and her head. She took a deep breath and turned. Cimmaron stood next to the wall. She tried to sit up, but a rush of air swooped up inside her head and she lay back down. Where was Isaac?

Perfie didn't know how much time passed. She felt the warm sun on her face and heard the horses milling around, searching the bare earth for something to nibble. She kept her eyes closed. Nothing was broken—she was pretty sure of that—but her head still felt funny.

"Perfie. Open your eyes. Please look at me."

She opened her eyes. Isaac was sitting down, and he pulled her head into his lap. "I'm okay." Her words came out in a whisper.

"Thank God." He stroked her head, pushing her hair back out of her eyes.

She waited for the scolding, the anger. She had run away from him. Remembering the sound of hooves pounding just behind her, she was pretty sure his horse had followed without him.

"I was so worried. I saw you lying so still." He rubbed his thumb across her eyebrow. "You hit your head."

"It was an elk. It scared us. I could jump that wall."

"I'm sure you could."

Her head felt better, but she didn't want to leave his arms. They were strong, holding her shoulders, spreading across her back. She remembered her father carrying her to bed when she was tiny. She remembered sitting in her mother's lap, rocking back and forth, Avelina's arms folded across her back like this.

It had been a long time since anyone held her.

She looked into his eyes, and the words gathered on her tongue. Don't leave me, don't leave me, don't leave me. She wanted to tell him how much she needed him, but she was afraid. If he loved her like she loved him he wouldn't consider going away. He would want to spend every minute of the day here, just like this, their warm bodies close together. If she told him she felt this way he might laugh, kiss her and leave her anyway. It was better to keep the words inside.

"Perfie?" He stared at her as she licked her lips and swallowed. "What is it?"

She pulled herself from his arms and sat up.

"Where's my hat?"

Five

Isaac needed to talk to Perfie about California. Eight months had passed since he first brought it up, but he had made up his mind to go. It was spring already, and he wanted to leave at the end of May.

Summer. I'll go for the summer and that way I won't leave the school short a teacher. If he could talk Lucas into letting him leave a couple of weeks early, that would mean three months to audition and be in a movie. If things worked out it would give his father time to hire his replacement before school started up again in September.

Perfie had reacted so strongly when he told her before. She seemed fine now, but something changed about her. He suspected their meetings weren't as much of a secret as they thought. Isabelle and Benjamin knew, but he didn't think either of them would talk. It was a small town. People noticed the frequent rides, all the time spent out on the property. Isaac knew his brother Enoch had even been worried that Isaac was interested in working the cattle, riding out with him on occasion. Enoch considered managing the cattle his role in the family.

Isaac had gone so far as to actually work the cattle. There needed to be a reason he borrowed Lucas's horse so often.

Saturday morning he met Perfie early. This was a day they could go on a longer ride, not just slip into the trees for a quick tryst. He packed a lunch and they headed up to Los Brazos, the high granite cliffs on the west edge of town.

He waited until they were seated on a ledge, the horses tied behind them.

"Don't run off."

"That means you're going to tell me you're leaving." Perfie stared off into the valley.

He nodded. "It does. But I want you to listen, please."

"Okay. I'm listening." He watched a dark cloud sweep over her face, her brows rigid and her mouth turned down in a firm scowl.

"I'm only going to go for three months, for the summer. I'll be back in September."

"Is that all the time it takes to make a movie?"

She might be only fourteen, but she was no fool. He knew he should be honest, but her reactions could be so intense.

"I don't really know how long it takes. I know I have to audition, work at some other job, maybe take some acting lessons."

"If you get the job, if you're a star or an actor, how long would you stay?"

"Until it's done. Then I'll come back, I promise."

"Why are you telling me this?"

"I thought, well, because you are . . . I am . . . I want you to wait for me." He wished there was a way she could go with him, but he didn't know how he was going to live. It would be better if she stayed here.

"What am I waiting for?"

"For me." He knew what she wanted. A proposal. The words hovered in his mouth. It wasn't like he hadn't thought about this night after night, but it was so complicated.

"And you? Off in California? What will you be doing? Waiting for me?" She squeezed his arm.

"Yes. I promise. I love you, and you are the only one for me." That was as good as a proposal, wasn't it?

Five weeks later Isaac tossed the worn brown suitcase into the bed of the truck and looked at his mother's face. Her mouth was a straight line, lips white from the tight pressure, and her pale brown eyes stared off into the distance. She looked sad, not angry.

At six feet Isaac stood ten inches taller than Carlotta, yet she towered over him with her presence. Carlotta brought to mind a dead tree limb, swaying in the wind, bound to come crashing down some time in the future. You just never knew when. Yet he had seen her tender side, especially when she held babies or nursed a sick dog back to health.

"Your father and I, we are old, Isaac. Old and tired. We can't last much longer."

She hadn't seemed old last night when she raged and threw a plate across the kitchen.

"Adíos, Madre. Things will be good. You'll see." He leaned in and kissed her cheek, keeping his excitement balled tightly in his chest. Superstitious by nature, he did not want to show any emotion that might curse his escape. She might suddenly say, *I've changed my mind, you must stay here and take care of me.*

He had waited until the last minute to tell his parents about his plan. Eli, Levi and Benjamin had known about the trip to California. He hadn't told Enoch, because his brother wouldn't keep a secret from Lucas and Carlotta. Naomi was still living with the Hughes family. Yesterday he went over to say goodbye.

"Does Madre know?" His beautiful sister asked, eyes wide.

"I'm planning on telling her tonight."

"She won't understand. She's never even seen a movie. How are you going to explain things to her?"

Naomi was right. It was hard to explain why he wanted to be in a movie when his mother didn't even know such things existed. T.A. was so backward. You had to drive to Española or Santa Fe to see a real movie.

"Movie? What is that? It sounds sinful." Carlotta had set down the potato she was peeling and wiped her hands on a dish towel. She pulled up a chair and sat down across from Isaac.

"It's not, Madre. It is like a book, only real life. You act out the stories, just like on stage, but people all over the world can see it." He didn't mention that he loved horror films like Frankenstein and Phantom of the Opera. His mother *would* think those were sinful.

"Isaac. Your father saved money to send you to school. This was so you could be a teacher here and help him out." Her voice was deep. This was not a good sign. "Are you going to throw that in our faces? Disrespect us like that?"

He knew what would come next. The deep growl would grow higher.

"None of your brothers has deserted us."

He wanted to argue this wasn't true. Levi was married and lived in Española. Benjamin had left and returned, but he seldom helped out unless threatened or broke. Only Enoch and Eli stayed and helped without complaining.

But arguing with his mother at this point would not work in his favor, so he let her rant while his father sat without a word. It was only after the plate crashed in the sink that his father spoke.

"I can't give you any money. Do you really think you'll be back by September? I need someone to teach."

"I promise, I'll be back by September." Isaac didn't add that if he decided to stay he would let them know in plenty of time to hire another teacher. His father would figure that out himself.

Now he flashed a grin at his mother and hopped into the truck. Turning to Eli, he let a smile escape, and his eyes lit up with excitement. He waved a hand in front of his face to clear the thick smoke from Eli's pipe and missed Carlotta's reaction to this motion. He didn't see her raise her hand slowly to return the wave.

Eli threw the truck into gear with a clunk and gunned the engine, laughed and off they drove.

The brothers didn't speak as the truck climbed the hill out of the Chama Valley, dropped down through the pass and headed south to Española. As Tierra Amarilla fell behind them, Isaac drew a deep breath and felt his chest and lungs expand and relax. His legs buzzed with excitement, needing to move, and he stretched them out in front of him as far as he could within the confines of the truck.

Isaac rotated each ankle and stared at his polished brown leather shoes. With five brothers ahead of him, he seldom had such a treat. These shoes had belonged to Levi. Purchased for his wedding in Española and never worn again. Levi stayed down south with his bride, Anastasia Luchetti, and worked in the orchard owned by the Chavez family.

Isaac had been filled with joy when he found out his brother was marrying a Catholic girl. And Italian too! He hadn't let his parents know about Perfecta, although he suspected his father was aware of the relationship. Maybe Levi's move would pave the way for him.

When Anastasia and Levi came to Tierra Amarilla to visit last month, Levi handed Isaac the shoes, wrapped in brown paper. All it took was a good soak and stretching to make the leather fit his big feet. Now the shoes were comfortable.

"Nice. You're one sharp dresser." Eli spoke without taking his eyes from the road as it twisted through the narrow canyon between the high bluffs. "I guess movie stars need to dress fancy. It could help attract some of those starlets."

"No women for me. I have Perfecta waiting. But you're right about image. I think you have to catch everyone's eye if anyone is going to notice you. That would be easy for Bennie, but for me. . ." Isaac shrugged and smiled, holding his empty palms up in front of his chest.

Eli scowled. "I still think you're making a mistake to keep her waiting here."

This was nothing new. Excited about Isaac's trip to California and happy that his brother had a chance to escape New Mexico, Eli had spent the last month encouraging him to break any ties to this god-forsaken place.

Isaac didn't want his brother to think Perfecta was holding him back. "I can't describe my feelings for her. I know it's the right thing for me. I just know."

Cooled by the wind blowing through the open windows of the truck, the brothers continued the drive in near silence, occasionally commenting on the view but avoiding the subject of Perfecta. Closer to Española, the temperature climbed. May afternoons were hot in the high desert.

They spent the night with Levi and Anastasia. Levi didn't feel the same way about Perfecta as Eli did.

"She seems like a nice girl, Hermano. A little young and maybe a little. . . spunky." Levi was careful with his words. He glanced over at Anastasia. She was young too.

Isaac was relieved to have at least one brother's approval—even if it was only because Levi was in love and happily settled in his marriage.

Rising early the next morning, they gulped the strong coffee Anastasia brewed. Her eggs were runny and the bacon was burned—part of having a young bride, no doubt. Things would improve, Isaac was sure.

He wished his brother well and gave Anastasia a hug before driving off. Isaac wanted to catch the ten o'clock bus.

The journey from Espanola to Santa Fe was flat desert rather than the high bluffs, and the ride was smooth. It wasn't long before Eli pulled the truck to a stop in front of the bus station.

"Do you need me to go in with you?" he asked. "I'd like to beat this storm back through the pass." Black thunderheads loomed in the north.

"No. You go. I'll be fine." Isaac leaned over and gave his brother a hug.

Eli stiffened, keeping his hands on the steering wheel. When Isaac unclasped his arms, Eli reached out his right hand for a handshake. Isaac laughed. His brother had told him repeatedly that hugging wasn't manly. He shook Eli's hand with a quick jerk, grabbed his hat off the seat and hopped out of the truck.

He placed his new gray felt hat on his head, tipping it to one side while he leaned into the bed of the truck and lifted his suitcase. This was his new look. He had bought the hat with money he needed for California, but like he told his brother, a man had to have an image. A smile filled his face. It was finally happening. He was on his way to Hollywood to be a star.

He turned to look at Eli one more time, raising a fist with his thumb up.

"Adios, Hermano!"

Six

"Come on Perfie, there's a dance tonight." Isabelle made a face. "Enough of all this boring stuff already. Let's do something fun."

"I want to finish this." Perfie sat at the kitchen table, holding the soft gray wool of the shirt she was making for Isaac. Since quitting school she worked for Tío Luna on his ranch, and she didn't have much time to sew.

"I suppose it's for *him*." Isabelle huffed out the last word in disgust. She spun, her red skirt twirling. She held her arms up and danced with an imaginary partner. "Come to the dance. You can imagine you're dancing with him. It won't do any harm."

Perfie stopped sewing and watched Isabelle's waltz. Her cousin was happy these days. She seemed to have bloomed, showing an interest in men like never before. Did her cousin have a secret lover, too?

She thought about Isaac. *I wonder what he's doing right now?*

Who would have guessed that promising to wait for someone meant turning off your life? Isaac had been gone for almost four months. At first he sent a letter every day. The weather was great; the place he found to live was terrible, but cheap; he found a job waiting tables in the evening so he could work at being a star during the day. But in the last month there was only one short letter. *I'm sure I'm about to make it into a movie. Remember your promise, my darling.*

As if she could read Perfie's mind, Isabelle spun over and grabbed her hand. "It's not a betrayal to have a life. Do you really believe he's just sitting in a room in California, staring at the wall, dreaming of his love for you? If you think that, then you sure don't know men."

Perfie laughed. Since Isabelle had gone on one date with Miguel Santos, she suddenly knew men. There must be more to it.

But she supposed Isabelle was right. Look at Joe. Out every night, a different woman every time. There weren't that many women in T.A. Joe must have started all over again at the beginning of the list. When Primitivo asked about his plans for the future, Joe laughed. "There is no future, there is only now." Primitivo left Joe alone because he was only the stepfather, and Joe was an adult.

She pictured Isaac out with another woman. Maybe even right now. There were night clubs in Hollywood, not just a dance hall like Jicarilla Hall here in T.A. The image grew vivid in her mind—women straight out of the magazines—tight fitting dresses, sequins, pearls, hair high off their necks, or bobbed. No cotton prints, tiny embroidered white collars or black sensible shoes for those California girls—instead high heels and slim legs showing through the slit in the side of the gown. In T.A. the girls wore their church dresses to the dance. No one owned anything else.

She imagined Isaac asking a beautiful woman to dance, his hand placed on the silken fabric just where it came over her shoulder. She saw his eyes wander to the woman's long, smooth neck. Compared to this imagined woman, she looked like a school girl.

Perfie tossed the wool shirt down on the table, scattering her threads and needles onto the floor, and looked at Isabelle.

"You're right. We need to have some fun."

They went upstairs to get ready for the dance. The closet she shared with Isabelle held six dresses, three for each of them. She picked out her favorite dress, the one with small pink flowers in the print. The color brought out the roses in her cheeks. Slipping it on, she stood in front of the mirror.

"I look like some sort of freak in a dress. My legs are so stubby." She wished she had a red skirt like Isabelle's.

Isabelle laughed. "You're beautiful, Prima. Your body is perfect. You must be looking into an enchanted mirror because it lies to you."

"That's it. An evil spirit lives there." Perfie ran her hands over the bodice of the dress, starting just under her arms and ending at her hips. She gave a practice swirl, twisting her hips and holding her hands out just high enough to avoid blocking the floating fabric.

She reached behind the chest of drawers and fumbled for the lipstick she kept hidden. Her parents didn't approve of makeup, as if pink lips were a sin.

Perfie ran the cylinder lightly over her lips, pressing them together with a small smack to spread the creamy pink evenly across her mouth. Tonight she didn't care what they thought.

Arm in arm the girls walked down the dusty road. It felt good to be out. The sun was setting beyond the distant mountain range, and the sky was a brilliant red. The air smelled fresh after they had spent days confined to the stuffy house.

Isabelle squeezed Perfie's arm. "You should listen to your wise old cousin more often."

A fox ran across the road in front of them and disappeared into the culvert. Its long tail waved in the dim light.

"Fox!" Isabelle cried out.

Perfie stomped her right foot three times, then her left twice. Isabelle did the same. Both girls twirled around, then holding hands up in front of them, clapped palms together three times. Breaking into giggles, they howled up at the sky.

"You two howling coyotes going to the dance?" Joe came striding up behind them, his guitar slung over his shoulder.

"We saw a fox." Isabelle told him.

"Oh, that old superstition. Stomping and spinning going to save you? I think the two of you are going to need more than that to keep trouble away." Joe smiled and ruffled Perfie's hair.

She pulled her head away from his hand. "Hey, don't mess with that, it took us hours to get ready."

Joe took her arm and the three of them walked on to the dance.

Isabelle sat on the wooden chair next to Perfie, her shoulders straight and her hands folded in her lap. She scanned the row of young men standing across the room and waited for that single raised index finger accompanied by eye contact and the invitation to dance. Perfie wondered who would catch her cousin's eye tonight.

Perfie sat slumped forward, her hands in her lap, both feet flat on the floor. She didn't look at the men across the room. She had felt good walking here, but now she couldn't keep her mind off Isaac. This reminded her too much of the guilt she felt when she betrayed her mother. Or did it? The problem was she didn't feel guilty and she thought she should. She tried to make herself feel guilty, but she really wanted to dance.

Her ruminations were interrupted when a sharp elbow poked her in the ribs.

"Pay attention." Isabelle tipped her head across the room.

Perfie looked up. There stood Benjamin, Isaac's older brother. He held up a finger and stared directly at her.

Oh no, she thought. Now word would get back to Isaac that she'd been out dancing. She tried to think of an excuse, something she could tell Bennie to justify her being here. The wrinkle on her forehead deepened, and her lips turned down in concentration. The elbow poked her again.

"Don't just ignore him. You've got to be crazy to ignore him."

Perfie looked up and met his gaze. He slowly crooked the top joint of his finger back and forth, beckoning to her. She needed to explain herself somehow, and sitting here wasn't going to do it, so she gave a slight nod of her head. When he crossed the room and held out his hand, she remained sitting.

"I just wanted to tell you—"

Bennie reached down and grabbed her hand, then pulled her up. He was so handsome.

"Dance, then talk." He led her out into the swirling crowd, placed his hand around her waist and spun her quickly into the rhythm. His black suit jacket swung open as he moved his hips smoothly to the guitar and drums. His feet shuffled quickly back and forth to the lively tune the trumpet player belted out. He was a good dancer.

Perfie responded, twirling her skirt and matching her feet with his quick moving steps. Her mind emptied as she melted into the music, and the cloud of bad air which had surrounded her for the past month swept away as if a refreshing north wind had blown through the dance hall. Where Bennie's hand touched her she glowed; the energy of the dance and his smile made her feet light.

The music came to an end, and the dance monitors scurried among the couples to collect dimes into their payment baskets. Benjamin reached into his pocket and pulled out a smooth leather wallet. The wallet was like his suit, something from a big city, not the little town of T.A. She watched as he unzipped a section and tipped a handful of dimes into his palm.

He spoke to the monitor as he dumped all the coins into the basket. "This should do for the rest of the evening. I like dancing with this young doe. Her feet are lively." He smiled at Perfie and grasped her hand in his as the music started up again.

All thoughts of guilt fled her mind. Benjamin's hand was warm as he grasped hers, and she felt a tingle run up her spine again. When the music slowed and he held her close, she could smell his cologne. It was a sharp scent—no smell of horses or hay or sweat on him.

At ten thirty there were only four couples still on the dance floor. Perfie sighed as the music ended. That was the last song.

"Gracias. I just want to say—"

Benjamin put a finger to her lips, and squeezed her hand. "Sshh. I know what you're going to say. Something about Isaac. But let's just leave him in California for now, why don't we?"

She pulled her hand from his and looked around for Isabelle.

She spotted her brother packing up his guitar. "Joe, can you walk home with me?" she called out.

He glanced her way and grinned.

Bennie put his hand on her shoulder. "I'll walk you home."

Perfie hesitated. She didn't want to leave the magic feeling behind. But she shook her head and stepped back from him. He smiled and shrugged as he reached out with one finger and stroked her cheek. Then he turned and walked over to a group of young men who were passing a bottle and smoking. As she watched him walk away, her eyes on his strong shoulders and slim hips, she felt her heart squeeze. She reached up and touched the track of his finger, her face hot.

She closed her eyes and drew in a deep breath, the image of Isaac filling her mind. Then she snapped her eyes open and walked over to Joe.

"I can't find Isabelle," she told her brother.

"While you were otherwise engaged she left with Carmella and Luisa. I promised her I'd keep an eye on you."

"Keep an eye on me?"

"Yes. You seem to have a weakness for Martinez men. You are treading in the danger zone again, my sweet." Joe rolled his eyes. "You better be careful. The Ogre might find out, and your backside will pay the price for your aching heart."

Joe was right. Primitivo would not be happy with her behavior. But she wasn't so worried about him.

She was worried about Isaac.

Robin Martinez Rice

River of Tears

Seven

Tierra Amarilla, New Mexico, August 1925

Joe burst through the back door, kicked off his muddy boots and pushed them to one side. "Hey, did you hear who's back?"

"What?" Perfie looked up from the sink, tossing a potato into the green ceramic bowl. She was cutting out the bad parts, trying to salvage enough of last year's potatoes to fry up for dinner. She looked at the mud Joe tracked in. Where did he find mud in the middle of August? "Couldn't you leave your boots outside?"

"Your beau. He hasn't been to see you yet?"

"Isaac?" Perfie didn't believe her brother.

"Yes, of course, Isaac. I saw him down at Hughes' store just now. Dressed in that fine suit he likes to wear—a new hat, too. Something Hollywood no doubt."

Perfie wiped her hands and set the knife to one side. Joe grabbed her arm as she reached to untie her apron.

He shook his head. "Don't go running down there, *Hermanita*. Make him come to you." His eyes were serious, and his mouth turned down.

Joe was right. Why hadn't Isaac come to see her? Didn't he know how hard it was for her? Sixteen years old and waiting for more than a year?

She'd gone to more dances. Perfie convinced herself there was nothing wrong with a dance. Trouble was, she seldom danced with anyone other than Bennie.

Now Isaac was back in town, and he hadn't come to see her. Benjamin probably told him about her betrayal—about the dancing, her laughter and her disregard for the promise she had made.

All that waiting. More than a year. And now for nothing because Isaac would consider the promise broken. Add that to the fact that her father was barely speaking to her and her mother rocked silently in that chair all day.

I'll wither away here, an old maid caring for two ancient parents. This was the price she would pay for the sins she had committed. She kicked at the wooden chair with her toe. She'd messed up again.

"Don't worry, he'll come." Joe's voice broke into her thoughts. "Perfecta, you're the most beautiful girl in Tierra Amarilla. You are smart and full of life. A wise man knows he will never be bored with you."

Of course Joe would say that, he was her older brother. She'd waited for her beauty to appear, like it did with some of the other girls when they were her age. But it hadn't come. Each year passed and she still wasn't beautiful—her drooping eyes and her round cheeks stayed the same. She wished for high cheekbones, like Carmella, who had a face like a queen. She hated the way her hair fought its way into curls no matter what she did to it. Her mother wouldn't let her cut it off, so she braided it or put it into a tight bun, but that wild frizz around her face—nothing could be done about that. No smooth bob for her head.

Smart, Joe has said. Quitting school in eighth grade? What man would think this was a sign of her intelligence? Things were just as her mother had warned.

Perfie flicked the dish towel at her brother's leg. "You don't have to lie to make me feel better."

The sound of footsteps on the wooden porch brought a grin to Joe's face. He headed toward the door even before the three sharp knocks announced the arrival of a visitor.

Perfie smoothed her skirt and her hair and quickly sat at the table. She concentrated on her mouth, relaxing the muscles around it into an expression which she hoped reflected boredom, or what she supposed was a hard-to-get look.

But when Isaac followed Joe into the kitchen with a small bunch of flowers clutched in his hand and his eyes shadowed by the funny flat hat he wore, she sprang from the chair and ran into his arms, tears flowing down her cheeks. The "I-don't-care-so-much" expression slipped off her face as she flung her arms around him and pushed her body against his chest.

He held her wrapped in his arms, his head tipping down so that his lips pressed against the top of her head. She felt his hot breath as he inhaled the smell of her hair. He squeezed her harder, and she felt herself melt into his very soul.

Joe shook his head as he stood and watched. He grinned, but the wrinkles at the corner of his eyes didn't follow his smile.

"My Perfecta." Isaac whispered. "Let me look at you." Unwrapping his arms from around her he held onto her shoulders with both hands and the bunch of wildflowers bumped her cheek. A sharp leaf poked her in the eye.

"Ouch." Perfie reached up to rub her eye. "Not Perfecta."

Isaac quickly lowered the hand with the flowers, keeping a firm grasp with the other. He leaned forward. "Let me fix it." He kissed her eyelid.

Perfie laughed, although her eye stung from the prick of the leaf. She twisted from his grasp and went to the counter, dipping a clean rag into the water bucket. She wrung out the rag, but as she reached to hold it against her face, Isaac took it from her.

"Really, it's my fault. Let me do this. You sit." He sat down, pulling her into his lap. Perfie leaned against him as he held the rag to her eye.

Joe stood watching for a moment, then without a word he turned and left. Perfie settled her cheek against Isaac's shoulder.

So quiet was the figure in the other room that Perfie forgot about her mother. Avelina sat in the rocker by the window, eyes piercing the dim light of the living room as she watched her daughter through the open doorway.

At supper Isabelle placed the tortillas on the table and stared at Perfie's face. "What's wrong with your eye?"

"Nothing. I banged it, that's all." Perfie tucked her chin, slid the platter of pork smothered with red chili onto the table and dropped into her chair, her head turned away from her father.

"What happened today?" Perfie's head shot up at her father's loud words, the boom of his voice startling her. Even though it had been a long time since he struck her, she couldn't stop herself from flinching.

"Nothing, what do you mean," she said, not really asking a question. He couldn't know about Isaac's visit. Joe would never say a word to his stepfather, and Isabelle hadn't been there.

"Your mother." Primitivo tilted his head toward the living room as he scooped a spoonful of pork onto his plate.

Isabelle and Perfecta both looked through the door to the living room.

Perfie couldn't remember when her mother had withdrawn from the family. For the past year Avelina had just gradually faded away. It started with her asking the girls to fix the meals on their own, although at first she sat at the kitchen table and directed them. Somewhere along the line she quit coming into the kitchen. The girls made the meals without her guidance.

Avelina never sewed or knit anymore; she complained her fingers hurt and her eyes were bad and she wouldn't wear the glasses Primitivo brought for her, saying they gave her a headache.

For a while Perfie still heard her parents talk at night, the low voices rumbling up through the floor of her room. Her father would lead Mama to bed, helping as she slowly removed her clothes. Her arms and legs moved as if in need of oil at the joints. Mama's voice seemed to come from some far-off place, her tone flat and weak, as if every word had to be pulled from some deep well, hauled up hand over hand by a frayed rope. But Perfie hadn't heard their voices for months. Isabelle always put Mama to bed now. Her father came in late each night.

If he came home at all.

Perfie tried to talk to her mother. She would fix her peppermint tea, pull her chair close to the rocker and tell Avelina about her day. But Mama wouldn't answer, and her eyes faded away while she stared off, not really looking at anything as far as Perfie could tell. So Perfie quit trying.

Now, as their eyes followed Primitivo's nod, Perfie and Isabelle heard a loud sudden creak, almost a bang, as Avelina rocked vigorously. Her feet were planted firmly, and her hands gripped the wooden arms of the rocker. She pushed with bent knees, back and forth, back and forth. The tip of the left rocker banged against the wooden end table, and the chair traveled backward with her movement.

"She does seem upset." Isabelle rose to go to Avelina. "What is it, Tía? Is something wrong?" Perfie and Primitivio listened, although they didn't expect Avelina to answer.

"Sinner." Avelina's voice carried into the kitchen.

Perfie gasped.

Her father's eyes snapped to her face. "You obviously know what she means." He waited.

"No, no." She shook her head. "I was just shocked that she spoke." Perfie suddenly realized her mother had been watching when Isaac came to visit. Why hadn't she thought of that?

She no longer thought of her mother as a person. Avelina had been sitting at that window for so long, she seemed like a piece of the furniture.

There had been no words of guidance from her mother—no scolding, no love for the entire year Isaac was gone.

Now, once again, her mother was accusing her of sinning. She couldn't feel the guilt her mother seemed to want her to feel. How could she? She thought about the pure pleasure of Isaac's hand holding the cool rag to her eye.

"You'd best tell me now." Her father continued to eat, a much better sign than putting his fork down beside his plate.

"Joe was here today."

"Ah, Joe. So he's the sinner?"

Perfie was silent. Joe protected her secrets. Things had never been good between her father and her half brother. She didn't want to feed that fire.

"Protecting him, as usual." Primitivo turned to his niece, raising his voice. "Isabelle?"

Isabelle came back into the kitchen. "I was out today." She sat down and picked up her fork. "She didn't eat any lunch, wouldn't even look at the food. That was before I went out."

Avelina was quiet now, but her rapid rocking continued.

Primitivo pushed his plate away and stood. "See if you can get her to eat. Feed her if you have to. I'm going out. I'll be back late."

The girls remained silent.

Suddenly Primitivo turned, and with a movement so quick Perfie didn't have time to duck, he struck her across the face with the back of his hand. Isabelle jumped up and fled to the doorway.

Not again. The words flashed through Perfie's mind as she grabbed her fork from beside her plate and pushed out of her chair. She stumbled back, trying to put distance between herself and her father.

"You stay away from me!" she yelled, waving the fork and trying to keep her balance.

He grabbed her arm. She twisted and swung the fork, catching the side of his cheek. The tines tore at the skin just above his whiskers. She scrambled backward, trying to get away from him.

Isabelle screamed. Perfie looked up and saw her father raise his hand to his cheek. Blood poured out from between his fingers.

"God damn you." His voice was strained and quiet.

She stood where she was and tightened her grip on the fork. With a sudden move, he jumped forward and grabbed the fallen chair. He flung it toward her.

Isabelle's screams filled the kitchen. "No, no, no, Stop!"

Perfie dodged the chair and ran out the back door. She thought she could stand up to him. All of the fear and hatred of the past sixteen years filled her body. Her arms and legs shook, and she couldn't breathe. No way was she going to stay and let herself be hit again. As she ran out of the yard and down the road she could hear Isabelle's screams echoing behind her.

It was after midnight when she came back to the house. She walked slowly up onto the back porch and peered in the doorway. Her father's coat and hat were gone. She was surprised to see Isabelle sitting at the kitchen table, only a small candle for light.

"What happened?" Isabelle looked at Perfie. "What did Avelina mean?"

"Nothing." Perfie stared straight into Isabelle's accusing eyes. "Nothing at all."

Eight

Tierra Amarilla, New Mexico, April 1926

Perfie ran down the street to Hughes' Mercantile. It was spring, and the days were mild. Green shoots poking out of the yellow earth and tentative blossoms called everyone outdoors.

I forgot the baking soda, the screw fell out of the back of this frame, I need another pound of sugar for the cookies, I need a little bit of air. Excuses flowed easily off her tongue, although in truth the family bought very little from the mercantile. With the cow, the garden and the dried and canned foods in the pantry, there was little to be added to the self sufficiency of this household. Today Perfie felt like her feet had wings, like that Greek god, whatever her name was. Or maybe it was a man—she couldn't remember. Her heart beat with such force she could feel it all the way down to those winged heels as she rushed down the packed dirt road to the center of town.

Behind the hardware counter Isaac was weighing out nails and helping customers find just the right color of paint. Although he had returned to T.A. last August with plenty of time to teach again, his father had different ideas. He had a full house of teachers and students now. Isaac was too late —there was no longer a spot for him. And he couldn't work the cattle; Enoch had that under control.

"I guess it's their way of punishing me for leaving." Isaac told Perfie. He explained he wasn't a movie star. Yet. But he had come back for her. "Next time, you come with me. There are little apartments we can share. If we both work we'll have plenty of money for one of those."

A little apartment. Perfie imagined the kitchen, painted yellow, a shiny new stove, pots and pans hanging from a rack above a tiny wooden table for two. She cut a picture out of Good Housekeeping and tucked it inside her Bible.

In the meantime, the two met in secret.

Perfie slipped into the store, shuffled around the aisles and picked up nails, rolling them between her fingers as she waited for all the customers to leave.

"Can I help you, miss?" Isaac put his arms around her and pulled her to him, his kisses coming fast, covering her face and neck. She kissed him back, her hands pressed against his chest. His heart beat as hard as hers.

The tinkle of the bell on the door interrupted their passion, and Isaac turned his attention to his customer.

Perfie left the store and walked home, kicking up the dust as she savored the memory of Isaac's embrace. It was so hard to see him for just a minute, a brief second of his warm arms and soft lips, but it was better than nothing.

They still met out by the ditch when they could. She would sit with her feet dangling in the water until Isaac appeared, sneaking up behind her and running his long fingers up the sides of her neck. A shiver would start at the base of her spine and shoot up through the top of her head. Her tongue would press against the back of her teeth in anticipation. They would kiss, sometimes so soft she could barely make out his lips, other times he pressed with such force he left her mouth swollen and red.

After these meetings she wore a scarf wrapped around her neck. It covered the marks where Isaac bit and sucked at her tender skin.

But as much as she loved their passion, she also looked forward to their conversations.

"Tell me about the beach."

"It's different every day. Sometimes the waves are small, slipping up onto the shore with barely a sound. That's when I liked to take off my shoes and walk in the water. It's cold, though. Always cold." He brushed her hair off her forehead. "But when a storm is coming the waves grow. They are as angry as thunderheads, booming and crashing down, sucking everything back into the ocean with them. I still liked to watch them, but from a distance."

"Why did you stay away so long?" She held his hand and studied his round fingernails. She liked to trace the even moons which marked each one.

"I kept thinking it would happen, my lucky break. I went to so many auditions. You have to stand in line, then do whatever they ask you."

"Whatever? Like what?"

"Walk fast across the room, smile, frown, read something. Then if they like you, you do it all again for the camera."

He had been in one movie. Just part of a crowd, but this was what made him think his big chance was around the corner.

"Why can't we go back now? Maybe I could be in a movie, too." She scowled. "But they probably only want pretty girls."

"You are pretty. But I have to save up some money first."

"I have some money."

Isaac sat up and took her hands. "How much?"

"Twenty-seven dollars."

He sank down, his grip loose. "I appreciate the offer, but that's not enough." He kissed her again.

She couldn't stay away from him, couldn't say no to him. She sneaked out when the chance of being caught was high, making up stories which didn't even sound believable to her own active imagination. She left by the back door, not wanting to pass the front window where her mother continued to rock and stare.

The expression on Avelina's face never changed, but her rocking would speed up when Perfie was near, her knuckles white as her hands tightened on the arm rests. Perfie didn't want to see this. She didn't want to think about her mother locked in whatever world she was in. She knew her mother still judged her, knew Avelina continued to think her daughter was a sinner.

In the Chama Valley region there are five catholic churches and three priests. Masses are staggered, and if a soul is particularly troubled and has a swift horse, then prayers are available every day, twice on Wednesday, Saturday and Sunday.

Father Matteo Gonzalez was at least eighty years old. No one knew his real age, including the old Padre himself. He was a tiny man, although some said he had shrunk with age. It was impossible to imagine he had ever been anyone other than the bent elf he was now with his fuzzy white hair sticking straight out all over his head. He insisted he was able to cover mass at more than one location, but he finally agreed to let George Tafoya take him from church to church in a wagon. This was only after the old Padre arrived at the wrong church several times, standing at the altar in front of empty pews, while his flock gathered eight miles away in another sanctuary altogether.

The second priest, Father Gabriel Carona, had arrived in Tierra Amarilla fifteen years earlier, riding into town on the back of a large black mule. It was said that he had followed Carlotta and Lucas Martinez from Taos, although no reason for this was ever offered. Why would a priest follow a Presbyterian circuit preacher? Perfie knew he ate dinner at the Martinez house once a week. She thought he was in love with Carlotta.

Father Gabriel seldom smiled. There was no one in Rio Arribe county who felt forgiven after confessing their sins to him. His masses were poorly attended, but the older residents of the valley came to hear him because he delivered the service in Spanish.

Father Thomas White, the youngest of the three priests, was considered the newcomer to Tierra Amarilla even though he had been here for nearly five years. Carmelita White of Los Ojos was his aunt, but her brother moved away to Oregon and married an anglo, so Father Tom had little of the Spanish heritage to fall back on. The people thought he was returning to his roots when he came to T.A., but the young man's refusal to learn Spanish (he spoke English to the oldest residents even when it was clear they didn't understand a word) led folks to believe there was some hidden reason he appeared in their town. School children had their own theory: he stayed because he was in love with Sister Maria Esther. Perfie was amused that the people of her town wished love for these men who were denied the solace of a woman due to the nature of the stern religion.

On Saturday, Perfie went to confession. "Forgive me father, for I have sinned." She chose the time when she knew Father Gabriel was traveling to small parishes. Only the new priest, Father Tom, was present at the church. She hoped if she confessed in Spanish he wouldn't really catch on to what she was saying.

She spoke rapidly, her folded hands in front of her mouth to further muffle her words. "I have taken great pleasure in sinful activities. I have used the Lord's name in vain, I have not respected my mother and my father, or even my cousin for that matter. I've been kind of lazy, too."

There's so much I can't tell you, she thought, her mind racing well beyond her words. I have no excuse, but tell me Father, why is something so wonderful a sin? How is any person to stay away from the best thing in the world? I'm in love, Father, in love. I'm not willing to give it up. I'm willing to burn in hell for it. Not even that is too high a price to pay.

She raised her mouth from her hands and spoke out loud. *"Límpiame, Señor. Perdona mis pecados, por favor. Yo me lo merezco. Yo soy una persona buena, Usted sabe eso."*

Father Tom cleared his throat. "Slow down, my dear."

Good, he's having a hard time understanding me. Perfie stopped her tirade, lowered her head to clasped hands and whispered a prayer to herself. "Please God, tell me it can't be so."

When she lifted her head she realized she had no idea what Father Tom was saying; she hadn't been paying attention. He was directing her with some Hail Marys and prayer.

"Gracias, Padre." She touched her forehead and shoulders in the sign of the cross, stood up and slipped out of the confessional. Maybe she was in the clear now. Wrapping her bright blue woven shawl around her shoulders, she hurried out of the church.

She could hardly wait to see what Isaac thought of this shawl. Knit from yarn he had given to her, she had made a special stitch along the edges for added glamour. It was bigger than her usual shawls, hanging down to the back of her knees. While pulling the yarn over and under her needles she had imagined it big enough to encompass both her own shoulders and Isaac's, keeping them warm as they snuggled together.

Two nights later Isaac admired the new shawl. They walked farther than usual on this crisp April night, following the horse trail which led up into the rocky bluffs of the Martinez property. Isaac found a spot on the smooth shale where they could lean back against a large rock, reclining together to look at the stars. Perfie listened to him talk about the heavens. He studied some astronomy in college, but he didn't know as much as Joe. She didn't care. She loved the sound of his voice. She snuggled up closer to him, his arm over her shoulders. Her tongue darted out and she licked the stubbly skin of his neck, just under his chin.

"Perfie, are you listening to me?" He laughed and licked her back, his tongue gliding in a smooth line across her forehead. He lowered his lips to hers and kissed her with such softness that her whole body responded, heat pulsing from her pounding heart.

"I was just wondering if you tasted like peanut butter," she said.

He laughed. "What?"

"You have this special smell. It's warm and nutty—you smell like peanut butter." She sniffed his neck.

He licked her again. "You taste like all the sweetness in the world."

She pushed him away. "But what does that mean? What does that sweetness taste like?" She wanted to make sure there was something more to this than just romantic words.

He put his finger to his chin, his thoughtful pose. "Like the honey of a bee that has just filled up on a juniper blossom, mixed with the fresh apple and cinnamon of the pie you are going to bake for me tomorrow." He leaned into her, his lips on hers once more.

The shawl came in handy as a bed beneath them. Perfie didn't think about his sincerity anymore. She didn't think about anything other than his touch, how magic all of this was, as she caressed, kissed and licked him.

"Perfecta, wake up, it's late." Isabelle's voice broke into her sleep. She felt a hand shaking her shoulder.

She moaned and tried to retreat under the quilt. Just an hour ago she had crept into the house as the sky was turning from black to deep purple, the sun about to show its face over the eastern horizon.

"Leave me. I can't get up."

"Your mother talked to your father last night."

Isabelle's words broke through the fog. Perfie sat up, eyes wide.

Her cousin continued. "I don't know what they said. He was sitting with her and I could hear mumbling, two voices. Then he took her into the bedroom." Isabelle shook her head. "She wouldn't get up this morning. She's not in her chair; she's in bed."

Perfie flung back the quilts, dressed quickly and followed Isabelle to the kitchen. Her father sat at the table, his back rigid, cold eyes staring out the window. She went to the pantry to get food for breakfast.

"That can wait. Sit. Both of you." Primitivo's voice was low. "Avelina has taken a turn for the worse."

"What does that mean?" Perfie spoke with a low choking whisper.

"She spoke with me last night. She asked to be moved to her bed. She doesn't want the doctor. She's praying she can go to the Lord soon."

Thoughts slammed around in Perfie's head like the angry hornets whose nest was upset last summer. A strange buzzing filled her ears. Her mother wanted to die. The soft touch of Avelina's hand, the gentle kiss at night, the silly stories meant to teach a lesson—those had been gone for a long time. But to lose her mother altogether—that was different.

Perfie let out a small breath, but her lungs were still tight. Avelina hadn't told her father about her—hadn't told him what a sinner she was.

Isabelle reached across the table and took Primitivo's hand in hers. "We'll take care of her."

He glanced at her and pulled his hand away. "Perfecta, what is this about you and the damn Presbyterian?"

Perfie didn't answer. She waited to see just what her father was asking. Since that night last August when he hit her, the two had kept away from each other. She hadn't initiated a conversation with him, and she never met his eyes.

"Sinner. Your mother repeatedly told me you are a sinner. To top that off when I was at the courthouse yesterday, Sergeant Torres asked me if I was still attending mass, now that my daughter left the church. What does this mean?"

Perfie pressed her tongue tightly against the back of her teeth while she thought about her answer. This was rare for her, she who spoke so impulsively, but she didn't want to say something which might jeopardize her relationship with Isaac. And she certainly didn't want to be attacked.

"I was dancing with Benjamin Martinez—maybe that's what they're talking about. It was just a dance. I danced with lots of Catholics too."

Isabelle's face turned red, and she twisted her hands together. She stared at Perfecta.

"How would your mother know about that? What is the sin she believes you have committed?" Primitivo was not fooled by Perfie's lie. He turned to his niece. "Isabelle, do you know anything about this?"

Isabelle continued to clasp her hands, her head down. She bit her lower lip. Perfie watched her cousin struggle. What would she say?

"Well?" Primitivo didn't let Isabelle get away with silence.

"I think, maybe, Perfecta and Isaac Martinez, they might like each other."

Eyes dark and jaw tight he turned back to his daughter.

"Not only do you meet with a man much too old, and *un pagano*, a heathen, but you lie to me." He stood, holding his hand out in front of his chest, palm facing Perfecta.

As Primitivo's voice grew loud, Perfecta ran her fingers along the tiny raised crescent, just above her left eyebrow. Everyone said they couldn't see it, but she knew this wasn't true. It was apparent when she looked in the mirror. It was a reminder of the need to stay out of Primitivo's way when he was in such a mood. Although she had been only two years old when she got the scar, too young to remember her mother always said, she did remember. She remembered it all: the sun shining through the kitchen window, the soft swish of the dish cloth as her mother washed each of the colorful bowls and plates and the tiny block of wood she played with. She remembered leaning against her mother's leg, the warmth filtering through Avelina's thick stockings onto her back.

Her father's voice had been loud, so loud, and her mother's leg began to tremble. As he came close, Perfecta had pressed between the cupboard and her mother's legs. When he spoke his tone was angry. Then the yellow bowl crashed to the floor, shattering, one piece flying up to slice her tiny eyebrow. It was the only time she had heard him speak that way to Avelina.

Now, as she heard the anger in his voice and looked at his clenched fist, she looked around the table for a weapon. Only the cloth napkins remained; there was nothing she could use to defend herself. She slid her feet in front of her and leaned her weight onto her toes, ready to run if he moved toward her.

"This will stop. You are not to leave this house. Do you understand?"

Perfie felt tears leak from her eyes and drain down her cheeks in spite of her effort to remain in control. She couldn't think of what to say. How would she fight her father on this?

He waited, his eyes burning holes into her as she sat silently. When she could bear it no longer, she nodded. He turned and left the house. The screen door slammed closed behind him.

A week later, as Perfie was mopping the kitchen floor her thoughts were interrupted by her father's appearance. It was mid morning, a time when he was usually off on patrol several miles out of town. He stomped up onto the back porch and through the door she had propped open to let the spring air dry the floor.

"Pack your bag. Where's Isabelle?" He continued on through the kitchen toward the front room.

Pack a bag? What could this mean? Was the family leaving town?

"You," he barked the word out, turning and pointing his finger at her, "are going to stay in Antonito." He turned and left the room.

Antonito? With Tía Emilia? Why would she go there?

She let the mop fall from her hand, the handle banging the bucket of water.

To get her away from Isaac. That was her father's plan. Did he know she was still seeing him?

For the last week she had borrowed Joe's hat and jacket, pulling them on over her own thick trousers and climbing out the window each night. If she was spotted no one would recognize her; they would think she was a young man out cruising the town. Each night Isaac met her. He brought a brown wool blanket with him, and what had started that night on the bluffs —the caressing and hands probing under clothing—was now more intense. Perfie rushed through each day, praying for the time to pass so she could feel that explosive sensation which took over every part of her soul when she was with him.

Now her father was sending her away. Tía Emilia was old. Her daughters had left, and her husband had died. She lived in a tiny house in in the middle of the small town of Antonito, and she smelled bad, like burnt toast. What would Perfie do there? Die of boredom and loneliness, that's what.

Perfie hurried after Primitivo. "Don't send me there. Don't do it, please, Papa. What have I done to deserve this?"

Her father ignored her. "Isabelle, I'll be gone overnight. I'm riding the train to Antonito with Perfecta. If you need any help with Avelina, Señora Alvarez will be next door."

He picked up his worn leather satchel from the chair in the corner of the room, tucking some papers and a book into the large pocket. "Perfecta, if you are planning on taking anything with you, pack now. We have just time to catch the train."

"How long will I be there?"

"As long as it takes."

He didn't speak to her on the train ride through the Sangre de Cristo mountains. Not a word to her as the smoking black engine wound through the narrow valley then plunged forward across the flat plains. Perfie was fearful on this ride. She didn't like the tracks so close to the sheer drops down to the river or the high trestle bridges they crossed, and she didn't like the raging heat coming from her father's rigid body.

She sat with her head against the window, eyes closed, dreaming only of Isaac. She pictured his face—his bright blue eyes with that special sparkle just for her. She hadn't even had a chance to tell him she was going. Tonight he would wait for her, blanket rolled tightly under his arm, his foot tapping impatiently.

As her father was rushing her from the house, Perfie tried to make Isabelle understand that she wanted a message delivered to Isaac. But her father had not left them alone, and she never had a chance to talk to her cousin.

My life is over. I will be an old maid. Well, not a maid exactly—that was no longer true. Isaac will find someone else, she thought, and no one else will want me now that I'm a soiled woman.

A sinner, that's what I am. Mama always told me God would punish me. Now I know she was right.

Nine

The pounding in her temple was so strong it woke her from sleep. Irritation filled her when she realized it was not yet five o'clock—too early to get up. She didn't have anything to do here in Antonito, and getting up early just added to the long stretch of hours.

She had spent the first week cleaning the house and polishing Emilia's wooden furniture, scrubbing the cracks between tiles and dusting hundreds of books. The second week she worked in the garden, trimming dead blossoms, loosening the compacted soil and digging up the hoards of weeds which had taken charge of the yard.

Each afternoon she arranged tea and crackers on the inlaid wooden tray Emilia had brought home from her trip to Texas, the one trip in her lifetime. Perfie heard every detail of this adventure three times, even though it had taken place more than thirty years ago. She would sit with her aunt and the other old women of Antonito, Emilia's friends, listening to the gossip about people she didn't know. She felt she couldn't bear another round of stories, but what else was there to do?

Three days ago she discovered a small lake at the edge of town. She had wandered up a trail in search of some distraction.

The lake became her sanctuary. She wished she had her paints, but with the quick departure she hadn't thought to pack them. Her father purposefully left her with no money, telling Tía Emilia she couldn't be trusted.

"Don't spoil her, Emmy. She's manipulative and crazed by men. You'll need to keep a close eye on her and make her work." Perfie kept her head down and bit her cheek as her father spoke. If she was so manipulative she'd like to know why everything had turned out so terrible for her. And she was crazed by only one man.

By late afternoon her headache had cleared a little, so she walked out to the lake. She sat on the bank and stared at the distant mountains. The water was a brilliant blue one minute, changing to a deep green as the clouds covered the sun.

She contemplated her life as she stared at the lake. Everything changed so fast in nature. Tall trees were reflected in the lake—a reversed world hiding in the deep water. If only my world were reversed, she mused. I would be a good person, instead of always getting into trouble. My father would be the sick one lying in that bed, and my mother would be in charge. I would be with Isaac right now instead of here in this lonely place.

If my father had never moved to Tierra Amarilla, then I would never have been born.

What *if* Primitivo had never met Avelina?

There was someone who could tell her their story.

Emilia was not really her aunt; she was a distant cousin of Primitivo. But everyone in these parts was a distant cousin. Emilia was very old, and her wrinkled skin was the color of coffee con leche—a result of mixed blood and so different from the dark of the Tewa or Apache or the pale white of the Spanish. Her brown eyes were pale too, as she stared at Perfie from under folded lids.

"Tía Emilia, how did my parents meet?"

"Ask your mother."

"I have asked her. I've asked everyone, but no one wants to tell me anything. What's the big secret?"

Emilia seemed to be considering. Perfie knew her aunt to be a gossip, and the slack cheeks and half-closed eyes told her that a story might come if she held her tongue and waited.

"Your father isn't from around here."

"I know that. All the relatives are related to Mama, not him. Except for you. But where is Papa from?"

"Texas. He came here to be sheriff of T.A."

"Texas?" Was Emilia's big trip related to her father? She was his cousin, after all.

Emilia settled back in the chair. This was a good sign; now she would talk.

"I think it was around the turn, 1897 or so. Maybe later. Manuel had left, so the boys were born already."

Perfie knew Manuel was her mother's first husband and Joe and Mannie's father.

"Avelina wasn't an easy one to live with. She was never pleased and always sad about something—so different from when she was young. Manuel was a wild one. He never should have got married in the first place. He wanted to sing and play music, not have the responsibility of a family."

Like Joe, Perfie thought. She had a sudden flash of Isaac. He didn't run around with other women, but he sure didn't seem ready to commit to her.

"Anyway, he rode off and no one ever heard from him again. Oh, we heard he was here and there, Taos or down in Socorro. Avelina had a hard time of it. He didn't leave her with anything. She was lucky when she got that house."

"How did she get the house?" Perfie wanted a house. If her mother could get one maybe there was a way for her to do it, too.

"An uncle died. His kids moved away, and no one wanted the house. She stepped up and saw a way to make some money letting out that bottom room. Happened someone moved out just when Primitivo came into town. It was a good spot for him to live, so close to the jail and all."

"When did they fall in love?"

"In love? Can't say I remember that part. All I know is one day I come to visit and she's not sleeping upstairs anymore. I knew her first, you know, even if he is my cousin. I grew up in T.A."

"So they got married?" Perfie wanted to hear more about her parents.

"No, not then. That came later."

Perfie choked, spilling tea onto the napkin. Later? Her mother was sleeping with her father before they were married?

"*Tía*, are you sure of that?"

"I know, *m'jita*. It's a shock, but it's true. They didn't get married until you came along."

"But she was married to Manuel. She told me he was dead, but now you say no one knows for sure."

She was a bastard. Her parents weren't married. No wonder her father hated her so much. She was cursed. She would never go to heaven, no matter how much she prayed.

Emilia continued. "If a man is missing so many years, the church will assume he's dead. She is married to Primitivo now. They married in that church you have there, Santa Christy or whatever."

"Santo Niño." Perfie set her cup down on the table. This changed everything. The next time her parents lectured her, told her what a sinner she was, she had a weapon to fight their displeasure.

"*They're* sinners."

Emilia shook her head. "No. Don't think of your mother like that."

"But from what you told me they are!"

"Your mother was such a sweet girl. She went to church every day. She was very young when she met Manuel. A handsome man like that, he could charm anyone. She was so beautiful." Her aunt stared out the window. "Her life, so hard. She lost her pretty smile."

"I never see her smile."

"She wasn't that way as a girl. She was gay. I remember how she would sing all the time. She had a good voice."

Perfie thought about the hymns her mother sang—they were melancholy, not gay.

Emilia went on. "How that girl loved to dance. I remember the skirts she made. She sewed for hours, making more ruffles to spin."

Perfie watched her aunt's gaze drift further into the past. "What happened next?"

"After the babies Manuel stayed out even more. Then one day—gone, just as I said."

Perfie tried to imagine her mother as a young girl, smiling and twirling. But all she could see was the straight lips and drooping eyes Avelina wore now.

"But what about *my* father? After Manuel was gone?"

Emilia shrugged. "He moved in, and they got married. It was a good thing; she needed help with those boys."

As far as Perfie could see, her father didn't help much with Joe or Mannie. Her oldest brother had left home at age fourteen. She had been a baby, and she didn't really know him until he started coming back to visit. Primitivo and Joe seemed to hate each other.

Tía had more to say. "As long as I'm spilling the beans I might as well tell you the rest."

The rest? What more could there be?

"It's said Primitivo had a family back in Texas."

"Did his wife die?" This was crazy. If he had another wife, then her parents weren't married after all.

"Supposedly."

Supposedly. How convenient. Perfie pictured a sad woman in Texas, waiting and waiting for her husband to return. Then she imagined her mother as that sad woman, waiting, too, here in New Mexico with Joe and Manny, little boys without a father. Primitivo must have been attractive, a welcome addition to a woman living alone.

Maybe some man had come along to that mystery wife in Texas. Maybe it was just a big game—men moving around, women waiting.

Emilia patted Perfie's arm. "There were children. Two boys and a girl. They're your brothers and sisters."

Family. She had *more* family? She pictured some children standing next to the sad woman. That wasn't right. They would be older than her, much older. Grown up.

"Do you think I can find them?"

"I don't know. Do you want to find them?"

Was more family the answer to this bitter taste in her mouth? Perfie shook her head. "I don't know, Tía. I really don't know."

Three weeks later Perfie found herself on a return trip to Tierra Amarilla. She chose an aisle seat and kept her eyes forward in anticipation, avoiding the windows. She looked at the clothing of the other passengers, noting the details of the sleeves and colors, but her mind was really on Isaac. Her whole body was pulled back to T. A, as though Isaac were a magnet. It had been a shock when Tía told her she was going home.

"Perfecta, tomorrow you will take the train back home." Tia Emilia stirred her tea, the spoon clinking in a tink, tink, tink rhythm on the side of the cup. She dipped a spoonful of honey and added it to cover the water's strong sulfuric taste. The odor of eggs was present in everything.

"Is Mama okay?"

"Your mother is poorly. I think it best you go back."

Her aunt refused to say more.

When the train pulled into the Chama station, Perfie was the first one off. She looked around the platform for Joe. She didn't see him, so she looked for her father.

She walked up and down the platform five times. Everyone else was met by relatives with hugs and laughter and kisses of welcome. Some of the travelers hopped into the waiting wagons or walked off down the muddy road. She stretched her neck and looked up and down one more time. Why was no one here to pick her up?

A cold wind blew across the platform. She shivered and pulled her shawl close around her shoulders. Something really terrible must have happened. No one was here to meet her.

Whatever it was, she wasn't going to stand here and freeze. She lugged her suitcase to the cafe across the street. Tía Emilia had given her some coins for the trip. A cup of tea would be nice.

A few minutes later she was seated at a table by the window. She pulled the chair around so she could keep watch of the street. Her father would be angry if she wasn't waiting. She could run out the moment she saw him.

"Going on a trip?" A smooth voice broke into her thoughts. She turned as Benjamin Martinez pulled out the other chair and slid into it. He was very close, the two chairs at right angles, his knee bumping hers.

His smile was charming. Although she longed for Isaac, she couldn't help but feel a warm flush where his knee touched her.

"I just came back. Is Isaac with you?" She turned her head and glanced around the cafe.

"No, just me. Guess you'll have to be satisfied with the older, smarter brother."

Benjamin teased and chatted as she finished her tea. Still no sign of her father. "Are you going back to T.A.?" she asked. "Can I have a ride?"

"Of course. You can't begin to imagine how I would love to give you a ride."

Ignoring his flirting, she picked up her bag. She was worried. What was going on at home?

Less than two hours later Benjamin pulled the wagon to a stop in front of her house and carried her suitcase to the front porch. "I'll just be off now."

"Gracías, I really needed the ride." She had enjoyed him in spite of her worry. She appreciated the distraction of listening to him go on and on. "Can you tell Isaac I'm back?"

"Now why would I want to do that? Ruin all my chances with the prettiest girl in T.A.?"

"Please."

He was suddenly serious. "Of course. I would never interfere with such a strong love."

She waited until he was out of sight, picked up her suitcase and walked around the house to the back door.

Isabelle turned in surprise as Perfie walked into the kitchen. "Perfecta! What are you doing here?"

"I'm home. Why didn't anyone meet me at the train station? How's Mama?" Perfie set her suitcase down and took off her coat. She placed it on the hook near the back door and noticed that her father's coat was not there.

"We didn't know you were coming home. Does Tío know?"

"He's the one who sent for me." Perfie brushed a stray hair from her face. Her cheeks were flushed from the wind. Things must not be too bad if Isabelle was sitting there reading.

"He never said a word to me."

"How is Mama?" Perfie repeated. She didn't want to see her mother without some preparation.

"The same. She doesn't leave her bed, but she's eating a little more."

Perfie walked into the bedroom. Propped with pillows, Avelina didn't look toward her daughter. She sat without moving, staring at the painting which hung on the wall close to the bed.

Perfie studied her mother for a moment. Then she turned her gaze to the painting.

It had hung on this wall for years, but Perfie had never really looked at it.

It was the lake in Antonito.

"Were you there Mama? Did you sit by the lake?"

There was no movement from her mother.

Mama didn't look good. Her wrists poked out from the ruffled sleeves of her flannel nightgown, and her fingers curled into claws. Her jaw was slack.

Perfie felt a tightness in her chest. A wave of longing swept over her.

She remembered her mother brushing her hair, working it into long braids with her fingers and perching a hat on the top of Perfie's head to protect her fair skin from the sun. *We don't want you brown like an Indian*, Mama would say, although Perfie secretly longed for the smooth brown skin of the Indians, and she hated the hat, taking it off before the end of each day. Perfie felt pale and sickly compared to the other girls. They had deep brown eyes, nearly black, while her own green eyes looked washed out, without meaning.

Isaac said her skin was beautiful, comparing it to alabaster. He said her eyes were like gems; they reflected the light, sparkled. Of course he didn't have brown eyes either. His were so blue, like that funny foreign cat Señora McNeil brought back from Santa Fe.

Perfie walked to the side of the bed. "Mama, it's me."

Avelina turned her head, and her eyes grew wide. She brought her hand to her mouth, then moved it down and pressed it to the center of her chest. Her mouth opened and closed three times before words came out.

"You have broken my heart."

Perfie didn't speak or move. It wasn't fair that following her own heart would lead to breaking her mother's. She tried to think about all that Tía had told her. About her mother being a sad young woman, left all alone.

"I'm not the one who broke your heart. It's time to stop blaming me."

Avelina turned her head away from Perfecta, back to the wall, and closed her eyes.

Perfie had imagined that punishment for her sins would catch up with her sometime in the future. She was wrong. The punishment was now: yanked from Isaac, hated by her father, and causing shame to her mother.

Should she apologize or confess, or do something else to make up for it?

It wasn't right to lie in confession. She couldn't say she was sorry for what she'd done, because it wasn't true. She didn't regret one moment of her time with Isaac. She could hardly wait to see him again, to be held in his arms, caressed, kissed, loved. It was all that mattered to her any more.

She wanted to scream at Mama. Talk to me, tell me what you're thinking. Tell me about your broken heart. Fight with me. Fight for me.

But the thin figure, now curled in a tight ball with eyes closed and chin tucked under the quilt, didn't offer much fight.

Perfie turned and left the room.

It soon became clear to Perfie that her father had *not* sent for her.

His eyes shot off the usual sparks, and he raised his clenched fist. "What are you doing here?"

"Tía Emilia sent me. She said I had to come home right away. I thought there was something wrong with Mama."

He stomped his foot and lurched toward her. "Of course there's something wrong. She's dying; she has been for a long time. You're a foolish girl. You've made her worse just by being here." He turned and went to the door. "Don't unpack your suitcase, you're not staying."

Perfie turned to Isabelle. "Tiá Emilia gave me a ticket and said I was to come home right away."

Isabelle shook her head. "I don't know. You mother was doing better. She was talking and eating."

Perfie was angry. She had done nothing, nothing at all. She was just a girl. She had done what her aunt told her to do. Why was she being punished for this? She hadn't killed anyone, put poison in a cup and served it up. She hadn't stolen anything. And most of all, she hadn't done anything to her mother.

"Perfecta?" Isabelle put her hand on Perfie's arm.

"What?" She didn't like the tone of Isabelle's voice.

"There's something else you should know." Isabelle hesitated. "It's your horse."

"Cimmaron?" Perfie felt every cell in her body buzz as if about to explode.

"Your father sold him."

Perfie shook her head back and forth as the sobs burst from her. "No! He wouldn't do that. Not Cimmaron, not my horse." The pain seared through her body as if the world were on fire. It seemed her plan to stand up to her father had failed. He would win no matter what.

Although she didn't believe Isabelle would lie about something like this, she jumped up and raced to the back porch. In the corral out back stood the gray gelding and the little burro. There was no funny white horse with splotches decorating his body. She sank to her knees and pulled at her hair. The screams tore out of her body. When Isabelle came and put a hand on her back, Perfie pushed her away.

"Leave me alone. Just leave me alone."

Two hours later she was in the wagon on her way to who knew where to be dumped on another cousin. She was numb and rode in silence, her head turned to one side. Her eyes were open, but she didn't see anything. She couldn't believe her father had put her on a wagon that traveled at night, but Señor Chavez drove this route every week. The moon was bright, and the horse knew his way.

Would Isabelle tell Isaac what was happening? I have to let him know I'm still waiting for him, she thought, not daring to admit what she really wanted was to know that he was still waiting for her.

She couldn't trust her cousin. Isabelle seemed frightened, as if she didn't dare to upset Primitivo. Maybe with Perfie gone he had turned some of his frustration on her, although it seemed she was doing quite a job at being the good daughter. Just what she always wanted.

Perfie grasped the side of the wagon and tipped her head back, looking at the stars and praying to that God who was supposedly up there.

Isaac will wait. We made a promise. I waited for him, now he will wait for me.

But what about Cimmaron?

Robin Martinez Rice

Prayers

Ten

Chimayó, New Mexico, October 1929

"**P**erfecta. Your brother is here." Paula Luna wiped the corner of her eye with a stained handkerchief. "Your mother, she doesn't have long."

"Joe is here?" Her mother must be bad off for her brother to come all this way. Perfie dried her hands on a worn dish towel. Cousin Paula didn't have much in the tiny house where Perfie had spent the last two years. What she did have was old and worn out. Perfie tried to convince the gruff woman that new dish towels could be made from flour or rice sacks, but Paula never bought in quantity. She made daily trips to the tiny mercantile in Chimayó, filling a small cloth sack with the few items they needed. It didn't take Perfie long to figure out that her cousin also filled the "medicine" bottle she carried with her.

Joe crossed the room and folded her into his arms. "Perfie. We should hurry. It's a two-day trip, and she didn't look good when I left."

It only took a few minutes for Perfie to stuff her belongings into the old suitcase. Since her father had exiled her from Tierra Amarilla three years ago she had grown accustomed to moving around.

She followed Joe out of the house. A shiny black mare hitched to a buggy stood out front.

Joe noticed the questioning look on her face. "Not mine. I borrowed it. It's faster than the wagon. She's a quick one." He pushed her suitcase into a small space in the back of the seat, then turned to help her in. Perfie wasn't sure if "she" referred to the mare or the buggy.

Cousin Paula stood on the wooden porch and sniffed. "Adíos. Say goodbye to your mama for me. I wish I was able to go and say goodbye myself."

As Joe clucked to the mare and they started off up the dusty road, Perfie realized she should have thanked Paula. But she wasn't thankful for the time spent in Chimayó. At least at Tía Emilia's there had been conversation, books to read, and the lake. Paula was a grouchy old woman, and Perfie was glad to leave.

She thought about the last time she had been in T.A.—the day she lost Cimmaron and her father sent her away. That time it was to Albuquerque. She had lived with three sets of "cousins" there, never lasting long with any one household. Her resentment made her a poor house guest. But at least there were young people and busy days, even if she didn't have time for much fun.

Here in Chimayó there had been only work. She was expected to tend to the large garden that supported Paula. It was her job to grow the garden, put up the harvest in the jars and man the fruit stand. The sick and infirm who traveled to El Santuario de Chimayó in search of the healing dirt were hungry by the time the pilgrimage had brought them this far, and they bought the food.

There were some young people here—cousins who invited her on picnics or for a swim in the river. But Paula refused her this pleasure, letting her know that all the work must be done before she could run off with them. And there was always more work.

The old Perfie would have gone anyway. But she missed Isaac so much, and she felt the weight of her mistakes. Maybe if she tried hard to do the right thing her life would change.

She attended Mass again, although it was different here. The Santuario was always filled with strangers, and the priests were very busy. She never felt they really listened to her confession. With this life of all work and no play she didn't have much to confess anyway. She should have felt forgiven.

She didn't. But she still couldn't accept the idea that God would be angry with her all the time. It just didn't feel right.

She hadn't seen Isaac in over two years. The last time had been so short. She was in between exiles, and he was in between jobs. He came to see her in Albuquerque, but they only had a few hours together, just long enough for another promise to wait.

Did she remember him as he really was? Maybe she had built him into a prince, riding into town to rescue her on his white horse. If only she had a photograph or something to remember him.

She turned to Joe. "Is Isaac there?"

Joe shook his head. "No. He's in Albuquerque. But I heard he's due to come back. That young teacher, Rafael Montoya, he's going to leave to marry a girl back in Tennessee. Lucas wants Isaac back at the school."

Perfie sighed in relief. If he was coming back then they could be together again.

A buggy might move more quickly than a wagon, but it was small and her back ached from the constant jarring pace. They spent the night in Abiquiu at a home which doubled as an inn. Señora Ruiz got up early and served them bacon and eggs with red chili and potatoes.

"Did Mama . . ." Perfie wanted to know if her mother had ever come out of her trance, but she couldn't figure out how to ask Joe this without sounding harsh.

"Huh?" Joe used a piece of bread so soak up the chili.

"Mama. Did she come out of her mood? Wake up at all?"

"She hasn't left the bed in years. Your father is hardly ever there." Joe paused and took a breath. "He's different, Perfie. I don't know. Sad. Old. He's not doing well with this."

Perfie didn't reply. She thought about her father being sad. So what? Her mother had been sad for years. He hadn't made life a happy place for his wife or his daughter, in spite of how much he proclaimed to love Avelina. Maybe it was time he got a taste of his own medicine.

Joe continued. "Perfie. You should be prepared. There isn't much left of her. She doesn't open her eyes, doesn't talk. She's skin and bones. Isabelle gets some broth in her once in a while, but that's it."

Perfie nodded and pushed her plate away. Her stomach churned, and she couldn't eat the food no matter how tasty it looked.

It was a good thing Joe had prepared her. Avelina hadn't been much to look at when Perfie last saw her, but now she was no more than a skeleton with skin. Perfie couldn't bring herself to touch this person. She stood back from the bed. *This is not my mother,* she thought

"Mama. Perfecta is here. She came to see you." Joe sat on the edge of the bed and held Avelina's claw-like hand.

Perfie was awed by her brother's behavior. She hadn't seen the tender side of him, but now she saw how he helped Isabelle care for Avelina. The two of them lifted her and washed her, tenderly applying salve to the bedsores which covered her mother's body. He patiently spooned broth into her, although most of it ended up on the napkin, having dribbled out of her mother's slack mouth.

Neither said anything about Perfie's unwillingness to touch her mother. She stayed in the room as much as possible, but the odor of impending death made her gag. When Perfie dozed off she had nightmares, crazy dreams with huge witches chasing her and God sending thunder bolts down to earth.

On the third day Isabelle approached Perfie.

"I need to go to church. Can you stay with her? I won't be gone long." Isabelle, her face still as a mask, stood straight and stared at Perfie. Perfie suspected her cousin was trying to hide her disapproval of the fact that Perfie hadn't been helping much.

Joe was gone too. If her mother soiled the bed it would have to wait until he came home. But the day was warm for October, and the windows could stay open for a little while. Perfie decided she could handle caring for Mama for a short time.

"Of course. I'll be fine."

Perfie sat in the rocker, which had been moved into the bedroom. The chair felt haunted, seeped with Avelina's sorrow, but there was no other place to sit. She held her knitting in her lap but couldn't focus on the complicated pattern. She stared at her mother.

Perfie wanted to talk. She wanted to clear the space between them.

"Mama? Can you hear me?" The shallow breath seemed to speed up. "I want to tell you something." Perfie stood and pulled the rocker closer to the bed.

"Once there was an Indian maid. She lived a long life. The first brave she married left her and another one soon moved in. She tried to be happy with the new brave, but he was mean to her daughter. *Their* daughter."

Perfie watched her mother's eye lids flicker. She knew Avelina could hear the story. Suddenly Perfie felt mean for telling her mother this story now. Better to do this right.

"Mama. I want to tell you about Isaac and how much I love him. I want you to know that I know your story. I know you lied to me. I know you sinned. But I prayed last night. Prayed hard. God forgives you and he forgives me."

Perfie sniffed and rocked. This is every bit as much a tale as the Indian maid story. I'm almost as good a story teller as she is.

Was, Perfie thought before she continued.

"I had a sign, a sign from God. He says Isaac is the one for me and you should feel good about this."

"Ahhh." Avelina let out a feeble moan.

Perfie jumped from the chair. She stood next to the bed but didn't know what to do. She had avoided caring for sick people her whole life. There was always someone else to do it—first Mama, then Isabelle.

Spittle dribbled from her mother's mouth. She knew Joe wiped this with the napkin on the night stand. But even when she held the cloth in her hand she couldn't reach to touch her mother. She watched as her mother's body shuddered once and was still.

"Mama?" She leaned closer. "Mama, are you okay?"

Even as she spoke she knew the words were crazy. Her mother hadn't been okay for years, and now she was dead.

Perfie couldn't shake the feeling that Isabelle and Joe would think she killed her mother. When Isabelle came home from church, Perfie met her in the kitchen.

"She's dead."

"What?" Isabelle raced into the bedroom. Perfie followed slowly and stood in the doorway watching her cousin as she grasped Avelina's shoulders and shook. "Tía? Tía, wake up." Isabelle started crying soft sobs that reminded Perfie of their dog who had lost her pups.

Perfie walked out to the kitchen. What's wrong with me? Why don't I cry? She sat down at the kitchen table. I didn't even really know her. She didn't help me plan a wedding or hold her grandchildren. She didn't tell me the truth about her life.

Perfie felt her body turn cold. Her hands were numb, and she couldn't move. What had she done? There had been no priest, no last rites for her mother. Was it too late for that? She had condemned not only herself to hell but her mother to purgatory. She closed her eyes.

Maybe if I just think about something else. This isn't real. I'm far away; I'm on Cimmaron's back; I'm riding like the wind.

Isabelle's voice startled Perfie out of her thoughts. "We have work to do. We have to clean her."

"I . . . I can't do it."

"Perfie, she's your mother. You have to do it. Don't you love her at all?"

"Of course I love her. I can't do it because I love her. That's not her. Don't you see?" Perfie stood up. She needed to leave this house, or Isabelle would have her way.

"What's wrong with you? Of course it's her, your mother. In there."

Heavy footsteps on the porch interrupted them.

It was Joe. He looked at the two women.

"She's gone." His voice was soft and matter of fact.

"Yes." Isabelle stood and went to him. She wrapped her arms around him, but Perfie could see that his body remained stiff.

"She'll have peace now. It's for the best."

Were her brother's words true? Could years of torment be wiped away so easily? Perfie pictured her mother with an express ticket to heaven, but everything she had learned in the last few years made her question this. If God was kind and rewarded lots of prayer and many hours spent in church, then Avelina would be at his side, surrounded by angels. But this wasn't what her mother preached to her. You will pay for your sins when you die —or in Perfie's case before you die—forever in Purgatory or hell. Your soul might even be stuck on earth as a ghost.

"Shouldn't there be a priest?" Perfie looked at Joe, avoiding Isabelle's glare.

"He was here yesterday. He'll come after we have her cleaned up." Isabelle stepped back. "Which we should be doing right now."

"I told you. I can't." Perfie shook her head.

Joe nodded. "You best go find Primitivo. Belle, you and I will clean her up."

Perfie didn't let herself breathe a sigh of relief yet. Telling her father might be worse than helping with her mother's body.

But she didn't have to do either one. She searched the town for her father, checking the courthouse, the mercantile and the bar without finding him. When she walked past Solomon's house, she stopped in to tell him his cousin had passed. He hugged her and fixed her some tea. It was so comfortable sitting and talking with him that she forgot her task. By the time she walked home Primitivo had already been and gone.

"How did he take it?"

Joe shook his head. "Couldn't tell. He just stomped into the bedroom and shut the door. He was in there with her for awhile. I could hear mumbling. I don't know if he was praying or talking to her. Maybe he was saying goodbye."

They held the service on Saturday. The church was packed, but Perfie suspected people were there to stay on the good side of the town sheriff rather than to grieve Avelina.

She sat in the front row, sandwiched between Manuel and Isabelle. Manny hadn't been back here for years, and Perfie barely recognized her oldest brother. Joe must have known where to find Mannie, judging by how quickly he arrived. His hug was warm, and his kiss held the scent of tobacco and sweat. She liked the feel of his shoulder pressed against hers. Isabelle sobbed into her hankie as Father Tom droned on.

Perfie was angry that Father Tom led the service. Isabelle admitted Avelina had begged her to be sure Father Gonzalez or Father Gabriel would give her last rites and perform the service. But it was Father Tom who droned the words in English over her mother's body. Everyone kept going on and on about her mother's soul, but it seemed such disrespect to deliver these important words in a language her mother couldn't understand. Maybe she would be so confused that she wouldn't find her way to heaven. It seemed like one more road block, even after death.

Perfie bit her lip and didn't listen to Father Tom's words. She thought about Isaac, Joe, and Manuel. She wondered how long Manny would stay and visit.

Then it was time for communion. As she followed Isabelle to the altar and knelt, she glanced up at the stained glass window. The sun shone through and lit up the Virgin's halo. Perfie felt her legs start to tremble. As she staggered forward and knelt she folded her hands tightly to control the shaking. She couldn't take her eyes off the light as it moved from Mary's halo down to her face.

It was her mother. The turned-down lips of the Virgin lit up, and Perfie could hear her mother's voice. "A broken heart. I am left with a broken heart."

Sobs broke from her. She tried to stand and run, but her body refused to cooperate. She pulled her arms off the rail and pressed her head to the cold floor. Her sobs grew louder as she wrapped her arms around her head to hide.

Perfie felt a hand on her back. Was it the priest? Manuel or Joe? It was a large hand, rubbing her back softly.

"Come. Stand up." The voice was deep and sounded far away. Two strong hands moved under her arms and pulled her up.

She kept her head down and turned to follow the deep voice away from the altar.

It wasn't until she was through the door that she drew in a deep choking breath and stopped crying.

"Cry it out. You need it."

She wiped her face and opened her eyes.

It was her father.

He stood staring at the graves spread out beyond the picket fence, some with white headstones, others with rocks placed carefully over the spot where the body lay below the yellow earth. An open hole stood near the fence, ready for Avelina. Tears ran down her father's cheeks, diverted by three days' growth of whiskers.

She held her breath. This was her father—his hand on her back, leading her out here to look at the grave? Her head felt like it was clouded with the red mud that washed off the steep walls of a creek in a flash flood. Her thoughts bombarded her, even as they seemed to come in slow motion.

One thing was clear to her. Primitivo was sad. And he wanted her by his side to share his sorrow.

She reached her hand out to his sleeve, but just before she touched him he turned and walked away. She followed him to the front of the church. People were drifting out; the service had ended. He mumbled, and she stepped closer to hear what he said.

"What will I do without you? How can I be alone?"

He wasn't talking to her. She watched as he pulled his kerchief from his pocket and wiped his face. In an instant he was Sheriff Trujillo again, shaking hands and thanking people for their condolences.

But she wouldn't forget the tears of a husband who had lost his wife.

Eleven

The weeks passed as if Perfie had stepped into another place—one where time was erratic, speeding and slowing without warning. Her father's unexpected tenderness had vanished, and she wondered if she had imagined the whole thing. She hoped he would notice her now, that somehow the loss of Avelina would open his heart to her; even though something about this disgusted her. It was as if kindness could only be given to one person at a time.

But nothing happened. Isabelle went back to the university, and Primitivo spent very little time at home. He was civil to her, but he treated her like a servant. There were no more signs of tenderness.

And now Isaac wasn't coming home. Enrollment at the school had dropped. The crash of the stock market hadn't impacted Tierra Amarilla the way it had the rest of the country, but people were worried. Jobs were disappearing and families didn't have the money to pay La Acadamía's high tuition. Joe thought some of them just wanted their sons closer to home. Isaac was forced to find another job in Albuquerque, working at the train yard, and Lucas told him to stay and earn as much as he could while the job lasted.

Then Joe left town. With a quick goodbye, a suitcase and his guitar, he was gone. She heard rumors, but she didn't believe them until a woman approached her at the mercantile.

"Excuse me. Are you Perfecta Trujillo?" Two small children clung to the woman's skirt. Her belly stuck out in front of her; another child would be here soon.

"Yes." Perfie didn't know her. A Tewa, she thought, looking at the large, dark eyes.

"Do you know where Joe is?" the woman asked. Her gaze darted around the store.

"I think he went to Santa Fe." Perfie told the truth. She didn't know where he was.

"If he comes back will you tell him to please come see Maria? It's important."

"I'll tell him." She walked away from Maria quickly; she didn't want to hear more.

But there had been more rumors—not only that Joe was the father of Maria's baby, but that he was living in Española and was married to another woman who had just delivered a baby. How could this be? Not even a month had passed since he had left town.

With no one around and her father seldom home, Perfie was bored. She missed Cimmaron. If her horse were here she could ride. Unless she was willing to mount up on Burrito, she was stuck.

She sewed. She made three new dresses with patterns she drafted for herself: a blue silk with a belted waist and pleats on the bodice to slim her round torso; a creamy linen embroidered with tiny blue and green flowers on the neckline and a little cut-out faux cuff; and an everyday dress of a tiny green floral print with a wide bodice and a curving neckline that made it beyond the ordinary.

Soon the other girls were asking her to alter their dresses.

Perfie refused.

"I'm not the prettiest girl in town, but I can be the best dressed," she wrote to Isabelle.

"I know of one person who thinks you're the prettiest in town." Isabelle wrote back.

But the new dresses hung in the closet because that one person wasn't here. Perfie had nowhere to go, no special occasions. She hadn't been to church since her mother's funeral.

Primitivo didn't seem interested in going to church, claiming he needed to work each Sunday so that deputies with families could attend— more proof he didn't think of her as his family.

Isabelle came for Christmas. These were two weeks of pure bliss. They baked bisquochitos and carried the plates covered with embroidered dish clothes to all the neighbors. They stayed up late playing cards. The air was filled with their laughter.

But the holiday ended and Isabelle went back to school. The house was cold and empty without her.

By January Perfie felt numb. Her arms and legs were heavy with inactivity. She knew how people came to die of boredom, even if she still didn't understand how they died of a broken heart.

She thought about going to Albuquerque. She could get a job there, maybe at one of the hotels, or as a nanny. And she could be with Isaac.

There was one problem. Isaac hadn't asked her to come. Well, two problems. Finding a job was the second. She had worked as a nanny and as a maid during her exiles, and she had lost her job every time. She just couldn't handle bossy people who focused on details that weren't important. What difference did it make what the kids had for lunch, how long they stayed at the park or if the towels were folded a certain way? And if the old men who spent their days on the bench at Hughes' store told the truth, there were no jobs. Not for anyone.

She was stuck here.

One afternoon in February Perfie decided to make a pie with the canned squash she found in the back of the pantry. As she stretched up onto her toes to put the mixing bowl back on the high shelf, she felt a tingle in her spine. She turned then, and screamed at the sight of someone standing behind her.

"That's the greeting I get?" Isaac grabbed her around the waist and swooped her feet off the floor as he swung her around, cutting off her reply with his lips pressed against hers.

She wound her arms tight around his neck, laughing and covering his face with her kisses.

"Are you here to stay?" She asked as soon as he set her down and the kisses stopped for a minute.

"Yes. I lost my job. I'm tired of waiting tables and working on road crews. Bennie isn't much of a teacher; he hates it. Padre agreed to let me work at the school again."

He opened the bread box and pulled out half a loaf. "Do you have anything to eat around here? I came straight from the truck. What smells so good?"

"Pie." Perfie glanced at the clock above the door. "But you can't stay. Papa will be here for his dinner soon."

Isaac turned and put his hand on her shoulder. "I think it's time."

She held her breath.

"We need to face him sooner or later. He has to know we see each other. Everyone else in town knows it."

This wasn't what she was waiting to hear, but she considered what he said. Primitivo had changed. Maybe Isaac was right. They could stop sneaking around. They could meet in daylight and let their courtship be known. But what if that made Primitivo mad? The last few months had been boring, but she didn't miss her father's anger.

She shook her head. "Not yet. He's been calm since Mama died. It might ruin everything."

"Just think about it. Please." Isaac spread butter on the bread and took a bite.

So they met at night. Dark circles grew under Perfie's eyes. She no longer climbed out the window since the branch of the ash tree had fallen during a winter storm. She sneaked out of the house without making a sound, stepping over the creaking third step, handing Blanco a chunk of bone to keep him quiet, and slipping out the door. She met Isaac at the school house. He spread a blanket on the floor of the classroom close to the little stove in the corner where the coals left from the day's fire kept them warm. As the winter turned to spring the nights grew warm.

"I'm worried I'm not going to wake up in time to get home." She wasn't worried about being caught here. She couldn't imagine anyone coming here at night.

"Don't worry. I'll wake up." Isaac did seem to have an internal alarm clock.

"If he finds out I'm seeing you again I don't know what he'll do this time. He should know banishment won't work." The fact that her father kept a very irregular schedule these days added pressure. She worried she would run into him in the early morning hours, both of them creeping back into the house just before dawn.

Isaac rubbed her cheek. "I can fix that. Come with me to California."

"California? You can't do that. You just got back. Your father . . . Bennie . . ."

Me, she wanted to add, but kept silent.

"Did you hear me? I want you to come with me."

She waited for the next part. *Marry me.*

But he didn't speak those words. *Wait for me, come with me, promise me*—those were the offers. What would happen if she did go with him and he decided he didn't want her anymore? She would be stuck in California. Alone.

"What would I do in California?"

"You would keep me company."

"What would you do?"

"I'll find some work. I can't stay here, Perfie. My father won't let me teach the way I want. He says it's his school and he knows what's best for the students. He can find someone else. There are lots of men out of work now. When I try to talk to him about it he says I can always move out to work the cattle. That's not an option for me. Besides, I'd have to deal with Enoch."

Perfie couldn't understand why Isaac didn't want to be out with the cattle. He loved the property. What would be so bad about being out there?

"Don't go, Isaac. I can't bear it when you're gone."

"That is why you should come with me." He rubbed her arm with his hand and followed with soft kisses that moved up her arm to her neck. She sat still and waited, still hopeful that he would ask her to marry him. But after a minute, when he didn't speak, she finally turned her lips to his.

Nothing more was said about California. Or a wedding.

Twelve

Isaac cleared his throat and tapped the ruler on the desk. "Quiet."

The spring weather made the boys act like coyote pups, yipping and hopping and poking each other. They were certainly not in the mood to learn about plotting points on a plane or any other geometric surface.

"Time for a quiz." He spoke softly. Two boys in the first row heard him and groaned. The rest of the class continued their chatter and unruly behavior.

"Ah hem." Isaac cleared his throat and raised his voice. "Take your seats please. Chalk and slates ready. Ten extra points for the first correct answer."

A few more boys heard this time. They moved to their seats.

"What is the congruence of these points?" Isaac waved his hand toward the graph on the blackboard.

There was a scramble, and soon all fifteen boys were quietly working out the problem.

Two more months of this. Isaac didn't see how he would manage.

"Number two." As he read out the next problem he imagined Perfie's warm skin. Yesterday they spent three hours together walking back from the property as the sun set. She didn't seem to worry as much about people seeing them together, although she still refused to let her father know they were courting.

Courting. Such an old fashioned word.

He knew she expected marriage. And now that their relationship was at such an intimate level it was what he should do.

He loved her. That was true. He hadn't even thought about another woman for the last six years. No, seven years.

A seven-year courtship. Unheard of. And a twenty-eight-year-old man not yet married—that was even worse. People would talk, imagine terrible things about such a man.

Yesterday he had walked home from the school house in the early afternoon. His father was out in the yard chopping some of last year's dried wood into smaller pieces for kindling. As he came closer, he heard his mother.

"And don't think you can just fill that little box on the back porch. I need lots of kindling. It might be spring to you, but it's weeks more cold weather to me." The wooden screen banged shut.

He watched as his father stood with one hand pressed to his lower back. Lucas leaned on the axe handle and shook his head.

Isaac saw the look on his father's face. It was as if he had put a sweet pepper in his mouth only to be surprised by the rancid taste of something rotten.

It was this look, this feeling he saw in his father. This was why he couldn't ask Perfecta to marry him. He couldn't bear the thought of his own face pinched and sad. He didn't know what he wanted from life, but he didn't want to be trapped here in Tierra Amarilla.

Isaac planned to save up some money. When he had enough to move away, then he would ask her to marry him.

"Mr. Martinez?"

He snapped out of his trance. The room full of boys was quiet. All were staring at him. He had the sudden feeling he might have spoken out loud.

"Number four. What is the value of y in figure number three?"

That night Perfie didn't come to the school house. Isaac lit a cigarette and paced. She was often late. Primitivo might linger over supper or come home at the last minute.

Ten o'clock. Isaac was cold and grouchy. He didn't sleep well wrapped in the blanket on the school room floor. The early rising and rushing home to pretend he had been there all night was catching up with him. He had to convince Perfie they could meet openly.

Primitivo was a stubborn old man, but he would come around. Other people had finally accepted the Martinez family. Presbyterians might still be considered sinners, but La Academía had earned a name. Even now, with times so tight, parents scrimped to send their sons to the school. As sheriff, Primitivo wouldn't dare to go against the rest of the town.

Isaac knew there was more to Perfie's fear. He had witnessed the old man's treatment, watching from across the street when he happened to see them. Perfie said things were better now since her mother had died and Isabelle and Joe were gone. Surely this was the time to let him know about their courtship. He had a suspicion she was waiting for something more formal.

Marriage. He couldn't seem to get away from it. Damn.

Three nights passed and no Perfie. What had happened? At least when Isabelle was here he would get some sort of message.

On Thursday morning he kissed his mother on the cheek and grabbed his hat. "Got to get to school early. Some papers to mark."

He stood at the edge of the Trujillo yard and watched the house. It seemed quiet enough; Primitivo must be gone by now. But as he walked up onto the back porch the door flew open and the old man came out.

"What are *you* doing here?" Primitivo growled.

Isaac didn't say a word. He could see Perfie standing in the doorway behind her father.

She held a baby on her hip.

Suddenly Primitivo let out a loud guffaw. It didn't stop there. He snorted, and his laughter bellowed out.

"Caught you by surprise, I see. Didn't know your secret lover had a baby, did you?"

"Papa." Perfie's voice was sharp.

Primitivo turned back to his daughter. "You think I don't know what goes on? I might be deaf, but I'm not dumb." He pushed past Isaac. "Go ahead. Find out all about *el niño*. He's going to put an end to your nighttime romance anyway."

"Come in." Perfie moved the baby up to her shoulder and went into the house. "His name is Little Joe."

"He's Joe's baby?" Isaac had heard the rumors.

"No. Well, Papa says not. His mother is a distant cousin. She's in the jail for killing a man—maybe the baby's father."

"Why do you have him?"

"No one else came. I thought my father was being kind, bringing him here so he wouldn't go to the orphanage. But after that," she nodded her head toward the door, "I think he did it so I couldn't sneak out to see you."

"I guess he knows."

"Obviously."

"That's a good thing, Perfie. Now we don't have to be so secretive."

She looked down at the baby. He wiggled and smiled. She turned him in her lap so that he faced Isaac.

"I can't come out at night. I can't leave him alone. And you can't come here."

Isaac knew that he couldn't come here to sleep. But surely he could come to visit.

"Why?"

Perfie didn't answer.

"For dinner? To visit? What's the problem, Perfie?"

"I can't do it. I can't sit at the table with you and Papa." She kissed the dark head of the baby. "And Little Joe."

"I don't understand. Your father seems okay with it. I mean, he didn't kick me off the property."

A loud knock on the screen interrupted the conversation.

It was Marcus Gallegos, one of Isaac's students.

"Mr. Martinez? Are you in there?"

Madre de Dios. He had forgotten about his students.

Isaac jumped up and rushed out the door. He raced down the road to the school. Lucas stood with his arms folded across his chest. Fifteen students were lined up in front of the building.

Perfie was wrong. There were *no* secrets in this town.

Thirteen

Perfie wiped the mush off Little Joe's rosy cheeks. He giggled and reached for the cloth.

"Not now. We have to get you cleaned up. It's a good day for a walk." She untied the dish towel that held him in the chair and set him down where he could hold on to the wooden seat. He liked to stand, and he crawled like a busy spider, but there were no first steps yet.

She had cleaned up her old play wagon for him. He loved to be pulled around town, stopping in at the mercantile for a visit, then on to see Solomon and Ruth. Ruth always had a cookie for him. Their house had seen so many children; it was a safe place in which he could crawl around and explore.

"Ma."

"What?" Perfie looked down at Little Joe. "Did you say something?"

He smiled. "Ma," he repeated.

She scooped him up and kissed his cheek. "Yes. That's who I am now. Mama."

The summer days were long and hot, but Perfie didn't notice. With Little Joe to keep her busy, time flew by. Isaac came to the house now, stopping on his way home from the school for some pie or a glass of lemonade. He complained that they never had time together, but Perfie didn't care.

"I can't leave him, don't you see? He already lost one mother." She petted Little Joe on his smooth dark hair.

Isaac shook his head. "Mother? You're not his mother, Perfie. More like a nanny. She'll get him back, you know."

"Not if she killed someone. She'll hang for that. Besides that. . ." Perfie snapped her mouth closed. She didn't want to bring up the fact that she was glad they weren't sleeping together anymore. Maybe Isaac would get the message.

She felt better now that she was sleeping nights in her own bed. She kept Little Joe snugged to her side against the wall. If he fussed she rubbed his soft back until he went to sleep. His warm body comforted her, and she realized why women loved to have babies.

It was on the fifteenth day of September that God reminded her she was a sinner and must be punished. The sun was shining, and there was no hint that fall was just around the corner. No leaves had turned, and Las Nutrias was completely dry, without mud even in the deep curves. Perfie took Little Joe out early before the day became too hot for the toddler.

He was walking now, taking tiny steps while he held her hand and grinned at his accomplishment. And he was into everything.

"Baby Joe, you can't have that." Perfie jumped up and pulled the walnut out of his mouth. Primitivo had brought a basket home last night and one must have fallen onto the floor. "You'll choke. Let me crack it for you."

His mouth turned down at the corners, and his eyes filled with tears. His lower lip started to quiver. She looked around for something to give him before the screams started.

"No *pucheros*. Wipe that grouchy face. How about some of this?" She grabbed an apple from the basket on the table. "Yum. We'll have a little snack. Apples and walnuts."

He shook his head and powered up his lungs. She knew by his red face that the scream would be a whopper.

Just as the wail pierced the kitchen she heard footsteps on the front porch. Who would that be? If it was Isaac stopping by he would come to the back door.

It was her father.

"You sure about this? He's a handful, you know. Of course my daughter has spoiled him, gives him everything he wants." Primitivo was talking to a woman and man who came into the kitchen behind him. The woman wore a pale yellow dress with matching shoes. Her eyes were blue, and she had hair the same color as the dress and shoes. The man wore a summer suit, his face red from the heat.

White people.

Little Joe stopped his scream and scuttled over to Perfie, throwing his arms around her legs and burying his face in her skirt.

"Oh. He looks just like David." The woman stooped and called to him. "Jonathan. Do you remember me?"

"His name is Little Joe." Perfie didn't know why the woman called him Jonathan.

Primitivo scowled at Perfie and shook his head. "These folks are this boy's grandparents. They're here to take him home."

Perfie put her hand on Little Joe's head. "They can't be his grandparents. He's Spanish." Or Indian, she silently added.

"My son, David, he's Jonathan's father." The woman stood and smiled at Perfie. "His mother, she's the dark skinned one."

"Is he dead?" Perfie thought about the supposed murder.

"Dead? No, he's in New York."

The man didn't say a word. Perfie looked at him. She had to figure out a way to prove that these people had no right to Little Joe.

"She might have told you your son was the father, but she's lying. Anyone can tell he doesn't look a thing like either one of you." Perfie paused, keeping her eyes on the face of the man. She didn't dare look at her father. "My brother, Ramaldo. Joe. He's the father. This baby belongs to us."

Primitivo stepped forward and pulled Little Joe off Perfie's leg. The baby reached his arms around the sheriff's neck. He wasn't scared; this man was nice to him, even played with him. But Primitivo didn't hold on to him long enough for the hug to take place. He passed him to the yellow-haired woman.

Perfie stood frozen as she watched the woman hug the baby to her.

"I think it's best if you go quickly," Primitivo told the man.

He nodded and put his arm on his wife's shoulder. "He's right. We have a long drive. Let's go."

Primitivo turned to Perfie. "Get his things. Put them in a box." Her father's words rushed over her like a bucket of cold water. She didn't move.

"We don't need them. We brought some things." The woman looked at Perfie. "Thank you for taking care of him. I can tell he loves you and you did a good job." Her words were brittle, as if she read them off of one of Isaac's movie scripts.

Perfie felt her throat grow into a tight knot. Her heart pounded in her chest, and that funny light feeling swept up the back of her head. Her hands started to tremble, and she squeezed them into fists. This couldn't be happening. These people were taking her baby.

Primitivo snatched the blue quilt off the chair. Perfie had stitched each scrap together to make a soft covering for the baby. "He likes this." He handed the quilt to the woman.

Little Joe reached out and grabbed it. He pulled it close to his body as they left the house and walked across the yard to a fancy automobile.

Perfie finally broke out of her frozen state and ran out onto the porch.

"Little Joe!" She drew in a shaking breath and called out. "Please don't take my baby."

"Ma." She heard him answer as the women slipped into the car and slammed the door.

And just like that, Little Joe was gone.

Angels

Fourteen

Tierra Amarilla, December 1931

Perfie held the coffee pot over her father's cup, not pouring, but giving the pot a slight twitch with her hand. "I'm going to mass today. Do you want to go?"

Primitivo pointed to his cup, and she filled it. He shook his head, his eyes focused on the newspaper.

Relief swept over her. She didn't want him to go.

Over the past year Perfie and Prmitivo had resumed communication. It wasn't much: questions about meals, requests for certain household items, the occasional greeting. It seemed she didn't aggravate him anymore because he didn't really pay attention to what she did. As long as his meals were cooked and the house was clean, there was peace in the household.

Perfie started going to Mass again, but not because she hoped for redemption or had decided to confess her sins. She went because it was her only social life other than the secret meetings with Isaac—which weren't much of a secret anymore.

Isaac hadn't given up fighting the secrecy, but Perfie still wasn't ready to be out in the open about the relationship. Maybe if he would offer more than walks on the property, evenings in the schoolhouse, and apple pie on the back porch—maybe then she would give more. The fact was he had never even invited her to his house.

She glanced at her father. "Will you be here for dinner?"

Primitivo didn't look up. "No."

Just what did that mean? Would he want it later than usual? For supper? She needed to know if she was expected to cook something later today.

"I thought I might make a stew. You could eat whenever you're home?" She made sure this was a question, still cautious of putting demands on her father.

"That's fine."

So he would be here. She would come back after church and put the stew on. That would leave time to go out and meet Isaac this afternoon.

Three days before Christmas Mr. Hughes reduced the price of the holiday decorations he had placed on the shelves near the front of the mercantile. Perfie fingered the porcelain angels with delicate gold-edged wings. They came in sets of two. She looked at them every time she came in.

I could give one to Isabelle when she comes tomorrow. But even with the discount, the angels cost more than Perfie had saved.

She held up an angel and called across the counter to Mr. Hughes. "Will you sell just one of these?"

He smiled and motioned with his hand. "Come here."

Perfie crossed the store.

"Perfecta. How are you these days? You like the angels, do you?" He rubbed his hand over his bearded chin. "I'm going to need help the day after Christmas. All these things have to be packed and the store cleaned. If you help me that day you can have the angels."

She flashed a smile. "I can have the angels now?"

"Yes. But mind you, the work will be hard. I'll need you all day, and you'll have to get here early."

She placed the angels on the counter. "I'll be here bright and early, Mr. Hughes." The smile never left her face as he wrapped the two angels in newspaper and handed them to her. Now she had a gift for Isabelle, and one for herself, too.

Christmas morning dawned sunny but cold, with a heavy wind from the north. Perfie and Isabelle walked up the street to the church. Bundled in their thick shawls and with heads down against the cold, they stepped with care to avoid the mud puddles that spotted the street. It had snowed two days ago, and the sunshine that followed melted the ice and snow, leaving pits of sticky mud.

The girls had invited Primitivo to the holiday Mass, but he refused, stating this was his one day off and he was going to enjoy doing nothing.

They decided they would open the wrapped presents, which lay on the small wooden table in the front room, after Mass. Perfie had placed the angel for Isabelle and the shirt she made for her father next to two other wrapped gifts. Was one of these from her father? Had he thought about her?

Perfie listened to Father Matteo's deep voice vibrate through the cold church. *Quotiescúmque manducámus panem hunc et cálicem bíbimus, mortem tuam annuntiámus, Dómine, donec vénias*

Perfie knelt with bent head and pushed her folded hands against her chin. Unlike most of those in the same position, she was not thinking about the birth of Christ or the body of Christ—or about praying.

She bit her lip in an effort to control her queasy stomach. She hadn't eaten anything this morning because she and Isabelle were planning to cook a Christmas breakfast after mass.

A burning sensation rose from her stomach up into her throat, and she placed her hand tightly over her mouth. Maybe if she thought about something else she would feel better, but nothing came to mind. She curled lower behind the pew, bringing her head down in front of her chest.

Father Matteo's voice was quiet, and she heard the congregation stand and begin to sing. Scrambling to her feet she slipped past Isabelle and rushed down the side aisle. She tried to leave without anyone noticing, but half way to the back of the church she felt her stomach heave.

Perfie broke into a run and jerked open the small door on the side of the sanctuary. She pushed her way out, then turned and vomited just outside, trying to close the door before anyone heard. She hoped the singing would distract people from her rushed exit.

She staggered farther from the building to a large stone that marked the path leading to the schoolhouse. She sank down onto the flat surface of the rock and wiped her lips with her handkerchief. It wasn't unusual for her to have a sour stomach when she didn't eat, but did it have to happen today? She didn't want to spend Christmas with the blinding headache that usually followed the nausea. The only cure was to darken her room by hanging towels over the windows and hide her head deep under the blankets of her bed. Perfie decided she would wait for Isabelle here. Moaning and clutching her stomach, she rocked back and forth.

Isaac's voice broke through her moans. "Perfie? Are you okay? What is it?"

She looked up and shook her head. Where had he come from?

"It's my stomach."

Isaac hadn't been witness to one of her headaches, and she didn't want him to see her this way.

He reached out and traced a finger across her forehead. "Come to the house. I'll get you some water."

She followed him across the field that separated the Martinez house from the church. As he led her into the kitchen she heard voices and laughter coming from the next room.

Isaac pulled a chair close to the stove and held Perfie's shoulder before turning to add a log to the fire.

The smells from the kitchen—onions, chili, garlic—overwhelmed her. Her stomach clenched and threatened to rise up. She looked around the room. A bucket sat near the doorway. She jumped up and ran across the room. As she knelt in front of it and vomited, she felt a wave of embarrassment take over. Her neck and face burned at the thought of Isaac watching this.

Unable to get up Perfie kept her head close to the bucket. Her sides heaved in and out, and her knuckles were white as she clutched the edges of the bucket. She felt a band of pressure across her forehead. Maybe the headache would go away if she didn't move. Maybe everything would go away.

"What's this?" A woman's voice asked, her tone harsh and demanding. Perfie peeked under her arm to see who it was.

"Madre." Isaac turned to the tall woman who stood in the doorway. Her arms were rigid by her sides, and her navy blue eyes were on the girl leaning over the bucket. "This is Perfecta Trujillo. She was sick, outside the church. I brought her in from the cold."

Isaac's mother bustled over to Perfie. She placed her hand on the girl's forehead. "Come. Isaac, bring the bucket." She led Perfie to a cot in the corner of the room. "Lie down here and I'll get you some tea."

"Mother makes some special tea. Helps your stomach." Isaac placed the bucket next to the cot and pulled a blue wool blanket up over Perfie as she lay down and curled onto her side. She kept her face close to the bucket. He placed his hand under her head and gently lifted it to slide a cool pillow next to her cheek.

The cold pillowcase felt good on her pounding forehead. She pressed her head down into it, trying to fight the pressure building behind her eyes. Isaac sat on the floor next to her, his face close to hers.

Perfie shook her head slightly. "Not so close," she whispered, reaching one hand out from under the blanket and pushing on his shoulder.

"Do you think you can sit up for the tea?" Carlotta stood holding the steaming cup.

Perfie moved slowly, keeping her eyes shut into narrow slits, the bright light from the window stabbing through her brain. She sat and took the cup from Carlotta.

"I'm so sorry. I didn't mean to burst in on you like this. These headaches, they just strike, and my stomach gets upset." She sipped the tea, which had a pleasant minty taste. Her stomach tightened at first, then it relaxed as the warm tea settled it.

"That's quite all right." Carlotta looked from Perfie to Isaac and back.

Perfie sipped the tea and didn't say anything. Isaac didn't speak. Carlotta sat at the table and watched them both.

Suddenly Perfie pulled herself to her feet and shoved the cup to Isaac, causing tea to spill over the edge. "Isabelle! I forgot about Isabelle. She won't know where I am." She turned to fold the blanket that she had tossed behind her on the cot.

Isaac took the blanket from her hands. "Don't worry about that. Are you feeling better?"

"Much better. Thank you so much, Mrs. Martinez. That tea did the trick." She tried to smile. The truth was her stomach did feel better, but she could barely see past the shimmering bright light that floated in front of her eyes. Her head still pounded.

Isaac walked her to the back porch. "Since you're here, how about you see your Christmas present?"

See it? She just wanted to get home into bed. But his look was so hopeful. "Okay, but your present is at home. I thought we'd wait until tonight."

"This is better during the day. Close your eyes and follow me." He took hold of her hand.

"Can I keep them open until we get down the steps?"

"Yes." He laughed as they walked down the four wooden steps. "But now you have to keep them closed."

She slid each foot forward carefully as he led her across the yard. She heard him open the door to the barn before leading her in.

The barn smelled like winter. It was the smell of hay and horses and the strong sour smell of urine. Although she loved this smell, her stomach started to churn again.

"Okay, open them."

She opened her eyes and blinked. She couldn't see anything at all in the complete dark of the barn. Then she heard a soft nicker behind the wooden gate to the stall.

It was Cimmaron.

Perfie jumped forward and threw her arms around the horse's neck. He snorted and pushed at her with his long nose. "I don't have a treat, I never thought. . . ." Her mouth couldn't form any words. Tears streamed down her face. She turned to Isaac.

"How did you . . . where did he . . . I . . ." She still couldn't talk.

"I found him. I bought him back for you, Perfie. You can keep him here with our horses in the winter and out on the property during the summer."

"But your mother? What will she think?"

"She thinks he's my new horse, and you better believe she had a lot to say about my choice! Such a silly looking horse, she said. But he won her over, don't worry. I caught her sneaking out here to give him the apple cores after she made a pie."

Perfie wanted to stay with Cimmaron, but her head still hurt and she worried that Isabelle would be frantic or furious—or both. She kissed both of them goodbye—Cimmaron on his soft nose and Isaac on his sweet lips.

Isabelle was standing in front of the church with the rest of the congregation. Voices called out wishes for a Merry Christmas as people set off for home. Isabelle's head swiveled back and forth as she searched for her missing cousin.

Perfie glanced back across the field to where Isaac stood outside his kitchen door. Then she hurried to the front of the church.

"I'm here, Isabelle."

"What happened? Why did you rush out?"

"I was sick. I was getting one of my headaches, and my stomach was upset. I had to leave.

Isabelle noticed Perfie's glance across the field. She turned and looked. "Isaac?"

"It's not what you think. He happened to see me out there." She could tell Isabelle didn't believe her. She grabbed her cousin's arm. "But something wonderful happened. It's Cimmaron."

"Cimmaron?"

"Isaac found him. He bought him, Isabelle. He's over in the Martinez barn. I have my horse back."

"What will your father do?"

"What can he do? The horse belongs to Isaac now." Perfie felt the sharp pain in her forehead return. She let go of Isabelle's arm.

"Come on. I need to get home and lie down."

Fifteen

Three days later Perfie knelt on the wooden floor of her bedroom, her forehead pressed against the edge of the bed and an oxidized tin bucket held steady between her knees. She had spent hours in this position. She leaned into the bed to put pressure just above her right eye while keeping her mouth over the bucket. She didn't always have ample warning before her body clenched and she began to vomit.

Her headache hadn't let up since Christmas. The pain was worse just after breakfast and in the late afternoon. It had been three days without any relief.

At least I kept my promise to Mr. Hughes, she thought. It hadn't been easy working with the headache, but she had done it. They stood side by side wrapping items in newspaper and placing them in labeled crates, and he never said a word when she dashed outside to spit and dry heave off the back porch.

It had been a good idea—working there to pay for Christmas gifts. Isabelle liked the porcelain angel. She held the figure up in the light and turned it side to side to admire the delicate wings.

"There are two. We each have one, so when you are back in Española we can think about each other." Perfie had explained.

"What a wonderful idea. I will put her on the table beside my bed. You should do the same. That way we can say goodnight to each other." Isabelle gave Perfie a bright red silk scarf, long enough to wrap around her neck or use as a turban-like hat.

What a wasted effort the Christmas brunch had been. Perfie hadn't felt like eating a thing, Isabelle ate like a bird, and Joe didn't come home. Primitivo ate the scrambled eggs with peppers and onions, the warm sopapillas drizzled with honey and the fried potatoes as if they were made of cardboard. When he finished he pushed back from the table and left without a word.

At least Primitivo had been there while they exchanged gifts, although there was no sense of love or sparkle. He had unwrapped the shirt from Perfie and a pouch of his favorite tobacco from Isabelle, but he had offered nothing to the girls, not even a thank you or a Merry Christmas.

Perfie pressed her forehead harder against the mattress, moving it around to find a cold spot on the quilt. She didn't want to think about her father, not while her head hurt so much, but she couldn't stop the thoughts.

He didn't seem to have any feelings for her anymore, not even the disgust and anger he used to have. Even spite would be better than this total lack of emotion. In the past he had cared enough when she made a mess of things to be angry; he had expressed some hope that she might succeed at something. Now he just ignored her.

Perfie got some comfort from the fact that her father no longer showered Isabelle with attention either. He had glanced at her cousin with a smile as she chattered on about her plans to work in Española at the new high school now that she had her teaching degree. But there were no probing questions, and there was no longer any advice on subjects he didn't have any knowledge about. There was not even congratulations.

The thoughts stopped as Perfie leaned forward and vomited. Wiping her mouth with a damp rag, she finally faced what she knew to be true: this wasn't one of her usual headaches.

Perfie didn't cry, but as her head pounded and her stomach churned, she started to shiver.

A week later she met Isaac at the edge of town. He drove the Martinez family wagon up the muddy road and stopped near the ditch where they had met so many years ago. It was their favorite place. The hill offered a view in both directions and was passable in winter if there was no recent snowfall. Today they stayed in the wagon and left the reins loose so the old mare could snuffle around for traces of something to nibble. Perfie enjoyed the brief sunshine. She rubbed her forehead as she stared off at the Brazos peaks.

"What's wrong? You still have that headache?"

Perfie nodded her head. Yes, she still had the headache—not the sharp pain anymore, but a dull, nonstop throb. Isaac moved his hand to her forehead, gently rubbing the trouble spot on her temple.

As they sat in silence she could feel the power of the earth; everything was quiet and still in the brief winter sun. Nothing was growing now, but she sensed the seeds sleeping under the soil—seeds that would awaken in spring to become tiny yellow blossoms peeking out from under sharp shale or green shoots that would poke their heads out of vast expanses of rocky soil, their bright tips appearing on the cholla and sage brush. She was part of all this—a seed was growing inside of her, too.

She pressed her hand to her belly and said hello to the new life inside.

Nothing bad can happen now. I don't believe this new life that is waiting so patiently to come into this world is evil. It's untouched. Pure. My baby hasn't done anything wrong. She pictured Little Joe, his big brown eyes staring into hers. Maybe God was giving her a present.

Perfie drew in a shaky breath. There was no other way—she had to tell Isaac straight out.

"Isaac, I think I'm pregnant."

His hand left her forehead and dropped into his lap. He raised his eyebrows and let out a snort. Then he turned his head and stared off toward the mountains.

When Perfie had imagined this moment she pictured Isaac quickly taking her into his arms and asking her to marry him. But now his silence was painting a different picture. It seemed like hours before he shifted in the seat and finally turned to face her.

His voice was shaky. "Perfecta. I just don't know what to say. I didn't expect this."

What kind of answer was that? What did he expect after all those nights together. He was supposed to know what to say. He was the man.

She thought about the words of her mother and her grandmother—and the words of all of the girls and women she had ever known. *Don't give in to a man, don't let him have his way, he won't stand by you.* She didn't believe this would be true of Isaac. He was better than that. He kept his promises.

She tightened her lips as she considered what to do next. He hadn't really made any promises about this. They had never talked about it. But didn't "wait for me" imply marriage some day?

They continued to sit in silence. He didn't reach out to her, didn't touch her or rub her arm. She clasped her hands together. She bit the inside of her cheek, and the metallic taste of blood filled her mouth.

Isaac picked up the reins and clucked to the mare. "I have to think about this."

He didn't say another word as they made their way back to town. When he pulled up near her house, she thought he would help her out of the wagon. But he sat looking straight off into the sky as she wrapped her skirts around her legs and jumped down, running up the path with tears streaming from her eyes.

The next morning Perfie woke early. She left the house without bothering to fix anything for her father's breakfast. He was still asleep, and she planned to return before he woke up.

She walked down the frozen mud road to the church. Heading around the building, she entered through the small side door that was always kept unlocked. The church was quiet and dim, the faint light of dawn illuminating the stained glass windows lining the sanctuary.

Perfie knelt in the third pew. Avelina had always sat in the front row, towing Perfie behind her with a tightly clasped hand that was ready to give a pinch if there was any nonsense. Perfie didn't feel she could sit there now.

She needed to tell someone what had happened, and there wasn't anyone she could talk to. God was her last chance. Maybe if he listened she would know what to do. She bent her head to speak to him, but her words betrayed her to God.

"Mama, what do I do now? Why are you gone? I need you here to tell me what to do."

Perfie waited, her eyes moving up to the statue of the Virgin, past the bare feet, so pale and soft, bound to be hurt on the sharp rocks, up past the folds of the simple skirt Mary wore, to the hands which stretched out, pleading for something.

I'm like her, Perfie thought as she studied the abdomen of the statue. She doesn't look pregnant, but she must have been; The Virgin wasn't important before she got pregnant. She was just a girl, a teenager even younger than me.

Perfie studied the plaster face. Such a pleading look in her eyes, those hands begging for something, some kind of understanding.

Maybe once I have the baby I'll be important. Isaac will change his mind when he holds a son in his arms. He'll be so filled with love for me and the baby. He'll want to be married then.

Carlotta. She pictured the woman's stern face. The dark scowl could bring you down to the size of a worm. Maybe she would change, too. The baby would remind her of her sons when they were young. She wouldn't turn away her own grandchild, would she?

In the few times she had been to the Martinez house she hadn't sensed any tolerance of Catholics. It felt to her like the Presbyterians saw Catholics as wrong, just as her parents felt Presbyterians failed to conform.

Her father wouldn't understand. He had turned her away, and he would turn the baby away. Neither one mattered to him. He would only see evil in the whole thing.

Perfie sank from her kneeling position to the floor, turned away from the altar and settled her head atop crossed arms on the bench. "Please God, please," she whispered.

Her prayer filled her with shame. What right did she have to ask God for any favors?

She gazed at the wood grain, her eyes following the swirling pattern. She felt her joy for this new life slipping away—slipping like smoke that drifted off in a breeze and slowly disappeared to leave nothing behind but a thin odor. She pressed her cheek against the smooth wood.

I'm not really all alone, she thought. I still have Isaac. I just have to wait. He'll do the right thing. As she comforted herself with her thoughts, her eyes closed and she drifted into a troubled sleep.

Sixteen

Isabelle needed to see Perfie. It had been three months since Christmas. She knew things weren't right when she left Tierra Amarilla to return to Española. Easter break had finally arrived and she had convinced Joe to bring her home. He had shown up at her classroom the week before, no sign of the supposed "wife" or children. He laughed when she asked him about his life.

"One day at a time, Bella. That's the only way to live."

Now, after a long journey up the canyon, she followed Joe as he rushed into the kitchen.

"Where's that troublesome sister of mine?" He dropped Isabelle's brown suitcase next to the door.

Isabelle watched as he threw his arms around Perfie and squeezed her tightly. "Hey, little sister, you're getting fat. You just sit around all day and eat?"

"It's hard to stay skinny when I don't have anyone to torment me all day. Now that you're here I'm sure I'll be slim as a jackrabbit." Perfie pulled herself out of his arms. Isabelle saw her cousin tug the heavy blue shawl down around her hips. Perfie seemed to feel Isabelle's stare and turned to her.

Isabelle stood without moving, her lips turned down. What she had suspected at Christmas was true.

"Come on. Let's go sit in the front room." Perfie hurried out of the kitchen.

Joe picked up his guitar and turned to Isabelle. "What's the matter? You didn't even say hello to Perfie, and she rushed away from you like you have the plague."

Isabelle shook her head. "It's nothing." She walked slowly into the front room.

The three sat and chatted. Perfie asked Isabelle questions about her job at the school, Joe told tales about his latest escapades and Isabelle chewed on her tongue. Joe strummed the guitar, and the talk stopped for a while as the room filled with his lively tunes.

After he'd played for some time, Joe put the guitar down and looked at his sister. "Is that Martinez fella still in the picture?"

Before Perfie could answer Isabelle turned to her and looked directly into her eyes. "*Is* he still in the picture?"

"Yes." Perfie didn't elaborate.

"Has he talked to you about marriage?" Isabelle wasn't mincing any words.

"Sí, we have talked."

"When?"

Joe turned his head back and forth as if watching a game of tennis, staring at Perfie, then at Isabelle, then back to Perfie again. "Am I missing something here?"

Isabelle turned and looked at Joe. "Perfecta needs to get married soon."

She felt her arms and shoulders flinch as Perfie spat out a response.

"How dare you? You come here and jump into my business? You weren't worried when you left, leaving me here with that grouchy old man to be his slave. Now you come back and think you can make decisions? What makes your advice so special?"

Perfie burst into tears, jumped from the chair and ran out of the room.

Isabelle watched her cousin go. She pressed her fingers into the padded arms of the chair. "I didn't really handle that right."

Joe cleared his throat. "Are you saying what I think you're saying?"

Isabelle nodded her head.

"Oh shit." The words spit from Joe's mouth.

"My thoughts exactly."

Just after midnight Isabelle climbed the stairs to the bedroom. She and Joe had talked for hours, trying to come up with a plan to help Perfie. There wasn't a simple answer to this dilemma—her cousin was in for a rough time.

"Move over. I know you're awake." Isabelle pulled the quilt up and pushed Perfie with her leg as she slid into the bed. Without speaking Perfie rolled over and faced the wall.

"Perfecta, we have to talk. You can't ignore this."

Perfie's muffled voice was harsh. "I'm not ignoring it. That's quite impossible, thank you."

"You know what I mean. Is Isaac ready to get married?"

Perfie flipped over and faced her cousin. "What makes you think my father would allow that? 'That damn Presbyterian,' remember?"

"But with the baby, don't you think that's the way it needs to be?"

"With or without the baby, that's the way I want it to be. I want to be with Isaac." Perfie sat up. "If I want it, my father will deny it. That's the way it will always be for me. And God is even worse. If I love it, then he rips it away from me."

Isabelle didn't answer. She knew that Perfie suffered the loss of Little Joe, although everyone had warned her not to get attached to the baby. And she knew that Perfie missed her mother. But she had never understood why Primitivo was so harsh with Perfecta.

For Isabelle it was different. Her uncle had taken her in when her family couldn't afford to send her to school. He helped with her studies through high school and then paid for her to attend college. He listened to her ideas and her dreams and asked her pointed questions at times, but only to guide her in her own decisions.

Not so with Perfecta. His face changed when she was in the room. The heavy fold in his forehead thickened, his eyebrows pushed together and his pupils grew darker with the intensity of his stare. Isabelle couldn't think of anything to say in response to Perfie's accusation that her father would treat her badly. It was true.

"I think we're both tired. Will you promise to talk with me tomorrow?"

"Fine. You're the one who said we had to talk about it now." Perfie turned back to the wall and pulled the quilt up over her shoulders.

Four days later, at ten past three, Isabelle watched as Perfie left the house, probably to meet Isaac. It was the moment she'd been waiting for. She grabbed her coat, slapped her hat on her head and ran down the road to the courthouse.

She stood in front of the tall wooden doors for a moment. Was she doing the right thing? What else could she do? She reached out and pulled the heavy brass handle on the front door, then slipped inside. She removed her gloves and tucked them into the pocket of her coat, then looked around.

In all the years she had lived with the family she had never visited her uncle at work. His office was only a block from the house. When Avelina was alive he walked home for dinner each day at noon, then walked back for his afternoon hours. There had never been a reason for Isabelle to come here.

She stood in the huge hallway and marveled at the expense that had gone into building this courthouse. There was a marbled floor and a huge staircase leading up to the second floor. The rich red wood of the stair rail and window frames was polished to a brilliant gleam. At the bottom of the stairs, just in front of her, a young man sat at a large desk.

"I'm here to see Primitivo Trujillo. I'm his niece." The young man seemed about her age, but he wasn't familiar to her. The town had changed since she moved away. Even though she came back to visit whenever she could, she hadn't kept up with the people of T.A. Many had left, but some young people had returned when they couldn't find work in the cities.

"Why, yes Miss. No problem at all. You just walk up those stairs and down the hall to your right. You'll see his name on his office, five doors down."

Isabelle climbed the steps. She hadn't figured out what she would say to her uncle. She had decided that she needed to talk to him now. She would go back to work in two days, and she wanted to be here to protect Perfecta when he found out about the baby. She had tried to talk to Perfie about her plans, but her cousin was still angry. Isabelle hoped that Isaac knew about the baby. Surely Perfie had told him.

Heavy wooden doors with opaque glass in the upper half of each lined the hallway. Isabelle knocked softly on the door marked *Primitivo Trujillo, Sheriff,* his name painted in black block letters.

"Yes?" Her uncle's deep voice wasn't welcoming.

She opened the door and poked her head in. "Tío?"

"Isabelle! What is it?" He pushed his chair back.

"I came to talk with you." She entered the office and sat in one of the two heavy wooden chairs in front of his desk. Many people must come to talk with him.

She left her coat buttoned, her hat on her head. It was warm in here, but she felt the chill of what she had to do.

She cleared her throat and looked straight at Primitivo. She flinched at those steely eyes, but she noticed that the ice in them melted a little while he waited for her to speak. He probably didn't think anything she would have to say to him was very serious. With determination she kept her gaze fixed on his.

"It's about Perfecta."

He sighed and snorted. His eyes narrowed.

"I know she won't tell you this herself, and she'll be very angry with me for telling you, but it must be done." She chose her words carefully, watching her uncle's face for any reaction.

His voice was low. "It's the Presbyterian."

"Well, yes, this is about Isaac, but it's about more than him." Isabelle paused for a moment. She turned her gaze away from her uncle and stared out the window behind him. "Perfecta is. . . the thing. . . it. . . she's pregnant."

"*La Puta.*" Primitivo swore under his breath and shook his head.

No shouts, no slamming of fists on the desk.

His gaze swept past hers to some far off point above her right shoulder. "Isabelle, I'm glad you came to tell me. Now I would like you to do me a favor. Go home and tell her to pack her bags. It would be best if she's gone before I come home tonight."

"Pack her bags? But Tío, where will she go?"

"I don't care. I just don't want her there, under my roof."

Could he do that? Kick her out? The house belonged to Avelina.

But of course! With her aunt's death the house passed to him, not to Perfie.

"Uncle, please don't do this. Talk with her. We can work this out."

He shook his head as he stood, dismissing her from the conversation. "No, I don't want her there." He reached out a hand to Isabelle's elbow, urging her out of the chair and out of his office. "Do this for me."

"Uncle, please."

But he wasn't listening. She knew this as she felt him push her out the door. Surely he would change his mind? Perfie was his daughter. Isabelle's stomach churned and tears leaked from her eyes. She walked down the polished marble floor of the hallway and stopped at the top of the stairs to look back, expecting to see him at the door of his office.

The hallway was empty, and his door was shut.

Perfie stared at her cousin. Her jaw dropped and her eyes went wide. "What? Leave my house?"

"I'm sorry, Perfecta. I never thought he would do this." Isabelle hoped that Perfie could understand. She wasn't being naive; she had seen the kind side of Primitivo. She guessed he would be angry, but she never imagined anything as drastic as this.

"You never *thought* is right. I warned you. You lived here long enough to know how this would turn out. You always wanted my spot in this family and now you have it. Now you're rid of me completely. I hate you, Isabelle. I'll never forgive you." Perfecta turned and ran out of the room, her arms clasped around her belly, tears streaming down her cheeks.

Isabelle followed her up the stairs to the bedroom. If only there was something she could say, something she could do to make this better. "Perfie, you must believe me. I don't want to replace you. I would never want that. I feel so bad. I don't know why he's like this."

Perfie pulled her suitcase out from under the bed. She grabbed clothes from the drawers and the closet and stuffed things in without folding them.

Isabelle tried again. "Where are you going to go?"

Perfie didn't answer. She pulled the quilt her mother had made for her off the bed and wrapped it around her shoulders. She picked up the porcelain angel from the dresser. Finally, she turned and looked at Isabelle.

The two cousins stood in silence. Then Perfie put the angel back on the dresser and grabbed the suitcase. She stomped into the hall.

Isabelle stood in the doorway. Perfie was in the hall filling her arms with embroidered tea towels, tablecloths and pillow cases from the linen closet. Avelina had stitched these items, promising them to the girls for their weddings.

With her arms full Perfie struggled to pick up the suitcase. Isabelle stepped forward and reached out. Perfie glared at her and snapped her teeth together in a near growl. Isabelle watched as her cousin made her way down the stairs and out the front door. Isabelle stood frozen, unable to think of what to do next. But she had to do something. She ran out onto the porch.

But Perfie, loaded with her burden of linens and suitcase, was already halfway down the block, and Isabelle watched helplessly. She raised her hand to her mouth, her mind racing, her chest heaving. She could barely draw in a breath at the thought of Perfecta on her own.

Seventeen

Perfie set the bucket down with a thump and brown water slopped onto the floor. She leaned on the mop for a second before turning and swiping at the spilled water. She had worked hard and the floors shone. Carrying the heavy bucket of dirty water down the stairs proved more difficult.

Her belly extended far in front of her. Her lower back tightened, and the ache spread around her torso and down the back of one leg. I'll fall, she thought. Something could happen to the baby.

Maybe that would be for the best.

A strange shiver went up her spine as if she wasn't alone. Instantly she regretted her thoughts, rubbing the skin that pulled tight across her baby. Then she heard the sound of steps below her.

Carlotta stood at the bottom of the stairs, her brow creased.

Perfie took her hand off her belly and called down. "I've finished up here. I don't think I can carry this down."

"Never mind. I'll do it." Carlotta scowled, as if Perfie caused her trouble by cleaning. The old woman started up the stairs, pressed one hand on the wall and pulled up her long skirt with the other.

It's not a mountain. Perfie chewed at the inside of her cheek and rubbed her tongue along the back of her teeth. I need to stop thinking such negative thoughts about her. I'll probably be living with her forever.

"Gracias." She followed Carlotta down the stairs. "I can take it now." Perfie reached toward the bucket.

Carlotta gave no sign she heard the offer as she marched through the kitchen and out the door. Household water was poured onto the small vegetable garden at the edge of the yard. No one dared to waste a drop.

From the kitchen Perfie watched the straight back and rigid shoulders of Isaac's mother as she headed out the door. Perfie hadn't realized a body could show so much displeasure without speaking a word. Even Primitivo seemed tame compared to Carlotta. *Careful what you wish for, don't jump from the pan into the fire*—all those old sayings had meaning to Perfie now.

I can't win here. I don't know what to do. She sank onto the wooden chair, leaned her elbows onto her knees and put her chin in her hands. She waited for the next command from her someday-to-be mother-in-law.

On that cold night in March Isaac had found her in the church, where she lay sound asleep with her head on the hard wooden pew. Isabelle had sought him out, explaining Perfie had been exiled by Primitivo. Although Isabelle had tried to make things better, Perfie still wouldn't speak to her cousin. She couldn't believe that after so many years as friends Isabelle had betrayed her. She had trusted Isabelle—told her secrets she never told anyone else.

Now Perfie decided she shouldn't trust anyone, no matter how well she thought she knew them.

Isaac brought her to his house. As they stood in front of Carlotta, Perfie wished he would hold her hand, but he didn't touch her as he explained the problem. His voice grew quiet. "She has nowhere else to stay, Madre."

Carlotta shook her head, but she agreed. "For now. Clear out that spot behind the piano and set up the cot we use when Tío Francisco comes."

So Perfie moved into the front room of the Martinez house. She rose early each morning to dress and straighten her bed before anyone else was awake. She didn't want anyone to catch her sleeping.

Especially Benjamin.

She had been prepared to act as if they were strangers, but Bennie flirted with her every chance he could. She worked hard to make sure they were never alone together.

Perfie had hoped that Naomi would be a friend, although at thirty, Isaac's sister was older than she was. Naomi worked as a tutor for the McNeil family and doubled as their nanny much of the time, staying the night with the two small children when needed. When at home she made appearances at the dinner table every so often, but she was a quiet woman. No overtures of friendship had been forthcoming.

Perfie asked Isaac why she couldn't sleep in Naomi's bedroom when Naomi was at the McNeil's. *Not possible*, he said, with no explanation.

"What will we do when the baby comes? Will he sleep in a basket on the porch?" But Isaac ignored her questions.

Under the watchful eye of Queen Carlotta there was no opportunity for lovemaking or serious discussions. Isaac refused to talk about their future. When she brought up things, important things, he would caress her cheeks and neck, kiss her, and tickle her. Other times his face would grow dark and he wouldn't say a word.

Isaac left the house each day to help his father with the cattle or the school and seldom made it home for noon dinner. In spite of what he said about the limits Lucas put on him, he was still teaching at the school.

Perfie thought it would be different. She had been scared when she left her father's house, but she had faith that Isaac would step forward now that Primitivo had thrown her out. She had pictured him happy about the baby, finally, and could see the two of them moving somewhere and living in a little house.

She hadn't imagined Isaac's indifference. She hadn't dreamed they would stay in the Martinez house, the house where Benjamin lived, too. It didn't make things easier that Benjamin was nicer to her than Isaac was. And she sure hadn't pictured a life in which she felt more married to Carlotta than to the father of her unborn child.

Carlotta returned, dropping the empty bucket near the back door. Perfie cringed as the metal hit the floor, the clang so sharp that goosebumps ran up her spine.

She pasted a cooperative look on her face. "I think I'll walk down to the mercantile. Is there anything you need?" She had to get out of this house.

Carlotta frowned. "Do you think you should be walking around town in your condition?"

"It feels good to stretch my legs and get some fresh air. I'll be fine." As soon as Perfie spoke the words she realized her well being wasn't what Carlotta was referring to. It was the shame of being an unwed pregnant girl.

This was a small town. Everyone already knew she was pregnant, and they all knew Isaac was the father. It was no secret she was living with the Martinez family and that there had been no wedding. It might as well have been printed in the newspaper. She could see the headline—*Primitivo*

Trujillo Banishes his Pregnant Daughter from his Home. No reason for her to hide; her life was already wide open to the world.

She grabbed her brick colored hat off the hook, jammed it onto her head and fled the house.

Once away from the yard, Perfie slowed as she walked the short distance down the street to the mercantile. No need to rush. She needed to make this time away last as long as possible.

She wrapped her hands around her protruding belly and felt the magic of the kicking and shifting baby. Most of the time she felt waves of guilt and imagined she would burn in hell for all her sins, but just now, here in this moment, the wonder of the small life was so great that she forgot all those things.

"I can't wait to meet you, little baby. Will you have bright blue eyes like your father?" She sang and hummed as she continued toward the mercantile. It was impossible for her to feel bad about the baby.

When she was away from everyone else it seemed right to her. The baby would be a miniature Isaac, if it was a boy. If her baby was a girl she would love her no matter what, making sure her daughter talked to her about everything. She would find a teacher for her baby who was patient and kind; this child would do math and write perfect essays.

The road was quiet this time of day, the morning rush over and the dinner time crowd not yet out. Mr. Gallegos and Mr. Capella sat outside the mercantile on a wooden bench, smelly cigarettes dangling from wrinkled lips. They didn't speak to each other much, but there wasn't a day when they didn't come to the bench. They would stay here until 2:00 before moving to the bar across the street. These two sat in that spot every day for as long as Perfie could remember. The covered porch provided shade in the summer. Even the rain didn't stop them, as long as it wasn't windy or cold.

"*Hola.*" She greeted them politely, keeping her eyes focused just past them. Mr. Capella nodded in greeting. Mr. Gallego flipped his chin up to direct her gaze across the street. She turned and looked.

Her father stood on the steps of the courthouse, staring across the road. She met his gaze and wondered if she should go over and speak to him. Just as she decided she would try this, he turned and walked around the side of the building. Without looking at her again he got into an old Ford pickup. He had a truck now. She wondered what had happened to the gelding.

She stood and watched him drive off, the tires flinging mud and dirt behind them as he accelerated.

Her sunny mood vanished.

She walked into the store and wandered around. Her thoughts spiraled down even lower. She picked up various items from the shelves, examined them and put them down. A hat, a screwdriver, some nuts—her eyes didn't really see what she looked at.

I've never really belonged anywhere. Not in Tierra Amarilla, not in Española, not Antonito with Tia Emilía, not anywhere. I sure don't belong in the Martinez house. I wish I could just live out in the wild. Bile rose in her throat. I need to be out of this. A sharp kick in her ribs interrupted her thoughts. The baby didn't want to be here either. She turned and left the store.

Twenty minutes later Perfie leaned against the top board of the fenced coral on the edge of town. It had been mild for two weeks, and Isaac had brought the horses out to the property. The barn needed the airing after the long winter months. There hadn't been a chance to ride. She missed the calm feeling of being out on her horse.

Cimmaron pushed his warm nose against her shoulder and worked his way down to her pocket in search of hidden treats. She slipped the bridle off the fence post and over his head, then led him out the gate to the large trough of water.

The oblong trough had a pipe at one end that brought fresh water from the ditch. Perfie dipped her cupped hand under the pipe and sipped the cool water. Then she glanced around, stepped behind the fence and stooped to empty her bladder. Better take care of that now, too.

She climbed up onto the thin edge of the trough and balanced like a tightrope walker, hoisting her leg over Cimmaron's back. "Easy," she coaxed as she held onto his neck and shifted her weight. She grunted as the baby shifted and settled.

"No trotting today, my friend, but that doesn't mean we can't go out for a ride." She turned his head away from town and clucked to him, and the two set off up the road.

May was a fickle month. One minute the sun shone to tease her with its warmth; in the next, the wind puffed in icy gusts. She shivered and rubbed her palms up and down her bare arms to warm herself. Her teeth chattered.

But this breeze couldn't chill her spirit. It felt so good to be on Cimmaron's back—to be away from everything. She felt his firm muscles underneath her thighs as tremors of excitement shot up his withers. He was happy to be out, too.

They crossed the creek and started up the mountain. Following an old cattle trail she wound through the tall ponderosa pine trees up a narrow ridge. The mesas and bluffs looked flat from a distance, but there were steep canyons and narrow gullies hidden among the trees.

Perfie knew the way to the bluffs. This was Martinez property but it had been her secret playground for years. This trail led to the top of the world. There was a view in all directions: the low sprawling hills were surrounded by distant mesas to the south, and the long Chama Valley was topped by the tall peaks of Colorado in the north and the majestic cliffs of Los Brazos to the East. She stared out at the Chama River, which wound its way down through the valley.

She let Cimmaron stop to munch on the green shoots of grass that popped up here and there. He wasn't used to this. Usually when someone was on his back it meant work, gathering cattle or patrolling fences. She knew it was encouraging a bad habit to let him nibble, but today she wanted everyone to get what they wished for. When she started to sing he swiveled his ears back and twisted his long neck to one side to look at her.

"Hey, careful there, guy. It's not so easy to balance with this big belly." She patted his neck and they continued up the trail, climbing the side of the mountain.

When she reached the top of the bluff she let the reins fall loose and settled into Cimmaron's broad back. It was comfortable here; might as well stay. It would be impossible to get back up without something to stand on. The wind had died, and the sun took over. She fell into a peaceful trance as it warmed her body.

Perfie thought about Isaac. She had to get him to talk to her, to be serious about what would happen to them. She was twenty-two years old, and she had waited for him for eight years.

I know he loves me. He must love me. He told me to wait.

But what about those trips to California? Did he have another girl there? Another child? She let out a cry. Cimmaron lifted his head, ears erect.

"It's okay." She patted the horse on the neck, and he lowered his head back to the tiny blades of grass growing between the yellow rocks.

If Isaac had another family, he didn't spend much time with them, only a few months every two years or so. Maybe he was divorced. Presbyterians believed in divorce.

She felt there was something secretive, mysterious about him. Yet when she was with him he seemed so uncomplicated. He lived each day with such ease, never worrying about much at all. When things went wrong he simply shrugged and moved on.

This didn't work for her. There were times when he should be worried. Like now. He thought that because she had a place to live, her father throwing her out didn't matter. He didn't see anything wrong with her sleeping in the corner of the living room. His parents had plenty of money from the school. He didn't feel guilty about letting them pay for his food or providing him a place to live. His father paid him for his work, so he had money in his pocket. That satisfied him.

But what about her? She didn't have any money at all. She hadn't asked him for any, but she was running out of things she needed. The bar of special soap she used to wash her hair was nearly gone, and her socks were worn clear through. She'd let out the seams of her clothes to accommodate her rapidly growing belly, but all her clothes were worn thin.

What about things for the baby? Her time was coming soon. Most women had gifts from families: tiny nightshirts, blankets, knit sweaters and booties. She didn't even have fabric to make these things. And diapers. She needed to buy the thick cotton batting and wool so she could make them now, before the baby came.

She hadn't brought her sewing machine with her; it was heavy and took up so much space. She wondered about asking Carlotta for a place to put it. Isaac and his brothers could go to the house when her father was at work and move the machine. The three of them would be able to carry it up the street, although getting across the ditch might be a bit of a problem. They would either have to cross the narrow foot bridge on a direct route or go all the way to the end of the street where the bridge crossed, then return on the other side.

A wagon would be better, but that would require more planning and would be more visible. Someone was sure to question three men with a wagon moving things out of Primitivo's house.

I can go with them and get the rest of my clothes, my pictures, maybe even that little lamp by my bed. The idea grew. Those were her things, she deserved to have them. Primitivo had no use for them.

And she wished for the porcelain angel. Although she was still angry with Isabelle, in her heart she wanted the comfort of her cousin.

When Avelina died, Primitivo had made the girls get rid of all her clothes. Perfie had kept the tortoiseshell hairbrush and some of her mother's beaded necklaces and silk handkerchiefs, but none of the clothes. Why had she been so hasty in getting rid of everything? She could have made new things out of the fabrics.

She imagined moving her bed into Naomi's room. If Isaac's sister went to live with the McNeil family full time, she and Isaac would have their own space and could sleep next to one another each night, his body curled around her. I wouldn't have to leap out of bed in the cold each morning. I would snuggle down until someone else built the fire and the house warmed up.

"Cimmaron, the baby will have a beautiful wooden cradle, just to the side of the bed. I'll reach out a hand to touch her. She'll never feel all alone." The horse was a good listener so she continued. "I'll see her the minute I open my eyes. I'll have a closet full of beautiful dresses. I'll wear a different dress every day. Never a housedress for me.

Would Carlotta like a dress made by Perfie? Maybe Carlotta would be so grateful that she would take Perfie into her arms and kiss her, calling her "*M'ija*" and treating her like a daughter.

Cimmaron snorted and stepped forward, his head raised, ears alert. She shifted to one side, nearly falling off the horse. She grabbed onto his stiff mane to regain her balance. Three ravens rose up on the draft that hugged the steep rock wall of the bluff and rode the wind until they were level with her and the horse.

She stared at the ravens, hovered in a triangle formation and peering at her with shiny black eyes.

Three. Perfie licked her lips. Last year she had asked Maria Cortez, the town expert on symbols, about ravens. Maria had listened to Perfie's story of the birds.

"These birds are your totem, Perfecta. They are not good luck or bad luck, but merely messengers. You must study them and clear your mind. Then their message will come to you."

She stared at the birds. "What are you trying to tell me?" she whispered.

The birds seemed relaxed, the wind under their wings holding them up.

A loud boom of thunder made her jump and sent the birds flying off with loud cawing. The storm had crept over the mountains in the east, and the enormous white cloud was like the face of a giant, puffing winds out of his circled lips and blowing the branches of the sage and cholla, which rattled in annoyance.

Cimmaron wasn't afraid of storms. In the past the two of them had raced up the winding roads with rain pelting them and the sky exploding in huge bursts of lightning. She felt his body fill with excitement.

"Not today, my friend. I think today we're just going to get wet."

As she kept him at a steady walk down the rocky trail, the sky let loose torrents of rain. She was soaked to the skin already, so there was no need to rush and risk falling. The wind increased and the trees bent low, snapping back between gusts. The air filled with the sharp cracks of branches splitting and falling. This was a true New Mexico storm, appearing out of nowhere with a fierce intensity as if it were angry at the world. She knew it would be over as quickly as it started but hoped it would be sooner rather than later. She was cold again.

This is my life now. I can't outrun the storms anymore. I have to just sit and let everything rain down upon me. How do I run faster than doom? Why does he follow so close behind me? Tears rolled down her cheeks, but the rain kept the salt from burning her wounded heart. Maybe those ravens were signaling that something was going to change.

Suddenly she understood their message.

She had to get Isaac to ask her to marry him. Three. That's what the ravens meant.

Isaac, me and the baby.

All week Perfie tried to find time to talk with Isaac. But Levi and Benjamin were home and there was extra work to be done. With the house full of people she couldn't catch him alone.

Perfie spent the week evading Bennie. He was determined to make her blush with his flirting and smiles.

And Carlotta spent the week evading her. She figured Isaac's mother was angry because of the ride last week, Perfie gone for hours without telling anyone where she had been, coming home soaked and chilled. But today Carlotta didn't avoid her. She sat down at the table where Perfie was eating a piece of toast with butter and jam.

"Perfecta. I have set next Saturday for your wedding."

Choking on a rigid chunk of the bread, Perfie gasped and inhaled, then succumbed to a fit of coughing. She grabbed for her coffee and took a sip.

"My what?"

"Wedding, my dear. Don't you think it should happen quickly, before this baby makes his appearance?"

"I . . ." Perfie didn't know what to say. "Did Isaac talk to you about this?"

"No. I don't expect he will. That boy has his head in the clouds, as always." Carlotta ran her hands over the table, sweeping up the crumbs Perfie had scattered as she ate.

"I was going to clean that up."

"What?" Carlotta didn't seem to know what Perfie was talking about. "I was thinking, I have a green silk dress you can wear. You should try it on today in case we need to make adjustments. It will just be the family, those who are here now, and a supper here at the house after the ceremony. Do you have anyone you want to invite?"

Perfie was silent, her green eyes reduced to tiny slits as her brow grew tight. Carlotta didn't seem to notice, moving the pile of crumbs around with the edge of her hand and stopping to poke at a large crumb with her sharp fingernail. The crumb made a popping sound when it broke into two small pieces. Carlotta continued before Perfie could reply.

"Lucas will perform the standard ceremony, nothing special. I don't think that would be proper, do you?" Carlotta stopped looking at the crumbs and stared directly at Perfie.

I don't think it's proper for you to plan my wedding, that's what I think. Perfie kept the words to herself. Isaac still hadn't talked about marriage even though she had brought it up several times. Time was growing short. It was only another month before the baby would come.

"I'll have to speak with Isaac." Perfie stood, picked up her plate, held it by the edge of the table and swept all the crumbs onto the surface. Grabbing her empty coffee cup, she turned to the sink. Neither woman spoke as Perfie rinsed and dried her dishes and placed them back into the wooden cupboard next to their colorful mates.

Isaac denied knowing that his mother was planning a wedding. "She never asks me, Perfie, she tells me. But isn't that what you wanted?" He didn't seem to think there was anything wrong with Carlotta taking over.

"It's my wedding." Perfie chewed on her lower lip. "Our wedding."

They sat upstairs on the bed, the only place for a private conversation unless they walked out to the edge of town. Isaac took her hand and rubbed his fingers lightly across the palm. Her hands were red and chapped, much worse than usual. Back at home she had washed clothes and dishes, but she always had a bottle of wonderful lavender hand oil that had been her mother's. She would rub her hands each night, the scent bringing back the few sweet memories she had of Avelina.

She had brought the oil with her to the Martinez house, but she'd used the last of it two weeks ago. After she washed all those dishes, doing her best to help out in any way possible, her hands were chapped. She tried to use some of the bacon grease kept in the can on the back of the stove, but it just made her hands gummy.

Isaac stroked her cheek. "I know it's not exactly what you wanted, but is it so awful?"

"No, it's just . . ." How could she explain that all her life she had dreamed and planned for her wedding day? She had spent hours looking through photo albums of old wedding pictures, noting the lace, pearls and tucks of the elaborate dresses of her grandmother and her mother. She imagined a very light veil, tiny pearls sewn all over it. She imagined Isaac lifting it from her face, her green eyes bright and happy as he kissed her.

Now she would be wearing Carlotta's cast off, a green old-lady dress, quickly altered to fit her pear-shaped body. There wouldn't be a veil. Would there even be a kiss?

"Isaac, I'm Catholic. If your father performs the ceremony I'm not sure I'm really married."

He laughed and wrapped his arms around her, lifting her off the bed and onto his lap. "That's what you're worried about? I love you and you love me. That's all that matters. All the rest of this is just fancy stuff for the sake of other people."

"If it doesn't matter, then why can't we get married in my church?"

Isaac dropped his hands. He scratched at a red bump on his arm and rolled up the sleeves of his blue flannel shirt. Perfie stood and turned to face him.

"It's me you're marrying, Isaac. Not your mother. If you're going to be a man, have a family of your own, you must stop giving in to her. I come first now." Perfie realized she had placed her hands on her hips, like an angry old wife, and she quickly slid them around her protruding belly.

"Perfecta, isn't it nice to do things the easy way? Not cause any more excitement around here? My mother's letting us live here, in her house."

"Can't we move to a place of our own?"

"Money, my dear. That takes money."

"Don't you get money for working at the school?"

"Sí, a little. Just enough to take you out dancing, buy you some pretty things. Not enough for a house."

Perfie did like the pretty things he brought home to her: the silk handkerchief, the little statue of a burro, a lapis blue comb for her hair. She patted the kicking baby. "I don't think we'll be going dancing anytime soon."

Isaac stood, grasped her face betweens his hands and kissed her, pressing his lips hard against hers. He was out the door and down the stairs before she could say another word. The subject seemed to be closed.

On Saturday Perfie stood alone in the downstairs bedroom. This room was so nice; the smooth wooden headboard matched the tall armoire and the framed mirror. There was a deep magenta quilt on the bed and a big window to let in the sunlight. Maybe someday Isaac and I will sleep in a bed like this, Perfie thought as she looked at the green dress Carlotta had laid on the bed.

Perfie had worked on the dress yesterday, letting out the side seams and pulling up the length by tacking the hem at ten-inch intervals, giving the bottom of the dress a southern bell look. She thought about trying to change the neckline—it was so old fashion with its high stiff collar—but there wasn't time. And she didn't think Carlotta really wanted her to change the dress much. She suspected after the wedding she would be asked to return it to its original condition.

She stood in front of Carlotta's mahogany-framed mirror. The wood shined from years of polishing, and the glass was smooth and flawless. The girl that looked back at her was sad and tired, and her green eyes drooped. Her blue flowered dress was faded, and it remained unbuttoned in the back so that it could stretch around her body. Only her shawl covered her white skin and Isaac's old undershirt that she wore underneath. Her bras didn't fit anymore, and she felt naked putting her dress on over her bare skin. She pulled the shawl off and dropped it, then stepped up to the mirror and stared directly into her own eyes.

She opened her mouth and studied her teeth. They were white and shiny, prettier than Carlotta's yellow teeth. She licked her finger and smoothed out her eyebrows. They were a little bushy.

She saw Avelina looking back at her from the mirror.

"Mama, I need your help."

Perfie imagined her mother's warm hand stroking her head, soothing the sharp pounding that hammered against the inside of her skull. She closed her eyes. Her mother's voice was singing a song to her—what was it? A nursery rhyme? She imagined herself a tiny girl, head in her mother's lap.

The gentle hands had disappeared at some point in her life. Was it when she was old enough for Primitivo to scold? When he started picking on her, following her every movement, correcting everything? When had her mother quit stroking her hair back from her forehead and started telling her to run upstairs and brush it herself? When had her mother's eyes faded, the green turning to dull grey as she sat, rocking, rocking, rocking in that chair by the window?

A hymn. Suddenly Perfie remembered the words—*Just as I am, and waiting not, To rid my soul of one dark blot, To Thee whose blood can cleanse each spot, O Lamb of God, I come, I come.* Why had her mother sung this as a lullaby?

Perfie imagined standing next to her mother in church, Avelina holding the hymn book low so she would follow along. Mama didn't need to see the book; she knew every hymn by heart.

"Perfecta, almost ready?" Isaac's voice drifted through the closed door and she opened her eyes. Turning from the mirror to look at the green dress, she knew this memory was a sign, a message from Mama.

"Just as I am," she said out loud, and slipped back into her faded dress.

She would not be getting married today. She didn't know how long it would take, but she would have the wedding she had dreamed of, and it would happen *after* Isaac proposed.

Spring Rains

Eighteen

Tierra Amarilla, New Mexico, November 1936

Isaac stood in front of the house, bowed deeply and extended his arm like the doorman of a fine hotel.

"Your castle awaits, my Queen."

He watched as Perfie grasped the smooth frame on the edge of the door to steady herself, balancing on the flat red stone that served as a temporary step. He hadn't built the back porch yet. He and Enoch had worked late last night to finish the plaster, and he was anxious for her approval.

It had been nearly five years, five long years of living with his parents. Now he could finally give her what she wanted, a house of her own.

"Oh." Her hand flew up against her chest. "It's wonderful. So bright. So clean."

He watched as she sniffed, drawing a deep breath and taking in the pungent odor of the white paint. It had a heavenly glow, lighting up the room as if there were sunlight pouring in through the ceiling. The dirt floor, not yet covered with boards, seemed to shine from the glow of the walls.

"I don't think the floor will shine like this once we walk on it." He balanced his chin on her shoulder and peered through the doorway. "We wet it down last night and used the trowels to smooth it, but once we walk on it, it's going to turn back to dust. I'll have those floor boards on soon, though. Don't worry."

Perfie stepped down onto the shining dirt. Isaac followed her as she made her way through the kitchen. He stopped, stood in the center of the room and turned slowly, inspecting the walls. He noticed a thin spot up near the ceiling. Probably going to have to do a little touch-up painting. It had been hard to see those thin spots last night. The glow of the lantern had cast shadows on the walls.

Perfie turned back to look at him from just inside the living room, her eyes traveling to where Isaac's gaze was focused.

"We missed a spot."

Isaac tensed at the use of the "we" and at the implied criticism.

Perfie continued. "Have you decided if we should paint the floor or not?"

He looked at her face, but her eyes were still focused on the ceiling. Was this her way of saying he better hurry up with the floor boards?

She walked back into the kitchen, wiped her hands on her apron and stopped in the doorway. "The plaster is a little uneven there, right at the top. Do you think that's why we missed it?" She ran her hand up and down the door frame as she studied the walls.

Isaac focused on her hand as she stroked the wood of the frame. He tried to erase her complaints from his mind. He'd sanded the door frames, but building the house was taking so much longer than anticipated, that he'd done it quickly and the pine was likely to have some splinters. Just what I need now, he thought—for her loving caress of her new door frame to end with the pain of a sharp point puncturing her hand. He watched her hand glide up and down, but he didn't issue the warning perched on the back of his tongue.

"Do you think you'll get to those floorboards today? It would be nice to move the bed over." She turned to him. "I was thinking, once we move the bed we can stay in the house."

"What about the kids? Our clothes? Cooking?"

"We could still do that in the tent, but we could sleep in the house. The boys can sleep on the mats and the girls can sleep with us."

Isaac had asked Benjamin to help move their things. His brother had committed to a Saturday of labor—two weeks from today. This would give Isaac and Enoch enough time to lay the floor boards, build the porches and finish the kitchen cabinets. All that work to do, and Perfecta was already talking about moving in.

"Perfie, give me two weeks, then Ben can help."

"Two weeks? I'm so tired of living in that tent. My back is permanently crooked from stooping." Her tone held a sharp clang but changed direction, like a hummingbird mid flight, before darting into a whine on the last note. "Just part way in, just enough to stand up straight once in awhile. Come on Isaac, the boys will be so excited."

"You love these white walls, don't you? Imagine moving in here with these dirt floors; how long do you think the walls will be so white? Picture them with brown handprints all over them." There had been four children in four years, and Perfie was pregnant again. Isaac wanted to move out of the tent, too. But two weeks wasn't much longer to wait.

Perfie rolled her eyes and walked back into the living room. No longer moving her feet so carefully, she crossed the eight feet of dirt to the doorway of the bedroom. She walked across the room to the perfect glass window and gazed out to the hill where the tent stood.

Isaac stayed where he was, watching her through the doorway. He hadn't imagined life could be so demanding. He thought that once they moved out of his mother's house, Perfie would be happy.

Those two, he didn't get it. He never saw them fight. Carlotta was her usual demanding self. He figured she had to be like that to survive raising six sons. It seemed like Perfie and his mother did things together, cleaning and cooking. But every night for the last five years Perfie complained— *Carlotta didn't approve of the way she cleaned, Carlotta thought she was stupid, Carlotta didn't like her.*

He had hoped Roberto's birth would change how the two women got along. Wouldn't Perfie be distracted with the care of the baby? His mother enthralled with a grandson?

That hadn't been the case. Soon Perfie was complaining that Carlotta was trying to take over raising their son. When Roberto started walking, Perfie would take him and baby Arturo and leave the house every day. One night she refused to come down for dinner. With each baby he thought things would get better and when the third was a girl, well, he had hoped that would be the magic cure. But Betty, and then Karleen, hadn't made any difference, even though Perfie could have used Carlotta's help with so many children.

Perfie was protective and didn't give an inch when it came to Carlotta.

It had been a relief when Lucas suggested they move out to the property. Enoch and Isaac started working on the house right away. Although she was pregnant again, Perfie pitched in, carrying the thick mud from the creek and mixing in the straw for the adobe bricks.

Building the house didn't go fast enough for her.

"I can't do this, I can't live with her." Perfie had sobbed one night last July.

"It won't be long. Besides, it's better if you are here to have the baby."

Then two months ago the "huge explosion" had occurred.

It was a Friday afternoon. Isaac and Lucas had cleaned up the classrooms and were walking home from La Academía. He remembered they were talking about fishing. As they approached the house they could hear the shouts.

Lucas turned to Isaac. "Do we run toward the house or away from it?"

Isaac shrugged and walked up onto the porch. His mother's voice came through the open window.

"*Eres una niña odiosa.* You are a hateful girl. Does your Catholic God teach you to disrespect your elders, or was it that pathetic mother of yours? I have raised six sons. I know what I'm talking about."

Isaac couldn't believe his mother would insult Perfie for being Catholic and then go on to call her mother pathetic. He hurried toward the kitchen.

" No wonder Primitivo kicked you out. I kick you out, too."

"Madre!" He pushed through the door. "What are you saying? Kick us out of the house? Calm down."

Roberto was crouched under the kitchen table with his hands covering his head. Little Betty leaned against him, her thumb stuck in her mouth. Arturo sat on one of the wooden chairs, where he was tied into place with a cotton dishtowel. At nearly three years old he refused to sit still for even a minute. His eyes were as wide as a hoot owl, staring at his mother and his grandmother. Isaac could hear Karleen crying in the other room.

Perfie stood facing Carlotta with her arms held out from her sides and her shoulders forward. He could see her hands shaking and her lips pressed so tight that the skin was white around her mouth.

She rushed to him and broke into sobs, but only for a second. Pushing off from his chest, she turned back to Carlotta.

"My mother was a kind and gentle woman. People loved her. I don't think the same can be said about a woman who thinks only of herself, thinks it is her right to control everyone around her."

He reached out and took hold of Perfie's arm, but she wasn't finished.

"You have raised six sons, six cowering men who are afraid to make up their minds about anything. I won't let you do that to my sons."

Isaac pulled Perfie out the back door, while Lucas led Carlotta into the bedroom.

That night Perfie had packed their meager belongings and taken the children out to the back porch.

"Come back in. You can't stay out here. The kids need to go to bed." He picked up Arturo.

"No, I'm not staying here anymore. She hates me, and the feeling is mutual."

"Don't be ridiculous. She wants us here." He tried to think of a way to put his feelings into words. Life hadn't been easy for Carlotta. Lucas had been married before. When he took up with Carlotta, the people of Taos, where they lived at the time, didn't approve. His father had told him things were so bad that the couple had been forced to move. Not only had they come to Tierra Amarilla where they had no family, but they were one of the few non-Catholic families in town. Carlotta had added a baby to the family each year, and many had died. She threw herself into raising her remaining sons and Naomi. God knows that was not an easy task. Isaac suspected his mother was jealous of Perfie, a beautiful young thing with life ahead of her.

He had hoped the two would get along, that they could be compassionate toward each other because they had both had it hard. Perfie left her family, just as Carlotta had. But instead the conflict seemed overwhelming to both of them.

He turned back to Perfie. "Where do you think we can go? I don't have anything, Perfie. My mother is what I have. We should be thankful to her. With the way you talk to her, I'm not surprised that she isn't the one packing our bags and throwing us out."

Perfie wouldn't answer him. She sat with her lips pressed tight as she rubbed Betty's head. The toddler sat beside her and dozed slumped over into her lap. Isaac didn't know where Perfie thought they would go. The house was barely started, and they had four children in tow. Too many bodies to squeeze in with friends or relatives.

But his father knew the two women had to be separated. Lucas pulled the old canvas tent out of the barn and suggested to Isaac that they set it up on the property until the house was finished.

Isaac looked out the window of the nearly completed house. He wanted to please Perfie. He didn't want his next child to be born in a tent in the middle of winter. Maybe she was right. They had been lucky with the mild weather, but the snow could be here any day. He had disappointed her again.

His thoughts were interrupted when he felt Perfie's arms wrap around him. She grasped his arms, untwined them, and placed her cheek against his chest.

"Thank you, my love. It's beautiful. It really is a home."

Nineteen

Tierra Amarilla, April 1937

Joe pointed up to the sky. "Up there. Do you see the scoop?"

Roberto shook his head. Joe knelt and put his arm next to the boy's head, his finger level with Roberto's eyes.

"Follow my finger. See the bright star?"

Perfie was happy that Joe was here for a visit. It had been years since she had time with her brother. When he suggested they go for an evening walk, she jumped at the opportunity to get out of the house. Arturo and Karleen were already asleep, tired from the long day, but Roberto had begged to come with them.

"Of course, you can come." Joe encouraged the boy.

"No one is going to carry you. You have to walk the whole way." Perfie knew that a walk to town was a long way for Roberto. It was hard to believe he would be five years old soon. He was always excited to go places, but he was a whiner, that one, begging for her to carry him even if she was already holding Karleen.

But she couldn't walk fast, or far either. Since Betty's death in January, she had lost all her energy. The walk and the time away from the house would do her good.

She had thought her kids would be safe out on the property as long as she could keep them away from rattlesnakes and out of the ditch, but the chicken pox had arrived in spite of her efforts and Betty had been unable to recover.

She knew women lost babies all the time. But that didn't make it any easier.

Shaking the thoughts from her head she looked at the sky. The stars were bright tonight. She remembered the first time Joe had taken her to see the stars. How she had loved his lessons.

She thought about her plan to have Joe as her teacher when she quit school after eighth grade. It had never come to pass.

It had been a mistake not to go back to school. The world changed, with people writing so much more. And math! She needed numbers to manage the small amount of money she and Isaac had saved. But at the time she hadn't thought she would ever need all that ridiculous knowledge.

Perfie vaguely remembered one of her mother's stories. She still couldn't figure out what most of them meant, but this one had been about trying harder at school. Something about winter storms eroding the earth that didn't have strong pines to protect it and spring rains gradually sweeping away what was left. The strong pines must have been the knowledge from school work. The erosion must have been the slow problems that develop when someone can't do math or write an essay. The spring rains seemed to represent something sweet, but they could be deadly in the long run. Just as deadly as quitting school and not considering the future.

The Martinez family was all about academics. This came from running a school. Family dinners involved discussion, arguments really, on all matters of things. She often felt left out because of her ignorance.

How many times had her poor math skills turned into ammunition for attacks from Carlotta?

"Can't you even count the change?" Carlotta stared at the coins in her hand. Perfie would just drop her head or mumble excuses.

Stop thinking about her, she chided herself. You have your own house now and you're out here with Joe. You have Isaac to yourself now. Just forget about everything else.

The house was finished and they had saved enough money to buy some nice things, a beautiful bed and a new rocking chair. She could make herself sad if she thought about Betty. Or her father. Or that she missed Isabelle. Best to keep those things out of her mind.

Joe and Isaac had been talking about Germany bombing Spain, but that seemed so far away to her. She spent time each day sitting on the front porch and staring out over the creek. She loved the house, but she still liked to be out in the open. No walls boxing her in.

Walls to protect or walls to contain? I guess they can do both. She hadn't known that about a house.

Roberto's voice interrupted her thoughts. "I see it! I really do!" He hopped up and down as he squinted at the stars.

"Your mother thinks that heaven is out there, too. Up there, in that big sky." Joe rubbed Roberto's head.

"Heaven? Like where Abuelo says Jesus lives?"

Perfie didn't go to church or let Isaac take the boys, but it seemed Lucas had been talking to Roberto about some things anyway.

"Time for a rest." Perfie walked to the edge of the road and sat on a log. Joe lifted Roberto to sit between them.

"Mama, what is heaven like? Abuelo says we'll go there someday."

"When we die, that's when we go there." She didn't imagine the boy understood. "Like Eli's dog. Remember when Wolf died?"

Roberto nodded. "We digged a hole and put him in." His face pinched up and his eyebrows rose. "But heaven's in the sky, not in the ground."

"Your spirit goes up into the sky, while your body stays down in the ground."

"Like a ghost?"

What else had Lucas told her son? "Who told you about ghosts?"

"Dad. He told me the ghosts come out at night."

"A spirit is different than a ghost. You can't see it. It leaves and doesn't come back after it goes up to heaven."

"Where Wolf is?"

This was tricky. Did dogs go to heaven? Sure, why not.

"Yes, and where your Abuela Avelina is." She had told the boys about her mother, and they had seen her picture in the carved wooden frame.

"Is Abuela Abba..abbalina playing with Wolf?"

"Probably not. She didn't care much for dogs."

Joe laughed. "To put it mildly," he added.

"What else?" Roberto wanted to know more.

"Well, in heaven everything smells good." Joe looked over at her as she spoke, his grin wide. "You get to eat whatever you want, and your clothes are always clean."

"Don't like clean clothes." Roberto shook his head.

He did hate wash day; she knew that. It was a day with short tempers and a hot house. Carlotta and Perfie worked hard to do the laundry not only for themselves but for five men and all the kids. Roberto had taken to finding a hiding place. Last week she had to search for nearly half an hour before she found him. Still, it was easier to do the laundry in town than it was at the house. Isaac loaded the clothes in the wagon and drove everyone in each Thursday. She was glad she had let Isaac talk her into making some sort of peace with Carlotta. Washing the clothes in the ditch was impossible. Roberto and Arturo jumped into the water and made such a mess.

"You have to take a bath every day in heaven." Joe teased. "Nothing dirty allowed there."

"Uh uh. Then I'm not going. Don't want a bath every day." Roberto folded his arms across his chest, and his green eyes sparkled at his uncle's teasing.

Perfie punched Joe's arm. "You hush. No, you don't have to take a bath every day unless you want to. You know how Mama loves to soak in the hot water? Well, in heaven I get to take a bath every day, but you get to skip it. Guess what else? You won't be dirty, even if you skip your bath."

"Okay. I'll go."

"Ready to walk some more?" Joe asked.

Roberto raced down the road.

"So, sister of mine. I guess Benjamin is clean out of the picture, now that you have all these kids."

She glared at Joe. Why would he bring up Benjamin?

"Don't get mad, now. It's just, I don't seem to remember being invited to a wedding."

"You know there was no wedding."

"Well, last time I checked, there were two Martinez men courting my beautiful sister. Are you sure you settled for the right one?"

"Joe, don't even say such a thing. Isaac is my husband, well, just like my husband." She stopped, remembering the sad young woman who had come looking for Joe. "Speaking of which, what about this Maria? Did she have your baby?"

Joe's smile left his face in a hurry.

Just then Roberto ran back to them.

"Carry me." He lifted his arms up to his uncle.

"Roberto! I told you no carrying. You're big enough to walk." Perfie shook her finger at him.

But she could see that Joe wasn't going to pass up the chance to be the fantastic uncle—or the chance to avoid answering her question. He scooped Roberto up onto his shoulders.

Perfie shook her head. "I don't want spoiled children. You can't go around me like that."

"He's not a peach, Hermana. He won't spoil, I promise."

Just as well, she thought. I didn't want any more questions about Benjamin. He's out of my life and it's going to stay that way. The truth was, she wasn't tempted by him anymore. His antics were childish, and she couldn't imagine him stepping up to the responsibilities of being a husband or father. Not like Isaac, who took his family seriously.

They walked slowly down the road, Roberto jabbering to his uncle from his perch. Perfie let her imagination drift back to heaven.

There wouldn't be laundry, nobody would argue, there would be no housework. There would be a creek flowing with warm water, where she would float. Like the ditch, only so much better.

She scowled. But she wouldn't be there. She was a sinner. She would never feel that warm water flowing over her body.

Slowly, with her chin down to her chest, she followed Joe back to the house.

Twenty

Perfie sat on the ground with her legs spread into a v-shape, her palms pressed flat against the earth between them. If she sat very still she could feel the spirit of Betty, whose tiny body lay below her hands, deep within the earth and far away from her mother's arms.

I should have held her more. I should have sat and rocked her all night. God, I know I'm a sinner, but did you have to take my baby? She was an *innocente*. No tears fell from Perfie's eyes; there was only a dull, never-ending ache deep in her chest.

With Grace it had been different. She was gone before they ever got a chance to know her, swept away in a sudden gush of fluid and blood four months before she was due to be born.

Perfie was lost in her grief, but she could hear Roberto and Arturo throwing rocks into the ditch water just down the hill. She hoped they were watching Karleen.

Earlier that day she had said "Let's go for a walk." She wrapped Geri in a cotton sheet and looped it over her shoulder, then called to the boys and Karleen. They walked on the cattle trail up to the ditch and crossed over on the old board.

"You play here. Watch your brother and sister." She instructed Roberto to stay at the bottom of the path that led up to the graves. She wanted to be alone with Betty and Grace. She thought about leaving three-month-old Geri with the boys; she was asleep. Even if she woke, she wasn't crawling yet, and Perfie would hear if she cried. The graves were just a short way up the hill, but Perfie decided to keep the baby wrapped in the sling and carried her up the steep slope.

At the top of the hill she had laid the sleeping baby next to a tree where she would be covered by shade.

Then Perfie prayed.

"Lord, forgive me for my sins. I'm with a Presbyterian, and for that I no longer take the Holy Communion." She spoke softly, her voice a whisper. "I take no pleasure in these sins, Lord."

She opened her eyes and tilted her chin up from her position of prayer. *Now I've lied to God. Another sin to add to the list.* This thought pulled her out of her purposeful lament. She didn't want to face the fact that she wasn't really sorry. She had to keep hold of her guilt if she wanted God to forgive her. With a shake of her head she returned to her grief.

"I have prayed for forgiveness, prayed that you show me the way to cleanse my soul, prayed that you, Lord, will see what a fine man Isaac is, what fine children we have. I left the home of my father. I knew my mother was ill when she sat rocking in that old chair every day, staring at the wall, not even turning her head to the window. Yet I did nothing to stop her from dying of a broken heart. The heart I broke."

She felt sad again, but sadness felt better than guilt. *I was a young woman then,* she thought, *and not meant for taking care of the old or the ill. I needed to start my own family. Oh God, for this you make me pay with my babies?* She managed tears and a strangled gasp, but her crying was interrupted by the sound of feet on the gravel.

Isaac's voice broke into Perfecta's list of sins. "Here you are. What are you doing?"

She looked up, straight into the bright sun. She could see the outline of Isaac but not his face, for it was in the shadow of the blinding glare. Was he mad?

Isaac reached down, grabbed her arm and pulled her to standing.

"You have to stop coming every day. Didn't you hear the boys? Arturo fell in the ditch. Luckily Roberto pulled him out, Perfecta, or you would have been visiting three of your children on this hillside. I can't believe you left them there alone." He held Karleen on his hip.

She hung her head to avoid his eyes. Isaac stooped down and scooped up the sleeping Geri with his other arm and set off down the slope.

She followed him to where Arturo stood shivering in wet clothes. Roberto hung his head but looked up as they approached. His green eyes were wide.

"Come on." Isaac called to the boys, and they fell into line behind him. Perfie brought up the rear.

Back at the adobe house, after Arturo was changed into dry clothes and dinner was started, Perfie stood in the kitchen rolling out the dough she had prepared in the morning. Sopapillas would go with the beans and beef that were cooking in the pressure cooker on the stove. She noticed that Roberto sat very still on the back step. He hadn't come into the house. Setting the dough aside she opened the screen and stood above him.

"What are you doing here?"

"Nothing." Roberto glanced over his shoulder to the hook on the wall beside the door. On the hook hung a four inch wooden paddle, the one she used for punishing the boys.

"Did your father talk with you about playing in the ditch?"

"Yes. He said it was good I pulled Arturo out."

"What about playing there in the first place? Where did I tell you to play?"

"You left us by the ditch."

"Roberto! Don't tell such a lie. Surely God will hear you lie."

Roberto was silent.

"Let me tell you a story." She saw him roll his eyes, but continued. "Once upon a time there was a brother. He was supposed to watch his younger sister." She stopped. How did that story go? She was sure her mother had told her something about one child taking care of the other.

"They were Indians, so his sister was a little maiden. Anyway, their father, the chief, told him to watch over her because there were coyotes and rattlesnakes that could kill her. But he didn't watch over her, and one day when they were playing by the river she disappeared."

"This is a stupid story. It doesn't make any sense at all." Roberto glared at her.

She shut her eyes. I need something. Take a breath, she thought. But she couldn't. She felt her lungs freeze, not able to take in any air. She snatched the paddle off the hook and grabbed his arm.

As she swung the paddle and struck Roberto on the hip she screamed, "You will listen to me. I'm your mother. I'm in charge. Don't you ever disobey me again." The words continued to pour out of her mouth as her arm swung up and down, up and down.

Usually when she spanked Roberto he sobbed. Such huge tears this boy could weep. But today he didn't cry out. He stood with a stubborn look on his face, his eyes growing as dark as the thunder clouds over the valley.

His brow wrinkled and his hands curled into fists. She could see he was prepared to battle her.

She dropped the paddle onto the floor and wiped her hands on her apron. "The little girl, the maiden, she was never seen again. The chief told the boy to leave the tribe and never come back."

Roberto stood staring at her, his breath ragged.

"Do you understand this?" She felt a sudden pull deep inside. Did she understand it? She thought of the stories her mother told and the fear her father left inside of her. Why couldn't Roberto just understand? If he would follow her rules he wouldn't ever have to feel like she felt.

Suddenly there was a loud bang from the kitchen. The house shook. Both Roberto and Perfie looked at the door.

"The meat!" Perfie cried out as she ran into the kitchen.

Thinking she would be near to watch the pot, she had left it over the hot flame, but the old pressure cooker didn't like that kind of treatment. The lid had blown off.

Meat and beans covered every surface of the stove and the walls. Isaac stood in the doorway, Karleen in his arms and Arturo peering around him.

"What happened?"

"I think it got too hot. It exploded."

He pointed up to the ceiling.

Wedged into the soft wood above the stove was the glass stopper that had previously been in the center of the pressure cooker lid.

Isaac shook his head. Then he started to laugh.

Arturo jumped up and down laughing. Karleen giggled.

Perfie looked around the room at the mess. She picked up a rag and started to wipe off the stove top. Isaac set Karleen down and grabbed the mop.

Nobody noticed that Roberto hadn't come into the house. He sat on the step, staring out across the sage at the slope where his little sister Betty lay sleeping forever.

San Francisco Bay

Twenty-One

Albuquerque, New Mexico, June 14, 1940

Perfie woke with a start. As soon as she opened her eyes a nervous feeling pulsed through her arms and legs. She hadn't been able to get settled last night, dropping into bed late after a long day of packing for the trip. She had tossed and turned for hours, not expecting to fall asleep at all.

The top edge of the scratchy wool blanket rubbed her chin. It smelled like old mutton and smoke. She missed her smooth cotton sheets. Somewhere in all the moves they had been left behind, and she didn't have the money to buy more. This stinky blanket would be left behind today; the good quilts were already packed in the trunk.

Perfie wiggled her shoulders and nudged her sleeping daughters, who were curled into tight balls on each side of her. She pulled the blanket up even though the morning was warm. It had been a hot spring, and the June evenings didn't offer any relief from the endless heat.

She peered at the window. There was a faint light coming through the torn cotton curtain.

It was morning, she decided—the morning of her last day in New Mexico.

None of the previous moves had felt like this; this one hovered over her like a dark thunder cloud, pregnant with pending downpour. In the past, she had known she could go back even if she had to apologize or agree to something she didn't want. Some act of contrition had always worked before.

Not this time.

She pushed her body down into the lumpy mattress and turned her head to smell Geri's sweet breath. Even at seventeen months her daughter had the breath of milk and innocent dreams.

I won't miss this life, she thought. I can never catch up, never keep everyone happy. Danger follows us. Maybe the curse of this place will stay here in New Mexico, not come with us to California.

There were things she would miss. She thought of the babies she would leave behind, buried up on the hill in T.A. She thought about the long walks along the river and about riding the hills on Cimmaron.

The truth of the matter was, she had left these things behind long ago. Cimmaron was skinny and old. She had moved him next to the adobe house, but she never rode anymore. He entertained the boys by letting them climb on his swayed back and walking them slowly around the fields. He would be happy now grazing with the summer cattle, and Lucas promised to move him to the barn during the winter months. Still, she was saddened to think that she would never see her horse again.

Since Isaac had gone to California she had moved the kids three times. They had been staying with Tía Consuela on a nice farm in Chimayó when he left. It seemed the perfect place to wait for word from him. *It won't be long*, he had promised.

But she had lost her temper. Again. Consuela had yelled at the kids for making too much noise and refused to let them play outside or enter any room other than the kitchen and the single bedroom they all shared. Perfie hadn't been able to look the other way. After a screaming argument, she packed up their belongings and boarded the bus to Albuquerque.

They spent a week in the chicken coop of Marcella and David Cortez, friends of Isabelle. There was an outhouse and a source of water, but the odor of the former residents was more than she could bear.

One day Perfie stood with her four children at a bus stop. She struck up a conversation with a woman there and mentioned that she was on her way downtown to look for work. The woman nodded in understanding but gave a questioning glance toward Perfie's four children. Not the best recommendation for a job.

"Katrina Dominquez," she introduced herself and told Perfie of a place where they all could live together. They moved in with Katrina.

Perfie tried to find some work, but her efforts proved fruitless. Mending clothes was the only thing she could do with all these children to watch. The small amount of money she made didn't just trickle away: it was swept away. She stretched her cash out the best she could; she shared a propane stove with Katrina, cooking one pot meals—watery soup, fried potatoes and eggs. But still the money vanished as soon as she earned it.

On top of that, there had been no word from Isaac. She was angry with him for leaving her alone, and she scribbled frantic letters to him.. He had deserted his family again; that's how she saw it.

In the seventeen years she had known Isaac, he had been to California three times. But all three trips had been before the children came along. She had hoped that his sense of responsibility would keep him here with his family, but as things grew worse in New Mexico she watched California pull at him once again. Six months ago she heard the words she had been dreading. He was going to go find a better job and would send for them when he had some money. Her ranting, crying and begging had not stopped him from leaving.

Last week she finally received a letter from him. It was time for Perfie to bring the children to California, he wrote. He had a job with the Navy, filling insulators with asbestos. She guessed it had something to do with building ships, but the letter was vague.

For a week she had fretted about the trip. She felt as if she were about to walk into a long, dark cave, her hands reaching out to touch damp walls, fearful of spiders or other creatures, her feet inching forward over an uneven surface, rocks popping up to trip her. She moved toward something new, with little knowledge of what this future would hold.

Isaac's brief letter included instructions: which train to take, which day to leave so that he would be there for her arrival, how to get the money he wired to her. But the letter told her nothing about what to expect: where they would live, what Oakland was like, how much money they would have.

Enough of this, she told herself. Pulling back the blanket slightly, she slipped out of the bed. Stay asleep, please stay asleep, she thought, glancing at the children. She needed time to get ready before they drained her with their demands.

Her prayer wasn't answered. As she slipped her arms into her green wool sweater she heard a hissing whisper.

"Mom?" Roberto sat up, his eyes wide.

He had probably been lying there awake as she had, thinking about what the day might bring. Yesterday he had followed her around endlessly.

"Will Dad be waiting for us? Where will we sleep? Is Abuelito going with us?"

Impatient with him, Perfie had spoken sharply, pushing him with her hands as well as her words out the door, away from her. Fears transformed into anger at the questions he asked. She didn't have the answers. Now that he was awake the questions would start again.

"Hush. Don't wake the girls." She walked over to the worn mat on the floor where Roberto and Arturo slept. She tucked the quilt around Arturo, who slept in a tight ball, his thin arm covering his face. "Come help me get ready." She motioned Roberto out of the bed.

"Will I get to sit up front in the truck?"

"We'll see."

She handed Roberto his pants and sweater while stooping to look for his shoes and socks. "Put these on and come outside, but don't let the door bang."

Perfie avoided the loose boards as she made her way down the length of the wooden porch. She didn't want to make any noise that would disturb the other families that shared the building.

She thought about the adobe house in Tierra Amarilla. It had been wonderful while it lasted. She hadn't appreciated the white walls, the water just up the path, the view from the porch, the separate bedrooms.

As most things in her life, the house hadn't worked out as expected. She couldn't believe it when Carlotta moved into the house part time to "help." The whole purpose of the house had been to create privacy for their little family. But Carlotta couldn't leave her son alone; she didn't trust him or Perfie to take care of themselves. And she made it very clear she didn't think Perfie was taking good care of the children. Not with two babies buried on the hill.

The fights started immediately. Perfie had given Isaac an ultimatum. Either he get his mother to move back into town, or she would move back into the tent.

Unfortunately, it was Carlotta's house. Even though Perfie had made the adobe bricks herself, stooping low over her pregnant body, and Isaac had built the house, the land still belonged to Carlotta.

But it was later that Isaac decided to try the west again, or so Perfie thought. There had been something bothersome at the time, something that nagged at the back of her mind. Only now, in retrospect, did she see it as a sign he was thinking about California.

As soon as the kids could talk Isaac had insisted they call him "Dad" instead of the usual "Papa" or "Papí." He spoke English to them, but they spoke only Spanish. He was practically the only one in town other than Father Tom who didn't speak Spanish. Maybe this was a sign that Isaac had been planning the move for a long time. Then Roberto started calling her Mom.

When Carlotta didn't move out, Perfie was miserable and Isaac decided to try something else. They moved to Española for a short time, then over to Chimayo to help on a cousin's farm. It was here that Isaac had decided to try for his fortune in California or at least when he finally told her what he was planning.

Now it was six months later, and she was here, alone in this fruit shed. As alone, that is, as anyone can be with four children and five other families.

Stepping off of the wooden porch Perfie made her way through the yard full of tangled weeds. At the outhouse she banged her shoes on the wooden step just loud enough to chase off any rodents or spiders that may have moved in during the night. After relieving herself, she went to the pump in the yard and pulled an embroidered handkerchief from her pocket to wash her face.

She heard the door shut quietly as Roberto came out onto the porch. She waited for him to use the outhouse before washing his face with the cloth.

"Mom? I'm the oldest. I get to sit up front in the truck." She noticed he had gone from asking to telling. At nearly eight years old he was moving out of childhood. With Isaac gone for so long, Roberto had been told by many well-meaning relatives that he was "the man" of the family. This new behavior, this telling his mother what was to be, had developed when they had moved to Albuquerque. Perfie didn't like it.

"Roberto, there's a lot to do first. We'll see. Now, help me finish tying up the bundles before we wake the others." She led the way back into the building to pack for the journey. Behind her she heard a soft whisper.

"I *am* sitting in the front of the truck."

"Arturo, please stay up here on the blanket."

Perfie grabbed her son's arm and pulled him up out of the straw that filled the truck bed; she didn't want an asthma attack now. She was already exhausted, and the journey had just begun. She hugged Geri close to her chest with one arm and supported Arturo with the other.

The truck stopped with a lurch, causing her to lose her grip on Arturo, but he kept himself from falling back into the hay. She heard the door slam, and the driver's footsteps crunched in the course sand as he came to the back of the truck to help her out. Roberto followed close behind him.

"Mama, is this California?" Six-year-old Arturo must think the ride was long enough.

"No. You're stupid." Roberto sneered at his brother. "This is Santa Fe, we haven't even got on the train yet."

Perfie handed Garcia, the truck driver, two dollars and pushed her kids off the road onto the steps of the train station. Then she turned back to Garcia. "I'll be back as soon as I have the labels for the crates."

"Sure thing," he nodded.

She stood for a moment, the three children surrounding her, the bundled clothing in a pile at the bottom of the stairs. She set Geri down and tossed each bundle to the top of the platform.

"Go on, up to the top and pick up your things."

The children climbed the steps. Roberto lifted his bundle up to his chest with both arms. Arturo and Karleen grasped the ropes and pulled their bundles behind them. Perfie took a deep breath, shifted Geri up to a firm spot on her hip, picked up her suitcase and walked to the door of the station.

She scanned the signs and spotted the arrow pointing to the ticket counter. She glanced back at the kids. They followed her like chicks after the hen.

"Mom, this is too heavy." Roberto dropped his bundle to the ground.

"Pick that up, Roberto. We have to find the spot to buy our ticket."

"No, I won't. You have to carry it."

She turned and glared at him, her voice taking on a high pitch. "Now."

He crossed his arms and shook his head.

Perfie plopped Geri down on the wooden floor and walked back to Roberto. She grabbed his arm and pushed him toward the abandoned bundle. "Pick that up. I won't have this today. Shape up right now."

Roberto stomped his foot and started to wail. This was his fake cry. Before she could stop herself, Perfie's hand shot out toward him, but he knew what was coming and ducked his head to the side.

"Fine. Stay. See if I care." She dropped his arm, pulled Geri back onto her hip and walked away. Arturo and Karleen dragged their bundles across the dusty floor and trotted to keep up with her.

She walked down a wide hall and entered a large room. She spotted the ticket counter on one side.

"Mama, Roberto is back." Arturo spoke quietly.

Perfie rolled her eyes to one side without turning her head. She could see Roberto trudging around the corner with his bundle dragging behind him.

"Can I help you?" The man behind the counter seemed impatient. She didn't realize he had asked this twice already.

"Oh, one ticket to Oakland, California." she said. "I have six crates out on the platform."

"Have they been weighed?"

She shook her head. "Where do I do that?"

"Round by track seven. They'll give you a slip. Bring it back here to pay."

The man was silent as he took the thirty dollars for her ticket. "Platform six," he said, as he slid the blue ticket across the counter.

Perfie turned and walked in the direction he had pointed, and the children followed. She glanced toward the clock on the wall. 12:50. The kids hadn't eaten lunch yet, but there was plenty of time before the three o'clock train arrived.

She saw a bench ahead and made her way to it. She set Geri and her old brown suitcase on the bench, reached for Karleen and put her beside Geri.

"Watch the girls." She tried to make her voice firm, her I-really-mean-this-and-don't-you-dare-disobey-me voice. "I'll be right back."

She hurried to the front of the station and told Garcia where to unload the crates. Pacing and tapping her foot while the men slowly weighed everything, she felt her heart pounding and her breath tight.

"Boy, that's a heavy one." The men complained when they unloaded her washer. She hadn't been willing to give it up. Isaac promised they would get one in California, but she no longer believed his promises. His sense of "soon" was very different from hers.

She snatched the slip of paper from the loaders and raced back to the counter. The kids were still on the benches. Well, near them anyway. Arturo was twirling and Karleen was curled up underneath the wooden seat.

The stern ticket seller studied the slip of paper. "Let's see, you're allowed 150 pounds with your ticket, but you have 320 pounds, so that will be another five dollars."

She slid five wrinkled bills across the counter. This was more than she had expected, and she worried about the dent it put in her cash.

"Boarding in thirty minutes."

She walked back to the children.

"Mama, I gotta go potty." Arturo's dance now included rapid hopping, which meant he had waited too long.

After shuttling all the children to the toilets, Perfie found a bench close to Platform Six. She leaned back and closed her eyes, imagining the end of the journey when the family would be with Isaac again. The children already whimpered: *I'm hungry, I want to sit there, quit pushing me, he touched me.* She reached her hand to her throat, rubbed the silver cross with forefinger and thumb and mumbled a whispered prayer. "Please God. I need you to help me through the next two days."

Perfie opened her eyes and sat up to check on the children. Arturo was under the bench, but Karleen and Roberto sat next to her. "Everyone sit. Listen and I'll tell you a story." Geri climbed into her lap.

"Once upon a time there was a mother and her two children, a boy and a girl. They were going on a long trip. First they walked, then they rode in a wagon, then they got on a train. Now the mother, she told the kids how dangerous the train was. It was big and fast and it couldn't stop, not for nothing. Nope, that old train was so heavy it took about a mile or so for it to stop. 'Don't play on the tracks,' that mother told her kids. But do you think they listened?" She looked at Roberto, but he was watching the trains.

"Yes, Mama. They listened to they mom." Karleen seemed to be the only one really paying attention to the story.

"No, Baby. They didn't. They ran away from their mom, right in that station. They ran across the platform and down the stairs. Then they ran back up. They thought this was so much fun until the boy stumbled and bumped his little sister. And the worst thing ever happened. That little girl fell right off the platform and onto the tracks just when the train was pulling into the station. And that train ran right over her. Chopped her in two."

Karleen's eyes grew big. "Made her two people, Mama?"

Arturo popped his head out from under the bench. "No, it killed her, dummy. There was blood and guts, and she was dead."

"Like Bronco?" Karleen had seen the old bull after Isaac had thrown that fateful rock. There hadn't been any guts when the bull keeled over.

The rock had been meant to stop his endless bellowing, but it struck him directly in the forehead and killed him instantly. The kids stood along the bank and watched as Isaac and Levi butchered the animal. Unfortunately, it had been the neighbor's bull. After Lucas paid the man for the murdered beast, Perfie and Isaac owed him even more money. But there was fresh meat for dinner.

"Yes, and that's why all boys and girls must stay with their mother when they're going to ride on a train." Her story was interrupted by the sound of the engine approaching the station.

"This is it, time to get on the train. Time to go to California." Her fear turned into excitement, and she tried to share it with the tired children. Arturo and Roberto jumped off the bench and grabbed the bundles. They were on their way to a new life.

Several minutes after the train moved away from the station, the conductor came down the aisle.

"Tickets, tickets please," he called out in a singsong voice. Perfie held out the blue ticket.

He punched her ticket and handed it back before extending his hand out to her again. Perfecta smiled and held the same ticket out.

"No ma'am. I need the tickets for the children."

"Tickets for the children? But they're children, surely they don't need tickets?"

"For local rides one child can travel with a parent, but you're headed for California and you have FOUR children. The children must have tickets."

"Oh, I didn't know." Perfie fumbled in her bag. She knew she had exactly twenty-five dollars left, and that was not enough for four more tickets. She held the money out to the conductor. "This is all I have."

He counted the bills and looked at the children. "Well, let me see. Children are half the adult price, and if the baby sits on your lap, I think this will just about cover it." He pulled three more tickets out of his leather pouch, punched them and handed them to Perfecta. "Have a good trip."

"Thank you." Perfie was grateful, but she felt the ice creep up into her heart again. Her excitement was frozen by her dread as she tried to imagine how she would make it through two days without any money at all.

Twenty-Two

Roberto blinked his eyes and used his finger to work the crust out of the corners. He pulled his cheek away from the cold glass and swiped the back of his sleeve across his chin to catch the line of drool that had gathered there sealing his cheek to the window. He shifted his legs from under his brother; Arturo was slumped against him snoring softly.

He looked out the window at the landscape rolling by; the reddish tinge spreading across the bare hills told him morning was almost here.

Licking his dry lips as he sat up, he lifted his face to look at the back of his mother's head. Some of her brown hair had escaped the clip that held it behind her neck, and her head leaned to one side, flopped back against the edge of the seat. She was still asleep.

Roberto tugged his shirt down from where it had crumpled beneath his back. He pulled his arms and legs free from underneath his brother and stretched his neck. Arturo mumbled "I can't, no, I don't understand," his arms twitching in defense of whatever demand was being made in his dream. Roberto patted his pocket to make sure the small cotton drawstring bag was still there.

Mama had handed him the sack when they first left Tierra Amarilla. *Put what is most important in here*, she told him.

He put the smooth rock with the gold seam in first. He remembered the day he had climbed up to the bluff with his abuelo. This rock was different from the others, and Lucas had stooped to pick it up. The bluff was mostly made of sharp broken rock, all shades of yellows and reds. This smooth stone seemed to come from the bed of a river; its gray center faded into a blue tone around the edges and the gold seam divided it into two, like a tiny river running through a valley far below. One side of the stone was rough, as if it had split into two, but the rest of it was smooth.

He liked to hold it in his palm and rub it with his thumb while he imagined his abuelo's tall thin figure walking up the trail through the piñon pines and aspen.

He had added the rest of his collection to the sack: a feather he liked to imagine was from an eagle, although he suspected it was from a turkey; a blue stone so round it was like a small globe; a smooth piece of wood which looked like a hawk; a rusted chain with a ring that held nothing and whose links spiraled into small intertwined eights; a tiny pine cone still tightly closed. He had folded a faded piece of blue fabric into a very tight roll and tied it with a small piece of hemp rope, but when he tried to place it into the sack, there wasn't room. The swatch was all that was left of the blanket he left behind in T.A.—the one he had slept under for most of his life.

His father had slipped a silver quarter into his hand on the day he left for California. Isaac had warned him to keep this a secret from his mother. Roberto had added it to the sack.

Now, satisfied that his treasures were still secure, he looked around at the other passengers. The man who had smiled at his mother yesterday was awake, and he met Roberto's eyes. Holding his index finger up to his lips, he winked.

When Mama made this sign it was usually accompanied by the hissing "shhh." Roberto nodded at the man to show he understood, yet his face remained still, his large green eyes unblinking, just that slight tip of the head to show the stranger that he also enjoyed the peace before his family woke up.

A few minutes later passengers began to shift in their seats, heads lifting from slumped positions, arms and legs stretching, coats and collars being adjusted. A young woman held onto the edge of each seat as she made her way to the back of the car. Roberto noticed her strange yellow hair, dry and stiff, sticking out from her head like the hay he fed the cattle each day back home. As her hand rested on the back of his mother's seat, his attention was drawn to the sparkling ring on her finger. She noticed him watching and moved her hand down to her side as if ashamed she had to grasp the seats to move down the aisle. Or maybe she was fearful he would steal the ring.

No longer interested in her, Roberto looked to the front of the train where the sliding door opened with a "whoosh." A cold draft made its way down the length of the car, leaving behind it a stirring in the slumbering passengers, as if icy fingers gently shook each one awake. With a rattling bang, someone entered the car pushing a cart with fruit, cookies and hard-boiled eggs in a blue glass bowl—a feast.

The man who pushed the cart was dressed in a dark blue suit with gold buttons. He stopped the cart with a thunk of his heel to push down the brake on the wheel. His hair was as white as Dad's handkerchief—it hugged the sides of his head, poking out from under his square hat that sat like a little box upside down on his head. He had the darkest skin Roberto had ever seen.

The funny man looked expectantly at the passengers in the first set of seats. A gray-haired man in the crumpled black coat picked out an apple and an egg, which he handed to his wife. Roberto felt a surge of excitement run through his stomach. There was going to be breakfast!

The gray-haired man then picked out a bag of nuts before reaching into his pocket and handing the man with the funny hat several coins. Roberto slumped back into the seat.

You had to buy the food.

He turned his head back to the window and stared out at the passing land, which was now devoid of any hills—just a long flat land filled with those scratchy round tumbleweed plants.

Roberto's stomach rumbled and he could hear the cart coming closer. *Mama, wake up now.* He tried to use his thoughts to wake her, but when that didn't work he raised his feet and pushed them against the back of her seat.

"Huh hmm." He heard a throat clear. He looked up to the frown of the stranger across the aisle.

With his face burning, he pulled his feet back down. Sliding to the floor he curled up and peered under the seats.

I'm so hungry, he thought. Why doesn't Mom give us some food? She's mean. It felt as though his stomach had been empty forever—ever since Dad left.

He didn't really understand why they had moved away from T.A. Mama said it was because they were poor, but he had never been hungry back then—only since they left and started moving from one place to another. He was tired of changing schools and tired of sleeping in smaller and smaller rooms. And he was really, really hungry.

It had been okay when Dad was still here. At least he took him fishing or for long walks, and told him stories. Mama only told scary stories, like the one about that witch, La Llorona, coming in the night to steal bad boys.

At least that stupid witch lived in New Mexico and wouldn't be there to haunt him in California. He liked to sleep near the window so he could open his eyes and look out at the stars, but at home he made Arturo take that side of the bed so that La Llorona would get him first.

Roberto stared at the bottom of his mother's loafers. Her shoes had holes like his. He looked past her legs. The man in the next seat had black shiny shoes, but they were worn thin, too. Dad told him most people didn't have much money, but yesterday he saw a man pull a big wad of money out of his pocket to buy some nuts. Some people had lots of money; why didn't his father?

He turned his head and stared across the aisle at the stranger's shoes. They were black and shiny, but he couldn't see the bottom. Suddenly the foot tapped and the toe turned toward him. He pulled his head out and looked up at the man.

The stranger was smiling now. That was good. At least he wasn't mad.

Roberto pulled himself back up onto the seat. He leaned over to pull his jacket out from under Arturo.

Just as he pulled, his brother shifted in his sleep. Roberto's arm shot back with the release of tension, his elbow slamming into the side of his mother's head. The man with the cart moved it up the aisle and stopped next to his mother just as her hand flew up to her cheek and she cried out.

"I'm sorry, I'm sorry." Roberto's shoulders rose up and he cringed away from the expected blow.

The stranger stood up and leaned over the cart.

"Excuse me, Miss. It was an accident."

Roberto watched his mother stare at the stranger. Did she think the man had struck her?

Maybe he could distract her. "Mom. I'm hungry. The food man is here."

"Mama, I'm hungry." Karleen piped up.

Arturo's head bumped Roberto's shoulder as his brother grasped the back of the seat and pulled himself up. "Me, too." He blinked and rubbed his nose.

Roberto watched his mother pull her bag into her lap and rummage through it. Didn't she remember there was nothing in it? They begged for food last night and she had looked then.

"There's no more. When we see Daddy he'll have a big fine meal for us. It won't be long now."

He watched Geri climb into his mother's lap and burrow her head into Mom's chest. It seemed his little sister remembered that at one time there was food for her there.

"Mama, there is food." Roberto pointed to the porter and his cart. He didn't call her Mom this time: she didn't like it and now wasn't the time to push things.

"We don't have the money for it, Roberto."

He thought about the silver quarter in his bag. He was hungry. How much food would twenty-five cents buy?

"Besides, we don't need to eat that food." Mama's voice sounded funny, as if even she didn't believe what she was saying. He looked back at the cart.

The stranger reached out and took four eggs, three apples and two oranges. He handed the porter a bill. "Keep the change."

The stranger had money.

The porter smiled and nodded "Why, thank you very much, sir," and moved down the aisle. He didn't look at Mama.

"Here." The stranger passed the oranges to Mama. He handed each boy an egg before pulling a small knife out of his pocket and flipping open the blade to slice the apples.

"You don't . . . ." Mama's words stopped.

No, Mama. Don't say it. Don't tell him he doesn't have to. Roberto longed to scream out the words, but he kept quiet.

"*Gracias.*" Mama turned and stared at Roberto. "Say thank you to the nice man."

He could see the fire burning in the back of her eyes. He would be in trouble later, but for now he would eat his egg. He took tiny bites to make it last while he listened to the stranger and his mother.

"I'm Jorgé Montello," the stranger introduced himself.

"Perfie Martinez. *Muchas gracias.* Eh . . . thank you so much for the food. I didn't . . . I don't . . . ."

"Not a problem. Your children are a wonderful bunch. It has made the trip pass quickly having the chance to watch them. Where are you headed?"

"*Vamos a*—we are going to Oakland. Mi esposo—my husband has been there for six months, and now we finally have enough money to join him. At least I thought we had enough money."

Roberto saw Mama's hand close into a tight ball. Why was she telling the stranger about their money?

"I'm headed to Oakland, too. That is home for me. I travel for work so I make this trip several times a year."

"Can you tell me where we are? I lost track when I fell asleep."

"We're near the spot where we'll change trains. In fact, it's soon. That's why the porter brought the breakfast so early."

"Oh. I better get everything ready."

"There's enough time for the children to finish eating." The stranger, Jorgé, smiled at Mama. He was nice. And this was the best egg Roberto had ever tasted.

Roberto held Karleen on his lap. "No, you stay here. Mama said so." His sister wiggled and kicked. Arturo sat next to him on the wooden bench with Geri held tightly in his lap. Mama had told them to watch the girls while she made sure the crates were moved onto the next train.

Mama and Jorgé were coming back. She was shaking her head and her fist. Roberto could hear her voice. Her mad voice, rising to a loud, high pitch before tapering off to a growling quiet. He leaned forward and looked down the platform.

"I just want to make sure everything is on the right train. What kind of rule is that? No one allowed back there? Those are my things—my life. I can't risk losing anything."

Roberto watched Jorgé pat his mother on the shoulder. "I'm sure it will be fine, Perfie."

Just then Roberto felt something warm and wet on his leg. "No!" he cried out, pushing Karleen off his lap. She fell to the floor and started screaming.

Mama and Jorgé came running.

"What did you do to her?" Mama's angry voice pounded down on him.

"I didn't do anything, she—."

"Why is she crying if you didn't do anything?"

Mama didn't even let him finish explaining.

"Roberto peed his pants." Arturo was pointing at his brother's wet crotch. His mother looked down at him.

"You peed your pants? Why didn't you wait? How much more trouble are you going to cause me?" She was winding up now.

"I didn't."

"Don't lie to me. I can see it with my own eyes."

"Ahhh . . ." Roberto let the scream escape. He closed his eyes tight and wished himself anywhere else, away from his crazy family. As he drew in his breath for a second bellow he felt a hand on his shoulder.

"Now there. Calm down. Perfie, I don't think it's this child that peed." Jorgé had a deep voice, and his touch felt good. Roberto opened his eyes and swallowed his scream.

Jorgé was pointing at Karleen, now held in her mother's arms. The back of her dress had a huge wet spot spreading across it.

"In fact, I would say that Roberto got peed *upon*." Jorgé smiled and shook his head.

Roberto was about to demand that his mother open the bundle and find him new pants when the loud whistle of the train, followed by the *All Aboard* call of the conductor, interrupted him.

"Come on. Pick up the things, hurry now." Suddenly Mama was in a hurry. And although Roberto hated the wet patch on the front of his pants, he just wanted to get back on the train.

Thirty minutes later Roberto and Arturo were sitting next to Jorgé showing him the treasures from the little white sack.

Mama and Jorgé had talked about the war. There had been a big attack, and everyone on the train was passing around newspapers. The Nazis had done another bad thing, this time in Paris. Señora Garcia, back at school, had shown them on a map where the bad stuff was happening. Roberto was glad it was on the other side of the world so they didn't have to worry about it. But today all the grownups seemed worried anyway. He wondered if Dad would have to be a soldier, instead of just working with the army guys. He would like Dad to have an army gun and not just a rifle for shooting coyotes.

Mama sat in her seat, the girls asleep beside her. She was looking out the window. Roberto turned and looked out the window on his side of the train and listened to Arturo tell Jorgé about his collection of lizards back home.

Roberto was tired of being on the train, and his eyes kept shutting. He stared out the window to stay awake. He didn't want to fall asleep like the babies did.

Outside there was a river, thick and wide, then farms, and then big buildings that were built close to each other. The train passed over a bridge, and suddenly the window was filled with the view of buildings. Beyond the buildings he saw green hills covered with trees of every color imaginable. He had never seen so many different colors.

Passengers began to gather belongings.

"Not long now," Jorgé told them.

Mama got busy. She tucked arms into coats and placed hats on heads. Roberto had a hard time sitting still. They were almost there.

He would finally see his father again.

Twenty-Three

Perfie and the children moved toward the steel steps to exit the train. Thoughts of Isaac filled Perfie's mind. It had been so long.

She stopped thinking about Isaac as she realized it would take some planning to get herself and four children, plus all the belongings, through the narrow passage. What was it about traveling that made things multiply?

Perfie realized that over the two days of travel they had taken things out and not put them back. She should have been repacking, but it was too late now. Distracted by the conversation with Jorgé, she hadn't planned ahead. She couldn't keep the smile from her lips as she glanced over at the handsome man. It had been nice to talk to an adult.

She picked up the sweater Arturo had dropped.

"Come on, Mom!" Roberto, in the lead, stopped at the top of the steps, set his bundle of belongings in front of him and gave it a push. The bundle tumbled end over end down to the concrete platform below. Roberto jumped after it. Arturo was next, and as always, followed his brother's example. Just as he set his bundle on the top step, she snapped out of her distracted state enough to realize what he was about to do.

"Wait. No, Arturo!"

Her warning was too late. Arturo kicked the bundle down the steps. The cotton rope holding the bundle came untied. Faded sweaters, mended socks, and a variety of undergarments, gray with age and many washings, flew out to land on the steps and the platform below.

"No!" she cried out. Then she felt arms reaching from behind her to take Geri. She turned to find Jorgé standing in the narrow aisle.

"Come on little one." He grasped Karleen's hand while he switched Geri over to his hip and spoke to Perfie. "You grab the case and I'll worry about the girls."

Perfie gasped, somewhat horrified, mumbling a "No, no" protest, even while she hurriedly squatted on the top step to gather the scattered clothing. As she made her way down each step, she hurriedly stuffed the items under her arm. She didn't dare to look up until the clothing was gathered.

Heaping the clothes on the platform next to Roberto, where Arturo also stood with his quivering bottom lip, she gave them a stern look. "Stay put and don't you dare move an inch." She turned back, stretching her arms out toward Jorgé and the girls. As she did this she realized that the old brown suitcase blocked the top of the steps.

Jorgé shook his head. "I'm fine. You get the case. I told you, let me worry about the girls."

Perfie looked around at the people gathered on the platform.

Isaac. There he was, taller than everyone else and looking worried. Did he think they wouldn't come? She watched his face as he spotted her. It broke into a wide grin as he pushed his way through the crowd.

"Dad" yelled Roberto, running to Isaac and throwing his arms around his father's waist.

She watched Isaac's gaze move around, then stop on Jorgé and the girls. The smile slipped from his face and his forehead creased.

Arturo ran toward his father. Isaac's face was like a stone, lips turned down, no twinkle in his eyes. She felt her head begin to shake back and forth while she silently screamed her denial. This was not at all how she planned the scene of reuniting with Isaac.

Her exhaustion overwhelmed her, and Perfie felt tears forming behind her pulsating forehead. That will only make it worse, she thought.

She took a breath and forced herself to smile through her dismay. She set the suitcase down and rushed across the platform to Isaac. She flung her arms around him, trying for a loving hug, but Roberto and Arturo were wedged between them.

"We had cookies, Dad. Two each!"

Isaac's body was rigid as he whispered closely into her ear, "Who is that?"

She kept her voice low in the hope that Roberto and Arturo would not hear her reply. "Just some gentleman from the train who helped us out. I don't even know his name."

Jorgé approached. She turned and reached for Geri, but Isaac stepped past her, his arms held out for the baby.

The baby didn't remember her father. She buried her head in Jorgé's neck. Isaac's arms dropped to his sides. He looked down at Karleen. She kept a tight grip on Jorgé's hand and moved her body behind his legs.

"Girls, say hello to Daddy." Perfie coached.

Jorgé seemed to read the situation and pulled Karleen from behind him. He pushed her toward Isaac. As Karleen let go of his hand and moved to her father, Jorgé peeled Geri away from his neck and handed her to Perfie. With a brief, somewhat sad smile, he turned and walked down the platform toward the exit.

"Adíos Jorgé," Roberto called out. Jorgé waved over his shoulder without turning his head.

Isaac's eyes flashed. "Don't know his name?" His voice was tight.

Perfie turned away. Balancing Geri on one hip, she started to bundle the pile of belongings. She spread the piece of cloth out on the platform and piled the clothing onto it before drawing the cotton rope tight around it, working awkwardly with one hand. She didn't want to put Geri down. The baby was like a protective shield against the crazy events.

Arturo and Roberto hopped up and down next to their father and started asking questions: *where are we going to live, do you have anything to eat, do we have a car, are you a movie star now?* Perfie used the distraction to avoid talking to Isaac—to avoid answering his question.

Isaac turned his attention to the boys. He tucked Roberto's bundle of belongings under his right arm, picked up the brown case with his right hand and grasped Karleen's hand with the left. "Come on. I have a surprise for you—hamburgers."

As the family left the train station, Perfie knew he was not done with the issue and that her hope for a new start in this new place would be tainted by the old problems.

Isaac pulled a key from his pocket. He led the family across the road to a dirt parking lot.

I wish I knew where we were going, Perfie thought. But how do I ask him? What do I say when he says nothing at all? Oh, why did I ever talk to Jorgé? Now things are all wrong when they should be right.

Isaac stopped in front of a truck. The color was questionable, and the rust spots, randomly spaced in blue oceans of the oxidized paint, were like the continents on a map of the world. On the bed of the truck the rust land masses had deep dark lakes in the center; these proved to be holes, Perfie saw, when she got a little closer.

Isaac banged the door with the heel of his hand, and as it swung open he grabbed it with the other hand to keep the sagging hinges from losing their grasp completely. Perfie walked around to the other side, noting the slick, treadless tires.

Would her children be safe in this vehicle? Too drained to protest, she lifted Geri, then Karleen, into the cab and settled them on a scratchy woolen blanket. When she pulled herself in, the handle came loose in her hand and she had to lean forward to keep from falling and squashing the girls.

The weak springs of the seat dropped her down four inches lower than she expected. She grasped the door frame and pulled it shut, then settled the girls in her lap.

Isaac lifted the bundles of belongings and the boys over the tailgate into the bed of the truck.

He moved the boys to the center of the bed near the cab. There was no window, just an open space, so the boys could talk to their parents. Isaac piled the bundles around them in a protective shelter.

"Sit tight," he warned.

He didn't speak to Perfie until he was in the truck.

"Off we go!" He turned the key, and the truck gasped three times before a cloud of black exhaust shot out the back and the engine grumbled to a start.

After they had collected the crates from the freight platform, Isaac drove the truck along the wide paved streets and listened to the boys chatter as they kneeled with faces pressed through the windowless space. He still didn't speak to her.

Perfie kept her face turned to the window. This world was so different from Albuquerque: bigger buildings, houses closer together and so much green. She could see trees covering the hills off to the west, and in the gaps between the trees were roads and houses built here and there. She wondered if the people who lived there came down much.

"How far do we go?" she asked Isaac. She still didn't ask him where they were going.

"I thought I'd take you on a little tour." At least he answered.

"I'm hungry, Dad. When do we get those things you said, those burglars."

Roberto quickly corrected his brother. "Hamgurburgers, you dummy."

166

Isaac smiled. "Hamburgers. Soon. I'm thinking a root beer will go good with those burgers."

They drove down a wide street to the west. As they turned a corner, Perfie gasped at the vast expanse of blue water in front of them. Was this the ocean?

But she saw the irregular shapes of buildings on the other side and realized her mistake. She hadn't known the bay would be so big; on the map it looked long and narrow.

"What's the name of that lake?" Roberto asked.

Perfie spoke up before Isaac could respond. "It's not a lake. It's the San Francisco Bay." Now maybe Roberto would have some respect for her.

"Can we go swimming?" he asked.

"Before the burgers?" Isaac teased.

"No!" The boys yelled.

"No." Karleen echoed.

"No, no, no." Baby Geri jabbered, and the Martinez family laughed.

Twenty-Four

Isaac sat on the edge of the bed. The room had seemed small before the arrival of his family—now it was miniscule. He had moved in two weeks ago. Daniel Noriega had agreed that they could rent this room for a month, just until they found a bigger place.

Now, with the boys sent out to the yard to burn off some energy, the baby asleep and Karleen playing on the dirty wooden floor, he couldn't see how they were going to manage. He had imagined everyone being so happy to be together that the tight space wouldn't matter. But only one hour in the room, and the walls closed in rapidly.

Isaac didn't have much money. Just the splurge on hamburgers would have been enough to buy food for a week. But he wanted to show them how much he missed them, how great California was, how nice it was to be a whole family again. He was thirty-nine years old and he had nothing. He hadn't felt that way a month ago with the thought of his kids and Perfie coming to be here with him. *My boys are the best, and my wife, what a beauty*, he had told the guys at the plant. But the way Perfie looked at him when she got off that train wasn't what he had dreamed.

And what about that man behind her who was carrying his kids?

Perfie hadn't said a word when he explained that the room was temporary. She set the sleeping Geri down on the bed, put her suitcase against the wall and lay down beside her.

Perfecta was pale and thin, but as beautiful as ever. He had been so excited to see her. He couldn't let it rest.

"So what about this Jorgé?"

She didn't raise her head from the folded blanket that served as a pillow. "He was just a man on the train. He felt sorry for us, Isaac. I was embarrassed. The kids were crying and I had no money to buy them food. You were here, enjoying these fancy hamburgers and all this fresh fruit.

Don't you dare pretend to know how it has been for me." She burst into tears.

He kept his voice quiet. He wasn't going to yell about this, but he couldn't let it go. "The way he looked at you. Do you think I'm a fool not to see it?"

"Why do you always have to be so jealous?"

He almost laughed. For years she had thought he had a girlfriend or even a whole family in California. Back in T.A. he couldn't even go out with Bennie or Eli without a week of silence from Perfie. He knew she hadn't been so faithful. Enoch had told him about the dances, about how she and Isabelle snuck over to Los Ojos to listen to her brother's band, and about how she flirted with Benjamin.

Isaac watched as her face changed, her forehead creasing and her eyes narrowing.

"You have a new girlfriend, don't you. You're trying to make it my fault so that you can leave me." She paused, but he could see she was working herself up, her breath rapid and her hands curled into fists.

She sat up and faced him. "Well it won't work, it won't work at all. We're here now, me and *your* four children."

This was unbelievable. She had managed to turn it around. He felt his patience drain. "How can you think that? I've been working day and night, extra shifts so that you could be here with me." He stood up and faced her.

She shook her head and jumped up, her face close to his. "Then why do you do this to me? Why do you greet me with such suspicion? I didn't do anything wrong. I never do anything wrong, but things just go wrong." Perfie clutched both hands to her chest as if struck with a pain in her heart. Her eyes rolled back in her head.

Not this again, he thought, and stepped forward to catch her as she slumped to the ground. He placed his hand at the back of her head to keep it from hitting anything. Once she was down he slipped his hand out from under her head and stood up, leaving her on the floor.

The fainting spells had started when they moved into the adobe house. He had pressed Perfie to see Doctor Green, but she had refused.

"It's just a spell, from all the pressure," she had said. "It won't happen if people quit upsetting me." She had brushed aside his concern and used the ailment to try to gain the control she wanted over him.

But the trick was old. He knew there would be no point in reassurance, no point in trying to be helpful, no point in being angry. He reached down and picked up the sleeping baby. Geri didn't wake as he draped her over his shoulder.

He held his hand out to Karleen. "Come on. Let's go for a walk." She looked up at him as if he were a crazy man. "Really, it's okay. Mama needs a nap." His daughter looked at Perfie lying on the floor, then, stood and took her father's hand.

Outside the house Isaac and Karleen walked along the sidewalk down to the busy intersection. This part of town was new to him, but with eyes forward he sauntered down the street without noticing the houses or buildings around him. He didn't want to think about the days ahead, so he let his mind go blank and simply enjoyed the feel of the tiny hand in his, the warmth of the baby on his shoulder and the rhythm of his steps as they took him away from his thoughts.

Buckets

Twenty-Five

Roberto pressed his chin onto the ledge of the truck bed and leaned his head out to feel the wind in his hair. He was wedged in a tiny space, all their belongings once again packed in the back of the truck.

Would this place have bugs in the beds? He didn't want to spend teach night crowded against Arturo and his sisters, all of them tossing and turning and scratching. Maybe it would have a light. That room at the last place was so dark. He wasn't a baby but he didn't like bumping around when he had to go pee. He wished they had never left New Mexico. He thought about asking if he could go back to live with Tito and Abuela. He would sleep on the back porch if there was no other room. Or maybe he could sleep up there at top of the house in Dad's old room with the slanting ceiling. Tío Bennie wouldn't mind.

He would go to the school, La Academia. He hadn't been old enough before, but he was nine now.

That was another reason he hated California. No one had even remembered it was his birthday today. No biscochitos, no present.

Nine was still too young for La Academía, but maybe because his abuelo loved him he would let him come anyway. Tito owned the school; that must mean he could do what he wanted.

Roberto knew he had another grandfather, Mama's dad. That abuelo didn't love him. Tía Bella had taken Roberto to see his grandfather. She had said they would go again, but that never happened. Too bad. Roberto knew Mama's dad was sheriff, and that meant he had a gun and got the bad guys. Mama had a fight with her dad and so they never got to see him.

He wasn't surprised. Mama had fights with everyone. She was so mad all the time. He tried to stay out of her way, but these places they lived didn't give him anywhere to hide. He played outside, but even then she would come out on the porch and yell at him: too noisy, too messy, not helping out. He couldn't seem to do anything right.

He pulled his head out of the wind and leaned against the wooden crate that held Mama's washing machine. Maybe there would be a kitchen in this place. Mama would cook a real dinner with three different things. He was tired of everything all mixed together in one pot. He wanted a fried egg, some bacon and potatoes with peppers. Each one separate.

When he closed his eyes he imagined the fork going into his mouth and he savored the memory of the sweet taste of the breakfasts he used to have.

"Happy Birthday," he whispered.

Twenty-Six

As Isaac guided the rattling truck through the streets of Oakland, Perfie looked at the run-down houses and old buildings. They soon left these behind and turned onto smaller streets that were lined with houses instead of businesses. Isaac pulled a crumpled slip of paper out of his pocket, glanced at it and tucked it back in.

"I wonder what Rose and Tom's place is like." She fished for details.

"This is a good neighborhood. I'm sure it will be fine."

Perfie was tired of moving. In the two months since she brought the kids to California they had moved seven times. Isaac had found friends and cousins willing to let them stay for a week or two. He kept promising a permanent place to live, but she didn't see how that was going to happen. They had barely enough money for food and his bus fare to work.

In most places they had a room to stay in even if they were crowded in tiny apartments with lots of other friends and relatives. But this meant all of them in one bed, or the kids on the floor if there was room. She hadn't slept a full night since they arrived in the Bay Area.

They just didn't have a way to earn enough money. It seemed that everyone else in the country had the same idea—find work in California. There were jobs; the ship yards and the auto plants were in full steam ,building things for the war that was taking over the whole world. But the housing situation was grim. Even a small apartment was three times what they could afford—and the chances of finding one at all were slim.

Isaac slowed the truck, looked at the street sign, then turned right. The street was treeless. Smooth sidewalks ran in front of the houses, which were built very close together. Each house had a small patch of grass in the front yard, with a concrete walk running from the front porch to the sidewalk. Some of the walkways were painted red, like giant tongues unrolling from the mouth of the house as if it would curl up and eat those who entered. The houses themselves were painted bright colors—pink, blue, green—unlike the earth tones of New Mexico. Some of the houses had rose bushes, hedges or flowers growing around the borders of the lawns.

As he drove the truck slowly down the street, Isaac checked the numbers. Perfie looked at each house. These were so nice she suspected he was in the wrong neighborhood. How would Rose and Tom afford a home like this? Her cousin had come to California five years ago, but as far as Perfie knew they weren't rich.

Isaac pulled the truck to a stop in front of a bright pink house. This one had a red sidewalk tongue. Yellow and pink flowers grew under the large front window and there was a lawn in front—deep green, thick and smooth as a carpet.

With the truck barely stopped, Roberto flung himself out of the truck bed, dropping onto the tiny strip of lawn that separated the sidewalk from the street. Arturo followed, landing like a graceful cat, and turned to open the door for his mother.

Perfie placed Geri into Arturo's waiting arms and reached for Karleen. The little girl slipped beneath her mother's reach, ducked her head down to escape Perfie's grasp and ran up the sidewalk. She was getting as wild as her brothers.

A screen door slammed and Perfie turned to see Rose standing on the porch with her hand raised to cover her squinted eyes as she stared out at the truck.

"Welcome. Welcome to California." Rose walked down the steps and opened her arms to gather Karleen and Roberto in a hug.

Perfie was surprised to see Karleen melt into Rose's arms. Karleen hadn't been this happy to see her own father. Roberto quickly stepped out of the hug, grinned and stuck out his hand.

"Men shake hands," Perfie heard him say. It was nice that he was picking up some good habits from the men in his life.

Rose was not put off so easily. "Oh, you are such a man, but you know you have to give your auntie a hug." With Karleen still in her arms Rose brought her lips to Roberto's cheek for a loud smacking kiss.

Perfie moved toward Rose with tears running down her cheeks. It had been many years, but she remembered her cousin. They used to play together during family visits until Rose would somehow make her cry, and that would be the end of it. Perfie had been desperate when she called her to explain that they needed a place to live.

"Oh, sweetie, what are these tears?" Rose embraced Perfie with one arm. Karleen reached her hand out to her mother's cheek and touched the wet trails.

"Why sad, Mama?"

"No, sweetie, not sad. Happy. Tears can be happy." It wouldn't do to start out on the wrong foot with Rose.

Isaac strode up the walkway and hugged Rose. "Thank you. This really means a lot to us. We won't be a bother. I'll make sure of it."

Perfie watched a funny look come over Rose's face. The bedraggled Martinez clan stood on the porch, waiting. Was Rose going to ask them to come in? Unload the belongings from the back of the truck? A hot wave of emotion swept over Perfie. Maybe she's not asking us in because she's changed her mind. Perfie licked her lips and tried to think of what to say.

"Are we going in the house?" Arturo spoke up, asking what they all wanted to ask.

Rose hesitated. "Of course, come on in." She turned and opened the wooden screen door and led the way into the house.

There was a tiny living room directly inside the front door. The walls of the room were lined with a long blue couch covered in plastic, an armchair, three round end tables strategically placed, and a wooden chair that seemed out of place. All this furniture left little room for standing. Perfie led the children to the couch and pointed.

"Sit, and don't move."

Roberto and Arturo rubbed their hands over the plastic and looked at each other with huge grins. They had never seen such a thing before. Embarrassed at the behavior of her sons, Perfie glanced at Rose, but Rose wasn't looking at them.

"I'll be right back. You all just sit right down here." Her flat heels tapped across the room and through a door.

Perfie looked across the room at Isaac, who was seated in the armchair. He raised his eyebrows, shrugged his shoulders and gave a slight shake of his head. She put Geri down on the floor and followed Rose out of the room through a narrow hallway and into the kitchen.

Yellow walls, a shiny linoleum floor, red tile counters and the most beautiful sink Perfie had ever seen greeted her there. The sink was white porcelain with a special drainer set in one end. It was large enough to bathe a small child. Rose opened the painted yellow cabinet and took out glasses.

"You're probably thirsty. Do the children need milk?"

"No, no. Don't go to the trouble. We stopped for some hamburgers on the way." Immediately she realized her mistake. What would Rose think of a family who begged for a place to stay and then spent money on hamburgers?

All Perfie really wanted was to see the room where they would stay. Then she wanted to lie down to ease the burning pain in her stomach.

"Oh." Rose placed the glasses back on the shelf. Turning to Perfie, she forced a smile onto her lips, but the smile never reached her eyes. "I see."

"Maybe you could show me where we'll stay? Isaac and Roberto can unload the truck."

"Okay." Rose turned and walked through a doorway and into a narrow room with a washer and a large sink on one side. She opened the door at the back of the little room.

Perfie followed, eyes wide with disbelief that there was a whole room dedicated to laundry and that there was even more to the house. It hadn't seemed that big from outside.

She quickly realized her mistake. The door led out onto a concrete porch. Rose was already down the steps and walking toward the edge of the house. As Perfie hurried to catch up with her she saw Rose walk around the corner.

When she turned the corner she saw her cousin reach for the handle of a slanted wooden door. A storm cellar? Why are we going down there? Perfie felt a sudden hopelessness sweep over her body.

They were going to live there. In the basement. Not even in a room of the house. This was worse than any of the places they had stayed.

Rose lifted the latch and used both hands to fling the large wooden door to one side. She made her way down a short flight of concrete stairs. Perfie watched as her cousin waved one hand in front of her, making wide circles in the dark room.

"There it is." Rose grasped a chain which hung in the center of the opening. With a tug she turned on a single bulb which lit the stairs. "Watch your step."

Perfie followed, straining to see what was below. Rose crossed the room to a switch and turned on a second overhead light. The room emitted a cold, cruel smell, like a deserted barn that had once been filled with cattle.

"Tom cleared some things to make room for you. I'm afraid there's no toilet or water down here. It's really meant for storage, you know."

Perfie looked around the room. The floor was concrete with stains spreading across it in random designs. There was a small window up near the ceiling, and a tiny bit of sunlight shone through it to leave a bright rectangle in the middle of the room—one bright patch on the gray floor. The air was cold and damp. She realized this room lay almost entirely below ground. The shelves that lined two of the walls were crowded with forgotten items: ice skates, a bent lantern, stacks of magazines, a hat box with a blue ribbon, rolled canvas that looked like a tarp or a tent. Old paint buckets were stacked in the far corner.

In the center of the room were two mattresses that had been placed side by side. A stack of blankets sat neatly folded in the middle of the closer mattress. There were two wooden chairs and a small table pushed against the wall that had no shelves. Next to the table sat a tin bucket.

Rose walked to the bucket and picked it up, turning to Perfie.

"You can use this to bring water down here. I'll show the boys where the spigot is—the one out in the yard, I mean."

"Gracias." Perfie walked over to the mattresses and placed her palm on the stack of blankets. "Thank you for the blankets. I was only able to bring a few quilts. We couldn't carry much on the train."

"Hello?" Isaac poked his head down through the wooden doors.

"Here. We're down here." She tried to keep her voice from shaking.

Isaac looked around the room, his usual grin in place. "Well, this is fine, just fine." His gaze skimmed over Perfie's face. Clearly he didn't want to meet her eyes. He walked over to the bucket. "This for water?"

"Yes. Let me show you where the spigot is." Rose hurried back up the steps and Isaac followed.

Perfie stood next to the mattress. It's only for a little while, she told herself. But she knew this wasn't true. They had used up the hospitality of all of Isaac's friends and the rest of the cousins. Rose and Tom were the last resort. They wouldn't leave this place until they had a place of their own—or until they were out on the street.

Isaac and the boys hauled the crates out of the truck and fit some into the basement and others into the garage behind the house. Perfie made up the beds by spreading the blankets over each mattress. She discovered that one of these makeshift beds was a box spring, not a mattress at all. She spread extra blankets across it; this would have to do for padding.

She moved some things to make space on the shelves for their clothes and pulled the table out from the wall. She placed one of the crates next to the wall and set the hot plate and the box of dishes on it. At least there was electricity down here.

Isaac seemed to guess that she was near the end of her rope. He offered to take the children for a walk.

"I believe there's a park just down the street. I think Mama could do with some rest."

The children followed him out of the basement. The bang of the heavy wooden door shot like a lightning bolt through her aching head.

Perfie eased herself down to sit on the mattress and stretched her feet straight out in front of her. Kicking off her shoes, she bent her knees and pulled her heels to the edge of the mattress.

Why did I wear these shoes today? As if I could impress Rose with how I dressed. She rubbed her hands across both her feet—they were hot and swollen.

She flopped straight back, leaving her legs draped onto the floor. The ceiling had been covered in some sort of plaster at some point in time, but now the plaster was chipped and stained. Perfie connected the dots randomly, searching out some sort of pattern. There really was no pattern at all, she thought. Not like the clouds, where she could see the shapes of animals or people. Not like the blue skies of New Mexico.

I need to make a plan. But her thoughts were like the ceiling; there was no pattern at all. She closed her eyes and let exhaustion move up through her body like a wave upon the sandy shore. A wave that sucked the last bit of her consciousness away with it as it slipped back into the sea.

Twenty-Seven

Perfie stood Geri in the small dishpan of water and used the worn washcloth to soap her squirming body. In four months her youngest child would be two years old—not much of a baby anymore. Geri tried to sit. She had been used to a much bigger tub, the large barrel Isaac had cut in two back in Tierra Amarilla. He had placed half of the barrel on the back porch there, close to the kitchen and the stove for hot water. The other half sat across the yard and was filled with water for Perfie's two milk cows. This way the cows would come across the flat pasture to get a drink and Perfie could catch them each morning for milking.

It had been a big job to bathe everyone, requiring many trips from the stove to the barrel. When they were finished it took both Perfie and Isaac to tip the water out over the edge of the porch into the small clay trough that led to the garden.

Now, here in California, this tiny dishpan was not even big enough for her smallest child to sit in. Using a cup to try to rinse the soap off of Geri, Perfie scooped water out of the pan near the toddler's feet and poured it over her head. Geri squirmed, her eyes squeezed tight. She nearly upset the pan, and water splashed out onto the table and floor.

"Stop it. You should be happy you get a bath." Perfie thought about how she would love a real bath instead of the rag and pan-of-water method. She was tired of sponging off a small section of her body, then dipping the rag into barely warm water to wipe down the next part.

She stood Geri on a towel and dried her off before dressing her in the worn blue flannel nightgown that had been Karleen's. The shoulders hung down to Geri's elbows, the hem past her feet.

The children were growing and this gown, which she had expected would fit Karleen for a while, was now so tight across her shoulders that she couldn't lie down comfortably. So Geri was in the gown, while Karleen used one of Arturo's t-shirts as her nightly wardrobe.

Perfie turned back to the dishpan, dipped the rag into the soapy water and wrung it out before wiping off her own face and arms. The water was still warm enough to feel good on the back of her neck, but she felt so grimy that this did little to comfort her.

She ran a hand through her hair and scratched the grit of the corn meal she'd brushed into her scalp in an attempt to clean her oily hair. It had been three weeks since she'd washed it.

She wiped the splashed water from the table with the washcloth, then lifted the dish pan and set it on the floor. Kicking off her shoes and sinking into the chair, she leaned back and dipped her feet into the pan. With her heels against one end and her toes slightly curled so that her feet could be covered with the remaining water, Perfie closed her eyes and tried to think of nothing at all.

But her mind bounced from one worry to the next. She had to do something about how they were living. Tomorrow she would talk to Tom. Maybe he would be sympathetic to her struggle to keep clean.

Perfie heard the screen door slam and the clickity sound of Rose's heels on the concrete stairs of the back porch. Rose's shrill voice broke into Perfie's conversation with Tom.

"Tom?" Rose called.

Perfie knew that Tom would have to go now, but she was grateful for his help. "Gracias. Thanks." She smiled at her cousin's husband.

"De nada. No problem at all." Tom turned and started back to the house just as Rose came around the corner. "Rose, what is it?" he asked.

Rose was holding a bag of food with carrots poking over the top. She looked at Tom, then turned and looked at Perfie. "What are you doing?"

Perfie felt fifteen years old, as though she were talking with someone else's boyfriend.

Tom answered. "I was helping Perfie with the lights. One of the bulbs burned out." He reached and took the bag from Rose. "Are there more?"

Rose cleared her throat and licked her lips and her eyes flashed sparks.

Okay, I get the message, Perfie thought. Stay away from your man. Don't worry, cousin, I have enough men to keep me more than busy.

She spoke aloud. "It was very dark in the basement without the light. I try to get work done when that bit of sun shines in, but today I was behind."

Rose glared and walked away.

Yep, Perfie thought. She got my message, too.

Later that night Perfie regretted her unspoken battle with Rose. If she made her cousin mad where would they live? She tossed and turned, pulling the quilt off Isaac more than once.

Isaac pressed his body close to Perfie's back, reached his arm over her and held her wrist. "What's wrong? You're bouncing around like a fish out of water." He tugged the quilt back over his shoulder.

"Isaac. I can barely save any money. We have to think of a way to get more. I have to work or we'll never get out of this place."

"It's not so bad, is it? The boys have a good school."

She was happy when she found out Roberto and Arturo could start at the school just two blocks away. Lockwood Elementary was in a new brick building with young eager teachers and desks for every student. There were no nuns teaching public school here.

The boys started late, missing the first two weeks of class. Rose had gone to the office and registered them, assuring Perfie that they wouldn't be too far behind. Perfie walked with them the first day but was afraid to go in and meet the teacher. She stood at the edge of the playground and watched her boys walk cautiously among the other children.

Perfie had never seen so many children in one place. And there were so many different kinds of kids. The playground had dark faces and light faces, colored children, Oriental children and white children. She saw girls with colorful flowers in their hair and kids with patched clothes like Roberto and Arturo wore. California was truly an unusual place.

On the second day Roberto had told her she couldn't walk with them. It was too embarrassing, he said.

"Hey, you still there?" Isaac's nudge brought her back to the present.

"Yes, I know. It's just . . ." She paused. "It's so hard to keep everything clean. We need baths, real baths, not just this rag and water thing."

"Can't you ask Rose? I'm sure she'll let you take a bath upstairs."

Isaac didn't understand the war between the cousins. He got along with everyone so easily. Sometimes it made her mad that he didn't see the insults that were made to his family. He tried to tell her there was no need for revenge, but Perfie was adamant that they needed to send the message that this treatment wasn't okay. She didn't want her family to be at the bottom of the heap.

That's where we are, she thought. We're at the very bottom of the heap. She pulled Isaac's hand up under her chin, kissed it and closed her eyes. She was too tired to listen to his easy answers, and she didn't want to tell him about her mistake of getting into a silent battle with Rose. No use causing him to lose sleep, too.

Twenty-Eight

"**M**ama, here's a letter from Miss Mary." Roberto handed his mother a cream-colored envelope.

"*¿Quién es* Miss Mary?" Perfie hadn't heard that name before. "What did you get in trouble for this time?"

"No, I swear, I didn't do nothing."

Perfie turned and looked at Arturo. "What did your brother do?"

"We both had to go to the office. A lady with a white dress looked at us. Her name is Miss Mary. She's nice."

A lady in a white dress? A nun? Perfie turned the envelope over in her hands, then set it on the table.

Roberto stood still, staring at her.

"Go! Go on outside. Take the girls. They've been waiting for you all day."

Arturo raced up the steps and out the door. She watched Roberto follow after taking a final glance back at the letter.

She sat at the table and smoothed the envelope with her hands. She knew it would be bad. Roberto had been in trouble three times.

With a shake of her head she stood and went to the box that held Isaac's sharp knife. She slit the envelope and pulled out a folded sheet of paper. She ran her index finger across the two creases where the page had been folded and smoothed the paper flat.

The furrow in Perfie's forehead grew as she moved her finger over the print and slowly read each word.

Dear Mrs. Martinez . . . Acc . . . accor . . . ding . . . to . . . sss . . . .cchhh . . . hhh. . . . code five seven two three, your chi . . . child . . . ren. . .

She wanted to figure this out before Isaac came home, but the handwriting, which was flowery, with extra loops and swirls, was hard to read. She struggled to read in Spanish, let alone English, and these words were so unfamiliar.

She skipped to the second paragraph, *tre . . . at . . . ment for this must be ap . . . ap. . . leeed for four days p . . . pree . . . or to re . . . return to . . .* there was that word again . . . *sss . . . chh . . . ool.* School, that's what that word was.

She read through the letter twice before the meaning struck her. This letter was from the school nurse, the lady wearing white. Her children would not be allowed to attend school. The bugs in their hair, and something else, something called scabies, must be removed before they could go to school. There was some kind of medicine she would have to use on them.

She thought about the coins in the can tucked behind the tarp on the shelf. How hard she worked to put away a few cents each week in the hope of having enough to rent a place of their own. She folded the letter and slid it back into the envelope. As she stood she pushed the wooden chair back so quickly it let out a harsh, rasping scrape over the concrete floor before teetering and falling with a crash.

Leaving the chair where it lay, she rummaged through her brown suitcase, found the small bible she kept there and put the letter between the pages. As she turned to pick up the fallen chair, she heard the voices of Isaac and the boys coming down the driveway.

"Is something wrong?" Isaac asked, ducking through the low doorway and looking at her.

She didn't answer right away, turning away from him. To avoid him she started picking up things, putting them down again and folding clothes that seemed to already be folded.

"Supper's ready. Sit, it will get cold." She didn't join the family at the table while they ate. Instead she bustled around the hot plate, buttered more bread and wiped faces.

"Perfie, is everything all right?"

"I'm fine."

"You've been jumping around like a *chichada* on a summer night. You only do that when there's something we should talk about."

"No, it's nothing. Rose was just on my case today." Perfie didn't know why she didn't want Isaac to know about the letter. "Isaac, we have to move out of here."

Isaac wrapped his arms around her. "I know, my flower. I was hoping to get more hours at work." He shrugged. "There are so many men here now, and all of them are wanting more work."

She tried to relax in his arms. If she kept her back rigid he would know something was up. She pushed her mouth and nose into his shirt and inhaled the smell of him. Underneath the odors of his day—dust, exhaust, cigarette smoke—she could smell his warm, earthy scent. She let her breath out through pursed lips and caused a damp spot on his shirt. He rubbed his hand across her shoulders. If only she could just stand here all night and not meet his eyes.

"Mama, I peed."

Pulling herself away from Isaac's embrace, Perfie looked down to where Karleen stood, stockings wet.

Karleen had accidents all the time. At four years old she should be over that by now, but moving so much had interrupted potty training. Perfie had brought home a dented bucket she found in the dumpster behind the grocery store. She put the bucket in the corner for Karleen to use. This way they no longer had to take her upstairs and were able to avoid the hated sighs and glares from Rose. Perfie would use the bucket herself if she had any privacy at all. In fact, when the boys were at school, she did use it.

Perfie pulled Karleen over to the table and lifted her to stand on the chair. Rummaging through the folded laundry, she pulled out clean underwear and stockings. As she peeled the wet clothes off her daughter, Isaac went outside for his evening smoke. It was almost time to put the children to bed, and Isaac would follow.

That night, as every night, Perfie was the last to lie down after double checking that all were tucked in, shoes were lined up by the door and the door was shut tight. She slipped into bed beside Isaac, who was already snoring.

Tomorrow would be soon enough to show him the letter.

Twenty-Nine

Roberto watched his brother race across the playground and join in with the other six-year-old boys, running around in circles and chasing each other. Roberto glanced over to where the older boys stood, too cool to chase each other. He knew he wasn't welcome to stand close to them, and he would feel silly playing with the little kids.

"Roberto Martinez."

He looked up at the sound of his name. Miss Jo, the office lady, stood at the open door.

"What are you doing at school?"

"Huh?" He stopped and stared at her. What did she mean? Why wouldn't he be at school?

He watched as Miss Jo looked across the playground. "Go get your brother and come back here."

What now? He started off to where Arturo was playing.

"Faster." Miss Jo walked all the way out into the courtyard and crossed her arms. He broke into a trot.

When he returned with Arturo, who wasn't happy that his playtime had been interrupted, Miss Jo shook a pointed finger at them.

"Did you give your mother the letter?"

They both nodded.

Miss Jo scowled and glanced at the office. "You can't wait in here. Go out by the flagpole and sit on the bench. Don't move from there."

Arturo was swinging his legs rapidly back and forth from his perch on the bench. "Mama's gonna be mad. What did you do now?"

Roberto didn't reply.

"Hello boys." Miss Mary stood in front of them. Her eyes scanned up and down Roberto's body. He thought about what she saw.

The shirt he wore had been red plaid at one time, but now it was only a faded gray with a hint of pink. It was held closed with three buttons, each one different; his mother had sewn them on when he lost the others. His frayed undershirt peeked out from the open collar. The denim jeans, black with grime along the tops of the thighs and frayed at the knees, were too big for him. He had a long leather strap gathering the denim into an awkward bunch around his waist,

Unlike the filth of Roberto's pants, Arturo's clothes were clean, but too small. His skinny wrists poked out from the sleeves, and the cuffs were worn all the way through. His brown corduroy pants were too short, but baggy nonetheless.

His brother jumped off the bench. He ran to the nurse and wrapped his arms around her waist. "Miss Mary!"

Roberto saw Miss Mary smile and shiver as she peeled his brother's arms away and pushed him back to the bench. Why was Arturo so happy to see her? She was the one who had sent that letter home.

Miss Mary bent down. "Hello, Arturo. Did you give my note to your mother?" She glanced over at Roberto, but he stared straight ahead.

Turning back to Arturo she asked, "Did she read it?"

"Miss Mary, I did give it to her. She put it on the table and told us to go outside."

"Did she talk with you about it?"

Roberto finally turned his attention to Mary. "You never told us what was in the letter." He rubbed the edge of his mouth with his fist. "Mama asked what I had done wrong, just like she always asks. But I didn't do nothin' wrong."

He watched her face to see if she was going to yell. He knew it was wrong to talk back to a grown-up lady.

"Oh, Roberto. You're right. I'm sorry."

Sorry? It must be something terrible. It had to be something Arturo did, because he hadn't done anything. Lately.

Arturo hopped up and down. "Yeah, Miss Mary. Why did Miss Jo make us sit on the bench? Usually bad kids have to sit in the office." Roberto could tell his brother didn't care that *they* might be the bad kids.

Miss Mary was quiet. Roberto watched as she licked her lips and then rubbed her forehead with one hand. Finally, she seemed to decide that she would tell them.

"You know how yesterday I looked at your skin and your hair." She paused. "What I found there was something called scabies. Lice, too."

Arturo's legs stopped swinging and he held out his hand to examine the blistered red rash on his wrist. He gave it a scratch.

"Your mother has to buy special medicine and put it on your skin and hair. Other children can catch it from you, so Miss Jo didn't want you to sit near them."

Roberto sucked in his breath and hung his head. This was the worst thing ever. Much worse than getting in trouble for punching. He should have guessed; he knew Miss Mary was a nurse.

"Did your mother talk to your father about this?" Miss Mary was frowning at him now.

"No." His voice came out a whisper; the breath didn't want to leave his throat. He squeezed his fists into balls and held them tight against his lap. A tear leaked from his right eye and slid down his dirty cheek where it left a glistening trail, like a slug on a leaf.

Arturo was swinging his legs again and focusing on watching his feet move up and down. "I heard of lice. That means we have bugs on us, right?"

"Yes. They are tiny bugs." Mary looked at Arturo. "You have little sisters at home, right? They'll need the special medicine, too. And your parents."

At this the single tear turned into many, streaming from both of Roberto's eyes. No sound escaped his lips, thin white lines pressed together.

"Roberto." Straightening her knees and standing, Mary reached a hand out to his shoulder. "The bugs aren't that bad. The medicine will make them go away."

"No, it's not that." Arturo hopped off the bench and balanced on one foot as he spoke.

"What is it?"

"We can't come to school anymore, right?"

"Just for a few days. Just while your mother puts the special medicine on. Then the bugs will be gone and you can come back to school."

"Nope." Arturo switched feet and teetered as he balanced on the left foot.

"Yes, Arturo, really. The bugs will clear up and you can come back."

Roberto let out a strangled sob. "You don't understand."

"What is it, Roberto?" Mary turned back to him and leaned down, bringing her face close to his.

He turned his head to the side. "We can't get it."

"Well." Mary hesitated. "You can. You already have it."

"No!" The word shot out of Roberto's mouth. "The special medicine, we can't get the special medicine."

He heard her draw in a sharp breath. Now he was going to catch it. He had talked back too much.

"Oh, the medicine. Yes, Roberto, your mother can. It's easy to get. The pharmacy is just down the street. I wrote in the note to her how she could get it."

"Nope." Arturo was now attempting to twirl in a circle while balanced on one foot.

Roberto unclenched his fists, brought his hands up and dropped his face down to wipe away the tears with his sleeve. He lifted his chin and looked directly at Mary. "We don't got the money."

Miss Mary stood quickly and looked away from him. He watched as she stared at the window of the office. When he turned his head to see what she was looking at, he saw Miss Jo at the window.

He would run away, go back to Tierra Amarilla where there were no bugs and diseases that lived on kids—except for the really dirty kids who lived up by the mine. He jumped when Miss Mary stepped forward and patted his shoulder.

"Don't you worry. I'll make it work out. You wait here for a few more minutes." Turning from the boys, Mary walked back up the concrete path to the office.

What now? Roberto punched his leg with his fist and moaned.

It seemed forever, but Miss Mary finally came back to the bench. Roberto continued to stare blankly down the street, while Arturo crawled on the ground and ran his fingers in the crack between the concrete walkway and the spongy green lawn that decorated the front of the school.

"Got one." Arturo held up a pillbug, rolled tightly in a little ball in his palm. "Miss Mary, look what I found."

"How nice." Mary glanced at the bug as Arturo put it into the pocket on the front of his shirt.

"You're so stupid." Roberto scolded his brother. "Why do you want more bugs on you when we already have bugs on us?"

"It's okay, Roberto. Boys, I am going to drive you home. I need to talk to your mother about the special medicine and about coming back to school. Come on." Mary looked at Roberto as Arturo turned and reached for her hand.

Roberto was silent. He used his flannel sleeve to wipe the tracks of tears from his eyes and cheeks. He finally turned to look at her and stood, but he remained next to the bench.

Arturo tugged at Miss Mary's hand. "Come on."

Miss Mary turned and walked toward the parking area. She didn't look back at Roberto. He knew he had to go with her, but this day was going from bad to terrible in a hurry. He wasn't about to hold her hand and he wasn't going to walk next to her.

His brother didn't seem to catch on to what was happening.

Arturo skipped along beside Miss Mary. "Rolly bugs aren't bad, are they? My dad says they're fine. They don't bite and don't hurt you."

"They are fine, Arturo." Reaching the car, Mary opened the back door and Roberto watched his brother scramble into the car. She turned and looked at Roberto. He walked around to the passenger side, opened the back door, slid onto the blanket-covered seat and pulled the door sharply with both hands clasped to the handle. Miss Mary reached over Arturo's shoulder and made sure the blanket was tightly tucked between the seat and the back ledge.

The boys were silent as Mary drove. Arturo had started to talk with her, but Roberto kicked him. His brother was now riding with his nose pressed to the window and experimenting with blowing warm breath and watching the steaming patterns. When Mary slowed to look at the house numbers, Roberto spoke up.

"It's the pink house, up on the right."

Mary pulled the car to the curb. "This one?"

"Yes." Roberto had the door open before she had even taken the car out of gear.

Miss Mary started up the front walk, but she stopped when the boys headed in a different direction. Roberto realized she thought they lived in this wonderful house.

"No, Miss Mary. Not that way, this way." Arturo waved her over to the side of the house. He walked with one foot on each strip of the concrete in the driveway and made a game of balancing by rocking back and forth, legs spread wide. Roberto walked on the edge of the right track and stared down at his feet.

Keeping to the cement, Miss Mary followed them down the drive. Roberto stopped next to the large wooden door that slanted away from the bottom edge of the house. The door had a wooden handle with a piece of cotton rope tied to it, the end hanging down about a foot. He grasped the handle as Arturo grabbed the rope. As they both pulled the door open, he heard his sisters' shrill voices laughing and screeching.

"Mom!" He called out loudly so she would hear them over the noise the girls made.

"Who's there? Who is that?"

Mama rushed over to the bottom of the concrete steps. Her bright green eyes looked up to see who was opening the door. He looked at her and was glad she wore her pretty dress, the one with yellow blossoms and green leaves. Her hair was pulled back tight, not all crazy and loose like it was sometimes. He wanted Miss Mary to see he had a good mother.

"Mama, it's Miss Mary. She drove us home. We can't go to school because of the bugs."

A frown creased his mother's forehead, and she grabbed hold of the edges of the apron that covered her dress. She rushed up the steps.

He watched as she stumbled on the top step and flung her arms out to catch her balance.

Miss Mary stepped forward and reached out her hand. Mama flinched, jumped up the last step and regained her balance. She twisted her shoulders to the side as if to evade Mary's grasp. He watched her scowl at Miss Mary. The nurse took a step back.

"Mrs. Martinez? Hello, I'm Mary Kent. I sent you the letter? I'm the school nurse?"

"Hola—hello." Mama stood very still, not reaching out a hand and not returning Mary's smile. Roberto bit his lip. His mother was rude to Miss Mary, too. Surely the nurse would get mad now.

"Mama, we got bugs. We can't go to school." Roberto spoke with authority to his mother.

"Roberto, does your mother speak English?"

Mama didn't wait for him to answer. "Yes. I do."

He saw Miss Mary's face turn red. "I'm sorry. I didn't mean, what I mean is . . ."

"It's okay. I know the boys have lice. I didn't want my husband to know."

Mama didn't want Dad to know?

"They can't come back to school until the treatment. Roberto told me you don't have the money for the medicine."

Mama's jaw clenched and her teeth made a grinding sound as her eyes swept over to him, then back to Miss Mary. "No, Mrs. Mary, we have the money. I will get the medicine."

"I can help if you like." Mary reached in her satchel and pulled out some bottles. "It is important that you follow the directions carefully, or the lice won't all be killed." She held out the bottles and waited for Mama to take them.

As Mama reached for the medicine, Miss Mary tapped the label. "Here, read this. It tells exactly what to do."

"Hello?" A high-pitched voice came sweeping around the corner of the house. Mama snatched the bottles from Mary and tucked them under her apron.

It was Aunt Rose. "I thought I heard voices."

Roberto couldn't help but notice how different she looked from his mother. She was dressed in a white blouse with that fancy stitching on the collar. She wore a sparkling necklace with a shiny pink stone dangling at the end of a golden chain. She looked like a fancy, rich lady.

Miss Mary looked at Aunt Rose. "Hello."

Mama glanced over at Mary and gave just the slightest shake of her head. Roberto saw Miss Mary nod.

"I'm Rose, the owner of this house. Can I help you with something?" Aunt Rose's hands went to her hips as she puffed out her chest and raised her chin.

"Hello. It's so nice to meet you. I'm Mary." Miss Mary paused. "A friend of Perfecta's. I dropped by for a visit."

Roberto sucked air in through his nose and watched Mama's eyes grow wide. Miss Mary was lying!

"A friend of Perfecta's?" Aunt Rose's tone made it clear she couldn't imagine such a thing.

"Yes," Mary replied. "I was in the area."

"Oh. Well. Nice to meet you." Rose stood still. Mama and Miss Mary stared at her silently. Rose glanced from face to face, then turned and walked back around the corner of the house without another word.

"Mrs. Martinez? Can we go inside? I'd like to talk to you." Miss Mary motioned toward the basement.

Mama twisted her apron and looked at Miss Mary. "If we are to be friends you must call me Perfie."

"And you can call me Mary."

His sisters ran to Mama and clutched her legs.

"Who do we have here?" Miss Mary crouched and smiled. The girls giggled and pushed their faces into Mama's skirt.

Roberto followed them in and stayed quiet. Mama would send him away if she noticed him. He watched her rush to the beds and pull the quilts straight.

"I'm sorry, it's such a mess in here," she said to Miss Mary as she hurried to the table and wiped it off with the edge of her apron.

"It's fine, really. Can we sit and talk?" Miss Mary waved her hand to the table.

"Would you like some tea?"

"No. I'm fine." Roberto saw her glance at the hot plate and camp stove set up on an old wooden trunk. A bucket of water sat next to it. No, no tea for her, thank you very much. He knew she was used to something much better than this. Even in New Mexico people didn't drink out of old buckets that sat in the corner.

When the two women were seated at the tiny table, Miss Mary jumped right to the point and asked Mama questions. *How long have you been living here? Do you have any toilet? What do you do for bathing? Water?*

Mama's answers were short, single yes and no, shakes of her head.

"Rose? The woman? Does she rent this place to you?" Miss Mary asked.

Suddenly Mama burst out, her hands waving in front of her as she spoke.

"Rose is good to us. She's letting us stay in her basement. It's better than the last place we lived. She's my cousin. Family. She did move the old paint cans and garden things. And the mattresses, she gave us those. The last place we slept on an old couch and the floor. I was lucky, there was some sale or something and she bought new mattresses for upstairs. That's how we got the old ones."

Miss Mary and Roberto both stared. What had come over Mama?

"I'm just asking. I'm a nurse. I need to make sure everything is—" Miss Mary paused. "Good. Everything is good for you and your children."

"It's good. She gave us a dishpan and some buckets, one for drinking, one for bathing, one for dishes."

"What about a toilet?" Miss Mary looked around.

Mama looked at a bucket in the corner.

"No." Miss Mary shook her head. "Not that?"

"Just for the kids. We can go upstairs." Mama waved a hand upward. "We use the toilet up there."

"What about washing the clothes?"

"I wash them once a week. Isaac, my husband, he set up my washer in the back yard." Mama hesitated. "I thought maybe Rose would let us use her washer. It's kind of amazing. It has its own room up there and is hooked up to drain down that sink. You don't have to haul water outside. She didn't want mine in the yard, but I guess she didn't want me to use hers."

Roberto noticed a change in Mama as she spoke. The scowl and suspicious attitude seemed to have flown out the narrow window. She liked Miss Mary, Roberto thought. Good, maybe I won't be in so much trouble.

He watched as Miss Mary smiled at Mama. "I think I do want some tea."

The change in Mama's face was wonderful to watch. Her green eyes lit up and the smile took over her face. He loved it when she looked so happy. She jumped out of the chair and went to the little camp stove.

Mama took out two china cups, one with pink flowers on it and one with a gold design. She turned and stood at the table. She held up one cup in each hand and tilted her chin to one side. She seemed to be considering something.

"Compared to everything else in our life, you could say that Rose has been a real saint to us."

Now Mama had decided to lie, too.

Robin Martinez Rice

Hot Springs

Thirty

Perfie lined up the bottles of chemicals and soaps on the table. She read the instructions three times. She felt like a mad scientist in a horror story. The process of ridding her children of scabies and lice was extremely complicated. And it wasn't going to take hours—it was going to take days.

Repeat the above after an interval of 2 hours. It seemed to her that it would take two hours just to get through the treatment once with four children. And then she had to do it all again.

She opened the bottle marked Sodium Thio-sulphite and sniffed it.

Although it looked like water it smelled like rotten eggs. This is what she was going to paint all over her naked children?

She opened the next bottle. A sharp, burning odor immediately filled the room. She looked at the label—Hydrochloric acid. She was supposed to put acid on her children? She tilted the bottle and dipped the tip of her smallest finger into the liquid. It did burn, but not as much as she imagined.

"Roberto. Come here."

"What stinks?" He wrinkled his nose as he came to the table.

"The medicine. We have to do the medicine today. Take off your clothes."

"No." He folded his arms across his chest and glanced at the girls. "I won't do it."

"Arturo, take your sisters out back to play." She grasped Roberto's arm and with one hand awkwardly started to unbutton his shirt. "You want to go back to school, don't you? Remember what Miss Mary said."

He shook his head, but he didn't run or struggle as she stripped him. His eyes grew large and he chewed his lip as she used the little brush to paint his body with the stinky egg solution. When she finished she spread a ragged towel on the floor.

"Sit. Now we have to let it dry before the next step."

"How long?" He smeared the solution when he folded his legs and wrapped his arms around his body.

"No! Don't rub. Be careful." She grabbed his hands. "Fifteen minutes."

"Will you put the clock where I can see it?"

"I will, but the others have to come back in now. I have to start on them."

She took the clock off the shelf and set it on the table. Then she headed out to the yard to get the others.

It seemed like barely any time at all had passed when Roberto called out "Fifteen minutes are done." Arturo sat in the other chair and held Geri in his lap. They watched Perfie paint the solution on the wiggling Karleen.

Not trusting Karleen to stay in one place if she set her on the floor, Perfie sat her on a chair, then turned to Arturo. "Keep her still. Keep her on the towel."

Arturo grabbed his sister's arm. "She's slippery."

"Don't move, *M'jita*. Stay put."

Roberto stood facing away from the others. With his bony shoulder blades and dropped chin, he looked like the wartime photos of children Perfie had seen in magazines. She uncapped the bottle of acid.

Although he shuddered a little as she painted on this solution, he didn't seem to be in pain. Maybe the shiny layer of stinky medicine protected his skin from the acid's sting.

"Finished. Sit." She realized she hadn't timed Karleen's first layer. "What time was it when we started?"

"It was 9:30. Or maybe just a little later."

She looked at the clock. 9:45. She could paint Karleen's next layer before starting on Arturo and Geri.

Roberto shivered. "Now how long, Mama? Another fifteen minutes?"

"Yes, and two hours. Figure out when it will be two hours."

"Two hours? I have to be naked for two hours?" His voice was high pitched. Forgetting his modesty he turned to stomp his foot.

"Sí, we have to do it twice today and again tomorrow."

"Then will we be done?"

"I can't remember. Here, why don't you read the directions while you dry." She handed him the blue paper, then turned back to Karleen. She carefully put her hands into the girl's armpits to avoid smearing the first layer and stood her back up on the chair.

Five hours later, the basement smelled as if a hundred rotten eggs had burst. It smelled like the sulfurous hot springs of Ojo Caliente. Imagine, people paid to sit in those springs. Perfie shook her head.

I wonder if sitting in the springs kills the bugs? It would be a much easier solution. Of course Ojo Caliente was in New Mexico, and she was in California. She didn't remember anyone having trouble with scabies back home, but there had been bouts of head lice.

Perfie thought about making tea but couldn't get her body in motion. The boys were playing and the girls had fallen asleep.

"Mama, this sticks." Roberto pulled up the sleeve of his flannel shirt.

She turned to him, but didn't answer.

He stared at her. "Don't you have to paint the stuff on you?"

Of course she did. But that would have to wait until Isaac was home. She would send the kids out and they would paint each other. A smile touched her lips. It reminded her of a book Joe had. She sneaked a look when he wasn't home. Crazy sex things that couples could do with each other.

Whoever wrote that book hadn't spent the day caring for four children.

When Isaac had finished painting the last layer of acid on Perfie, he took her face in his hands and looked straight into her eyes. "Don't panic."

"What?"

"We have to do the hair too."

She had forgotten about the hair oil and the little comb. It was bedtime and she just wanted to hurl her body down and cover her head.

Isaac went to the door and called the kids. They had been playing outside for two hours and were thrilled to be allowed to run screeching through the dark backyard. As they came back into the house, Perfie could see they were somewhat subdued.

"What happened out there? You didn't do anything to make Rose mad, did you?"

"No Mama, we're tired." Roberto had dark circles under his eyes. "Is it bedtime?"

"Not quite." Isaac patted his son on the shoulder. "We have to treat the hair."

Perfie pulled herself up from the chair and got the oil and comb off of the shelf.

Isaac lifted Geri onto his lap. Her hair was snarled into a bird's nest. He started to brush the tangles out.

She squealed and twisted. "No. Want Mama."

"Sshh. Sit still, it's nice." He rubbed her shoulders, but she continued to wiggle.

Roberto sat on the other chair while his mother worked on his hair with the nit comb. He hadn't had a hair cut for a long time. His brown hair curled close to his head. She had to grasp each spiral between her finger tips and pull it straight to get the comb down to his scalp.

Geri's voice grew louder and her body thrashed on her father's lap. "Mama."

Isaac looked across the table at Perfie. "Are you thinking what I'm thinking?"

"I suppose I am."

He set Geri on the floor and went to the small brown leather box he kept on the shelf. He removed the slender scissors with the tell-tale hook on the handle. These had been purchased years ago on one of his trips to Albuquerque when it was clear to the young couple they needed to save money by cutting each other's hair. Isaac kept the scissors sharp, and with all the haircuts he had given through the years, he had become quite the barber. Setting the scissors on the table, he turned and picked up an apple from the bowl on the shelf. He pulled out his pocket knife and cut it into thin slices.

"*M'ija*, here's a treat." He picked Geri up, set her on a pillow he had placed on the chair and handed her a wedge of apple.

Twenty minutes later the Martinez children had matching haircuts, as short as Isaac's sharp scissors could manage. Perfie put her hand to her throat. Her children really looked like war victims now. The shorn hair made their eyes stand out. The round circles with pupils turned upwards seemed so sad.

"What about yours?" Isaac held up the scissors and waved them toward her head.

"No."

"Let's get these imps to bed and I'll brush yours out."

Ten minutes later she sat with her eyes closed as Isaac searched for nits. The tiny comb on her scalp soothed her. Funny how time could make something like a treatment for head lice seem romantic.

The next morning the kids were up early jumping on the bed. Perfie rolled over and felt the empty space where Isaac should be.

"Isaac?" She opened her eyes.

"He's gone, Mama. He went to work." Roberto was sitting at the table, spooning cereal into his mouth.

"What time is it?" She sat up. Sun streamed through the tiny rectangle window. She looked at the clock. Nine. *If only I could just keep sleeping.* She flopped back onto the mattress and closed her eyes.

Within two seconds she felt warm breath in her ear. "Good morning, Arturo," she said.

"What are we going to do today?" He bounced beside her.

"I don't know." What *was* she going to do today with four stir-crazy children? Just the thought of having them home all week made her body tight and her head hurt.

She pulled herself out of bed and slipped into her gray shawl. The mornings were growing colder. Isaac didn't like to run the electric heater, but she usually turned it on when he left for work. She left it on just long enough to take the chill off the room.

"I made you tea." Roberto spoke around a mouth full of cereal.

She looked over at the camp stove. Water bubbled in the old pot. Tea leaves were scattered on the make-shift counter and the floor.

"You spilled my tea! That's what you did." She rushed over to sweep what she could back into the jar. But there was water spilled too, and most of her precious tea was wet and unsalvageable. "Why can't you just keep out of my things?"

She wasn't looking at Roberto, so she didn't see his jaw tighten. She only heard the slamming of the heavy door as he ran out of the basement.

Thirty-One

Perfie finished wiping off the table and looked at the tiny silver clock that had been a going-away present from Isabelle. 2:30. Mary Kent would be here soon.

"Please, God. Make it be today that we are through with all of this," she whispered the prayer out loud. I know the bugs are gone. How could they still be around after all that work? Mary had told her the boys needed a final inspection before they could return to school.

Perfie was exhausted, not only from having the boys home for two weeks, but from the constant mess they made and the added work of washing all the clothes and bedding. Isaac had helped her, but it was cold now and they both had chapped hands and aching shoulders from hanging heavy wet blankets on the line. Nothing was quite dry when the sun went down, but they had to use the blankets at night, so down they came.

Mary told her everything should be washed a second time a week after the treatment. And they need to be bleached, too, but that just wasn't going to happen. Isaac couldn't help her again, and there was a chance of rain.

The blankets looked terrible and had big faded spots after being bleached. She had used a tiny amount of bleach on the clothes, but they were so faded already that they didn't look much worse. Good thing most of their clothes were still packed away in crates and didn't have to undergo this treatment.

Perfie refused to bleach her mother's quilt or even to wash it with the harsh soap. She hadn't been able to bring much with her from New Mexico —only a few things of her mother's. Her father had never let her back into the house, but Isabelle had brought her the quilt and the tortoise shell mirror and hairbrush, probably without Primitivo knowing anything about it. That was when Isabelle had brought her the little white angel, although Perfie hadn't unpacked her since they arrived in California.

Yesterday, during the brief bit of time when the sun poked its timid face out from behind the rain clouds, Perfie hung the quilt outside to air and beat and shook it to remove all the bugs. She hoped that would do the trick, but she wasn't putting it back on the bed. The bugs must die eventually, she thought, with no fresh children to feast on. She folded the quilt and put it away in her trunk.

Arturo clattered down the steps, a trail of muddy footprints covering her clean stairs. "Mama, Roberto's throwing rocks over the fence."

Perfie held out her palm to stop him, but he ducked under her arm and raced to the table. "Arturo! Mud." She pointed.

He didn't even look. "I'm hungry. Don't we have any more apples?"

"Knock knock?" Mary's voice sang out. "Perfie?"

"Come in, come in." Perfie grabbed the broom and attacked the muddy prints, but all she managed to do was smear mud across the steps. Mary would think she was a terrible housekeeper. "Arturo, take those shoes off right now."

Mary stepped around the mess. "Oh, boys and mud. They just seem to go together, don't they."

Arturo slipped out of his shoes and ran up the steps, his socks sticking to the smeared mud. "Roberto, Miss Mary is here." he shouted when half way up the stairs. His voice bounced off the walls of the basement.

Perfie grabbed his arm and held him as she peeled off his socks.

"Go and sit. Don't move again."

Mary set a basket of oranges on the table and turned to Arturo. He peeled off his shirt and dropped it to the floor.

She knelt and examined his arms for the tell-tale rash. Perfie watched. She had checked him this morning; she knew his arms were clear and smooth. Mary stepped behind him and examined his scalp.

"Looks like your hair is starting to grow back." She smiled at Perfie. "How have things been going?"

"Fine."

Perfie held each of the girls in her lap while Mary performed the same careful examination. She felt the heat rise up her neck and settle with a burning in her ears when Mary examined her. She never imagined that her family would be so dirty, like the Ortegas, who lived on the edge of Tierra Amarilla in that awful shack.

"Have you been able to treat Mr. Martinez?" Mary hadn't met Isaac yet. Perfie explained to her that he rode the bus to work and didn't get home until after 6:00 each night.

"Yes. He shaved his hair off, too. He does my hair with the little comb every night."

"Have you found any more nits?"

"No. None since last Friday. That's when we did another treatment."

Roberto finally came in, kicking off his shoes on the top step and walking around the mud. He sat at the table without a word.

"Say hello to Miss Mary. Don't be rude." Perfie's hand twitched as she nearly reached out and slapped him. But to hit him in front of Mary would be more embarrassing than Roberto's rude behavior.

When Mary finished examining Roberto she wiped her hands off on the rag Perfie had provided. Last week, when Rose wasn't home, Perfie had taken Mary upstairs to wash her hands. But today she could hear footsteps up in the kitchen and didn't make the offer.

Since Rose found out about the scabies and lice she hadn't allowed the Martinez family to enter the house at all. The bucket that had been used for Karleen's accidents was now used by the whole family. The stench filled the basement in spite of frequently emptying the contents down the grated sewer out in the street. Isaac showed the boys where to pee in the corner of the yard and told them to make sure Rose and Tom weren't looking.

"Everyone looks good. I don't see any trace of lice or scabies. The boys can come back to school." Mary smiled at her. "I'm sure you're ready for that. But you need to do one more treatment in ten days."

Perfie didn't realize she had been holding her breath. Now she slowly exhaled; things could go back to normal.

"I have some more news for you," Mary continued. "I met with a friend of mine, and there is a way for you to get a place to live, a better place to live."

What could Mary mean by this? A place to live? Something better than this basement? Perfie held her breath again. But then she realized what Mary was saying, and the dream whooshed away as if a tornado had sucked it up.

"Isaac won't, I mean, *we* won't take charity."

"This isn't charity. It's something everyone is entitled to." Mary paused. "It's called public housing. It's for people who came here to work and don't have a place to live. You and Isaac will have to go to the housing authority office and fill out some papers."

Perfie thought about the awful bucket in the corner. "Where would we live?"

"There are several options. There are special places built for people who just need some time to get on their feet. Apartments for families." Mary leaned forward, her eyes wide and staring directly at Perfie. "Do you want me to come back tonight and talk to Isaac?"

She considered Mary's offer. Would Isaac be more likely to listen to the nurse than to her? Or would he just get mad at her for letting a stranger know about things he considered to be nobody's business?

But Perfie knew she couldn't live like this any longer.

"Sí. Yes. I think that might be a good idea."

Thirty-Two

"She's coming here?" Isaac gnawed on the chicken bone and slid it to the side of his mouth to bite off the joint with a loud crunch.

Perfie shivered. She hated that sound. "Why do you do that? What if you break a tooth? We don't have money for a dentist."

Isaac grinned and set the splintered bone down on his plate.

"Dad's like a dog." Arturo chewed on the end of his drumstick and made a growling sound.

"Now see what you do? Arturo will be the one to break a tooth." Perfie stood and cleared the plates. She wiped each plate off with a damp rag so that the water in the dishpan would last through the washing. Cold water, even with soap, didn't cut grease.

Isaac and the boys straightened the blankets and quilts while Perfie wiped the girls' faces and hands. Isaac convinced Karleen to use the bucket so that no accidents would occur while Mary Kent was visiting.

Perfie had explained about the housing to Isaac and he hadn't seemed angry, just disinterested.

Things were peaceful for a moment. The boys sat on the mattress and looked through a book Roberto had brought home from school. He turned the book to show the pictures to the girls. Isaac sat at the table shuffling a deck of cards, ready to engage in his nightly game of solitaire. Perfie took the moment to sit with her feet propped up on a chair.

When they heard the knock, Isaac jumped up to lift the heavy door.

He braced the door up over his shoulder with one hand and offered the other to Mary. "Hello, I'm Isaac Martinez."

"It's nice to meet you." Ducking her head to step under the door, Mary moved her satchel to her shoulder and reached out to shake Isaac's hand.

After giving hugs to the children and passing out books and sugar cookies, Mary sat down with Perfie and Isaac and placed a stack of papers on the table.

"I was able to talk the housing office into giving me the papers you have to fill out. This is just the start of it. Once you're approved there will be more."

Isaac picked up the stack and ran his finger across the lines on the top page. Perfie watched the feathery movement of his lips as he scanned the words.

Within a minute Isaac shook his head. "They certainly want a lot of information. I hate giving out so much to strangers."

"I know it's a lot." Mary's voice sounded slightly irritated.

Don't get into it with him; that's not the way it works. Perfie tried to communicate with Mary, but Mary didn't seem to read her thoughts. Perfie jumped up and went to the kettle.

"Would you like some tea?"

"No. I can't stay. I just wanted to answer any questions Isa—you two might have."

"What kind of housing is it?" Isaac pulled a pack of Lucky Strike cigarettes out of his shirt pocket. Mary and Perfie watched him as he used his long fingers to delicately remove a single home-made cigarette before slipping the package back into his pocket. He didn't light up, just rolled the cigarette softly between his thumb and fingers. Perfie looked at his fingernails and remembered how she used to love to stroke each of those fingers. They hadn't touched each other in a long time. His hands were stained now, and tiny cuts covered his knuckles

Mary tried to answer Isaac's question. "I believe there are several different areas. I think they try to keep you in the same neighborhood where you live now so you can be near work and the children don't have to change schools."

Isaac laughed. "A two-hour bus ride is not really near work, but it would be nice if the boys stayed at that school. They seem to love it." He looked over his shoulder at Perfie. "Matches?"

Perfie glanced at Roberto and Arturo before opening a white jar on the counter and removing a box of matches. She did this silently, quickly replacing the lid and walking over to hand the matches to Isaac.

"Don't leave them lying around." She stood next to him with her hand out. She didn't trust the boys not to get into trouble.

Isaac removed a match from the box and struck it with a quick flick. He raised the cigarette to his lips and puffed before extinguishing the match with a shake. He took a long, slow pull on the cigarette and then placed the box of matches back into her hand. With a glance at the children Perfie quickly walked back to the jar and slipped the matches in. She pushed the jar behind all the other items that covered the top of the crate: boxes of cereal, a bag of beans, a stack of plates and bowls, a salt and pepper shaker.

Isaac tipped his head upward as the blue smoke seeped from his nostrils. He lowered his chin and stared directly into Mary's eyes. Perfie recognized the look. He wasn't letting the nurse get away without answering his question, and he was letting her know he didn't appreciate her evasion. "What kind of housing is it?"

"Apartments." Perfie could see that Mary truly didn't know what Isaac was asking. "I think you might be able to get into Campbell Village. It's being built right now. The apartments are two-story with kitchen and living room on the ground floor and bedrooms upstairs. With four children you might be able to get a three-bedroom place."

Isaac removed the cigarette from between his lips and leaned forward. "The Martinez family doesn't take charity. Never been on the dole and never will be."

You had to give it to Mary. She didn't flinch.

"It isn't the dole. It's housing built specifically for those who have come to work here, whether at the shipyards, for the railroad, or for any other job that brought them to California. There aren't enough places for people to live, so these apartments have been built, and even more are being built. The rent is based on what you can afford. That's why you need to fill out the papers. There's no guarantee you'll get in, but they do take into account where you're currently living." Mary's lips were tight and her eyes flashed as she looked around the basement. "And I have to say, where you're living gives you every reason to find somewhere else for your family."

Perfie watched Isaac. The passive way he resisted an argument left the foe little recourse. But he didn't like confrontation, and he sat smoking his cigarette without saying another word. The taste of the blue smoke had his full attention.

Mary seemed to realize she had crossed some line. She stood and picked up her satchel. "I have to go. I'll just leave everything for you to look through. The address of the office is at the top of the page."

Perfie walked her to the door, where the two women bid each other a hasty good-bye and exchanged a meaningful glance. They would talk about this tomorrow.

Thirty-Three

Roberto threw the ball to Kevin. It felt good to have a friend. School was working out okay, but some of the kids liked to fight and call names.

He was happy Mrs. Colby had moved him to sit by Kevin. Kevin was good at writing, and Mrs. Colby said he could help Roberto when he needed it. And Roberto helped Kevin with his math.

This was the first best friend Roberto had ever had. Kevin loved baseball. He had lived in Oakland for a while and he knew everything about the Oakland Oaks. His dad even played on a baseball team, but just a local one.

Roberto wanted more time with his new friend. "Hey. Do you want to come over to my house after school? We can play on my street. There are walnuts in the back yard and they make good golf balls."

Last week Isaac had taken Roberto for a drive in the truck. He pointed out something called a golf course as they drove past a broad expanse of green grass bordered by trees. He explained to Roberto that rich men swung clubs at little white balls and tried to make the balls roll into little holes that were placed here and there in the grass.

Kevin was interested in coming home with Roberto. "You have clubs?"

"No, but I have some sticks, boards my father gave me. They work pretty good."

Kevin walked home with Arturo and Roberto. He liked to walk in the gutter and search for treasures. Sure enough, he found two pennies and a paperclip. Roberto walked behind him and wished he had the idea first.

"Wait here," he told Kevin when they got to the house. "My sisters might be asleep. I'll see if my mother will fix us something to eat."

Kevin sat at the top of the steps while Roberto opened the heavy door.

His mother was sitting at the table knitting. "Mama, Kevin is here to play. Can we have some sandwiches?" Roberto set his school papers on the table.

"How about some apples instead? Where is your brother?"

"He's outside with Kevin."

"Don't be too noisy. The babies are still asleep."

Roberto took the apples out to the porch and sat with Kevin and Arturo. After they had eaten the crunchy fruit, Roberto showed Kevin the boards and walnuts. They set up old cans and leaves around the back yard for their "golf course."

Kevin was good at the game, almost as good as Roberto. Arturo was bored. He couldn't hit the nuts where he wanted because he never stood still. It wasn't long before he wandered away.

Kevin was concentrating on getting his walnut over the little hump of lawn and into the can when a shrill voice interrupted the boys.

"Hey you! Get out of my yard. This is private property."

Roberto looked at the back porch. Rose stood there, shading her eyes with her hand "You. Colored boy. Get out of here before I call the police."

Suddenly Roberto realized she was yelling at Kevin.

"It's okay, Tía. He's my friend from school."

His aunt snorted and shook a finger at him. "I don't care who he is. No colored boys can play in my yard. Does your mother know he's here?"

Roberto nodded.

Kevin came up to him and handed him the board. "It's okay. I can go home now." He sprinted off down the driveway before Roberto had a chance to answer.

Later that night Roberto heard his parents talking about Kevin. Rose had complained to Perfie that she was neglecting her kids by letting them hang out with undesirable children. He didn't understand that at all. Kevin was Roberto's best friend. He crawled out of bed and went to where his parents were whispering.

"Dad. How come Rose doesn't like Kevin?" Roberto knew the answer, but hoped he was wrong. "She doesn't even know him."

"I know, son. Some people are that way. There are a lot of people who don't like colored folks."

"But we like colored folks, right?"

Dad patted his shoulder. "We like to make our decisions about people from what we know about them. What do you know about Kevin?"

"He likes baseball. He knows everything about the Oaks, and he's good at writing."

Mama interrupted. "But what about his family? Are they nice people?"

Roberto shrugged. He didn't know much about Kevin's family except that Kevin had some younger brothers.

"Go back to bed. Don't worry about it tonight. We'll talk about it more tomorrow."

Roberto crawled back under the quilt and pushed Arturo out of the way. He would just have to play at Kevin's house from now on.

Thirty-Four

It was Monday before Perfie had time to look at the housing papers. She sat at the little wooden table with the many pages spread in front of her. This was the only quiet time of day, when the girls were napping and the boys were at school. She sipped on peppermint tea to soothe the burning in her stomach. Her finger ran along each line of print as she puzzled out the words.

Isaac was right. These forms did ask for a lot of information. She figured out that public housing was for families like hers, families who could make some money right now but didn't have enough saved up to rent a decent place. If she was reading this right, they would be allowed to rent an apartment at a very low amount based on Isaac's wages. If the wages increased, so did the rent. You had to pay twenty-five percent of your income for the place to live.

Perfie picked up a pen and drew a circle on a paper bag she had folded after taking out the apples. She divided the circle in wedges, like a pie cut into four pieces. One piece for rent, one for food, one for everything else—laundry, bus fare, shoes and whatever else they needed. That would leave one piece of the pie to save.

She rubbed her head. It wasn't enough. Roberto and Arturo were so hard on their shoes that there wasn't anything left for Karleen. That meant buying new clothes and shoes for Roberto and Karleen and giving their hand-me-downs to Arturo and Geri. It wasn't *nearly* enough. More like half of their money went for food, and the rest went for clothes and other things. Perfie erased the lines and made the slice of pie representing food bigger. Then she drew a new pie, bigger than the first. This is what it would be like if Isaac got a raise. But after ten minutes of erasing and redrawing the slices, she crumpled up the bag and threw it to the floor. If the rent went up when Isaac's wages went up, they would never get ahead.

At least now she could save some of his overtime money and even use some for such things as cosmetics or a mirror. She hid some of the money in a jar behind the paint cans and tucked some into the little pocket inside her suitcase. She didn't dare hide it in only one place. What if someone found it?

Perfie wondered if she could earn some money herself without telling Isaac or the housing people. She could do something here at home and get paid in cash. She thought about cleaning houses or getting a part time job, but what would she do with the girls?

There had been a time when Perfie thought Rose would help take care of Karleen and Geri if she had work. But Rose could hardly bear the sight of the children. Only now that the lice and scabies were cleared up did she begrudgingly let them use the toilet upstairs again.

No, Rose was still upset. You could tell from the sharpness of her voice and the way she interrupted every time Isaac and Tom had a conversation on the back porch. *Tom*, she would screech, *I need you*, as if fearful something evil or lazy would rub off from Isaac onto her perfect husband. Rose didn't seem to realize that living just below the living room where she and Tom sat each night gave Perfie and Isaac a front row seat to all their arguments. Their angry voices were amplified through the wooden floor boards.

With a sigh Perfie turned to the second page of the housing application where she found a list of rules. It was definitely against one of the rules to make money on the side and not report it. You had to tell the housing authority if you were expecting another child. It was against the rules to let other relatives live with you. She didn't like that rule. What if Joe wanted to come for awhile? Or maybe even Isabelle?

She had written to her brother once to tell him how much she missed him. He wrote back saying he might make a trip out to California. He hadn't mentioned Isabelle or Primitivo in his letter, but he had talked with Benjamin, who sent his love. Love to her or to Isaac? Joe wasn't specific.

Perfie wrote to Isabelle all the time. Her letters had become a diary of sorts, spilling out to her cousin all the problems she faced. Isabelle wrote back often, encouraging Perfie to deal with things, just as she always had.

All couples applying for public housing must not have committed any crime or felony.

She read this again. Was it against the law to live together, to have children, without ever getting married? She had sinned. She was clear about that, but she didn't know if she had broken the law. In New Mexico there were plenty of people who didn't get married.

In fact, after hearing Tía Emilia's stories, Perfie was fairly confident that Primitivo and Avelina had never been married. No matter what her aunt said, she thought Avelina was still married to Joe and Manny's father, Manuel. And it was possible her father had another wife. It seemed like there was actually a family tradition of not being married.

Perfie flipped to the next page. There was something here about marriage. Both parties of the married couple must complete and sign the application. She read it again. They did have to be married to get a house.

I should have gotten married when I had the chance. She thought about that terrible day when Carlotta had been so angry. For some reason the old woman thought Perfie wouldn't marry her son because she didn't have the right dress or he wasn't good enough. Perfie never told her the truth, and all these years had passed without Isaac ever delivering the proposal she had been waiting for.

Life was so busy. Not only had there been the hard work of getting the house on the land ready to live in, but every year there was another baby. Then there was the sewing and housekeeping, not to mention the cows to tend—the list never ended.

Time passed and the chance to have an actual wedding slipped out of her mind. Perfie felt married. She had imagined the ceremony so many times that it seemed real to her—until now.

These requirements. She couldn't be a sinner and couldn't just imagine herself married—all of this stumped her. How would she fix things?

Her mind raced. Would the housing authority ask to see an actual marriage certificate? If she and Isaac lied and simply said they didn't have a copy, would all their chances be gone?

Perfie felt God inhale once again, his heavy breath sucking away her dream of a home for her children.

Bathtubs

Thirty-Five

Isaac flung open the heavy door and bounced down the steps into the basement. "My darling beauty, I have a surprise for you." His joy was catching, and the girls ran and hugged his legs. Roberto and Arturo jumped up from their building blocks and sent the half-built tower tumbling over with a crash. They raced to Isaac with their heads down and rammed at his legs, as if they were young goats.

A raise, let it be a raise. Perfie prayed to the God she swore she didn't believe in. She turned her attention to the stack of folded clothing, now teetering precariously on a chair as the children raced around it.

"What?" She picked up the stack and held the laundry in her arms while looking around for somewhere else to set it down.

"Grab your towels, my grubby little offspring. *Miss* Rose has agreed to let us take a bath upstairs." Isaac took the stack from Perfie's arms.

A bath! That was almost as good as a raise. She rubbed her greasy, limp hair.

Perfie was so dirty that her toes felt moldy. She soaked them every night in the dishpan after bathing Geri and Karleen, but she had to put the same socks back on, and with her shoes never airing out completely she felt as if she lived in a swamp.

"Really? Ike? How in the world did you swing that?" She couldn't imagine Rose letting them do this. No way, not in this lifetime. "Did she hit her head or something?"

Isaac looked around and set the stacked laundry in the center of the table. He pressed a kiss to her cheek before pulling his lips away with a loud smack. "I managed it with my amazing charm and good looks. And a fair amount of pull from Tom. Think of it as an early Christmas present."

"Come on, it couldn't have been that easy."

"Okay, if you must know I explained to Tom that there was no way for us to keep clean enough to prevent another outbreak of scabies. I guess he told her she would catch them too if she didn't let us take a bath." He turned his lips down in a playful scowl. "I'm sure she'll pour gallons of bleach down the drain when we've finished."

His face turned serious. "There are some rules. It wouldn't be Rose if there weren't some rules."

"Rules?"

"Not so much different from our days in the old place. We can only fill the tub once. She doesn't want us to use up all her hot water."

Perfie couldn't believe it. Not use up the water? Water that flowed freely from a tap and didn't have to be hauled from a ditch or a spigot in the back yard? She felt her mood deflate like a tired balloon.

Chin up, old girl, she told herself. It's still a bath.

Isaac went upstairs first. When he returned with wet hair sticking out from his head like a bewildered porcupine, he handed Perfie a large bar of gray soap. "I brought this home. Didn't want to use Rose's perfumed stuff."

"Not like she'd let you anyway." Perfie turned to the boys and picked up the clean pajamas and towels she had gathered. "Come on, our turn."

Roberto folded his arms across his chest. "I don't need a bath."

She reached for his arm just as Isaac spoke to him.

"I can see dandelions growing on the back of your neck. It's time to water them."

Perfie couldn't understand why Roberto was so in love with his filth. He would never remove his dirty clothes when she was ready to wash, and if his father wasn't around he would resort to hitting and screaming. It wasn't as if Isaac punished him. In fact, Isaac was soft on the kids. She tried to make up for it, to make them mind. The last thing she wanted was spoiled children.

With a kick at the bottom step Roberto followed her out of the basement. Perfie had to admit that Isaac's way worked.

She was glad she didn't see Rose or Tom as she led the boys through the kitchen to the bathroom. She didn't want to grovel right now. She pushed the boys into the tiny room and shut the door.

Such a bathroom: green tile edged with black and a white sink with a silver spigot and twin handles like funny elk with knobby antlers protruding out in all directions. Rose's towels were dark green. Four of them hung on a silver bar, and matching wash clothes were draped neatly over each one. There were two hand towels near the sink. They didn't look as if they were ever used. The bar of soap was green, too, and was in the shape of a fat turtle hunched at the edge of the porcelain bowl, ready to slide in if someone dared to touch him. The fuzzy green rug just in front of the sink was covered with huge brown footprints. Isaac had left a mess.

I'll deal with that later, she thought as she pulled Arturo's t-shirt over his head. Roberto quickly stripped off his clothes and a shower of fine brown dirt fell to the wet floor and formed swirls of mud. Perfie wrinkled her nose at the sour odor of little-boy sweat and grime.

"You stink. Hop in and sit."

Perfie rubbed the boys' heads briskly with the bar of gray soap and scrubbed every inch of them with the rough washcloth.

"Ouch, it hurts." Roberto scooted to the far end of the tub, sending a big wave over the edge and soaking her slacks.

"Now look what you've done!" She reached around Arturo to slap at Roberto, but he ducked behind his brother. "Never mind. Lay down and rinse."

Perfie reached for one of the towels to dry the boys off, but Roberto slipped behind the edge of the toilet and pushed her away with both hands. "Why do you have to treat me like a baby? I can do this myself."

"Then do it yourself. But hurry, I want my bath, too." She set his clean pajamas and underwear on the toilet seat lid. Roberto dressed quickly while Perfie finished drying Arturo.

"Go straight downstairs. Don't you dare get those pajamas dirty. No touching anything at all." Their feet were bare. No clean socks for them; she hadn't done laundry yet this week. She would wash their clothes out in the tub after her bath.

"Wait!" She looked at the toilet. "Use this before you go."

The boys stood at the toilet and giggled as they waved the twin streams of urine back and forth. When they were done they skittered across the wet floor and out the door.

Perfie waited at the bathroom door until the slam of the back screen signaled that the boys were out of the house. She picked up the rug and shook it into the pile of dirt that was already next to the tub. We should have hung that out of the way, she thought, and made a mental note for next time. She knew Rose would be mad.

Perfie rolled the damp towel tight to hold the dirt inside and used it to wipe off the floor. She unbuttoned her blue shirt, slipped out of her slacks and pulled off her bra and underwear. She carefully folded each item and made a neat pile on the wicker hamper by the door before standing in front of the mirror to look at herself. Her breasts drooped. She knew that nursing so many babies had done things to her body, but she hadn't imagined the long creases that now stretched from her shoulders down to the thickened brown nipples. She put her hands under her breasts and raised them back into the proud position she remembered.

I haven't looked at myself for a long time. Probably not since my wedding day—or make that the day I didn't have a wedding.

She pulled on the wrinkles at the edge of her mouth and stretched the skin down. She frowned. It wasn't much different from the permanent scowl that had taken over her face. She tried smiling, but she nearly cried when she saw how unnatural this looked. It was as if her face couldn't even imagine lips turning up or eyes crinkling with laughter.

Enough of this. I'm just making myself feel terrible. She turned to the tub and looked down at the brown water. A white layer floated on top of the water. The asbestos dust that coated Isaac each night. She thought about the clear ditch water back in New Mexico. Cold and far from the house, but so fresh and clean.

Perfie stuck a toe into the soapy mess. It was barely warm. Did she dare to turn on the spigot and add more hot water?

No. Why add it to this filthy mess when it wouldn't really make things better. And Rose was probably in the next room with her ear pressed to the wall. Instead Perfie rinsed out the yellow washcloth at the sink. She waited until the water ran hot and stuck her head under. There was no shampoo; the bar of soap would have to do. She rubbed the cloth on the soap, then scrubbed and rinsed her face, her neck and her armpits before tending to her more personal areas.

Perfie looked at the tub again. She reached down and pulled out the plug. Then she stood and watched the water swirl down the silver drain. All that was left was the line of brown scum, a line that seemed to mark the life in which the Martinez family was trapped—trapped and struggling to reach that white porcelain above.

With a sigh she knelt and wiped out the tub. Only when she felt the bathroom would meet Rose's standards did she turn and put on her clothes.

The clean underwear, bra and socks felt good against her skin even if she did have to slip back into the wet slacks and blue shirt.

Back downstairs the boys were jumping on the bed and the girls were laughing and running in circles. Everyone seemed energized from their bath. Isaac sat at the table with the newspaper spread in front of him. He looked up at her with a wide grin and his twinkling blue eyes.

"Felt great, didn't it?"

She tried to make her face look as if she had been able to dip herself into a clean tub full of hot water. "Yes. Of course."

"I think Rose will let us do this once a week."

She kept her face turned away from him as she hung the wet clothes on the wooden rack in the corner.

"That'll be nice." It was just as her father and mother had always preached, as if they had read the words off an ancient tablet discovered high in the mountains. "Once a week will keep a spirit clean."

But Perfie's spirit was covered with grime.

The following Thursday was Rose's shopping day. Wearing some marvelous flowery dress, she would leave the house at about 10:00 and back the car down the long drive. If she noticed Perfie looking out through the open door she would pretend not to see her. Her eyes would remain focused on her task as she looked over her left shoulder and concentrated on keeping the tires on the twin concrete strips. Rose was usually gone until 3:00. Perfie imagined Rose meeting friends for lunch. She pictured her surrounded by smiling woman, all sipping tea and spearing bits of food with shiny forks.

But today Perfie had a plan. As soon as the boys left for school, she dressed the girls and tied their shoes in double knots. "Let's go to the park," she told them.

She didn't put them in the wagon. She took hold of the two little hands and circled three blocks before stopping at the park they loved. Usually she sat on a bench reading a magazine while the girls kept busy in the sandbox or on the swings. But today she played with the girls. They all ran chasing and laughing around the sandy yard.

By the time the three had walked home the kids were tired and hungry. After a lunch of leftover beans wrapped in tortillas, she tucked them in for a nap. When both girls were asleep, she glanced at the clock.

One o'clock. Perfect.

Perfie grabbed a towel and opened the heavy door as quietly as possible. She made her way to the back porch, took the spare key off the hook inside the water heater closet and let herself into the house. Walking lightly as if she might be discovered at any moment, she made her way through the laundry room and kitchen and into the bathroom.

She left the door open and turned on the water to fill the tub. She remembered to hang the green fuzzy rug over the hamper before shedding her clothes and slipping into the half-filled tub.

A warm, wet heaven. Perfie sank down slowly and bent her knees. Taking a breath she pulled her head under the water, reached up her hands and rubbed her hair briskly. When it felt well rinsed she sat up so that her legs were under the water and reached down with the wash cloth and soap to scrub her feet. The tub was nearly full now, and she leaned forward to turn off the water.

She listened. No sounds from below.

I can't get enough of this, she thought, as she washed herself again.

Her head back under the water once more, she thought she heard something. She sat up quickly.

A cry.

She jumped from the tub, snatched the towel and swiped her body. She pulled her shirt and pants on without bothering with the clean underwear she had set on the hamper. Even though she was worried, she took the time to mop up the water from the floor with her towel. The tub was still draining; she'd have to deal with that later. She ran out the door.

Perfie jumped down the four steps of the back porch. Geri's cry sounded close, as if she was outside. Racing around the corner of the house, Perfie slid to a stop when she nearly crashed into someone.

It was Mary Kent, and Geri was on her left hip. One of Karleen's small hands held Mary's, the other was raised, thumb stuck in mouth. Mary's face was pale, and her eyes flashed lightning as she held her mouth open in disbelief.

Mary shook her head back and forth. "How could you leave them alone?"

"It was just for a minute. They were sleeping." Perfie felt her brief moment of relief give way to fear.

The sound of an approaching car added to her panic. The last thing she needed was for Rose to see her here like this, hair dripping wet, towel in hand.

"Come on, let's go in." She brushed past Mary and walked toward the basement.

She heard the car drive passed. Not Rose.

Perfie turned back and pulled Geri from Mary's arms, then reached out a hand to Karleen.

The little girl shook her head and pushed her body closer to Mary's leg.

I don't have time for this. Perfie grabbed Karleen by the arm and jerked her away from Mary. She heard another car. This time it was Rose.

"Come in the house. We can talk there." Perfie's voice was sharp. She pulled Karleen down the steps, away from Rose's prying eyes.

Thirty-Six

Mary followed Perfie down the stairs. She stepped past as Perfie turned to pull the heavy door shut behind them. Karleen let go of her mother's hand and ran to the corner to grab her doll.

Mary turned and looked at Perfie like a storm rolling over the mountains. "How could you—"

She didn't get any further than that because Perfie set Geri down and burst into sobs. She gasped as if to choke her cries back into her shaking body. She felt Mary's gaze on her and covered her eyes with her hands, but she couldn't stop herself, even though she was embarrassed at her weakness. When Mary stepped forward and wrapped her arms around her, Perfie sucked in a huge breath.

She stiffened and shook her head back and forth. She desperately wanted all of this to go away.

"What happened?" Mary asked when the sobs had turned to gulping hiccups. Perfie didn't answer.

Mary led her to a chair and pressed her into it before turning to Karleen and Geri. The girls stood side by side, Karleen with thumb in mouth. Geri's lower lip trembled.

"Where are your clothes?" Mary asked.

Karleen pulled her thumb from her mouth and pointed to the corner of the room. A bank of shelves stood there—shelves that held a variety of items such as vases, a set of hockey sticks and old shoe boxes marked with labels: Christmas, Summer, Thread, Whatnot. In between these were neatly stacked clothes.

Perfie watched Mary rummage through the folded clothes and find some pants and underwear that looked like the right size. The nurse slipped Karleen out of her urine-soaked stockings and replaced them with fresh clothes. Karleen's thumb was back in her mouth and a smile curved around it, causing a bit of saliva to run down her chin. Mary pulled up the edge of Karleen's shirt to wipe the girl's face.

"What's so funny?" Mary smiled at her.

"Not by clodes." Karleen mumbled around her thumb and her nose, which was stuffy from crying.

It took Mary a second to translate. "Oh. These do look like they might belong to Arturo, but I think they'll do for now." Mary rolled up the cuffs. "Do you think you can play with Geri while I talk with Mama?"

Karleen nodded her head and pulled Geri over to the corner of the room where the two dolls Perfie had made for them lay on a pillow. Perfie watched as Karleen handed one of the dolls to Geri and picked up a book. When had her daughter grown up so much?

Mary turned to the bed, removed the quilt with the wet spot on it and set it and the soiled clothing in a pile near the door. Then she moved to the hot plate and lifted the tea pot.

Perfie pushed her head down onto her folded arms and closed her eyes.

She listened as Mary searched through the clutter of food that covered the top of a trunk. She heard the clank of the tea pot lid, the strike of a match and the tinkle of the china cups.

When Mary set the cups on the table and sat down, Perfie lifted her head and rubbed her nose with the back of her hand. "I just wanted a bath. They were asleep. I wasn't gone long."

"Can't you take a bath when Isaac's here?"

"No." Perfie stared at her cup of tea before raising her gaze to meet Mary's. "Rose won't allow it. Only on Saturday night." Perfie picked up a spoon and stirred her tea, although she hadn't added anything to it. "The water was so dirty. I just wanted a clean bath."

Mary didn't understand. "Why was the water dirty?"

"Because we only get one bath a week. The kids are covered with an inch of mud by that time, and Isaac's not much better."

"But why would that make your bath dirty?"

Perfie looked straight at her. "You don't get it, do you? We only get one tub of water. No one has to haul it, but we still only get one tub." Fresh tears rolled down her cheeks.

Mary slowly nodded, understanding at last.

Perfie sniffed and continued. "I thought with Rose out shopping I could just sneak up, real quick. She would never know."

The two women sat without speaking, listening to the voices of the girls chattering in the corner.

"Was it lavender shampoo?"

Perfie frowned and squinted at Mary. Her eyebrows arched together, then relaxed. She nodded. "Doesn't it smell wonderful?"

"What will Rose do if she catches you?"

"Probably throw us out on the street. She's just waiting for an excuse."

"Why doesn't she want you here?"

Perfie leaned forward, placing her elbows on the table. She lifted her cup with two hands, raised it to her lips and blew. "It goes way back. You'd have to understand Tierra Amarilla, the way the families are— competitive or something. Everyone tries to say that their family is the best. Rose's family, they were at the top of the ladder, the first to get everything. When Rose married Tom and they moved out here, her mother —she was my mother's cousin—she just couldn't stop bragging about Rose. I guess I got so I hated her just because I had to listen to how wonderful she was all the time."

"That doesn't explain why she doesn't like you."

"No, that came later. They came for a visit, Tom and Rose. Drove out in a brand new car." Perfie's face turned red. "I wasn't very nice to her."

To her relief, Mary didn't ask for any more details.

"Perfie, you can't leave the girls alone in here. There's so much that could go wrong." Mary stopped.

Perfie bit her lip. Of course she knew that. Did Mary think she was stupid?

"What if I come after work and watch them while you take a bath?"

Perfie couldn't believe what Mary was offering. Then she shook her head. "Rose only shops once a week, but she's usually home by two or three. I have to work something else out. Maybe Isaac will let me bathe first sometimes."

Perfie stood up. "I'm sorry, but I need to hang that quilt out or it won't be dry tonight."

Mary glanced at her watch. "I have to get home." She carried the cups over to the makeshift kitchen.

Perfie grabbed a dishpan off the shelf and set it next to the hot plate. "You can put those in here."

Mary set the cups into the pan and turned to Perfie. "We'll think of something. Just promise me you won't leave them alone again."

Thirty-Seven

Isaac pulled out his handkerchief to wipe his forehead and leaned back against the worn seat of the bus.

"Hard day?" Dom slid into the seat behind him.

Isaac nodded. "I moved to the second crew. It's a few more hours, but my sleep times—impossible to sleep during the day with four kids at home."

"Pretty soon you'll be on third crew. That's the only way you can get ahead."

Dom had been on third crew for five months. Isaac had watched while his friend moved his way up the ladder in a hurry, while others stayed at the same low-paying jobs. Some said Dom's uncle had connections to the navy officer in charge of the insulator manufacturing crew.

Whatever the reason, Isaac wished he could make the kind of money Dom was making.

"You still living in that basement?"

Isaac had told Dom about wanting to move to a better neighborhood.

"Yeh. My wife hates it." Isaac had a thought. "Hey, she got some paperwork for this public housing. You know anything about that?"

"It's a rip off." Dom shook his head. "They want twenty-five percent of whatever you make as rent for an apartment. My place is way less than that."

"If I could find a place like yours I'd be there in a flash. But there's nothing like that left."

Dom nodded. They both knew that he had been lucky to find his apartment three years ago. People like the Martinez family, new to California, had to compete with hundreds of other workers. There were no reasonable places left.

"You get a raise, *they* get a raise. It's twenty-five percent no matter what." Dom rolled his eyes. "Best bet is to stay out from under the government thumb."

Still, Isaac thought. It would mean having a place of their own. Perfie would like that.

But when he asked her about the paperwork that night, she got a funny look on her face.

"Didn't you want me to fill it out? Try for that apartment?"

She shook her head and looked away. "It's too much money. I think we should wait and find a place like Dom and Monique got. She told me she would keep an eye out for something in their building."

"That could take a long time. We can try for the public housing and then move if we find something better." Isaac looked around for the stack of papers. He had skimmed through them the night Mary Kent brought them over, but he hadn't really been able to sit down and focus. "Where are the papers? I want to look at them."

"Put away." Perfie jumped up from the table. "It's time for dinner. Can you get the kids?"

Isaac let the subject go, but later that night when he was tucking the children into bed, he thought about Perfie's strange reaction..

"Daddy, you forgot to kiss me good night." Karleen giggled. He had kissed her twice already.

"A magic kiss for the princess." He tucked the quilt around her and kissed her forehead.

"Me too." Geri turned her head back and forth, flashing first one cheek and then the other.

He kissed them both once more. "That's it. Quiet time now. Close those eyes." He watched as his two sweet daughters squeezed their eyes tight. With a sigh he stood and looked at the boys. "Good night, my brave Californians."

"Night, Dad."

At least the boys had settled into their school. After all that worry about him being behind, Roberto had been moved up to third grade. Arturo loved his teacher, and his reports were good.

Perfie was washing dishes in the pan that was balanced on the edge of the crate they used as a counter. Isaac decided he would grab a quick smoke and then ask her once more about the papers.

He stood at the end of the driveway and puffed on one of the hand-rolled cigarettes he made each weekend. He didn't really like the taste of the funny tobacco, but it was all he could afford. Once in a while one of the men at the shipyard would give him a Lucky Strike or a Camel. How he loved those cigarettes.

Isaac coughed. He'd had this darn cold for a month now. Every time he lit up his cigarette his lungs reacted. After a few puffs things would settle down—until he went to bed. When he lay down at night his chest ached. Last week he had got out of bed and pushed a box against the wall. He wrapped himself in a blanket and tried to sleep sitting up. He thought about switching back to a pipe, but he couldn't afford to buy one right now, and he'd left his old one in New Mexico.

Finishing up the last puff, he stubbed the cigarette out on the sidewalk and headed back into the basement. He was surprised to find it dark.

"Perfie?"

"Mmm." She was in bed.

He kicked off his shoes and undressed, then slid in beside her. "Why in bed so early?"

"I'm tired. It was a long day." She pulled the pillow over her head.

He would have to ask her about the papers tomorrow.

Thirty-Eight

Perfie watched as Mary pushed her face into Geri's brown curls. They had grown in much thicker since the lice treatment four months ago. The nurse closed her eyes, and Perfie could see her inhale the sweet baby scent, just as she liked to do. Not that Geri was a baby anymore—she had turned two years old last week.

Perfie appreciated the nurse helping the family, but this was her baby, not Mary's. Irritation rose in her throat when she thought about it, and she couldn't stop her jaw from growing tense and her teeth from grinding together. She set the plate of cookies down with a bang, and two of the biscoquitos bounced off and left a sugar trail across the clean wood of the table.

Mary's latest idea, that Perfie take a job while Mary watched the girls, had been nothing short of a miracle. Not only was it a relief to go work for Mrs. Cooper three days a week, but Perfie had the chance to be away from the kids for awhile and away from the terrible basement. She had time to think as she dusted each of Mrs. Cooper's many knick knacks. There were dogs and horses and pretty women with parasols—even one of Jesus and Mary. The money Mrs. Cooper paid her went straight into Perfie's hidden stash.

Without Mary's help Perfie would never be able to have this job, but as much as she appreciated Mary, she wasn't sure about having a friend. Friends took up energy and she didn't have any to spare. Just cleaning up the basement before Mary came over was a pain. There were no closets for hiding things; everything was in plain sight.

She looked back at Mary, who was snuggling with Geri. Mary's eyes were glazed over, and her lower lip was caught up in her teeth. Something was bothering her.

How cruel I am to be jealous, Perfie thought. I need a friend no matter how much time it takes. I'll just be careful this time. She thought about how she had trusted Isabelle. She'd never tell Mary her deepest secrets, but that didn't mean they couldn't be friends.

She reached over and laid her hand on Mary's wrist. "Is everything okay?"

"Yes, I'm fine." Mary answered quickly, her tone bland. Then she turned to Perfie. "No, not really. I'm not really fine." She slid Geri off her lap. "Can I talk to you about it?"

Perfie knew Mary liked to talk about everything, and she herself looked forward to these conversations. They were so different from the talks she had had with her mother or Isabelle. With Mary there was curiosity and dreaming about the future. There were plans, and even silly jokes. It wasn't like the scolding or fear that had permeated her conversations with the other women in her life.

"Of course you can talk to me. What is it?"

"You're a lucky woman, Perfie. You have four fine children. I don't have any."

"Is something wrong?"

"I lost a pregnancy. More than that, I lost three, before we came to California."

"You lost a baby?"

Mary's eyes grew wide. She nodded. "I lost my babies. My Jenna."

"I've lost babies, too." Perhaps Mary thought she was lucky with four children, but that didn't dull the pain of the two daughters she had left behind in New Mexico. "Why don't you try again?"

"That's just it. I told John I'm ready to try again. He said no. He thinks I should work and save money." Mary leaned forward. "I didn't handle it well when Jenna died. He's afraid it will happen again and he thinks this is a bad time, with his job and all. He's too busy to help me if I need it."

Perfie knew all about Mary's husband. John was a psychiatrist at Highland Hospital. Mary hadn't explained all that he did, but she had complained that she didn't agree with some of the treatments John used on children. Mary also told her that he worked late many nights and didn't always come home for dinner.

"Is that why he works all the time? No chance to make babies?" Perfie thought about Isaac, how he petted and whispered when the kids were asleep. He wanted to make another baby, but Perfie couldn't imagine that just now. She pushed his hands away each night, telling him they couldn't do such a thing now that the kids were bigger and might hear them.

"No, we use birth control." Mary twisted her wedding ring around on her finger.

"Birth control? Oh, you mean only during your time of the month? That hasn't really worked for me."

"No, there are other methods. A cap, that's what I use." Mary seemed to think Perfie knew what she was talking about.

Perfie burst out laughing as she pictured Isaac wearing his knit cap to bed. That wouldn't make much of a difference down below. "A cap? What do you do with the cap?"

"No, you silly goose." Mary laughed too. "It's a rubber protector that I insert. It's shaped like a cap. It caps the cervix."

"Insert? Cervix? You forget I'm not a nurse. I don't know what you're talking about."

"It's a small device that goes into the vagina, into the spot where the penis goes. That way no sperm can get through."

Perfie blushed and looked away, studying the cluttered shelves as if there was something important there. No one had ever talked about these things so matter-of-factly to her before. "I know about the rubber tubes. Isaac won't use them even though I said he could. I'm barely a Catholic anymore anyway, so what the heck. But I don't know what this other thing is. I still don't know what you're talking about."

She turned to Mary and drew in her breath, exhaling slowly to steady her nerves.

"Really, Mary. I need to know about this thing. I keep pushing Isaac away and I don't know how much longer that will last."

Perfie was amazed at all that Mary explained. She wanted to get one of these things that would keep her from having another baby, but at the same time would make Isaac happy.

"Do you know how much it would cost?"

"Doesn't Isaac have some health benefits from his job? I'm sure you could get one."

"He gets the doctor covered when he moves to the next crew, the third crew. He's only at the second now."

Mary promised to help Perfie find out how to get an appointment. No more was said about the babies who had died.

The next day Perfie thought about her babies as she mopped the Cooper's floor. She had always thought her girls were taken because of her sins, although she suspected poverty had something to do with it. But Mary had lost three babies and she was rich. Maybe she had sinned. Perfie carried the dirty mop outside and rinsed it with the hose, then hung it on the line. She wished she knew more about Mary, but it didn't seem right to ask. She decided not to think about her babies anymore because it gave her a headache.

At least Mrs. Cooper was easy to work for. She understood about children since she had six of her own. They were all grown now with children of *their* own. Perfie had dusted the framed pictures of all the weddings, christenings and anniversaries. Such a loving family.

That day Mrs. Cooper stopped Perfie as she put on her coat and got ready to go home. "I have these for you, dear. A gift from Dr. Cooper."

Perfie opened the bag and looked in. Toothbrushes and toothpaste.

"Thank you. I know that Arturo has a bad tooth. Maybe this will help."

"If he has a bad tooth you must let Charles take a look at it." Mrs. Cooper put a hand on Perfie's shoulder. "Call the office and make an appointment."

"Thank you." Perfie smiled, but she was confused. Did this mean she could take him for no charge? Or was Mrs. Cooper drumming up business for her husband? Either way, it didn't matter. Isaac wouldn't take charity. "Can my husband and son do some work in the yard to pay for it?"

"I'm sure we can arrange that."

The toot of Mary's horn came from in front of the house.

"See you on Thursday." Perfie turned and hurried down the sidewalk.

"How was your day?" Mary asked as Perfie slipped into the car.

"Fine. Mrs. Cooper gave me some tooth things. Were the kids good?" She twisted to look at the girls. Karleen's hair was pulled into two tight braids and Geri held a new stuffed dog. Perfie had gotten past her jealousy of Mary and now appreciated what it meant to have someone to help.

"Angels, as always." Mary shifted and slowed at the corner. "I'm sorry, Perfie, but there won't be time for a bath today. John called and he's bringing a new doctor home for dinner."

"It's okay." Perfie was disappointed. She looked forward to the midweek bath at Mary's house. Once a week just wasn't enough, although at least she had finally convinced Isaac that he should bathe last. She didn't like the white dust that he left in the tub. And that cough! He said it was nothing, but it had gotten worse. She noticed he had abandoned the stinky cigarettes he smoked each night and had switched instead to a pipe. "John didn't bother to tell you about this earlier?"

Mary shook her head. "No, but I guess I should just be grateful that he thinks I can impress someone at a moment's notice."

"Is there anything I can do to help?" Perfie was too tired to help, but Mary did so much for them.

"No. I'll be fine."

Perfie wished she could think of something to do for Mary. The friendship felt so lopsided. Mary was doing everything for them, but the Martinez family hadn't found a way to repay her, either with money or favors. Perfie had offered Isaac's services working in the big yard where John and Mary lived. Their cottage was up in the hills on the property of Mary's aunt. The main house looked like a castle, and the green lawns and flowers stretched for acres. Perfie had never been inside any house bigger or nicer than Mary's cottage. She had spent many afternoons in the cottage since Mary had come up with the idea of watching the girls while Perfie worked and then bringing them all back to her place for a bath. It made her ache for a home of her own.

"Perfie, have you heard from the Housing Authority yet?" Mary glanced at her, as if reading her thoughts.

"No. Not yet. I've heard it can take a long time."

Perfie didn't dare tell Mary that she hadn't filled out the papers. How did she explain to her new friend that she and Isaac weren't married and wouldn't qualify for the house?

How could she tell Mary that she was a sinner, especially if Mary was a sinner too?

Thirty-Nine

"**Race ya?**"Arturo crouched with one foot forward, knees bent and fingertips touching the dirt in front of him. The huge expanse of lawn behind Mary's cottage provided a perfect place for the two boys to run and tumble without anyone yelling out the window to "mind the roses." The closely cut lawn was thick and spongy. It climbed up a small slope to the edge of a dense copse of eucalyptus and oak trees, with the occasional pine towering high above. Neatly trimmed rose bushes edged a path made with round stepping stones set evenly across the lawn and ending at a trail into the trees.

Near the cottage were flower beds with all colors mixed together: yellows, purples, bright pinks. Roberto didn't know the names of the flowers but he wished he could pick some for his mother to put on the center of the table like Miss Mary did. Miss Mary told the boys to play in back and to stay away from the big house up front where her aunt was lying down with a headache.

Roberto ignored his brother's challenge. Even though Arturo was younger, he always won the races. Roberto had a stronger body, but it was more suited to wrestling matches than to running.

"I wish we had a football," he said to his brother. It would be fun to run and tackle with the soft green carpet of grass to fall on. But they didn't have a ball and Arturo didn't like tackle. Roberto thought about golfing while he wandered to the edge of the lawn where a forest of trees spread up a hill. He inhaled deeply; the smell of eucalyptus was not familiar and he liked the pungent odor. It reminded him a little of the sage back home.

He found a thick, sturdy branch and a rock half the size of a baseball.

"Let's golf," he called to Arturo. He gave the rock a swift whack with the branch and sent it forward nearly six feet.

He knew he couldn't dig holes in the lawn, so he piled leaves here and there as the targets. Arturo found his own branch and rock, but he soon tired of the game and climbed to where the edge of the lawn sloped. He lay down on the grass and rolled down the hill with arms tight to the sides of his body.

Roberto kept his attention on golfing. He liked the challenge of making the rock go just where he wanted. He thought about a time when his Tío Joe had taken him fishing and how they had cast the lines into the river. Tío taught him how to keep his eye on the ebb near a rock and fling the end of his line to drop just at the spot where the fish were hiding. Roberto liked making something do just what you wanted it to do.

He hadn't been fishing since they had moved to California, but his father said he would take him when he had the time off work. But Dad worked all the time. He still had his job helping build Navy stuff, but now he worked on weekends, too, fixing up rich people's yards. Roberto went with him sometimes to help out, but his father was quiet while they worked. Riding in the truck was the only time he talked much. Roberto wished he could talk to his father about more things.

He wanted to tell him that he didn't like California. He didn't like the basement, where they all had to live crowded into one room. He missed having the creek, the ditch and the mountain as his playground. There were no adventures in the back yard of Tía Rose and Tío Tom's house, just concrete and a tiny patch of grass. Whenever he started to have fun someone yelled at him. *Stay away from the flowers, don't make so much noise, don't throw things.*

Don't live.

It was different here at Miss Mary's house. He knew he had to take care of this place, not wreck anything. Her house was fancy, and that big house, her Tía's house, was as big as ten houses.

He liked Miss Mary. Liked her a lot. At first he had been ashamed because of the bugs, but now his family came to Mary's house every week for a bath and to play, and he was happy. Well, he was happy about playing, but he still didn't like the baths. He liked to be dirty because it made him look tough.

But Mom was better now. She smiled more, and she didn't yell and hit as much.

He did like the school here. There were no nuns to slap his hands with the ruler, and you could raise your hand and go use the toilet whenever you wanted. Roberto remembered the shame of wetting his pants. It had happened back in first grade, and all of the kids laughed as the nun insulted him by calling him a baby. He was happy when they left that school.

But Roberto didn't have many friends here. He still played with his brother most of the time. The third-grade boys liked to play rough, and fights happened every day. Roberto didn't like fighting. He didn't like the feel of his fist when it made that crunching sound, and he really didn't like to *be* hit. It made him cry, and the other boys laughed and called him a girl. Not only that, he couldn't invite Kevin over to play anymore. He begged his mother to let him go to Kevin's house, but since both of his friend's parents worked, Mom wouldn't let him go.

"Roberto! Wait 'til you see." Arturo's call came from the other side of the cottage. What was he doing there? They were supposed to stay back here.

Picking up the rock and putting it into his pocket, Roberto swung his stick around in giant figure eights as he walked toward his brother's voice. Maybe Arturo had found a lizard.

Arturo came zipping around the side of the house waving something shiny. Roberto put out his hand and his brother plopped a heavy object into it.

It was a watch! Not the kind with the brown strap and round face like Dad wore, but the round kind with a chain like the one his abuelo carried. A pocket watch. He pressed the little latch on the side, and the cover sprung open revealing the face.

"Where did you find it?"

"Up there." Arturo waved over his shoulder.

"Show me."

Arturo led him around to the front of the house. The driveway here was like the one at home, just much longer. It led from the main road around the edge of the big house. A hedge grew along one side, and grass sprouted between the two strips of concrete.

Arturo pointed into the bushes. "It was in there."

How in the world did his brother come to be looking into those bushes? Arturo crawled and slithered like a snake most of the time. Maybe he had been pretending to be a car trying to park beside the house.

"It's very valuable." Roberto snapped the cover shut and rubbed the front. There was a picture of a sailing ship on a stormy ocean engraved in the gold.

"You think we could sell it? We could buy a dog." Arturo begged his parents for another dog nearly every day. He had hated leaving Flojo behind in New Mexico.

"No. You know we can't have a dog." A watch like this was worth a lot of money—maybe enough to buy a house. He knew his mother was saving. She thought the money hidden in her suitcase was a secret, but he had seen her sneaking to put coins into it after they came home from buying groceries.

Things would be so much better if they had their own house again. He thought about having a mattress to share with Arturo, no little sisters pissing in the bed, waking him up all night, crying and whispering. Maybe they would even have their own room again. He hated listening to the whispered hiss of Mom and Dad at night. Mom crying after the rumbling voice of Dad had answered her.

He couldn't sleep with the lights on, yet his mother made him go to bed every night at the same time as the rest of the kids. He told her he was old enough to stay up.

"I'll be quiet. I'll just read. I promise," he begged her every night, even though she had slapped him once and told him to be quiet and get into bed.

Arturo's voice interrupted his thoughts. "We could buy a new car. We need one of those. Maybe a race car."

His brother was such a baby. "We can't buy a race car. Dad doesn't know how to drive one and we aren't old enough."

Arturo tried to grab the watch. "Give it back to me. It's mine."

Roberto shook his head. "No, it's not. We have to give it to Miss Mary. It was in her yard. It's probably hers."

"Ladies don't carry watches, *estúpido*."

"You want a bloody nose?" Roberto didn't fight at school, but that didn't mean he wouldn't punch his brother. "It's probably her father's watch. Come on."

Roberto ran to the back door of the cottage and kicked off his shoes before going through the green screen door. He remembered to stop and hold out his hand so the door didn't slam. Mom told him he must always behave himself at Miss Mary's or they might not get to come anymore.

"Here come some young men who look thirsty." Miss Mary stood up from the table where she had been sitting with Mom. "How about some lemonade?"

"Yes, thank you, please." Roberto followed Miss Mary to the refrigerator. "We found something."

"I found it." Arturo came through the door and let it slam behind him. Roberto turned to glare at his brother.

"Don't let the door slam, pig."

"Don't call me a pig, donkey."

"Boys, boys." Mary scolded. "What did you find?"

"This." Roberto held out the gold watch. He watched Miss Mary's face and waited for her praise. Instead a furrow took over her forehead as she took the watch from his hand.

"Where did you find it?" Her voice was a gravelly whisper.

"In the bushes, where you park the car." Roberto waited, but Miss Mary didn't say another word.

"Is it yours? Can we keep it if it doesn't belong to anyone?" Arturo reached out his hand for the watch. Mom got up from the table and came to look.

"Of course not. It belongs to someone." Mom turned and looked at Miss Mary.

Miss Mary finally spoke. "Yes, it does. It belongs to my husband." She turned to Roberto. "Can you show me where you found it?"

Roberto led Miss Mary to the front of the house. His mother followed along with Arturo and his two sisters. He felt important, like a police detective. But as he approached the driveway he realized he didn't know exactly where Arturo had found the watch.

"Umm . . . right there." He waved vaguely toward the driveway.

"No it wasn't." Arturo ran to the edge of the drive, where daisies grew around some big green bushes. He pointed. "It was in here, stuck right in the middle of this bush. I saw it shine. I thought it was a weird flower."

Arturo turned to Miss Mary. "Are you sure we can't keep it? I'm going to use it to buy a dog."

Mom shook her head. "Arturo, it doesn't belong to you. It belongs to Miss Mary's husband."

"Okay." Arturo hopped on one foot and made his way down the narrow cement strip to the end of the driveway.

Roberto watched Miss Mary's face. Her lips were pressed together in a thin line, and her eyes seemed to be staring at something far away. She shook her head slightly, then turned and looked at him.

"Thank you, Roberto. Thank you for finding this and bringing it to me. John will be happy to have it back."

He felt his cheeks turn red with her praise. He should tell Miss Mary that it was really Arturo who found the watch, but he didn't say a word.

Sewing Machines

Forty

Perfie and Mary sipped the cinnamon tea they both loved. Mary seemed nervous about something, and just as Perfie was about to ask her what was wrong Mary jumped up and walked over to the low corner shelf where Karleen stood staring at the trinkets and glass animals.

Mary handed Karleen a glass dog that was no more than two inches tall. "We must be very gentle with these. They break."

Karleen held it carefully in her tiny hand. "It's a dog."

"Can you clean him off with your cloth and put him on the shelf?" Mary handed Karleen her napkin.

Karleen wiped the dog and used both hands to set him on the shelf just as Geri toddled over and reached for it.

"No!" Karleen slapped Geri's outstretched hand.

Perfie expected Geri to cry, but instead she simply went back to her toys in the middle of the carpet.

"You mustn't hit your sister," Mary said.

"She's bad."

"She's not bad, just curious."

Karleen stuck the tips of two fingers into her mouth, and her eyes filled with tears. "I'm bad?"

"No, you're not bad either." Mary bent and hugged Karleen. "You're my best helper."

Perfie felt her face burn red. It was obvious Mary thought her kids needed some kind of attention that she couldn't give them.

Mary returned to the table. "Perfie, there's something I want to talk to you about."

"I don't hit them. Only when they're naughty."

"I know. It's not that. It's about the watch."

"The watch?" It had been over a week since the boys had found Mary's husband's watch in the bushes.

"Oh, not even about the watch. About more than that. About our friendship and about John, and . . . oh, this is hard."

Perfie was silent.

"John thinks the boys stole the watch and then returned it. He doesn't understand about us, how we're friends."

Perfie felt a surge of anger from her toes to the top of her head. "My boys are not thieves. They found that watch. They returned it right away."

"I know that. I guess I'm trying to tell you about John—about how different he is from me. He thinks . . . he thinks that we can't be friends because of who you are and who I am."

"He doesn't want us to come here anymore? Because he thinks my boys steal?" Perfie could barely pull the words out of her tight throat. "Because you're rich and I'm poor?"

"That. And because I'm . . . you're . . . well, Mexican." Mary reached for Perfie's hand. "I don't feel that way at all. You have to believe me. But John does feel that way. I just didn't want you to think, I mean, you have me to dinner and I know the next step would be for all four of us to get together. I just wanted to explain why I can't do that."

Perfie wanted to jump up and run from the house. She wanted to grab her kids and go back to her lowly basement. But Mary had to drive them home. She bit her lip and stared down at the cup on the table. She didn't know what to say. Just last week Isaac had suggested that a picnic might be a way for them to entertain the Kents. Something up at Tilden Park.

To Perfie's surprise Mary started crying. Karleen jumped up and ran to her.

"Don't be sad. I'll be your helper."

Mary reached down and hugged Karleen. "It's okay. You play. Mama and I have to talk."

Karleen scowled and turned. As she walked back to the living room she looked over her shoulder at Mary. Mary wiped the tears from her face and smiled, waving the girl on.

"Oh, Perfie. John and I had a big fight about it. I never knew he was so prejudiced. But some of the things he said made me so sad. Like thinking about how hard you and Isaac work and how you won't ever get ahead. John said you shouldn't come to this house because you won't ever get to live in a house like this. He said I shouldn't make you think you could. And when he thought the boys would steal! I know you're mad about that. I'm mad, too. I know they wouldn't." Mary looked up. "I shouldn't be dumping this on you. It's not fair. But it's been like a stone on my back, so heavy. Perfie, you are my only friend. Since we moved here John has expected me to be a doctor's wife. But I'm not like those women. I can't talk about the things they talk about. It's not like talking with you."

Perfie was confused. One minute it seemed Mary was saying that they couldn't come to the house and the next that she was her only friend. Then she realized she needed Mary as much as Mary was saying she needed her.

"I know about not having friends. I guess you are my only friend, too."

John's opinion must not have impacted Mary much judging by how often the two women continued to get together. Perfie taught Mary to sew. Mary borrowed her Aunt Eugenia's machine, which Perfie expertly cleaned, oiled and adjusted so that the stitch was accurate.

Mary was eager to learn. "How about I start with dresses for the girls? That way if I make a mistake it's smaller."

"Smaller is harder, in some cases." Perfie hesitated. "You don't need to make dresses for them."

"But I want to," Mary coaxed.

"My sewing machine is in one of those crates in Tom's garage. I thought it would be unpacked by now." Perfie shook her head. "Isaac doesn't think it's a good idea to get it out because there's not really room in the basement."

"You know you can use this one whenever you want."

To her amazement Perfie discovered that she liked teaching. Mary listened and watched as she explained why things had to be stitched in a certain order or cut a certain way. It felt good when Mary did the things Perfie had taught her.

But the best thing of all was how excited Mary got when she found out Perfie knew how to make the patterns fit. When Mary carefully measured her own body and decided that a size eight would do, Perfie measured her again and made slight adjustments to different areas of the pattern. Mary had a long waist and slim, long arms.

"I look like a scarecrow," she complained to Perfie. "Look at these long arms! I can never get the sleeves right when I buy a dress."

Together they transformed Mary's yellow dress. It had not been out of her closet for two years because it didn't fit right. Now it was like a new dress with a waist that hugged her perfectly, a skirt that swished and twirled with a wonderful flair and a neckline that followed the slope of her neck and teased at what might lie below.

Perfie sat and embroidered tiny flowers onto the placket of the yellow dress while Mary looked through a magazine in search of her next project.

"Do you think I'm ready for some silky fabric?" Mary held up a picture of a shiny green dress.

"It's hard to sew—it wants to slide out of place all the time. I think with lots of pins and taking it slow you can do it." Perfie squinted and tied a knot in her thread.

"I saw a brilliant turquoise dress the other day. It was nipped in at the waist and had two little pleats to bring the skirt out before it dropped off straight. But the neckline, now that was amazing. It was asymmetrical, coming to a point just on the left with a bunch of gathering and no collar. There were little tucks in the bodice that brought it in for a close fit." Mary traced the shape on her neck with her finger.

Perfie picked up paper and a pencil and sketched. When she was done she pushed the drawing across the table to Mary.

"Almost. The neck line was a little different." Mary changed one line on the sketch.

Perfie examined the drawing and nodded. "We can make you this dress."

The following Tuesday the two women and the girls drove downtown to the Singer store.

It didn't take long for Mary to find the perfect material, turquoise silk with tiny nubs. While Perfie selected thread and buttons to go with it, Mary browsed through the bolts of fabrics. She walked the aisle with her fingers slipping over the silky edges. She stopped and stared, then pulled a bolt out of the stack and carried it over to Perfie.

"This fabric is perfect for you. Perfect for Perfecta." Mary laughed.

Perfie didn't smile. "It's very pretty."

"What's wrong?"

"It's nothing." Perfie turned back to the buttons.

"I think you should get this fabric. It's wonderful and it will be easy to wash. Wouldn't Isaac like to see you in a new dress?"

"I'm sorry Mary, but I can't spare the money for the cloth."

"Let me get it for you. It will be my gift for all the sewing lessons."

Perfie reached out and caressed the green fabric.

"I couldn't Mary. You already do my laundry and watch my kids."

"Let me think of something else you could do then. I know we can think of something."

Perfie took her hand away from the fabric. "No. I can't. Maybe after I work a few more weeks for Mrs. Cooper I'll be able to afford it." Why couldn't Mary understand there were lots of other things she needed the money for. Fabric for a new dress was not on that list.

After Mary paid for her fabric and notions she folded over the top edge of the pink and white shopping bag and smiled at the girls. "How about I treat everyone to some ice cream?"

Karleen jumped up and down and chanted "Ice cream, ice cream."

Geri made little hopping jumps while laughing at her sister and copying her moves. "Scream, scream," she mimicked.

Soon they were seated around a table at Fenton's Creamery. The girls were coloring with crayons and paper provided to keep them busy. Karleen worked on a picture while Geri scribbled circles and chewed on a red crayon.

Perfie sipped a cup of hot tea. "That Mr. Kamatsu makes me so uncomfortable."

"Mr. Kamatsu at the hardware store?" Mary held a spoonful of sugar halfway to her cup.

"Yes, that's him. He follows me around the store just waiting for the kids to break something. He probably thinks Roberto will steal." Perfie glanced at Mary. She had thought that, too. Well, John had, and Perfie still suspected that Mary had brought the whole thing up to see if it might be true.

Mary shook her head and dumped the sugar in her cup. "Mr. Kamatsu is a wonderful man. He walks around with me to help me find what I need. I'm sure he's doing the same for you."

Perfie shook her head. "I don't think so. You know how it is, with the war and all that. Those people are out to get us now. You can't trust them."

Mary scowled at Perfie. "Did you just say *those people*?"

Perfie stared at Mary.

Mary continued. "I'm sorry, but that's a sore point for me. It's something my mother always said. Did I ever tell you about my best friend Tulip?"

Perfie shook her head.

"She's a Negro. She was the only child I ever got to play with until I was sent away to school. She was my best friend. But people didn't like that. It just wasn't done, a white girl and a Negro being best friends."

"I've never known a Negro."

"That's just it. Most people who make that kind of judgement never have either." Mary stirred her cup madly even though the sugar had long since dissolved. She stopped and leaned toward Perfie. "That's what John and I fought about, you know."

"What?"

"He called you that. He said I shouldn't hang around with *those people.*"

"I'm not a Negro."

Mary shook her head fiercely. "It doesn't mean a Negro. It means anyone who is different."

"Different than what?"

"Different than yourself, whoever you are."

Now Perfie shook her head. "No. I think it means not white. And I am white."

Mary put her hand on top of Perfie's. "To me it doesn't matter at all, but that's not what some people think."

Perfie remembered what her father had always said about Isaac. Un pagano, discomformidad. When he said it he meant someone who wasn't Catholic—someone who didn't conform. She looked at her friend. "I think you're right. But in New Mexico we didn't say *those people.* We just didn't like them because they weren't like us."

She had never told Mary that Isaac was Presbyterian and she was Catholic. It would come to light that they hadn't married, and she didn't know how Mary would react to that. "But Mr. Kamatsu, he's Japanese. He's on the other side."

Mary shook her head. "Mr. Kamatsu has lived here all his life. He was born in Oakland. He belongs here more than you or I."

Perfie wrinkled her nose. She didn't agree with Mary.

The waiter interrupted Perfie as he placed bowls of ice cream in front of the girls. "Here we are. Creamy ice for the creamy ladies. Can I get you anything else?"

Perfie and Mary shook their heads.

"You were saying?" Mary wasn't going to let Perfie off the hook.

"Mr. Kamatsu. He still gives me the creeps. Japanese or whatever."

"But do you understand about people? How you shouldn't judge someone you don't know?"

Perfie snapped a napkin open and tucked it into the neck of Karleen's dress. "Mary, don't scold me. I'm not a child."

Mary flushed. "I learned something once from a friend. She taught me that it doesn't always work out to think one way or another. She accused me of thinking too positively about everything—told me that I was going to get hurt. Well, I don't agree with her. I keep my thoughts positive and it makes things better. But the opposite is true." Mary paused. "Perfie, you're my friend, you know that, right?"

Perfie nodded, and Mary continued.

"You think negatively and the world will do just what you want—it will be negative. Do you even really know Mr. Kamatsu? Do you know if he has a sick mother or a dying child or bills he can't pay?"

"Of course I don't know those things. But I do know that he's rude and suspicious of me and my kids."

"What does he do that makes you think that?"

"He scowls and clicks his tongue while he follows us around the store. He bobs his head up and down the whole time like he wants to say something but he's holding it back."

"What if, just what if, he scowls because he's worried about his son? What if he bobs his head because that's what Japanese people do? They bow, as a greeting, as a sign of respect."

Perfie stared at her friend. Why was Mr. Kamatsu so important to her?

Mary sighed. "I can't believe that you feel he's evil. Nothing is ever that simple. Good or bad, right or wrong, black or white. The world isn't really like that. Do you know anyone like that? Someone who's always right? Or always wrong, for that matter? Someone truly evil?"

Perfie's face turned pink, then drained of all color. She licked her lips.

"Mi padre," she said softly.

"Your father?" Mary asked. "He's evil?"

"He spent his life—my life—making things bad for me. Nothing I ever did was good enough for him."

"Did he beat you?"

"He never beat me. When I was young there were paddlings. I guess there was a fight or two when I was a teenager." Perfie turned and looked into Mary's eyes. "But it was more than that. It was the pressure, the waiting to see when he would strike next. I never knew what was going to be considered wrong and what would satisfy him. I was scared to try things, to do things that young people should be doing."

"But you seem okay, not afraid of anything now."

"It's only because I have Isaac now and we are far away from my father." Perfie's voice shook.

Mary was quiet for a minute, obviously thinking about what Perfie had just told her. Would she start talking about Mr. Kamatsu again?

But Mary took a deep breath and simply asked "When do you think we can start on the dress?"

Forty-One

On Saturday morning Roberto woke early. He opened his eyes and stared at the stain on the ceiling. It scared him, the look of La Bruja. His mother always warned him that spirits and witches could see him.

"I haven't done anything bad lately," he whispered to the stain with the long pointy nose and stringy hair.

He looked over at Arturo. How could his brother still sleep when Dad was taking them to the ball game today? He turned his head and tried to see Mom's old clock. She had set it on the shelf in an attempt to make this basement look like the kitchen back home. He couldn't see the clock from here, but he felt it was getting late. Why wasn't anyone else awake yet?

He thought about the house back home. He remembered the fun he and Arturo had running around outside. They never had to ask permission in those days. They just jumped out of bed and raced out of the house to visit the bull, throw rocks in the creek or build forts with the fallen cottonwood branches. Ever since they left T.A. there hadn't been as much fun. This place they were in now had a perfectly good back yard and a smooth sidewalk to run on, but they got yelled at for playing out there.

Today would be different. Dad promised for weeks he would take them to someplace new and exciting and today was the day. They were going to a real baseball game—with hot dogs and everything.

He nudged Arturo with his foot. His brother moaned and curled into a tight ball. Roberto slid out from under the blanket and looked over at the piss pot in the corner. That was another thing he hated. There was no outhouse here, and Tía Rose wouldn't let them use the bathroom upstairs during the night. Everyone had to use Leenie's bucket. He tried to decide if he could wait or not.

Nope, had to go. He looked at his mother and father. Both were still asleep. He tip-toed toward the door. He would much rather pee out in the yard than in the pot, but it was nearly impossible to open the heavy slanted door without making noise.

The door creaked, but no one stirred. He slipped through and lowered it slowly. The sun streamed over the back of the garage and cast a dim glow into the yard. It must be earlier than he thought. He stood near the side of the house away from the windows and peed. He liked the way it steamed in the early morning. He didn't feel like going back inside so he walked around and sat on the concrete step of the back porch. It was nice out here. Quiet.

A little black bird landed on the lawn and poked his shiny beak here and there. What was that saying that he had heard? The early bird gets the worm—that was it. This must be the bird everyone talked about, and he wondered why the bird was so special. His mother, his grandmother and even Mrs. Colby talked about this worm thing.

Mrs. Colby was nice. The second grade had been full of kids, most of them new like he was. He had been the tallest one in class. Good thing they made Arturo go to first grade 'cause he didn't want to go to the same class as his puny little brother. But now he had been moved to third grade, and there were even more kids in his class.

In fact there were so many kids that there weren't enough chairs to go around. Some kids had to sit on the floor. He liked to sit in the back corner of the room where he could lean on the wall and stretch his legs out. But it was hard to see the board when the teacher wrote on it.

The new school had so many books. There were even books they could take home to read. You had to sign your name on a little yellow card and put it into a box. Plus, you had to be really careful not to wreck the book. He kept his book on the highest part of the shelf so Leenie and Geri wouldn't get ahold of it. They wanted to read it too, but they ripped the pages.

Roberto knew his parents didn't have any money to pay for a wrecked book. They didn't have money for anything much at all, but somehow Dad must have saved up for the baseball game.

Thinking about the game again, Roberto jumped up from the porch. The early bird fluttered away, scared by his movement.

Time to see if anyone else was awake. "I'm the early bird, and I want that worm," he told himself.

Arturo jumped all over the sidewalk as they walked to East 14th to catch the bus that would take them to the ball field. What a baby, Roberto thought, as he walked beside his father.

"I'm good today, right Dad?"

"Yes you are. But you can jump around a little if you want. Get some energy out before we get on the bus."

"No, that's okay. I'd rather walk with you."

He wished he had a hat. His father always wore his, usually the gray felt one with the shiny ribbon. But on Saturdays Dad wore a different hat, more like a cowboy one with a big brim to keep the sun out of his eyes.

"Dad? Can I get a hat?"

"Someday," his father answered absently. That was the answer he always gave when one of them asked for something.

"Are we going to get hot dogs?"

"Yep. Told you we would, didn't I?"

"The bus. The bus is here. Run!" Arturo spied the big orange and white bus up at the corner. He started running toward it.

His father's voice drifted up the street like a lasso, roping Arturo to a stop and pulling him back to them. "Whoa, Arturo. That's not the one we need."

"That's not it?"

Dad shook his head.

When they got to the bus stop on the corner two more buses came, but Dad shook his head each time.

Finally their bus pulled up, and Dad reached in his pocket for coins. He handed them each five pennies and motioned them up the steps. Arturo hopped up first, and Roberto followed.

"It's empty! We get to pick any seat we want." Arturo dropped his pennies into the tall metal box and watched as they clinked to the bottom. Roberto added his pennies while Arturo headed down the aisle.

"Eeny. . . Meany. . . Miny. . . Moe." Arturo tapped each seat with his hand. "Catch a nigger by the toe," he continued.

Roberto felt his father push past him and saw him grab Arturo's arm to swing him around.

"Hush!" Dad sounded mad.

Then Roberto saw the man. He was seated near the back, over by the window. It was a colored man, and he had a mean look on his face.

"Sorry 'bout that," Dad said to the man.

"Should teach your boy that's not a polite word. He could get in some real trouble with that word."

"What word, Dad?" Arturo pulled away from his father's grip.

"Just sit here. We'll talk about it later." Dad pushed Arturo into a seat and sat down by him. He pointed to another seat. "Roberto, you sit here in front of us."

Roberto slid in, moving next to the window. He knew what the bad word was. Nigger. That's what colored people were called. Some kids at school had called a boy that, and the teacher made them stop. Those same boys had called him a Spic. He didn't know what that meant, but he could tell it was mean.

A few stops later the man stood and walked to the front of the bus without looking at them. He stood near the door and held onto the silver pole with his dark hand. When the bus stopped at the corner he got off, and a crowd of new people got on.

Dad tapped Roberto's shoulder. "You move back here with us so folks'll have a seat."

Roberto slid into the seat alongside his father and brother and looked at all the new people. There were colored people, but there were some Chinese and some whites too, not just the brown faces of New Mexico. He liked to look at the hair styles and the clothes. He watched the mothers hold their kids on their laps, and he tried to imagine what these people ate for dinner. But he didn't have long to think about this, because several minutes later Dad stood up and said they were there.

The baseball game was the best. Their seats were way up high, and Roberto felt almost like he was back on the bluffs in T.A. He could look out over the buildings and see the blue water of the bay. The crowd cheered and stood up, clapping their hands and yelling when a player made a good hit. He soon learned the best part of the ballgame. Yelling and screaming at the top of your lungs was allowed! Even the grownups did it. Dad bought them each a hot dog. He could have eaten two, but Dad said no, only one each.

There was a man selling navy blue hats with a red design. An Oaks hat! He looked at his father. Dad shook his head.

Maybe someday he would have enough money to buy his own.

When they got home it was late in the afternoon, and Mom and the girls were sitting out back in the sun.

"You should've seen that ball. Went right up to the clouds, didn't it?" Arturo looked back at him and waved his arms to show his mother how high.

He had something to tell her, too. "Mom, I'm not Roberto anymore."

Her eyebrows flew up and she covered her mouth with her hand.

"I'm a Californian now. I want to be called Bobbie."

"He just wants that because he's in love with Billy Raimondi. He wants his name to sound like that." Arturo knew what his brother was thinking.

"Bobbie," his mother repeated. "Not Robbie?"

He shook his head. "Nope. Bobbie."

"Well, I'm going to be Artie." His brother always copied him.

"Sounds good to me. Boobie, Artie, Leenie and Geri." Dad waved his hand toward each of them.

"No!" Why did Dad do that? "No jokes. Not Boobie. I'm Bobbie, and you better remember because I'm not answering to anything else."

He watched his mother. She was nodding her head up and down, a far away look in her eyes.

Forty-Two

Perfie picked up the shoes that were scattered around the room and set them by the concrete steps leading out of the basement. The kids had bickered all through supper, and she heard more arguments and crying from outside when she sent them out to run around before bed time. She was glad when they finally fell asleep.

She didn't know why, but she was bothered by the "American" names Roberto and Arturo had decided to adopt. "Bobbie and Artie," she corrected herself in a whisper.

"That's right, my American boys."

She hadn't realized Isaac was listening to her. He sat at the table smoking his pipe.

"Why does it bother you, Perfie?"

She sat with him. "I don't know. I guess it makes New Mexico feel so far away. Things aren't exactly how I thought they would be."

"The boys are adjusting. They like it here."

Even if you don't, she heard the reproach in his unspoken words.

"It's not that I don't like it," Perfie stopped. In many ways she didn't like it.

But there were lots of things she did like. She liked the schools, and she loved Mary Kent. She liked having a friend. She liked taking the girls to the park. She liked catching the bus and riding downtown to shop, even if she didn't have money to spend. She liked the grocery store with all the choices of fruits and vegetables, meats and candy. She missed the nutty, heavy bread from home, though. If she had an oven she would bake her own.

Isaac reached across the table and pressed his hand into hers. "Just give me some time. When we have our own house I know you'll feel better."

Perfie filled her lungs with a deep breath and slowly let the air out. She felt her shoulders relax. The quiet of the evening and Isaac's warm hand comforted her. The only sounds were the soft snores and gurgles of her sleeping children.

Isaac sucked in on his pipe before pulling it out of his mouth to speak. "The boys had a good time today, but I thought the day was going to start off bad."

"Why?"

"When we got on the bus there was a big colored man. Arturo called him a nigger."

"A nigger? He doesn't use those kinds of words. That can't be right."

"It was an accident, he was singing that rhyme, the one about choosing: Eeny, Meeny, Miny, Moe. When he came to the next part, the fellow wasn't too happy about it."

"Do you think he even knew what it meant?"

"No, but Roberto did."

"Mary and I talked the other day about people being different. It started out about the Japanese, but she really lectured me. She has a colored friend back east."

"I don't care what color people are, but I think I need to talk to the boys about it. I thought we had settled it after Kevin came to visit, but sounds like it didn't really sink in. There's some tough kids around here. Artie could get beat up if he accidentally says the wrong thing to the wrong boys. Dom told me there's an Italian gang running around his neighborhood."

Perfie wasn't worried about the Italians. "Isaac, what do you think about the Japanese?"

"Japanese? Well, I think we might end up at war with them. I know they signed that treaty, but I don't have faith in that kind of thing."

Perfie didn't keep up with the news. It was overwhelming to her. "What treaty?"

"The Soviets and the Japanese said they would stay out of things— stay neutral."

"Do you think they're our enemy?"

He squeezed her hand. "Don't worry. The war won't be here. Not in America."

She realized he was thinking about things happening on the other side of the world, while she was focused on things here, like Mr. Kamatsu.

"But what about the Japanese here, in Oakland? Do you think they'll do something? Attack from within? Or maybe they're spies?" She watched his face.

Isaac sat up straight and leaned forward. "Here? What are you afraid of?"

"Like Mr. Kamatsu, down at the hardware store."

"George?"

She shook her head. "I don't think that's really his name. That's not what his wife calls him. Genges . . . no, Genji, that's it."

"Well, he answers to George. I'm darn sure he's not a spy. He's just a fella who works hard, like the rest of us. Lucky guy to have that store." Isaac leaned back. "Is that what Mary told you? That the Japanese are spies?"

Perfie didn't want to admit to him that she was the one who thought this. "Enough for tonight," she said, yawning. "I'm tired. Let's go to bed."

Forty-Three

Rose had taken to placing what little mail the Martinez family received on the ledge of the front porch. The boys grabbed it and brought it to their mother when they came home from school.

Today there was a thin brown envelope, just like the ones Perfie used to see in the box Carlotta kept on the big desk in the living room of the Martinez house. She ran her fingers over the written address. Isaac Martinez. They were never addressed to her, these letters from Carlotta.

The handwriting was different—printed, and in a bolder script than Carlotta's.

Perfie held it up to the window where sunlight outlined the same bold handwriting inside, but she couldn't make out what it said.

It's for Isaac, not me. She placed the letter on the shelf and turned to make a snack for the boys. They were always hungry when they came home from school, and this morning had been so chaotic that she hadn't even been able to pack any lunches.

"Mom, hurry up. We want to go out." Roberto sat at the table and drummed his hands. Arturo followed suit, adding his heels against the crossbar of the chair to increase the noise. Geri screamed in glee at the antics.

"Hush, too much noise." Perfie cut up an apple.

"We want food, we want food." Arturo giggled and added the chant to the chaos.

She carried the egg sandwiches and apple wedges to the door. "You can eat outside today. Watch your sisters."

With the children out in the backyard she turned to the letter. It had been a month since Isabelle had written. Her letters were always filled with news about Primitivo and what was going on in Española, but she seldom wrote about Isaac's family. In her last note Isabelle had mentioned seeing Bennie pass through town on his way to Albuquerque, but there had been no news of the school or Isaac's parents.

Perfie put her fingernail under the seal and wiggled it back and forth. It was sealed tight.

I deserve to know what this says. She slid her nail farther and pried the sealed flap up. She pulled the letter out and stood near the window to use the sunshine as her reading light.

Dearest Brother,

It is with great sorrow that I must write this letter. Our beloved father, Lucas Francisco Martinez, has passed from this world. I know this must come as a surprise to you, as it was a surprise to us all. Just last week he patched the roof of the school and talked about a new class in Biology for the students. The doctor feels his heart gave out, although it had never shown any signs of weakness.

Mother is devastated. She paces endlessly and pours over the papers from the school. Eli is able to take over the running of the school since Papa trained him in these matters, but that doesn't seem to be of any comfort to her.

Although by the time you get this letter he will be buried, I think it might be a good idea if you come home. We are already short a teacher at the school, and with Papa gone things are tough. Our enrollment is good just now, and Eli is concerned about jeopardizing this just when we need it.

Your Brother, Enoch Martinez

P.S. I know you are wondering why we didn't telephone you, but the lines have been down for a week due to a crazy thunderstorm we had here.

Lucas dead! Perfie glanced at the clock. Isaac would be home soon. She should start supper.

Perfie could barely focus on the chopping and stirring, but she managed to get a pot of stew going. She turned the fire low, wiped her hands, picked up the letter and read it again.

Would Isaac want to go back to Tierra Amarilla? Did she want to go back? The thought of living under the thumb of Carlotta once more wasn't appealing, but maybe the old woman would be so struck with grief that her attention would be elsewhere. What about the house? Levi and his family had moved into their house, but if he was running the school wouldn't he need to be in town?

The adobe house seemed like a castle to her now. She had complained about walking to the ditch for water when they lived there, but at least she had been able to have the water without feeling guilty. She pictured herself standing out on the porch and looking at the cottonwoods and cattle, where the stream ran through the lowlands.

Benjamin was gone now—married and living in Denver with his wife and children. Perfie was happy that he had finally settled down and relieved to think that she wouldn't be distracted by him.

She wanted to go back.

She walked up the steps to the driveway and waited for Isaac. She didn't have to wait long.

"Isaac, Isaac," she called out as he came up the driveway

"What is it?"

"It's your father; he's dead."

"What? How do you know this?"

She thrust the letter to him. He read it, and read it again with tears streaming from his eyes.

"*Mi papa, mi papa. No tuve la oportunidad de verlo. Sólo una última vez, eso me hubiese bastado*. If I had just gone back one more time to see him." Isaac lifted his face to the sky.

Perfie tried to remember when Isaac had last seen his father. They had fought with Carlotta right before packing up and moving out of the adobe house. Had he gone to see his father before they left T.A.? Lucas would never take sides when the boys complained about their mother, but maybe he had said goodbye to his son.

"Will you go?"

"Perfie, I don't know. Give me a minute."

"Dinner is ready."

"Perfie, *please*."

She looked at Isaac, this man she had lived with for ten years. She could see the patient hand of Lucas in Isaac when his eyes sparkled and he flashed his crooked grin. She recognized the sly shrug which said *go ahead and criticize me—it doesn't sink in*. But she could also see the commanding disgust of Carlotta in the way Isaac looked away when trouble presented itself. His eyebrows pushed together, his lips pressed into a pale thin line and tiny wrinkles around his eyes gave away his despair.

Perfie had overlooked those wrinkles for many years. She never wanted to believe he had any weaknesses or anything other than love for his parents.

"You should eat something. Let me fix you a bowl of stew."

"You eat. I need to go for a walk." He turned and strode down the drive.

Isaac returned when the kids were fed and the dishes cleared. Perfie had left the pot of stew on the stove along with a bowl and a plate of tortillas. He had to eat—she would insist on it.

To her surprise Isaac served himself a bowl of stew without a second thought. He seemed calm, smiling and laughing with the children and bouncing Karleen on his knee in her favorite horsey ride game.

"Did you decide?"

"Yes, I will go. I know it will be hard, but I think I can arrange things."

"When?"

"It will take a few days. I think Saturday."

"Will you work at the school?"

"I just need to see what's going on. I don't know what Madre will be like." Isaac picked up his empty bowl and set it with the rest of the dishes. "Let's get these kids into bed."

Isaac read the children their current favorite story, The Coyote and the Owl, while Perfie washed Isaac's bowl and the stew pot. This was all happening so fast. To change how they were living again? She should be used to it by now, she thought. They had changed so many times over the years.

She wondered if this time would feel like they were going backward. She thought about the schools in T.A. Roberto was old enough to go to the Martinez family school now, but Arturo and Karleen would be back with the nuns. There was no one in T.A. like Miss Mary. And without Isabelle, Perfie wouldn't have a friend in town.

Mary had just helped her get the new job with Mr. Clark. Perfie had heard about it, but didn't know how to go and ask. Mary had given her the courage to talk to the man. Perfie would work three mornings a week learning upholstery. No pay while she was learning, but once she could do the job herself, the pay was good. Best of all, the work was done in a quiet workshop at the back of Mr. Clark's house and the kids could come with her. There wouldn't be that kind of opportunity in New Mexico.

There would be no one to talk with each day—no one eager to learn from her or to share those silly tales about difficult husbands.

Perfie would miss Mary Kent.

Forty-Four

Mary placed a cup of tea in front of Perfie. "Something is bothering you."

Perfie twisted her handkerchief tightly, then unwound it and used it to blow her nose. "Oh Mary, you're a good friend. You're what makes me want to stay here."

Mary sat down and reached for the sugar. "Where else would you go?"

"Back to Tierra Amarilla. We're moving back."

"What?" Mary's tone was sharp.

"Isaac's father died. His brother sent a letter saying they need him at the school."

Mary rubbed her fingers on the smooth surface of the china tea cup. Her shoulders slumped forward, and she shook her head slowly.

She finally lifted her eyes to meet Perfie's. "When?"

"Saturday."

"How will you get ready so soon?"

"I know. I should be home right now. Packing. I can't imagine leaving so soon, but that's what Isaac said." Perfie took a gulp of tea. "I just wanted to tell you how much I appreciate everything."

Mary jumped up and pulled Perfie into her arms.

"I can't bear it. Why does it have to be?" Mary sobbed into Perfie's shoulder.

Perfie hadn't imagined this kind of reaction. With tentative arms she reached around Mary and gently hugged her, but she was glad when Mary pulled her face away and sat up.

"I'm sorry. I'm going to miss you something fierce. But you're happy about it, aren't you?"

Perfie made a movement with her head, not exactly a nod. She shrugged.

Mary rubbed her eyes. "I don't mean to dampen your happiness. Really, I don't."

"That's just it, I'm not sure if I *am* happy about it. There's one part of me—I hate the basement and all, but the other part—I just keep hoping things will be better."

"Maybe you know more now. Maybe you can make things better, back in T.A., I mean." Mary smiled "You're going to know a lot more than Isaac's mother. Think about it—where has she been? What things has she done?"

"I hadn't thought about that."

"Picture this." Mary tipped her nose in the air and held out her hand, speaking in a gruff voice. "Perfecta, my dear, those children of yours are not respectful. You should give them a little beating with the belt to bring them into line."

Jumping to one side and smiling, Mary changed her voice. "Oh, Mamma Martinez, don't you know I've lived in California? All the children there are well behaved."

Perfie smiled. Her friend's manic mood seemed to catch her. She raised her hand in the air with a dismissive wave and used a gruff voice.

"Oh my dear Perfecta," Perfie drew out the end of her name in a sarcastic growl. "Books are meaningless to me. And other people's opinions? Why would I need that when I know everything there is to know about everything?"

Perfie looked directly at Mary. "Maybe that isn't really funny. I think Carlotta probably believes that. You know, I did argue with her about things until I saw how mean she could be and how she would go to any length to win an argument. To her, winning is not proving herself right. It is revenge."

"Then don't go back! Stay here with me." Mary stepped forward and put her hand on Perfie's shoulder.

Perfie wrapped her arms around Mary again—this time in a warm and desperate embrace, as she sought support from her friend.

"What a pair we are," Mary said as they leaned on each other

Perfie sucked in a breath and pressed her lips tight in an effort to hold back her tears, but the sobs broke loose anyway. The two women held each other tight and rocked back and forth.

Once again Perfie would lose what she treasured most.

Forty-Five

Isaac wasn't helping with the packing. Perfie stood at the top of the steps and watched him as he left for work on Thursday morning. He was so distracted that he didn't even turn to say goodbye. She bit back her words. Don't add to his distress, she told herself firmly.

There hadn't been a moment to talk about the move, and she needed to let him know her mixed emotions. Mary had put an idea into her mind. Her relationship with Carlotta needed to be different, and it was important for Isaac to realize this before they went back to Tierra Amarilla.

She didn't want to pack up dirty clothes, so she gathered the socks and shirts that were scattered around the room. She would have to run the washer by herself today

It was early afternoon by the time she hung the last of the clean clothes on the line.

Karleen tugged at her skirt. "Mama, let's go play."

Perfie had sent the boys to the park earlier. She decided to pack up the girls and go see what they were up to.

"Okay. Get your wagon and I'll give you a ride."

An hour later Perfie was wiping the sweat from her forehead as she pulled the wagon home. The boys had begged to stay at the park a little longer, but it was late afternoon now and she needed to do some more packing. Geri was asleep in the wagon, and Karleen shuffled behind with an occasional "Mama, I'm tired." It was a hot day for early June, and the trip had taken longer than she expected.

She heard the sound of a truck pulling up behind her.

"Thanks, John." Isaac called out as he hopped out of the truck.

"Where have you been?" He scooped up Karleen and held her on his hip, then took the handle of the wagon from Perfie.

"The park. The boys stayed. I did laundry all morning so everything would be ready to pack."

"I don't need much."

"Maybe *you* don't need much, but I don't want to do laundry the minute we get there. It would be silly to pack dirty clothes. Besides, now the washer is ready to pack."

Isaac stopped and turned to face Perfie. "Ready to pack?" His eyebrows bunched together in a question mark.

"Yes, I'm the one who does the laundry around here. I didn't figure we would have my washer set up until Levi and his family move out of the house."

"Levi move out? Why would Levi move?"

"It's our house, Isaac. They have to leave if we're coming back."

Isaac shook his head back and forth. "No, no, no."

"Where do you think we're going to be?" Perfie couldn't believe he was planning to live with Carlotta in the big house. Best to clear this up right now—she was not giving up her house.

She shook her head. "I'm not moving in with your mother."

"Oh, no." His hand flew up to his face and he rubbed the wrinkle out of his forehead with the tips of his fingers. "Do you think we're moving back?"

What was he talking about?

Suddenly his meaning hit her. She turned and screamed. "No way, never, never, never. You are not going to do this to me again."

Isaac grasped her arm. "Do what again?"

"Move away and leave me here. Abandon me."

"I'm only going to be gone for two weeks. I'm coming back, Perfie. My father died. I'm just going home to tie up loose ends." He let go of her arm. "Don't be so dramatic."

She felt her body start to shake. She gulped air into her lungs. She couldn't faint, not now. She needed to settle this with Isaac. But her eyes rolled back against her will and she slumped onto the plush lawn that bordered the sidewalk.

"Wake up," Isaac's voice interrupted her peaceful dream. She was riding Cimmaron along an unknown river, the air a swirling fog. Her body was completely relaxed and there was nothing in this world to cause any grief.

"No, I like it here." She felt a wave of pressure sweep over the top of her head. She kept her eyes closed.

"Mama, carry me." Geri's voice pierced through the fog.

"It's okay, just breathe and relax." A soft voice whispered in her ear. Mary!

Perfie opened her eyes. Mary's face was close and Perfie felt her head get lifted into Mary's lap. "Where did you come from? Are you an angel in my dream?"

"No." Mary smiled. "I was coming to see you."

Isaac's voice broke through the moment. "Get up. We need to get home. Then we can talk about all this."

"If you rush her, she'll faint again. You have to let the blood get back to her head."

"I know you're a nurse, but she does this all the time."

"She faints all the time?" Mary sounded concerned.

"She has for years—conveniently whenever there's something she doesn't want to talk about."

"I'm feeling better now. I think I can get up." Perfie wanted to put a stop to this conversation.

Mary helped her to her feet.

A few minutes later Perfie was sitting at the table drinking the tea Mary had made while Isaac fed the girls. "I'm not going back to New Mexico," Perfie told Mary.

"What happened?"

"Isaac is going, not me, not the kids. He's deserting me again."

"What? How can he do that?" Mary looked over at Isaac and frowned.

"It was a misunderstanding." Isaac didn't elaborate.

"It's still a misunderstanding. I don't understand you at all." Perfie's voice was high pitched and the words came out much louder than she intended. She didn't want to sound hysterical. Isaac already thought she had fainted on purpose, when in fact she had tried so hard not to.

He never talked and he never listened. Perfie wanted to have a real conversation. There needed to be a plan, and she needed to be a part of it. Did he think she could read his mind? She took a deep breath.

"Isaac, we have to talk about this. If you're going back and I'm staying, then it's the same thing all over again. What will I do for money?

The little bit from Mrs. Cooper won't go far. What about your job? You can't just leave it. You know there are men waiting in line for that job." Perfie glanced at Mary for strength, but her friend was watching Isaac's face.

Isaac frowned. "Once again, Perfie. My father is dead. *Dead.* Does that mean anything to you? Can I not go back and pay my respects?"

"I know that. Maybe I want to pay my respects, too." What she really wanted to tell him was that she was afraid he wouldn't come back. Carlotta had so much power over him. He had never been able to stand up to her in the past. What made him think he could stand up to her now?

"We can't afford it. Not with all the kids. And I made arrangements at work. We're allowed bereavement leave. I can come back to my job in two weeks. It will be tight, but we can do it. You just have to—"

Mary interrupted Isaac. "Perfie, it seems like there's something else bothering you. What are you thinking?"

Perfie was grateful that Mary understood. She turned to Isaac. "I'm thinking he always says this. It will only be a few days, a week, whatever, and it's always longer. Just look at the letter Eli sent. They need him at the school. Carlotta will talk him into staying, and I'll be stuck here. Rose is furious already. She wants us out of here. She'll probably kick us out while he's gone. She knows I won't be able to stand up to her. Where will we go? We'll be out on the streets, the kids and me." Damn, she'd been sucked into an hysterical tirade. She dropped her chin and looked away.

Mary and Isaac spoke at the same time.

"You shouldn't—" Mary stopped as Isaac continued.

"That is not going to happen. Rose wouldn't do that. What can I do to make you believe I will come back?"

"I would believe you if you had come back the last three times when you said you would, but it's too late for that." She wasn't going to give up on this. She wouldn't be deserted again.

Mary cleared her throat. "Maybe this isn't the time to bring this up, but have you turned in the application for the housing?"

Perfie and Isaac glanced at each other, guilt sweeping both faces.

"There's a little problem." Isaac started. He seemed to have trouble finding words, so Perfie took over.

"One of the things it says is that we have to be married. Well, I guess it's time you knew. We aren't married." Perfie watched Mary's face.

"Not married?" Mary's voice sounded just as shocked as Perfie imagined it would.

"No, we didn't ever have an actual wedding. It's kind of complicated." How could she tell her friend what it had been like, why things had turned out this way. Should she explain this to Mary now, when Isaac was already angry? Should she tell her how Isaac had failed to pass the test she'd secretly given to him?

Isaac's voice broke into her thoughts. "We can get married. Let's set the date right now, two weeks from now. You'd believe I wouldn't miss my own wedding, wouldn't you?"

"Married?" She looked from his face to Mary's. "Now?"

"Oh Perfie! How wonderful. I'll help out. You can do it at my house, in the garden. I know Aunt Eugenia won't mind. Two weeks is enough time to make a new dress for you and dresses for the girls."

This was like a bad dream, the kind you have over and over for your whole life, Perfie thought. Once more the plans for her wedding had slipped out of her control. If this was a proposal, it felt more like a bribe, and another woman was already planning the place, the dress and the details.

Isaac wrapped his arms around Perfie and whispered into her ear. "I love you, Perfecta Martinez. You are my wife. You will always be my wife. Isn't it time we had a wedding?"

Forty-Six

When Isaac stepped off the bus he was surprised to see Mary Kent standing on the corner. "Hello Mary." He wondered why she would be waiting for a bus instead of driving her car.

"Isaac. Can we talk?"

"Of course." He nodded toward the bench in front of the library.

They were barely seated when she pulled a stack of papers out of her satchel.

"I want to talk to you about the public housing. I think Perfie would be happy if you would fill out the application. I picked up another one. I thought. . ."

"You want me to do it without telling her." Isaac was beginning to understand a little about Mary.

"Yes. As a surprise. Maybe a wedding present?"

"Do you know why she won't do it?"

Mary shook her head and Isaac continued. "She thinks she's a sinner."

"A sinner?"

"Yes. It started a long time ago, when she was a child really. Her parents were very religious and stern. When we first got together it was even worse. I know it doesn't seem to matter as much here, but in New Mexico, with the Catholics and Presbyterians, that's just not done."

"Is that why you never married?" Mary's lips turned down.

"No. That's more complicated. At first I was afraid. Then when my mother planned a wedding, Perfie had some sort of meltdown. I think it had to do with sinning, not being married in the Catholic Church. She refused."

"Why didn't you do it later?"

"We never did it officially, but I can't think of two people who are more married than Perfie and I are."

Mary was quiet. She seemed to be considering something. "Isaac, I need to tell you something."

"Yes?"

"You don't have to be married to apply for the housing. It's stated as a requirement, but that's just so people don't go together to live, to only use one salary or something. If you live together and you have four children, the government sees that as the same as being married."

Isaac watched as Mary's face crumbled. He could tell that she thought he would withdraw his proposal.

"Don't worry, Mary. It's time we did this. I know it's what Perfie has wanted forever. I don't know if we can find a Catholic priest here who will marry us but if I can, that's what I want to do. Maybe she'll get over this sinner burden she has carried so long." He reached for the stack of papers. "If we fill these out right now can you turn them in for me?"

Mary nodded.

Forty-Seven

Perfie asked Mrs. Cooper to drive her to town. She told Mary she had some errands to run and asked her to bring the girls to the house at five o'clock.

"Forgive me Father for I have sinned," she whispered as she stood in front of the old church.

St. Margaret Mary's. A woman's name.

Perfie clasped her purse up to her chest. She didn't know if churches in California were open all the time. Did a priest live in the back, like at Santo Niño?

The front door of the church opened and Perfie quickly turned and walked down the block. She glanced back over her shoulder and watched a young man help an old woman down the steps.

Perfie walked around the block twice. She slowed down and stared at the tiny cross high on the pointed roof each time she passed. There were plaster angels guarding the windows.

"I need a guardian angel. Can't you fly down here and come home with me?" She looked back at the door.

God was everywhere. Did she have to go inside the church to ask for his forgiveness? She started around the block once more.

This time when she passed the little park beside the church she went in and sat on a stone bench. She didn't really want to talk to a priest. This wasn't about another confession of guilt.

She wanted to talk to God.

She wanted the true answers, not what her mother told her, or a nun told her, or even what a priest told her. Did God talk directly to them? If he would do that, then surely he would talk to her.

I have felt stuck for so long—since I met Isaac, she thought.

No. Longer than that. Since the day I decided I couldn't be perfect. "I'm not Perfecta anymore," she whispered now. But I'm not a bad person. I try so hard, God. I really do.

She decided to try something Mary had suggested once when Roberto was feeling bad about something.

Mary's words came to her. "Have him list all the good things—maybe even write them down. He needs to focus on what is right, not what is wrong."

"God, I have a list for you. One, I'm a good cook. Two, I keep that sloppy basement clean and warm for my family. Three, I save money. Four, I only lie when needed—you know, God, so that someone doesn't get hurt."

That was a short list. There must be something else good about her? I'm jealous, impatient, stubborn and revengeful. Suddenly her list wasn't good anymore.

Maybe changing her name to Perfie hadn't been right. Maybe she should have changed it to Imperfecta.

The honk of a horn interrupted her thoughts. She glanced at the road. A car was honking at a dog crossing the street. She noticed the sun was moving below the trees, and she saw the glow on something white behind the hedge.

Perfie stood up and walked to where the sunlight shimmered. It was a statue.

The Virgin.

The sun lit up the smooth plaster face of the sculpture. This young Mary was different from the one in Santo Niño. This Mary had a sweet smile on her face, and she looked out at the flowers that grew before her.

She looked as if she could appreciate their beauty.

"Mama?" Perfie whispered and walked closer to the statue.

She reached out her hand and touched the shoulder of the tiny Virgin.

This young woman who had given birth to Jesus, raised him then lost him—what did she have to smile about?

But she didn't lose him. Not really.

Perfie realized that although she had gone to church every week for all those years, she hadn't really paid attention. She had been busy thinking about how much she hated things, and about what she was going to do when she was finally free from her parents. She had been busy thinking about her next ride on Cimmaron and about Isaac.

I don't really know anything about this religion at all, she thought. I've been making it up as I go along. I only think I'm a sinner because my parents told me it was so. They weren't right about other things. Maybe they weren't right about this either. Maybe it's time I figured things out for myself.

The sun left the sweet smile of the Virgin's face as it moved behind the church.

It was late and Mary would be waiting with the girls. Perfie turned and walked back toward the church.

But she didn't walk through the doors. Instead she waited at the corner for the bus that would take her home to her family.

Train Tracks

Forty-Eight

Isaac felt pulled between Perfie in California and his mother in New Mexico as if his arms were attached to giant rubber bands. The tension grew as the train chugged away the miles.

"I'll be back, I promise. Nothing will make me stay." He had reassured Perfie over and over yesterday at the Oakland station, but even as he said the words he knew it wouldn't be so easy.

Isaac curled his body on the cracked leather seat and tried to sleep, but anxiety swirled around in him, invading his mind, his heart and his stomach. His thoughts scattered in all directions. He hadn't had the chance to say goodbye to his father; Perfie didn't seem to believe he was serious about the marriage; his mother was a widow now and Levi was in charge at home; the kids were growing up in a basement; barely making second crew after all this time. The list went on.

Anxiety turned to sorrow during the long night. He hadn't paid for a sleeper, and the hard seat of the train smelled like a three-day-old pork sandwich. The morning sun and the last few miles to Santa Fe did nothing to ease his aching heart.

After the endless train ride, the bus took him to Tierra Amarilla. He walked from the courthouse down the road to his parent's house. Home. He stood and stared. The anxiety had slipped down to his stomach, where it churned and ached as he pictured what awaited him inside.

"Ike?" Enoch walked out onto the porch.

Isaac shook the thoughts from his head. "Hey, Enoch."

"We're worried. You've been standing out here staring at the house for a long time. Is everything okay?" His brother frowned.

"Just thinking."

"Well come in. Madre is waiting."

He followed his brother through the door and crossed the room to hug his mother. He was shocked at how thin and tired she looked. It had only been a year, hadn't it? He quickly did the math. Well, closer to a year and a half.

"*Mi hijo.*"

"Don't cry, Madre." He didn't know what else to say. "I wish I could have been here sooner."

He wanted to ask about his father's death, but she seemed so frail. He was afraid he might push her over the edge.

Carlotta wiped her face with her lace hanky and seemed to recover her composure. "How are my grandchildren?"

Isaac was surprised. He couldn't remember when she had ever referred to the kids as her grandchildren. More like "that boy" or "your girl."

"They are good. Roberto is so tall, soon he will be taller than Perfie." He paused. "She's fine, too. She sends her love."

In theory, anyway, he thought.

"Perfecta. Does she like California?"

"I won't lie, Madre. It's hard for us. There isn't a good place to live. But soon, soon we will have our own house. An apartment, really."

He explained what an apartment was, but the notion was foreign to his mother. Carlotta said she couldn't imagine living with strangers but Isaac was pleased that she cared about what was happening in his life.

After a somber supper, a night spent in his old bed and a huge breakfast, he made his way out to the property. His brother was taking good care of the adobe house. Enoch had added a larger front porch and a split corral off to one side for two horses and a cow with her calf. His brother had built a rock-lined trench that brought water closer to the house.

Isaac climbed the hill to visit the graves.

"Hola, niñas." He sat on a flat boulder next to his daughters. The fresh mound of dirt where his father rested was close to the girls.

"Hola, Padre." Isaac choked and clenched his fists. "I'm sorry I wasn't here. I hope you know that I would have given anything to be here."

The smell of the piñon, the sugar pine and the sage—and the tiny breeze that dried the sweat on his face—these things went straight to his heart. For a moment he was a child again with his father's large hand clasping his as they walked through these hills.

"You were right, Padre. California is not easy. But things will work out. I know they will. I know you loved this land. I do, too. But I can't stay here."

Isaac told his father about the wedding, about the kids, about his job.

"There's someone there, Padre. A nurse. She's Perfie's friend and she is helping us. There are good people in California."

Isaac stood and walked to the wooden cross. He traced his fingers over the carved letters.

Lucas Francisco Martinez. b.1852 d.1941

"Padre? Why are woman this way? Why can't Perfie tell me what it is she wants from me?"

Maybe she already had.

He stood and dusted off his pants. It was time to tell his mother about the wedding.

Carlotta set down her tea so abruptly it clattered on the delicate plate. "You asked her to marry you? Don't you think you are married already?"

"I think that, but it's not the same to her. We never really made it official."

"Will you convert?"

Isaac was taken aback by his mother's question. He hadn't thought about religion.

"No. Of course not. Madre, you should know that religion, it's not something we really talk about. We don't go to church."

"Not at all? She doesn't go to mass?"

He shook his head.

"There's something I need to ask you, Isaac."

"Okay." He knew what was coming. He wondered what reason she would give for wanting him to stay here. He resolved to be firm. He had to go back to Oakland or he would lose his job.

Carlotta leaned toward him. "I want to come to California."

He choked. This was not what he expected at all. He had been sure Carlotta was going to ask him to help at the school.

A flood of thoughts nearly drowned him. He could see Perfie's angry eyes and spittle flying from her mouth if he brought his mother to live with them. He pictured the boys sleeping in the truck so their abuela would have a bed.

"Madre. I don't think you would like living in California. It's so different. And what about Enoch? Eli? They wouldn't want you to leave."

His mother shook her head. "Not to live, dear Isaac. You needn't look so scared. Just for the wedding."

His shoulders relaxed back to a normal position. He hadn't even realized they were clenched up to his ears.

"Of course." But even as he agreed, he could see the problem. Where would she stay? He would have to telephone Rose to find out if Carlotta could sleep upstairs.

But he didn't want Perfie to know. She would work herself into a frenzy and a week-long headache if she found out.

"There's something else." Carlotta reached for an envelope.

Isaac watched her trembling hands.

"Your father left this. He wanted you to have it now."

"What is it?" He reached out and took the envelope from her. A letter?

"It's your inheritance."

He slid his finger under the flap and pulled it lose. Money. A thick pile of cash.

"But Madre? What about you? Surely this isn't to come to me now?" He prayed that it would. There had to be well over two hundred dollars here. What a difference that would make. He would be able to find a place to live with this kind of cash. He wouldn't have to take the public assistance, and he could hold his head up with pride.

"Yes. Now is when you need it, so now is when it should come to you. It's what Lucas wanted and it's what I want."

"Gracias," he managed to whisper, picturing the tears of joy Perfie would weep when he handed her this envelope.

Forty-Nine

Isabelle wiped her hands on the dishtowel and carefully hung it on the hook near the sink. She poured herself a cup of tea and pulled the letter from her cousin out of her pocket. She had saved it to treat herself after finishing the work of cleaning up after Primitivo. Her uncle had partially recovered from his stroke, but he still required constant care. Her long-time admiration of him was fading as she watched him give in to his sudden illness.

"You can do it," she encouraged as she helped him from his bed to the chair in the living room. Isabelle thought he should be trying harder. The doctor had assured her that Primitivo would be able to recover his speech and movement with exercise and practice.

He refused at first. Finally he had started to talk again, but he wouldn't try to move out of his bed on his own.

Perfecta sent Isabelle a letter every month to update her on the latest adventures in California. Her letters shared intimate details—more even than she had been willing to share when the cousins had slept in the same bed years before.

Dearest Cousin, Isabelle read, *I hope all is well with you.*

Isabelle scanned the letter. She couldn't believe Perfecta was writing to her in English. Ever since she was a young girl her cousin had resisted changing languages. She always complained about the foreign language spoken by the nuns. Isabelle could remember the crazy dinners when Joe spoke English and Avelina shook her head because she didn't understand. These letters written in English were throwing a monkey wrench in Isabelle's plans. Primitivo still refused to talk about his daughter, but if Isabelle left a letter lying around, he would read it. He would sneak into the kitchen and stand by the window when he thought that she was busy elsewhere. Since the stroke, she had decided to leave the letters in the bedroom instead. But Primitivo couldn't read English. In fact, because of his role as sheriff, this had become an issue the prior year at the town council. The stroke had knocked him out of the job before anything was decided about his position. Isabelle felt the English issue had just been an excuse; the people of T.A. were tired of the stubborn old sheriff.

She needed to figure out a way for him to get the news of his daughter and to protect his pride at the same time. She turned back to the letter.

Are you still in town? I was happy to hear about your engagement to Michael Brown. He sounds like a fun man. Will you live in Española? Will you keep your teaching job? Does Michael want you to work or not? So many questions I have! I guess you will have to write back to me today. I can't wait for your letter.

Isaac is still working at Mare Island, even after the scare of some layoffs. Guess what—I have a job now. In fact, in a couple of weeks I will have TWO jobs. Mary, that nurse I told you about, found me a job as a maid. Can you believe it? It is true, even though you always said I was so messy The hours work out because I go in the afternoon when Mary can watch the kids. It gives us a little bit of money, which is nice. I found the second job myself. I start learning how to upholster furniture on July 22. I don't get paid at first, but once I'm trained I can make some real money. That should help a lot!

Rose hasn't changed much. She still glares at me all the time. I wish we could find a new place to live, but Isaac doesn't want to move until we can rent a place of our own. We finally get to use the bathroom again, even once a week for baths, but Mary lets me take a bath at her place, too, and I do the laundry there sometimes. That is an amazing thing. She has a washer that plugs right into electricity. It's so much quieter than mine, and there's no smell of gasoline in the clothes. I want one of these California washers.

I know this letter is short, but I have to get to bed. It seems I only have time to write late at night when everyone else is finally asleep, but Isaac doesn't like the light on.

Love Perfie

Isabelle wanted Perfecta to come back to New Mexico—not just because she missed her. When Primitivo was felled by the stroke Mrs. McNeil had called Isabelle instead of Perfecta. Isabelle had to take a leave of absence from her job, and she worried that the hard work she had put into her students would be lost with a substitute teacher.

And then there was Michael. At thirty-three years old Isabelle had resigned herself to being a spinster and to having her students as her only children. Michael wanted children of their own. At her age she couldn't afford to wait, and she needed to be back in Española with him, not here taking care of her uncle.

There had been rumors her uncle had another family before Avelina, but Isabelle couldn't get him to admit to this. She asked around, but no one seemed to remember anything. But even if she found some long lost relatives she doubted they would step forward to care for Primitivo.

Isabelle needed to have Perfecta and Isaac move back. Otherwise she would have to pack up the old man and move him to California. She couldn't imagine trying to do that. She waited, not wanting to tell Perfecta that her father needed her help. It didn't seem right to do this while Perfecta and Isaac had no place to live. It didn't sound like the basement of Tom and Rose's house would work with another person living in it. Isabelle felt the heavy weight of guilt on her shoulders. She had prayed, but she knew that the reason she hadn't told her cousin about the stroke was because she carried the knowledge of her betrayal. How would things have turned out if she had never told Primitivo that Perfecta was pregnant? Maybe Isaac and Perfie would still be here in Tierra Amarilla.

But too much time was passing, and she couldn't wait much longer to get her own life back. She would write to Perfecta soon. In the meantime she would try to talk her uncle into moving to Española.

Later that afternoon Isabelle pulled the curtain to one side so that the sunlight filled the room and fell onto Primitivo. "Would you like me to read you a letter from Perfecta?"

"I don't know anyone by that name."

"Well, I'm going to read it out loud. You don't have to listen." Tío was quiet while she read the letter. When she finished she waited silently, but his gaze never left the dark spot on the wall that seemed to absorb his attention.

"Tío, I need to talk to you."

"About what?"

"About me. You know I love you and I appreciate everything you've given me."

"That's good to hear."

Isabelle tapped the folded letter on her thigh and her leg bounced nervously.

"Michael asked me to get married and I said yes."

"Fine young man, even for an anglo."

Isabelle smiled at the thought of Michael as a young man. "Yes, Tío. He is a fine man. We plan to start a family right away."

"This is a good thing."

"The thing is, I need to be back in Española. I need to be with him. I've been looking at some places for you to live down there."

"Places? What kind of places?"

"Places for people who need some help."

"One of those old folks homes?"

"Yes." She didn't try to explain any more; she knew it was best to let him think about things, feel he was in control of the conversation.

The two sat quietly. She wanted to remind Primitivo what Dr. Garcia had said about being able to make gains so that he could live on his own. But her uncle hadn't been doing a very good job of living alone even before the stroke. He didn't cook much, and he never cleaned. When she had arrived a month ago the house was a mess. Until recently he had still been charming enough to find women to take care of his laundry. He had been eating down at Maria's Cafe for dinner each night, and Mario Hughes always brought him a donut and coffee every morning. But all that had ended with the stroke.

"Take me back to the bed."

She helped him from the chair. No use to argue that he had only been up for a little while.

Avelina's death had been the start of his decline. He had continued his stubborn refusal to make amends with Perfecta, even after she and Isaac had four children and it was apparent that Isaac was a good husband. It was his failure to recognize his grandchildren that hurt Isabelle the most. She had tried to talk to him about it many times, tried to get him to have a relationship with the kids, even had brought them to the house without their parents.

But he ignored them, and the kids steered clear of the old man. They were fearful of his icy eyes, his glare and his scowl.

Isabelle had been sure that Roberto would melt him. He looked just like his grandfather. He even spoke like him, curious and stubborn, always in charge, always determined to have the final word.

A knock at the door interrupted her thoughts. Who could that be? Isabelle pushed her hair out of her face and went to the door.

"Isaac!" Shocked at seeing him, just when she was thinking she needed Perfecta, Isabelle stepped into his hug. "What are you doing here?"

"Came home to say goodbye to my father."

She could see that the twinkle had left his eyes. "I'm so sorry. It was a wonderful service; the whole town was there. Everyone loved Lucas."

"I wish I could have been here."

Isabelle leaned and peered around him. "Did Perfie come with you?"

"No, just me."

"How is she? How are the kids?"

"They're all fine. The kids are growing like weeds."

Isabelle turned. "Come in, come in."

He didn't ask about Primitivo right away and instead chatted about life in California and about Perfie and the kids.

He finally said. "What about her father?"

"He's bad. He's in the other room, in bed."

"In bed? Here?" Isaac looked over his shoulder as if scared he might be attacked.

"He had a stroke."

"A stroke? Does Perfie know about this?"

Isabelle could see from his face that he suspected Perfie knew and hadn't told him.

"No, she doesn't know. I didn't write to her. I was waiting until you found a place to live."

Isaac was silent for a moment. "What are you saying?"

"I can't take care of him. I don't know if you heard, but I'm getting married."

Isabelle watched as Isaac finally understood what she was trying to tell him.

"How bad is he?"

"Not so bad. Most days he's up and sits in the front room. Today is bad. He didn't want to do anything."

"I need to talk to him. He can still talk, can't he?"

"Yes. Let me see if he'll get up." She went into the bedroom.

Primitivo was asleep. She placed her hand on his shoulder and bent down close to his head.

"Tio, wake up. You have a visitor." When there was no response, she shook him slightly. "Tio," she repeated. His eyes slowly opened. He licked his cracked lips, and she offered him water from the glass she kept on the night stand. She propped his head on some pillows and wiped the spill that ran down his neck.

"What is it?" he asked.

"A visitor. Isaac is here."

There was no recognition in Primitivo's eyes.

"Husband of Perfecta, your son-in-law." Isabelle knew the two were not married, but she also knew her uncle had been led to believe they had married long ago, before Roberto was born.

"What's he want?"

"He wants to see you, to say hello." She straightened the blanket. "Do you want me to bring him in here?"

"No. Help me get up."

Ten minutes later Isabelle led Primitivo out to the front room. Isaac stood at the window, staring out. When Isabelle had the old man settled into the arm chair, Isaac sat in Avelina's rocker.

"No, not there." She shook her head. "Why don't I get you a chair?"

"I'll do it." Isaac went into the kitchen and came back with two chairs.

"How about some tea?" Isabelle asked the two men, heading for the kitchen before they could answer.

She could hear them talking as she poured water into the pot and set it on the stove.

"Do you miss her?" Isaac asked.

Isabelle couldn't imagine Isaac would ask such a question of Primitivo.

"Yes, every day. Even though I look at that chair where she rocked herself to death with her broken heart, I think about how she looked when I first met her. So beautiful. Not a young woman—neither of us was young —but a regal woman. She held her head high in spite of what that rotten pig did to her."

Isabelle realized that Isaac had asked about Avelina, not Perfecta.

"And now, I'm sure Isabelle told you I had a stroke. Struck down out of the blue."

Some people would think Tío was joking, but she knew better.

"I'm so glad I have Isabelle," Tío continued. "She's all I have left."

"You have Perfie and me."

Isabelle walked into the room with the tray and set a mug in front of each man before turning to leave.

Isaac grasped her hand. "Please stay."

She sat in the chair he'd placed next to his.

"I was just telling Primitivo that, while it is wonderful he has you to care for him, he also has Perfie and me."

"Puh." Primitivo shook his head. "Perfecta wants nothing to do with me." He leaned toward Isaac with some of the same old glare in his filmy eyes. "You're a good man, Isaac. But I lost my daughter years ago."

Isabelle was shocked. Had Primitivo actually complimented Isaac?

Isaac rubbed the back of his neck. "Why do you say that?"

"Why did I lose her? She's the one who left. I guess we could say that's your fault, couldn't we." Primitivo's voice quivered.

"Yes, I got her pregnant. But we weren't the first and we won't be the last. You didn't have to cut her out of your life."

Isabelle shifted in the chair and gripped her mug. Her uncle didn't back down. "She was stubborn from birth, reminded me of my mother." Primitivo turned and stared out the window.

No one spoke.

Isaac glanced at Isabelle before turning back to Primitivo. "Was that a bad thing?"

"My mother was a cruel woman. She saw things her own way. She was stupid and uneducated, and yet she felt she was right about everything. She made my life hell." Primitivo's hands began to shake. "I wasn't about to let my daughter grow up to be like that."

Isabelle had never heard this story, never heard him talk about his parents at all, or even mention the supposed life in Texas.

"But Perfie is *not* her. She's not your mother and she isn't evil." Isaac's voice was soft.

"You're wrong!" The shout startled Isabelle and she jumped back, spilling tea onto the edge of her skirt.

Primitivo leaned forward and yanked open the small drawer on the end table. He fumbled through the papers he kept there and pulled out a photograph that looked like it had been crumpled into a ball and then smoothed out. With a shaking hand he thrust it toward Isaac.

Isaac took the picture, and Isabelle watched him study it for several minutes.

"Is that you?" he asked Primitivo, as he handed the picture to Isabelle.

It was a photo of a young woman and a small boy. The woman had a stern face with large, round eyes. She seemed angry or frightened. Her lips were pulled into a circle, and her eyebrows pressed together forming a sharp v-shape above her nose. By her side was a boy about two years of age. He looked terrified. The boy's white shirt wrinkled at the shoulder with the woman's tight grip. He leaned away from her, as if to escape. The woman did look a little like Perfie.

"Yes, that's me. And my mother. Can't you see that my daughter is that woman born all over again? Come back to haunt me?"

Isaac shook his head. "I don't see it."

Tío snatched the photo from Isabelle's hand. He crumpled it and threw it down. "I don't know why you can't see it. I knew it from the day she was born. Avelina screamed in pain when that baby came, as if the devil himself were ripping her apart."

So that was it, thought Isabelle. He had been there watching his beloved Avelina suffer the birth of their daughter.

"Tío." She reached forward and put her hand on his arm. "All women suffer when they give birth. It is a painful thing, but one soon forgets."

"No, that's not so. No woman suffered like she did." She saw the color drain from his face. His hands shook.

She stood. "Come on Tío. I think you should lie down."

Isaac stood. "Let me help."

After the two of them settled the old man into his bed, Isaac moved the chairs back into the kitchen. Isabelle gathered the tea mugs and stood at the sink to wash them.

"Isabelle, I'm going to go now." Isaac stood beside her.

"Just let me dry my hands." Wiping them on her apron she turned and hugged him. "Thank you for coming. You'll tell Perfecta?"

Isaac reached into his pocket and pulled out an envelope.

"Use this. Put him in a home down in Española. I'll send more when I can." He pushed the money into her hands. "Don't tell Perfie. I'll figure out a way to let her know."

Fifty

During the next two weeks Perfie felt her nose shift out of joint many times, but soon gratitude moved it back to the center of her face. It was good to have Mary helping with the wedding. She was surprised when Mary showed up with Aunt Eugenia's sewing machine and that wonderful green fabric. Mary proved to be supportive, but she didn't hover. They spent several afternoons working on the dress, but her friend wasn't around much after that.

Today Perfie needed to get out of the house. She folded the old gray army blanket into the bottom of the wagon and set the girls on top.

"Let's go to the store. We'll make something special for dinner," she told them as they set off down the smooth sidewalk.

She pulled the wagon past bright green lawns that were mowed as short as if sheep had nibbled each blade close to the black soil. Like everything else, the California dirt was different too—it was black and so moist that it clumped together and stuck to everything, especially the shoes of her children.

She studied the twin front windows of each house. They were like eyes looking out at the world. No names were attached to these homes. It was different from New Mexico, where the same families inhabited the houses for generations. The Chavez house, the Hughes mansion, the Luna farm. Here, Perfie kept track of the families by the curtains: Mrs. White Lace, Mrs. Blue Gingham and Mr. Green Plaid.

"We'll have turquoise curtains in our house," she told the girls. "Just like the sky back home. I'll stitch a red design along the edge to remind us of the bluffs."

"Will we have a creek?" Karleen asked.

"No, I don't think so." She watched as her daughter gave a sigh of relief. Perfie remembered all the warnings she had given the little girl when they lived on the banks of Las Nutrias. This must have stuck with her.

When they got to the corner Perfie stopped and searched for cars. She warned Karleen and Geri to hold on tight as she pulled the wagon off the curb.

"Perfecta?"

The deep voice came from behind and surprised her. Her purse caught on the handle of the wagon and dropped to the street. Hairbrush, cup, handkerchief, glasses and her tin of coins—all spilled onto the asphalt.

"I'm sorry. It seems I'm destined to help you pick things up."

It was Jorgé.

He was as handsome as she had remembered from their train ride. The brown of his eyes was so deep that they were nearly black, and they seemed to penetrate her as they gazed out from under his firm and confident brow. His square jaw, punctuated with a cleft in his chin, was like that of a movie star.

"You grew a mustache." The words embarrassed her as soon as they were out. She bent and scrambled for her spilled belongings.

"I didn't mean to startle you." His smile was warm.

Karleen climbed out of the wagon and ran to wrap her arms around his legs.

"Hello, Niña. You remember me." He scooped her up.

Perfie felt as if her tongue puffed up like a frightened gila lizard. What should she say to him?

"Can I have a cookie?" Karleen's voice broke into her thoughts.

"Hush," she said. "There's no cookies."

Jorgé laughed. "No cookies, little one. But let me see." He patted the pocket of his gray jacket. "Here we are." He pulled some wrapped candy out and presented it to Karleen.

"Now let's get this train out of the street." Jorgé pulled the wagon to the curb. Perfie followed, stuffing items back into her purse.

Jorgé wanted to talk. He asked her if she would go down the street to Mimi's Cafe and have a cup of tea.

"No, no. We, the girls . . ." she fumbled for words. "We're on our way to the store. We're going to fix a special dinner for Isaac, my husband."

"Daddy's gone away." Karleen still held tight to Jorgé's hand.

Perfie felt her face turn bright red. "His father passed on. He'll be back. He's just gone a short time."

She watched as a shadow came over Jorge's eyes and he gave a slight shake of his head. "Well, it was nice running into you again. Say hello to Roberto and Arturo for me." He hesitated and Perfie held her breath.

"Adios, Mrs. Martinez. Goodbye, niñas."

Why does he make me feel this way? I love Isaac. I'm getting married in a week. But Perfie couldn't stop her self from thinking about the choices she had made in her life. She imagined running away with this handsome man and leaving everything behind. It was only when Karleen tugged at her hand and called out "Mama?" that Perfie sighed and walked home.

The Coopers were on vacation, so Perfie wasn't working this week. She hadn't heard from Mary for several days, but Friday afternoon her friend showed up unexpectedly, ready to chat and to finish the dress.

"I don't have the courage to have a fancy wedding," Perfie told Mary. "I have been living in sin for so many years, and I have four children. "

Mary didn't see it that way.

"Every woman needs her wedding to be special. People will celebrate, you'll see." Mary stitched tiny pearls onto the bodice of the green dress. "If they don't share in your happiness, Perfie, promise me you'll just brush them away like a nasty fly." Mary wouldn't let Perfie be trapped by her worries.

For two days Perfie felt like she could go through with it; she could have the wedding she had always dreamed about. If the details were different from her old fantasies she was different, too. She wasn't some silly girl anymore. She made a new list of the good things about her now: a mother of four, a working woman, a friend. She voted, she knew how to repair almost anything, she was a seamstress and she was learning upholstery. There would soon be a good job with real money coming in, not just a housekeeping job.

Mary suggested they have the wedding in her yard and invite lots of people. Perfie dictated while Mary wrote names in a notebook she kept just for wedding details.

But the next day Perfie changed her mind.

"No," she told Mary. "That might be the dream wedding for some women, but not for me." She couldn't imagine herself standing in front of a crowd. She wanted to do things her way this time. To her surprise Mary didn't argue.

"Where will it be?" Mary asked.

Perfie considered for a moment. "Do they have weddings in the courthouse here?"

Mary nodded. "That's what you want? The courthouse?"

"Yes. But I want you to be there. And I'll wear the beautiful dress. A judge does it, right? He won't care that we're a Catholic and a Presbyterian?"

"Oh, Perfie, no one cares about that. It will be fine."

"What about the fact that we've been living in sin for so long? There isn't a law that says we can't get married now?"

"No, no law like that. You just fill out some papers, pay the three dollars and there's a quick ceremony."

"But will we be married, really married? In the eyes of God? If it's not a priest, I mean?" For a moment Perfie heard her mother's disapproving words, but Mary's voice pushed the ghost aside.

"I believe it will, but the important thing is, do you believe it?"

Did she? She thought about the church, the nuns, her mother. The rules seemed clear cut: Catholics married Catholics. The only way around it would be for Isaac to convert.

But there wasn't time for that. Even if there was, he would be coming home from saying goodbye to his father. His Presbyterian father. He had lost a lot and would be leaving his brothers and Carlotta behind once more. She could only imagine the worst if she asked him to change his religion.

Perfie thought about how the Jewish people were being treated. She knew so little about her own religion let alone about other religions. She didn't really even know about Presbyterians. In New Mexico it had felt the same with Presbyterians as it did here with the Japanese or the Jews. They seemed like the enemy.

I should have gone to their church and listened to what Lucas had to say.

But Isaac hadn't offered to come to Santo Niño either.

Stubborn, both of us, Perfie thought.

That settled it. She wouldn't be Catholic anymore. She would find some other sort of religion that didn't care who you married. California had a lot to offer, and she could make up her own mind.

Perfie wondered what was right. She thought about the smile on the little statue's face—the smile on the happy Virgin, not the tortured one. The happy one carried a secret inside, and suddenly Perfie knew what the statue's secret was. She just lived. She talked directly to God and listened to the happy things.

She pictured Isaac's face as he hugged her goodbye before boarding the train. He had found a window seat so that he could wave to her as the train moved away. She pictured his face from the first time she had ever seen him, back at the ditch when he was coming out of the sage like a coyote.

He loved her. She loved him.

In the end, that was all that mattered.

Isaac called once from New Mexico. Rose came down to the basement with a scowl to let her know there was a call.

"Hello, my wildflower." Isaac's voice echoed in the black receiver.

"How is it?" As always her voice was too loud when she talked on the phone. She cleared her throat and tried to speak with a softer volume. "They know you're not staying?"

"Yes, don't worry. I've been clear about that."

"What's your mother like?"

"She's sad. She seems so much older. Levi's in charge now."

Perfie discussed the plans for the wedding with Isaac. He agreed to everything she told him and reminded her that he would like to invite Dominick Couto. He told her how to leave a message at a neighbor's phone since Dom didn't have one.

"We aren't really having guests, Isaac. It's at the courthouse."

"Mary's coming, right?"

"Yes."

"Then I think it's okay for me to have a best man."

"She's not a bridesmaid. She's a guest. We have to have a witness."

"We have to have two witnesses. Dom will be the second."

She agreed to leave a message for Dom.

"Have you seen my father?"

"Yes. I didn't want to tell you this by phone, but he's had a stroke."

Her father had a stroke?

She thought about the possibility of Primitivo dying. Would she feel grief or would she feel free? He hadn't been a part of her life for many years, but there was still a sense of longing that lived deep within her.

"Is he dead?"

"No, not dead. Isabelle is here taking care of him."

"Isabelle? What about her job? What about Michael?" Perfie knew the jealousy she felt was ridiculous. She hated her father, and yet she was still jealous of her cousin—jealous of someone taking care of a sick old man. Was there no end to these crazy feelings?

"She was waiting until we were settled, then she was going to tell you she couldn't care for him anymore."

"What does that mean? She wants him to come here?"

"No, not to California. He's going to go to Española, to an old folks home."

Perfie tried to picture Primitivo in an old folks home; a crocheted afghan on his lap, sitting on a long porch with white haired old women. She couldn't see it happening.

"Perfie? Are you there?"

"Yes, I was thinking. I just don't know. What do you think?"

Isaac cleared his throat. "He's different, Perfie. He's an old man now. It's like he's shrunk, not just in size, but in that way he had. You know, how he always had to tower over everyone with his mood, be in control. He talked with me, actually opened up."

"What are you saying?" she asked.

"Just . . . it would be nice if you could see him again."

"Come there?"

"Not now, but someday. I just think it would be good for you to settle things with him."

Perfie imagined her father smaller, without the evil glare in his eye. She had a strange vision of someone who looked like a cross between Santa Claus and a raven.

Isaac continued. "Anyway, just a thought. Don't worry about it now. Isabelle can handle things and I'll be home soon. I love you."

Home. His word struck her. She realized she still thought of New Mexico as home. But he considered this cramped and dingy basement their home.

Two days later Perfie stood at the station in the same spot Isaac had stood a year ago. She waited for the seven o'clock train to arrive and tried to keep the unpleasant thoughts from her mind.

What would she do if he wasn't on the train? The wedding was just three days away. The initial excitement had been replaced by a dull ache. She still felt so out of time, as if she were a step behind on the dance floor. Not only was she getting married after having lived together with Isaac for so long and after having six babies with him, but now she was planning a wedding with no groom around. She pictured herself standing on the steps of the courthouse with flowers in hand and waiting for Isaac to show up.

At least she would be wearing her own green dress.

She shook her head to get the image out of her mind. Of course he was coming home.

A bell rang—the train was here. She stood and scanned each window as the cars pulled into the station, but she could see only the backs of heads. The travelers were standing and gathering bags from shelves in their readiness to get off the train.

She spotted Isaac when he stopped at the top of the steps and looked out over the small group of people gathered to greet the travelers. His eyes found hers. She smiled and waved.

His grin was stiff as though it were forced on his face, and his eyes didn't twinkle as she expected. She dropped her hand to her side but didn't push forward through the crowd. She watched him turn back into the train and say something. He moved down the steps to the platform, then stopped and turned, reaching his free hand back.

She watched as a hand reached for his. A woman's hand! A flash of jealousy struck her like lightning just seconds before she realized this wasn't the hand of a young woman.

It was Carlotta.

No, no, no, no. In disbelief and desperation she shook her head back and forth. Isaac and his mother approached her, and with great effort Perfie forced her head to remain still before her mother-in-law-to-be could lay eyes on her.

She rushed to Isaac and smashed her face into his shoulder as tears choked her throat—tears that she hoped would be interpreted as tears of joy

"Perfie." Isaac's arms were around her, squeezing. They stood still, breathing into each other's ears, clasped in embrace. Minutes passed, but she couldn't let him go. She didn't want to turn her face to Carlotta, didn't know how to paint a look on it that wouldn't reflect the thoughts racing through her head. Where was the woman to stay? In the basement? Was she here for good? To live with them? How could Isaac do this without asking her?

She cried harder. The wedding would be off again. She wouldn't do this. She wouldn't be trapped back under the horrible thumb of Carlotta. She wouldn't go back to being that scared little girl.

"Hush, it's okay." Isaac moved his lips very close to her ear. "She's just here for the wedding, not to stay."

Perfie felt a shudder start deep in her stomach and move up through her before it was released from her body with a shake of her shoulders. Isaac had understood what her tears were about. She took a deep breath and removed her arms from the embrace, then turned to Carlotta.

"Mama Martinez. I'm so surprised. How are you?"

Carlotta answered her with a frown and a nod, no expectation of an embrace.

Things hadn't changed a bit.

Fifty-One

Carlotta stayed upstairs with Rose. Perfie realized now that Rose had shared the knowledge of Carlotta's visit with Isaac, and this secret had kept the smile on her lips all week. It appeared everyone but Perfie knew Isaac was bringing his mother here.

Mary apologized. "I wanted to tell you. I knew you would be upset, but Isaac made me promise not to let you know." She had stopped by to check on Perfie.

"She's been okay. Having her upstairs with Rose seems to work. They don't really know each other, so they're both on their best behavior. Rose even fixed a dinner for all of us. Can you believe it! She used the dining room instead of the kitchen. You should have seen her. She never took her eyes from the kids. I was ready to jump up and rescue things if anyone knocked over a glass or dropped something."

"What did she serve?"

"Nothing fancy. She's really not a very good cook. We had some very tough meat and potatoes, bland and blander. Isaac asked for chili to go with it. You should have seen the look on Rose's face." Perfie reached down and placed a hand on her stomach.

"Feeling okay? Is it giving you any important messages today?" Mary asked. Perfie had told Mary about her gut, how it churned to warn her when things were going wrong.

"Nope, it's in good shape. Churning a little, but with excitement." Now that Isaac was really here, home in the flesh, she could anticipate the wedding tomorrow without the dreaded visions of being alone.

"I'm excited, too." Mary reached out and pulled Perfie's hand away from her stomach. "It's going to be wonderful."

Perfie was glad she had finally talked things over with Mary and told her how she worried about being a sinner. Mary understood and helped. She arranged for Perfie and Isaac to meet with Reverend Mike, a pastor at Mary's church.

Perfie thought about the conversation with Reverend Mike. He had described the courthouse ceremony and explained about the signing of the marriage license and the expectations they should have as a married couple. The next thing he talked about was rather silly: he gave them information about living together and about sex and children. As if they needed that!

"Do you have any questions?" Reverend Mike folded his hands on his lap.

Perfie bit her lip and summoned up her courage. "Yes."

She glanced at Isaac. "Father, we're not of the same faith. My mother, that is, I was led to believe that this is a sin, to marry outside the faith."

"There are some who believe this."

"I don't know if I believe it or not. How do I know what is the truth?"

"I think you find your truth deep in your heart. You and Isaac have four beautiful children. Would the Lord bless you with this if he were angry with you?"

She looked down, licked her lips and rubbed her palm across her forehead. "We had more children. Two sweet daughters. He took them as my punishment." She kept her head down as she spoke.

Reverend Mike was quiet as he reached out and took her hands in his. "It *is* a sad thing when He takes children. But you mustn't see this as punishment. He's not punitive in such a way."

"Why would he take them? My Betty? Little Grace?"

"It's particularly difficult when a child dies. I know it's of little comfort, but you must rest assured he had his reasons." Reverend Mike paused. "Not as a punishment, that is never the reason. You are blessed, Perfecta. I know your faith has left you with guilt, but Catholics are eventually forgiven, just like everyone else. Maybe this is the time to put all that behind you and move forward."

Perfie felt better after the visit with Reverend Mike, but she wasn't completely convinced that she was guilt free.

The loud clatter of someone coming down the back steps toward the basement shook her out of her daydream. Perfie and Mary looked at the door.

Rose stormed into the room and stood in front of them, her hands balled into fists, her face bright red, and her breath puffing out of her like a locomotive.

"You sinner," she hissed.

"What?" Perfie asked, shocked to hear Avelina's words coming out of Rose's mouth.

"You, all this time, living here in my house, a sinner."

"What are you talking about?" Mary asked.

Rose turned to face Mary. "*She* knows what I'm talking about, and apparently so do you. Not married, that's what."

Carlotta. She must have told Rose about the wedding tomorrow.

"You're right. We aren't married. But we will be tomorrow."

"That's beside the point. I want you out. Now. Today." Rose shook her fist in the air.

Perfie couldn't believe this. Rose would kick them out? Today? Just like that?

Mary walked toward Rose and reached out her hand. "Calm down, Rose. Let's talk about this."

Rose stepped away from Mary. "I'm not talking. I want her out."

"What about Carlotta?" Perfie was all too familiar with having to move out of a place at a moment's notice. She knew she could do it again, although she had no idea where they would go, but this time it included Isaac's mother.

"She's out too. She's not even my relation since you and Isaac aren't married. Why should I put up with her?"

Just yesterday Rose had been all smiles and compliments when she talked about how much she enjoyed Carlotta's company. Things sure changed in a hurry.

Mary stepped in front of Rose. "Rose, you can't do this. Not today. The wedding is tomorrow. They don't have anywhere to go."

"Why don't you take them in? Don't you have a house?" Rose waved a hand and pointed a finger into Mary's face.

Perfie turned to Mary.

Mary shook her head and looked away. "No. I don't."

Perfie felt her heart sink. Sudddenly, when the family needed her most, Mary wasn't there for them.

Spigots

Fifty-Two

Perfie and Isaac sat on the sagging green couch with their hands clasped between them. She was exhausted. Only one day had passed since moving and getting married—and since Mary had said they would not be welcome in her home.

Hard to believe it had only been yesterday when Rose had stormed upstairs after insisting the family move out of her basement immediately. Mary had followed and soon returned with Carlotta.

Isaac's mother had reached a hand toward Perfie. "I'm so sorry, Perfecta. I didn't know."

Perfie was tempted to take her hand, but she was still in shock over Rose's demand and Mary's betrayal. It had to be John, she thought. Mary couldn't ask them to come because her husband hated them.

But that hadn't been it.

"Perfie. I have to tell you something." Mary sat back at the table, and Carlotta sat next to her. "I'm not living in my house anymore. I moved out. John and I . . . we're not together anymore."

Perfie gasped. "What?"

"I didn't want to tell you now, but I moved out last week. I couldn't stay there. I'm renting a room, so you see, that's why I can't take you in."

Perfie tried to feel sympathy for Mary, but she was too worried about her own family. "I don't know where we're going to go. There are no more relatives. We've used everyone up."

Now, just a day later they were here in Mr. Bentley's kitchen, and Carlotta and Mr. Bentley were washing the dishes. Mr. Bentley, the old man with the big house where Mary rented a room.

At first Mr. Bentley had been reluctant to let the family stay for a night, but now he seemed pleased with the company. He insisted on a wedding dinner for the couple and their family and that they stay one more night.

The day went well in spite of everything that had happened yesterday. The kids were on their best behavior at the courthouse, and no rules had surfaced against getting married when you had already lived together forever. Carlotta hadn't even said a word to Perfie about how crazy the day had been—a day filled with packing and moving, not to mention a wedding. In fact, she had pitched in and helped by entertaining the girls while the rest of them were busy loading the truck.

Now, the long day had come to an end. The children were in the corner of the room where they would make their bed. Mary laid blankets over them and treated them to hot chocolate and a story, They fell asleep piled like a litter of puppies on the big pillows from the couch.

Mary looked exhausted. She slumped down into the green stuffed chair and let out a huge sigh. Perfie smiled as she reached out to touch Mary's knee. "My day was perfect, all because of you. You're wonderful, Mary. We'll find somewhere to go tomorrow, I promise."

Mary glanced at Isaac. "Now?"

He nodded, and Mary reached for an envelope that was tucked under her book on the end table. She handed it to Isaac with a smile.

"I have a present for you," Isaac said to his new bride.

Perfie stared at the envelope. "A present? I didn't get anything for you."

"No need. This is for both of us." He handed it to her.

Perfie removed the papers and scanned them quickly.

"Gracias. I guess we can turn this in now that we're officially married." Perfie looked at Isaac with a smile and a shrug.

He reached over, flipped to the second page and pointed to the bottom where something was stamped in blue ink.

"Approved?"

A huge grin filled Isaac's face. "Yes, yes, yes. We have a house."

"A house? But . . ."

"We turned it in before I left. Mary did it."

"I thought it took weeks for approval?"

"Not when you pull some strings." Mary smiled. "Dr. Cooper was willing to step up for you when I explained your situation."

"You mean we have a place? Where? When can we move in?" Perfie sat up very straight now and clutched Isaac's arm.

"Two weeks. It's close by, so the kids can go to the same school."

Mary smiled at Perfie. "It's an apartment, not a house, but I know you'll love it. There's a playground, an activity center for the boys and lots of room outdoors."

"It's really true? We really have a place to live?"

"Sí, we really do." Isaac kissed her cheek.

"What about the two weeks? Where will we go?"

"We'll figure something out. Don't worry tonight. Tomorrow is soon enough to think about it."

Perfie and Isaac slipped into bed. Mary had insisted they sleep in her room. She would be on the couch next to the children.

"It's your wedding night." She smiled as she pushed them into the room.

"Isaac. I'm so happy about the house, the apartment." Perfie had to remember to use the correct word. "But what about tomorrow? Where will we go?"

"Perfie, I don't want you to tell Mary. She's already done enough." Isaac rubbed her arm. "We'll stay in the truck. As long as it doesn't rain we'll be okay."

"In the truck? But where?"

"I'll find a place. I will. I'll take the bus tomorrow. When Mary goes to work I want you to take the kids and go park at Dom's house. Leave her a note. Tell her you won't see her for a couple of weeks because we have to stay with someone, a cousin, far away."

"Far away? Where?"

"Napa. We'll stay with cousin Frank in Napa. Tell her that."

"Lie?"

"Just a little white lie, Perfie. It's for her sake. She'll get kicked out of here if we don't leave." Isaac paused. "It was a white lie, too, you know, when Mary never even told us she had left John. Everyone does it once in a while to keep from hurting someone. Now hush and kiss me. It's our wedding night, remember?"

The next afternoon Perfie drove the loaded truck across town. At the corner of Foothill and 23rd she pulled hard on the stiff gear handle before stomping on the brake.

Roberto complained about the abrupt stop. "Mom, you're breaking my neck."

Like all children in T.A., Perfie had learned to drive on the farm, but she had never driven in traffic. She kept the truck at a steady twenty miles per hour and stopped at each intersection to check the pencil drawing Isaac had given to her that morning.

Carlotta hadn't said a word since piling into the truck with the kids, but she spoke up now. "Sit still and hush."

"I think we're almost there." Perfie pushed Roberto's legs to the side and changed gears with the knob on the long shaft.

Karleen stood behind Perfie's shoulder on the seat, and Arturo was curled on the floor between Carlotta's knees. Carlotta held Geri on her lap.

Dom lived on the west side of town near the bay. The houses were run down there, and apartment buildings were crammed onto lots between the houses. There were no yards at all. Perfie wondered if their apartment would look like this. Where was all that outdoor space Mary talked about?

She pulled the bucking Ford to a stop in front of a building whose paint was so peeled and faded that you could barely tell it had once been green. There was an old washer and a pile of garbage sitting on a patch of dirt in front of the building.

"I think this is it."

Carlotta pulled on the door handle.

"No, stay in."

"Aren't we staying here with Dom?"

"Not until Isaac gets here."

Roberto leaned over his grandmother to peer out the window. "Why did we have to leave Mr. Bentley's house? I liked it there." Carlotta elbowed him back to his spot. He turned to his mother. "Mom, why did you make us leave again? You're always making us leave the good places. I *loved* it there."

"I did, too." Arturo said. "I loved Mr. Bendy's dog." Perfie had dragged Arturo in from the yard the night before. He would have slept with the old shepherd all night if she had let him.

"Not Mr. Bendy, stupid."

"Hush, don't say that to your brother. We can't live there. Be thankful we have this truck." Perfie leaned her head back and rubbed her neck.

Once the words were out of her mouth she realized what she had done to Roberto. She had told him to be grateful for something terrible. Life had a funny way of turning you into your own worst nightmare. She saw the shimmery light hovering off to the right of her face and felt her jaw tighten. This was a terrible time to get a headache.

"But he has so many rooms." Roberto wasn't going to let up. "Dad would have let us stay there."

She felt her heart pound. Why did Roberto always think Isaac was so wonderful and she was so mean? She was afraid she might say things she would regret, so she didn't answer him. She took a deep breath and counted to ten.

Truth was, she felt the same way. Mr. Bentley had been kind to fix them dinner and let them stay, but it wouldn't have hurt him to invite them to stay longer.

Carlotta lifted Geri from her lap and pushed her past Roberto to Perfie.

"Just where *are* you going to live?"

"I don't know. I'm just doing what your son said to do. He told me to load up and drive here, so that is what I did." Perfie kept her eyes closed.

It had been another long day. Perfie finally let the kids get out of the truck to run around on the dirt patch. She did her best to keep the girls away from the pile of garbage, but it was hopeless trying to keep the boys from it. They pulled things out of the pile and used what looked like a part of a bicycle handlebar to dig in the dirt. They stacked some old cardboard boxes up for a target and found rocks to use as weapons.

Carlotta never left the truck.

"Mama, I need to pee pee." Karleen clutched at herself.

Perfie looked around and wondered if Dom's wife and kids were home. She didn't know for sure which place was theirs. Finally she led Karleen to the curb beside the rear wheel of the truck and slipped the little girl's underpants down.

"Pee here." She could see Carlotta's look of disgust in the side mirror.

She was helping Karleen pull up her panties when a rock went whizzing past her head and banged into the side of the truck.

"Stop that right now." She saw Arturo run around the side of the house when another rock flew through the air and struck her just above her ear.

"You little bastard!" she yelled as she ran after Roberto, her exhaustion turning into fury. He followed his brother around the side of the house, and Perfie was half way to the back yard when she realized she would never catch him.

"You better keep running all the way to China. You'll pay for this," she yelled as she trudged back to the truck.

Carlotta was standing on the sidewalk. Geri was on her hip, and Karleen was holding her hand.

Carlotta frowned at Perfie. "Don't do what I did. Show them you love them, *M'jita*."

Perfie stared at her mother-in-law. My daughter? Had Carlotta actually addressed her with a term of affection?

"Did you see what happened? That rock hit me!" Perfie rubbed the sore spot on her head.

"This isn't easy for you, but it isn't easy for them, either." Carlotta's face was white. "It's too late for me. I didn't tell my kids I loved them or show them how important they were to me. Now Lucas is gone. All he ever wanted me to do was be sweet to them, overlook the bad parts and focus on the good parts."

It hit Perfie that this was what Mary had talked about that day at Fenton's. She had talked about seeing people in a different light.

Carlotta was in pain. Perfie knew Carlotta had lived with an overpowering grandfather, a helpless mother and a father who was gone much of the time. Isaac's mother was an only child; her mother had never been able to carry another child to full term.

Perfie thought about the photograph that Isaac kept of his mother. He had never bothered to display it anywhere, just as she never displayed the photos of her parents. Carlotta's children did love her, but they were not close to their mother. Instead they felt more of an obligation to her. In the photo Carlotta was only twenty-two years old and already a mother of four. She was an heiress, and she was about to make the decision to move away from her family to a place where she didn't know a soul. She made that decision, and the people of the new town shunned her.

Carlotta's heart was deeply hidden from years of building a stone wall around it, but Perfie could see that she had one. Her mother-in-law felt both pain and love, though these feelings were hidden deep below a layer of ice like the strange formations that remain frozen in underground caves.

"Gracias." Perfie said softly. She wanted to reach out, to touch Carlotta, but she didn't have the courage to make the final move.

Fifty-Three

Dom didn't have a room for the Martinez family.

"We'll sleep in the truck," Isaac announced "If we park here in front of his house the police won't make us move."

Carlotta sat in the front of the truck and slept with a rolled-up blanket to support her head. Arturo and Roberto lay wrapped in a blanket under the truck, close to the curb. Thank goodness this wasn't a busy street, Perfie thought from her spot in the bed of the truck. The two girls were wedged tight between her and Isaac. Isaac was unable to straighten his legs and lay uncomfortably on one side with bent knees. Thank goodness Mr. Bentley had let them leave some of the crates in his garage, or else they would have even less space to sleep.

Perfie listened as the girls' soft breathing grew deeper and Isaac snored and moved his legs now and then in a futile attempt to find a better position.

She knew this would be a rough night, but she eventually drifted off into a light sleep, only to be wakened twenty minutes later by a grunting sound. A man was standing beside the truck.

"Isaac," she hissed.

She heard heavy breathing, throat clearing and hacking as the man spit behind the truck. The sound of a zipper and a stream of urine brought her to her feet. This man was peeing just where her boys lay sleeping.

"What are you doing?" she yelled from where she stood in the bed of the truck. Geri and Karleen started to cry. Isaac jumped to his feet and let out a yell that could have woken the dead.

The startled man ran down the street with his fly open. Perfie vaulted herself over the edge of the truck bed and reached for the boys. She was sure they would be covered with urine.

"What's happening?" Isaac was fully awake now.

"I can't stay here. We can't make our children sleep where drunks do their business."

Isaac tried to calm her, but she insisted the boys sleep in the truck bed. Karleen was moved into the front where she curled up on the driver's seat next to her grandmother and draped her feet over the gear shift bar. Perfie sat up so that the boys and Isaac could lie down. She held Geri in her lap.

"I won't be going back to sleep anyway," she insisted.

The next night Isaac slept under the truck. Carlotta insisted that both girls sleep in front with her. Perfie lay in the truck bed next to the boys. All night long she heard the sounds of the neighborhood: dogs barking, men and women fighting and children crying.

Perfie longed for the whitewashed adobe walls, the dusty roads and the high bluffs of Tierra Amarilla. What she wouldn't give to be on Cimmaron's back, winding her way up to the hills again. Coyotes and bears were easy to deal with compared to what was surrounding her now. Here she didn't know what to fear, so she couldn't plan ahead to protect her family. It seemed that every place she had lived before—the corner of Carlotta's living room, the tent on the hill, and even the fruit shed in Albuquerque—had been better than what she had encountered in California.

With silent, salty tears dripping down her cheeks, Perfie drifted into sleep and melted into dreams of long ago.

Wednesday was their third day in the truck. That morning Carlotta folded the blankets and put them in the truck bed.

"How do I catch a bus in this place?"

"A bus?" Perfie was confused. Where in the world did Carlotta plan to go?

"Yes, that big vehicle that has four wheels and takes people around from place to place." Carlotta actually smiled as she joked.

"Where are you going?" Perfie asked.

"I'm going out, and that's all you need to know."

"But you'll need to speak English to get around. The drivers don't speak Spanish."

What happened next came as a complete shock to Perfie. Carlotta answered her in nearly perfect English.

"I have English, enough to make my way around this town. There's a lot you don't know about me, my daughter."

"The bus stops down at the next corner, but I can take you in the truck if you need to go somewhere."

Carlotta didn't bother to answer. Perfie watched her mother-in-law's rigid shoulders as the woman marched her way down to the corner to board the next bus.

Perfie wondered what she would tell Isaac if she lost his mother?

That day dragged on as Perfie worried about Carlotta. She sat in Dom's yard and watched the girls, while the boys played on the street and ran up and down the sidewalk.

"Don't go past the corner," she warned Roberto and Arturo. "Stay where I can see you."

"Okay, Mom. Don't worry." Arturo called over his shoulder as he ran around the building and disappeared from her sight.

"Oh, Lord. How did I ever get into this mess?" She watched Geri pick up an unidentified black object, a car part, maybe. "Put that down," she yelled.

Geri dropped the grimy thing back into the dirt and smiled. Nothing makes that child unhappy, Perfie thought. I wish I could be more like her.

"Cookie?" Geri asked, as if expecting a reward for her compliance.

It was getting late. The kids would be hungry, but with nowhere to cook she had to rely on Isaac bringing food home when he got off work. The crackers in the truck would have to do for right now.

"Okay, let's get a cookie." She made her way back to the truck.

Three days in a tightly packed vehicle had lead to chaos. Their belongings—clothes, toys, books, and what little food they still had—lay scattered around the truck bed. She tried to rummage through the mess to find the crackers, but standing on the curb made this impossible, so she climbed in.

"What a disaster. You stay right there." Geri sat on the sidewalk and picked up a rock.

Perfie folded clothes and stuffed them back into sacks. When she at last located the crackers she climbed back out of the truck and handed one to Geri.

"Where's your sister? Let's give her a cookie, too." Perfie looked around for Karleen.

"Leenie?" She walked around the truck. "Karleen!"

Her heart pounded in her chest.

She heard Arturo and Roberto around the side of the building. Scooping up Geri she ran toward their voices. "Karleen? Come here right now."

She ran around the apartment building.

"Is your sister with you?"

The boys stared, their hands behind their backs.

"No, Mom. She's not here." She saw Roberto drop a rock. So that's what they were doing back here. She would have to worry about that later.

"Help me find her. She's gone."

The boys ran down to the corner where their grandmother had caught the bus and called out their sister's name. Perfie's cries took her down the street in the other direction. When she reached the corner she looked down the busy street. East 14th was a major road, and cars were speeding by. Karleen was in danger if she had wandered down here.

"Please God, whoever you are, whatever you are. I didn't mean it about not being Catholic. I'll go back if that's what it takes. Just find my baby, please find my baby." Perfie prayed out loud, gasping sobs punctuating her words.

She continued her bargaining. "I'll go to Mass every day. I'll make the children be Catholic. Anything. Please, oh please."

Perfie looked south, but the long sidewalk was empty. She turned around and looked north.

She could make out two figures, one small and one large, walking together two blocks away. The small one was wearing a blue dress.

"Karleen!" Perfie started to run, clutching Geri to her shoulder. She saw the little head turn.

It was the man who had urinated by the truck the other night. He looked back at her and quickly picked up Karleen before starting to run.

"Stop! Somebody help me!" She ran faster. "He's stealing my baby. Stop him."

Geri started to cry.

Perfie saw a blue car pull over near the man. An accomplice? If they got into the car she'd never catch them. She ran faster, Geri screaming as they raced down the sidewalk.

Someone jumped out of the car. She saw the figure swing a large black bag and hit the man across the face.

It was Carlotta.

The man pushed at her, but she managed to get another direct hit. Perfie watched in amazement as the old woman reached out and grabbed his hair.

Perfie was closing in. The man was dressed in filthy rags. He was young and very thin. Perfie screamed out as she got closer. "Leave them alone."

The man dropped Karleen to the ground and pushed Carlotta. The old woman teetered on the edge of the curb. Karleen crawled under the car.

Perfie was out of breath, but she was nearly there. The scruffy man turned and bolted down the street.

Perfie set Geri down and glanced under the car at Karleen. She looked scared, but not hurt.

"Ohhh . . . ." Carlotta let out a moan. She wasn't moving.

"Madre. Don't try to move. I think you hit your head." Perfie reached down and put her hand on Carlotta's forehead. A huge bumped swelled between her ear and her eyebrow.

"Karleen? Is Karleen safe?" Carlotta struggled to sit up.

Perfie heard pounding feet. The boys raced in her direction.

"Mom! What happened? Why is Abuela on the ground?"

Karleen crawled out from under the car and threw her arms around Perfie's legs.

Perfie sänk onto the sidewalk, pulling Karleen next to Geri. Roberto helped his grandmother to sit up and lean against the bumper of the car.

"You saved her." Perfie met Carlotta's eyes over Karleen's soft brown hair. "I was so scared."

Carlotta turned a shade of green and vomited in the gutter. Perfie saw her mother-in-law's hands shaking. She wanted to get up and help her, but Karleen was still holding on tight.

"It's okay, Abuela. Do you want to use my handkerchief?" Arturo patted his grandmother's shoulder and offered her the dirty rag from his pocket.

"Is everything okay here?" Perfie turned in the direction of a deep voice that came from behind her.

A tall man wearing a blue uniform stood on the sidewalk.

"No. It's not. A man tried to steal my little girl. If it weren't for my mother-in-law she would be gone."

Much later that night, the Martinez family found themselves miraculously gathered around Mr. Bentley's kitchen table. The kids scraped the last of their ice cream out of blue bowls and Mary washed the dishes from dinner.

Perfie held Isaac's hand. She couldn't let go. She had told the whole story to the policeman and to Isaac and Mary. Carlotta helped fill in the blanks. She explained how she happened to be driving by in Mr. Bentley's car. She had gone to see him, and when she described their circumstances he agreed to let them stay at his house again. He even offered to let her use his car to go back and tell them. She explained that she had heard the screams of her daughter-in-law and the baby just before seeing the man race down the street with her granddaughter.

Perfie knew Mary was upset that they hadn't told her the truth about where they were going. Exhausted and relieved, Perfie didn't have the energy to deal with this now. Tomorrow would be soon enough to repair the friendship.

That night Perfie prayed silently as she lay with Isaac and her two daughters on the folded pile of blankets.

Thank you, God. I'm sorry for all my sins. Please don't punish me anymore. It's okay, right? Isaac is a good man. His mother saved my baby. You made her do that, didn't you? She thought about what Reverend Mike had said about God not punishing us. But if he didn't punish, she wondered, would he also chose not to come to the rescue?

Perfie felt a cool breeze on her hot cheeks, and when she opened her eyes she saw a light flickering on the ceiling above her. The light seemed to be in the shape of a hand. She was sure now that God had heard her prayer and had forgiven her. Carlotta had saved her family and that meant that God watched over Presbyterians, too.

Shifting her arms so that she could feel Isaac's shoulder and Karleen's soft hair, Perfie closed her eyes and thought about the sweet smile of the Virgin. "Thank you for stepping in. I think God listened to you," she whispered as she drifted into sleep.

Fifty-Four

Roberto peeled the tape slowly from the edge of the package. When the newspaper wrapping tore, he glanced nervously at his mother.

She smiled. "It's okay. You can rip it."

He pulled the rest of the paper off and opened the box.

It was a hat—navy blue with a red logo. The Oaks.

He put the hat on his head and looked at Dad.

"Now you are a true Californian."

It was hard to believe that more than a year had passed since they left New Mexico. Roberto tried to picture his *abuelo*. He was sad that Lucas had died and he would never see him again. But *Abuela* was here, and she was nice now.

"I have something for you, too." *Abuela* handed him a little cloth bag.

He loosened the drawstring and slid out a shiny rock. It had a gold stripe down the side like the one his grandfather had given him a long time ago. He pulled his lucky stone out of his pocket.

The rough sides fit together.

"He told me about the stones," his grandmother said, "and how you found them on your hike. He kept that half in his pocket, Roberto. He missed you. He would take it out and rub it and tell me stories of how smart you are and about the adventures you two had together. I think he would want you to have it so that someday you can give half to someone special." Tears ran down his grandmother's face.

"*Gracias, Abuela.*" He kissed her wrinkled cheek.

"Happy Birthday to you." Singing came from the other room as his father turned out the lights. Mary and Arturo carried in a big cake lit up with ten candles. They walked slowly across the room and stopped in front of Roberto.

"Make a wish!" Mary smiled.

"What?" He was confused.

"It's tradition. You make a wish and blow out all the candles. If you can do it in one breath your wish will come true." He saw Mary look at his mother.

Mom shrugged.

"Better hurry. We have a big fire going here." Mary nodded. "Make a wish in your mind. You don't have to say it out loud."

He thought he might wish for a home, but they got that already. Next week they would move to the apartment, although he wished they could just stay here. He liked it at Mr. Bentley's house. There was a big back yard and a dog.

He would have wished for a hat, but now he had that, too.

He thought about wishing to move back to New Mexico, but he found he could barely even remember Tierra Amarilla anymore. He only remembered the mean nuns at the school. No, he didn't want to go back there.

He looked at his smiling mother and his father's twinkling eyes.

"Go on. Do it," Dad said.

Finally Roberto knew what he would wish for.

Make it stay the same. Just like this.

He drew in a breath and blew out all the candles.

Fifty-Five

Mary was holding a letter that looked as if it had been crumpled up in a tight ball, then smoothed and placed in the envelope. Her face was as white as the paper.

"What is it?" Perfie rose from her chair.

Mary shook her head and handed the letter to Perfie.

Lawrence lost his job at the mill. The strike didn't help any. I'm working two jobs now, and he watches the girls. I'm scared, Mary, so scared. How will we manage?

It was a letter from Mary's colored friend from back east.

"She's having a rough time, Perfie. She wants me to come home." Mary sat down at the table. "I told her about John, about moving out."

"What about John? I thought you were going to keep trying."

"I know I told you that, but he hasn't even called or come by. I think he's glad, Perfie. I think he wanted out, too."

"But shouldn't you try harder?"

"I don't think so. I don't think that's ever going to happen." Mary looked so sad.

"It definitely won't work if you're in some other part of the country."

"I know you don't approve, but I think I'm going to ask him for a divorce."

"Oh, Mary." Perfie shook her head. "I'm so sorry."

"It's okay, really. I truly think this is better."

By the next day Mary's decision was final. "I have to leave, Perfie. Everything is pointing that way. Sarah Green, she wants the job back, now that her mother died."

Perfie looked puzzled.

"She was school nurse before me," Mary explained. "She only took a leave to care for her mother. So, you see, I don't have a husband or a job."

What about me? Perfie wanted to ask, but instead she turned away and grabbed the broom.

A moment later she turned back to Mary.

"I'm sorry. I know this must be right for you."

Mary blinked rapidly. "You'll be busy with the new place and your new job. I promise I'll write."

Perfie nodded and went back to the sweeping so that Mary wouldn't see her tears. She couldn't talk about this anymore.

Mary spent the next two days making arrangements for her trip. She wrote a letter to John asking him for a divorce. She gave most of her things to Perfie and packed up only what could fit in her little Ford. Perfie watched Mary slip the last parcel into the trunk of her car.

"There's one last thing we have to do."

Mary drove Perfie over to look at Lockwood Gardens—the new project where they would live.

Perfie sat in Mary's car and looked out at the green apartments and the newly planted grass that carpeted the wide areas in between buildings. Some of the apartments were already occupied.

Perfie watched the kids playing on the grass. "I don't see any colored people."

"Negros aren't allowed here. Whites only." Mary added. "I think it's terrible."

Perfie was silent. In spite of all Mary's best efforts to convince her that prejudice was wrong, she knew that Mary herself didn't consider the Martinez family white. But Perfie didn't consider herself different even though many of the so-called-whites did. There were restrictions on buying property up in the hills. Not only Negros were excluded, but also Asians, Italians, Portuguese, Jews, Roman Catholics and just about anyone else who hadn't sailed over on the Mayflower. Unless they were the live-in help, there was no place for them in those hills.

It had been no problem at all for a family with the name of Martinez to secure a place in this whites-only project, so Perfie felt justified in her thinking.

She wished Mary could stay to see the family move in. The kids were so excited. But today, with hugs and tears, Mary said goodbye to them.

"I'll be back, I promise."

318

Perfie saw this as one of those white lies. She knew Mary would never come back to California and that they would never see each other again.

Still, something felt different, even after Mary had driven Perfie back to her family and walked out her door for the last time. Perfie was sad to lose her friend, but she was also thinking about the new adventures that lay ahead. She thought about her mother, Little Joe, and even Cimmaron, and she remembered all the places she had lived, all the complaints she had each time.

Then she thought about the sun shining today and about Isaac and the nutty smell she missed. She looked at him, settled into the rocker on Mr. Bentley's front porch, reading the paper as if nothing was changing. Maybe he could get a different job soon, one that didn't make him cough all the time.

"Once there was an Indian Maiden," she said out loud.

"What?" Isaac looked up from his paper.

"Nothing. Just a story I need to tell myself." She leaned over and kissed him.

Fifty-Six

Perfie followed Carlotta and Isaac up the walkway to the apartment. It had been ten days before Isaac finally came home with the key. Perfie didn't want to wait until the next morning to move, but it was past dinner time and Isaac needed help loading the crates in the truck.

"Always in a rush, my dear." He smiled and gave her that look that said *I love you in spite of your faults.* "Tomorrow morning, first thing. Dom is coming over and we'll be on our way."

Carlotta cleared her throat. "It would be a good idea if you and I cleaned up this house, as a way to thank Mr. Bentley."

Carlotta was able to look beyond the immediate, and somehow the old woman managed to get just what she wanted in the process. Thank goodness Carlotta had bought her ticket home the day before. She would stay until the next Tuesday, just long enough to see them settled in.

Perfie wondered if she had misjudged Isaac's mother all these years. If she had, then what about her father? Had she misjudged him as well?

She felt her shoulders tighten in reaction to the memory of her father's cruelty. She still didn't understand why he had been so mean to her.

Perfie tried to imagine her father as a young man. She wondered how he had treated the children of the mystery woman in Texas. He'd been the father of those children, too.

She knew he had deserted them, and the thought filled her with disgust. She imagined what her life would have been like if he had deserted her—if he had left her and Avelina. Perfie sighed as she thought about her mother. She was sure her mother would have come to accept Isaac. She would have loved her grandchildren and would have spoiled the boys with extra chunks of meat in their bowl of stew. She would have sewn frilly, silky dresses for the girls. She probably would have insisted on taking the kids to Sunday mass. Perfie imagined arguing with her mother about that, the two of them not speaking with each other for days.

But Perfie also knew that time would have erased any disagreement, just like the wind could leave a smooth surface in the desert sand.

She thought about what Isaac had told her when he was in New Mexico. He had wanted her to make amends with Primitivo.

She could still picture the last time she had seen her father, just before she had left Tierra Amarilla with the children. She had run down to the Mercantile to pick up some yeast so that she could bake bread for the trip. With Geri on her hip and Karleen in tow, she was about to push through the swinging screen doors when she felt a shiver run up her spine.

From the steps of the courthouse, her father stared at her and started to raise his hand just as she looked his way.

To wave to her?

She hadn't looked long enough to find out. She had grabbed Karleen's hand and hurried down the length of the long wooden porch. When she turned to look back a moment later, he was gone. Had he wanted something from her—to talk to her or to meet his granddaughters?

It didn't matter. Isaac was wrong. It wouldn't be good for her to see him again. It would just open a wound that had finally scabbed over. She didn't want fresh blood to pour from her heart.

Perfie wished Mary were here. She thought about what she had told Mary about her father. She had glossed over how many times he had hurt her. In fact, she had thought at times that he would actually kill her. Why hadn't she told Mary how bad it really had been?

The answers were buried deep within her, and she didn't want to dig them up. Primitivo was hundreds of miles away. Leave him there.

But now she wished she could talk to Mary and get her advice on all the questions racing through her mind.

Her friend's departure had been so sudden. She knew Mary was unhappy here, but Perfie wondered if she herself should have talked to John. Mary had said she was ready to try again, if only John would make some sort of effort. But the only communication she had had from him was the strange letter he had sent agreeing to handle the paperwork for the divorce.

No, it was probably best that Mary was back where her parents and that friend of hers could take care of her for awhile.

Perfie's thoughts came back to the present as Isaac turned the key in the lock and the sharp click broke the silence. Three adults and four children held their breath as they prepared to enter their new home for the first time.

The kids poured into the house before Isaac could push the door all the way open. They raced ahead, feet clattering in the empty rooms.

Geri squirmed her way out of Perfie's arms, eager to be part of the excitement.

A huge room with a shiny hardwood floor opened out in front of them. Off to the right a staircase led up to the second floor. At the far end of the room Perfie could see a shiny refrigerator through the open doorway.

Roberto came running down the stairs. "A bathroom, with a tub. And so many rooms Mama, bunches of rooms. Where do I sleep?"

"Hold on. We'll figure that out in a minute."

She watched as Carlotta ran her hand over the wall and walked into the kitchen. "Let's look in here first."

The kitchen was more than Perfie could ever have dreamed of. There was not only the refrigerator, but a stove and a shiny white sink. Painted yellow cupboards surrounded two sides, and a blue linoleum countertop covered the lower cabinets. So much space! There was a spot with two windows in an L-shape, just right for the dining table.

Perfie opened a door next to the stove and entered a little room with a door out the back. A laundry room!

She walked back into the front room. Isaac carried her rocking chair in and set it in front of the window.

"No!" She bit her lip and lowered her voice. "Sorry. Not there. Okay?"

Isaac looked at her and nodded in understanding. "Of course not. How about over here?" He moved it to the corner by the kitchen.

She nodded. She could rock Geri and keep an eye out the window from a distance.

"Mama, hurry up, you have to see." Arturo tugged her arm.

She followed him up the stairs. At the top there was a bathroom, complete with a shiny tub. She smiled and rubbed her hand over the porcelain. The toilet was brand new, as shiny as the tub.

"Can I pee in here?" Arturo danced up and down.

"Yes, but let the rest of us leave first."

Roberto tapped her arm. "Can I take a bath tonight? All by myself?"

Was this Roberto, asking her if he could bathe?

"Of course. We all can."

"By myself?" he repeated.

"Yes, by yourself." She walked down the hall.

There were three bedrooms up here, each with a big closet and a window. The biggest room faced the front of the building, where a window would let in the late morning sun. The other rooms were smaller, but still plenty large for two kids each.

"Mom? Can this be my room? Arturo and me?" Roberto stood at the window of the back bedroom. She walked over and stood beside him.

Outside the window was a tree, its upper branches level with the roof of the apartment. Across the lawn stood another line of apartments, just like this one. Separating the two lines of buildings was a wide expanse of lawn filled with kids running and riding bikes, throwing balls and chasing each other.

"Yes, this can be your room."

"Mom?" Roberto looked at her with a slight grin.

"Yes?"

"Once there was an Indian boy."

"There was?"

Roberto nodded. "He had to travel a long way and he was mad and hungry. He didn't want to leave New Mex—the river."

Perfie waited.

"But one day he found a new cave to live in. And it was a really nice cave with a better river and lots of deer and foxes and trees."

"Did he like that?"

Roberto slipped his hand around her arm. "He did like it. A lot. And when he walked around, when he explored the new place, he found out there were lots of other Indian kids. And there was this even better thing and it was called baseball, and all the kids and the braves and even the maidens, they all played ball every day."

He leaned toward the window. "That's a good story, right?"

"Yes, Bobbie. That's a good story."

He grinned and ran out of the room.

Perfie looked out the window. She was almost afraid to be excited. Was it possible things were going to go right for awhile?

A black shadow caught her attention. She turned her head and saw a raven perched on a thin branch of the tree. His black eye was focused on her, and he tipped his head to one side and let out a squawk. There he stood, unfolding and spreading his wings and, looking like Isaac when he shrugged and held up his hands, palms to the sky.

"What will be, will be," Perfie whispered, repeating her husband's favorite saying, as the raven folded his wings and flew away.

She turned from the window and walked back down the stairs toward the sounds of laughter and chatter coming from the kitchen. As she walked into the room, she watched Carlotta scoop Geri into her arms and kiss her soft cheek. Bobbie was at the sink, watching the water run from the spigot.

"Mom?"

"What now, Bobbie?"

"Thank you for bringing us to heaven." He smiled and hugged her waist.

Then he ran off to join Arturo, who was racing out the back door and across the lawn toward the laughing children.

Perfie watched Isaac place two wooden chairs next to the table he had just carried in from the truck.

"What do you think of this castle, my Queen?" He smiled. They both remembered the words spoken so long ago at the adobe house.

"I think . . . ," she hesitated and thought about Roberto's warm hug. "I thank you for bringing us to heaven."

That afternoon, after Dom and Isaac had moved all the furniture from Mr. Bentley's garage and from the other various storage spots, there was a surprise.

A blue truck pulled up and unloaded three new beds.

"Where do you want these?" The young delivery man was smiling at Perfie as though he knew a secret.

"Isaac? We can't afford these." Perfie had hoped to be on good enough speaking terms with Rose to talk her into giving them the old mattress and box springs.

"Don't look at me." He shook his head.

Carlotta looked up from the paper she was cutting to line the kitchen drawers. "One in each of the rooms upstairs," she told the delivery man.

Carlotta smiled. "*Felicidades, y les deseo a los dos que sean muy felices.* It's your wedding present."

"But . . ." Perfie stopped herself from telling Carlotta she shouldn't have. Instead she walked over and hugged her. "Gracias. Thank you Carlotta."

As the delivery men carried the beds and mattresses up the staircase, Isaac went to the back door and called the boys. Bobbie and Artie, followed by a third boy, came running into the kitchen.

Artie tugged at Perfie's arm. "Mom, I can be Japanese if I want to, right?"

Perfie looked at the young boy with walnut-colored skin and almond eyes. His face was covered with dust, just like Arturo's face. Both of them looked up at her.

"Hello," she greeted the newcomer.

"I'm Ichiro Nakamura. I'm an American. But Artie can't be Japanese."

"Uh-huh. I can if I want, right Mom?"

She heard Isaac laugh as he walked into the kitchen. "What's this all about? Japanese?"

"Yeah, Dad. Ichiro says he is American and Japanese. I'm American, too, right? I want to be Japanese, like Ichie." Artie threw an arm over the boy's shoulder.

"Nice to meet you, Ichiro." Isaac stuck out a hand.

Ichiro stepped forward and shook Isaac's hand. Then he took a step back and bowed. "That's the Japanese way."

Artie bowed, too.

"Well, the way I see it, Ichiro is Japanese, and you, Artie, are Spanish." Isaac pointed to each boy as he spoke. "But you are both American."

"I can speak Spanish. *Hola, Ichie. Yo soy tu amigo.*" Arturo bowed again.

Ichiro giggled and covered his mouth with his hand. "Soy sauce."

Isaac laughed. "Ichiro, how about you run home and ask your mother if you can come have a Spanish dinner with us?"

"Okeydoke. That's American for yes." Ichiro giggled again. His laugh was contagious and soon the whole family was laughing.

While Perfie had organized the kitchen, Carlotta had made up all the beds upstairs. Carlotta lay with the girls in their new room on the new bed. Her mother-in-law had the sense to order a rubber sheet for Karleen's bed and she convinced them it was nap time by reading them a story out of one of Bobbie's school books. Perfie took advantage of the lull to go up to her own room.

She opened the trunk and pulled out her mother's quilt. It would need to be aired again, but for now she wanted to see it on the bed. When she had spread it over the mattress and smoothed it, she turned back to the trunk and took out a small box.

Perfie unwrapped the porcelain angel who had been confined to her safe space for so long. Maybe it had been a mistake not to let her out, not to put her on some crowded surface in each of the many places they had moved over the past year. But the thought of her being broken had been too strong, so Perfie had left her asleep in the safety of the cotton batting and the box and the trunk.

"We're here, Mama." Perfie set the angel on top of the chest of drawers. Now she could think about her mother and Isabelle. She would like to have the tiny guardian on the bedside table, but with Artie's habit of jumping on the bed, that seemed like a bad idea. Up here on the tall chest was a good place for the little angel to watch over her as she slept each night.

Two hours later Perfie was setting plates on the table when she heard a soft knock at the back door.

"Welcome, Mrs. Martinez." A smiling Japanese woman stood at the door with a large bowl. "I am Mrs. Nakamura."

"Come in." Perfie stepped back from the door. Ichiro and Artie followed the woman into the house. Did Ichiro invite his mother to dinner?

Mrs. Nakamura held the bowl out to Perfie. "For you."

"You didn't have to—" Perfie stopped. She knew some people considered it rude to say you didn't want their gift. "Thank you." She forced a smile and took the bowl. Although she knew it was wrong, this Japanese woman frightened her. What if she was a spy? What if it wasn't safe to eat this food?

"My son, Ichiro, he will eat dinner with you?" Mrs. Nakamura smiled again and nodded.

"Yes, we would like that." Perfie nodded back, but she was still nervous about the food.

"Thank you for inviting Ichiro."

"Well, thank you for the . . . food."

"I would like for you to come to my home for lunch? Just you and me?"

Perfie felt herself start to nod again. Everything Mrs. Nakamura said sounded like a question.

"That would be nice."

"Tomorrow?"

Perfie was surprised. She had thought Mrs. Nakamura's invitation was just a token gesture. A Japanese woman inviting her to lunch?

"So soon?" The words burst forth before she could rein them in.

"Too soon? Maybe Monday?"

Mrs. Nakamura didn't give up easily, and Perfie didn't want to seem rude.

"Can I let you know? I'm not sure," Perfie waved her hand toward the crowded kitchen. "The kids . . . the unpacking . . ."

"Yes, of course." Mrs. Nakamura smiled and left.

The children and Carlotta gathered around the table while Isaac served the plates with beans, sopapillas and fresh cucumbers.

"My mother brought some kiritanpo." Ishiro pointed to the bowl Mrs. Nakamura had left.

"It smells delicious." Isaac scooped a dollop of the noodle mixture onto each plate.

Perfie opened a cabinet door and ran her fingers across the smooth yellow paint. She took a glass pitcher to the sink and turned on the faucet.

Clear, cold water ran from the spigot. Perfie held the pitcher under the stream of water and watched it fill while the colorful voices of her family echoed around her. She heard Ishiro say something, and the whole family burst into laughter. It had been so long since they all had sounded this happy.

Perfie carried the pitcher to the table and poured water into each glass.

"Ishiro. Please tell your mother Monday will be fine."

* * * * * * *

Acknowledgements

Special thanks to all my friends and family who made writing this book possible. Thanks to my draft readers: Roberta (also known as my mother), Marlene, and Kate, as well as my proof readers, Marlene, Shirley and Cindy. (Yep, Marlene helps me a LOT!) Thanks to the people of Tierra Amarilla, including my wonderful cousins, Doreen and Manuel, and all those who put up with my visits to Three Ravens Coffee House and my endless questions about life in Northern New Mexico (and thanks to Paul for introducing me to all those folks.) Thanks to Writers of the Storm for so many nights of wonderful critique, and to both of my Sierra Writers critique groups. Thanks to Barbara, my muse and massage therapist (her magic hands never fail to put me in my most creative space.) A special thanks to Leslie and Dan for giving me a space in the yurt to write (and re-write.) Thanks to my children, Liz and Vic, for adding width, length and depth to my life.

But most of all thanks and love to my husband, Dan, for giving me the support and freedom to follow my dreams.

ABOUT THE AUTHOR

Robin Martinez Rice has dreamed about writing since learning to read. She has a million stories to tell. Born in Oakland, California, with a family heritage in Northern New Mexico, she worked as an Educational Psychologist and Marriage Family Therapist for twenty-nine years, before retiring and venturing out into the literary world. She lives in Northern California with her husband, Dan, Ollie the Boston Terrier, three cats and eight chickens. She seeks out new adventures whenever possible.

www.robinmartinezrice.com

PO Box 5818
Auburn, CA 95604-5818

17070312R00199

Made in the USA
Charleston, SC
25 January 2013